"Stop playing games."

Without moving a muscle, Jack Merlin managed to make Cassie feel about an inch tall. He was asking her to let a man who might be a criminal go free, and he was well aware that if she needed his help badly enough, she would do it. He knew his own worth very well. "You leave me no choice," Cassie said.

"But you do have a choice, Cassie. Forget about this whole unsavory mess. Drop your story. Go find something or someone else to dig your sharp talons into."

Cassie gave a bitter smile and shook her head. "Not a chance. Get used to the feeling of them digging into you, Mr. Merlin. Because they're in to stay."

ABOUT THE AUTHOR

Linda Stevens loves mixing intrigue and romance, never knowing what might turn up around the next corner as the books develop. The author's story ideas come from many sources, particularly newspaper and magazine articles, but most of them start with the simple question: What if? Linda Stevens lives and works in Colorado Springs, Colorado.

Shadowplay
Linda Stevens

Harlequin Books

TORONTO • NEW YORK • LONDON
AMSTERDAM • PARIS • SYDNEY • HAMBURG
STOCKHOLM • ATHENS • TOKYO • MILAN

Harlequin Intrigue edition published January 1990

ISBN 0-373-22130-4

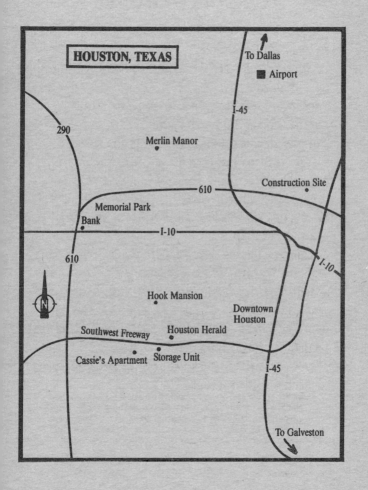

HOUSTON, TEXAS

To Dallas

■ Airport

I-45

290

Merlin Manor

Construction Site

610

Memorial Park
Bank

I-10

I-10

610

N

Hook Mansion

Downtown
Houston

Southwest Freeway

Houston Herald

Cassie's Apartment   Storage Unit

I-45

To Galveston

CAST OF CHARACTERS

Cassie O'Connor—She was determined to get a story... and revenge.

Brian Fenton—His death set the ball rolling in a deadly game.

Jack Merlin—He was known to be a loyal friend, and a dangerous enemy.

Patrick Rourke—His name was the lever Cassie'd found to move Jack Merlin.

Mrs. Carlyle—Was her newspaper empire no longer enough for her?

Stan Lockwood—Cassie's editor was a hard man to get around.

Leonore Xavier—Her charitable contributions were an inspiration to everyone.

Anthony Knox—He'd do anything, if the price was right.

Marilyn Hook—Would Cassie's research reveal a ruthless family business?

Flynn—He lived in the shadows, and preferred to do his fighting there.

Chapter One

Cassie O'Connor made a mental note in her *Guidebook for Amateur Criminals*: "When sneaking into a man's bedroom, don't forget to bring your own rope."

"Damnation."

She stood outside the closed door, pondering the problem as she waited for her eyes to grow accustomed to the almost total darkness. Improvise. Make use of what was on hand. After all, she'd done all right so far, hadn't she?

Hiding in the trunk of the baby-sitter's car had been the hardest part. Compared to that broad-daylight escapade, it had been a snap to wait for nightfall in a musty garage. Prior planning had made it a simple matter to slip past the guard dogs. But gaining entry to the house itself had been easier than it should have been. Though the place bristled with alarms, the night was warm and someone had thoughtfully left a kitchen window ajar.

In fact, the only time the insanity of what Cassie was doing really hit her came as she picked her way through the sleeping household without being caught, despite creaking stairs and groaning floorboards.

Compared to coming through all that without a slip, what was a minor oversight like forgetting your rope? There would be something she could use in his bedroom, providing she managed to work up the courage to go inside.

It was much too late to chicken out now. Cassie turned the knob, slipped into the room and closed the door behind her. How was she going to find anything in here? Though it hardly seemed possible, his bedroom was even darker than the hallway had been. As she inched forward into the gloom, however, she discovered that not having any rope was the least of her problems.

The floor was littered with booby traps. She tripped over one large shoe, stumbled, took another tentative step and immediately found the second shoe. Cassie just barely managed to catch herself before she fell flat on her face.

Crawling would be the safest course. As she sank to her knees, however, a sharp cuff link dug into the tender palm of her hand, giving her second thoughts. Its mate would be around somewhere, waiting to jab her, as well. She might even cry out and wake her sleeping victim. Stifling a moan, Cassie sat back on her heels.

Were cat burglars allowed to cry?

Thoroughly disgusted with herself, Cassie held her breath, listening for the slightest movement or sound. Nothing stirred. Luck was still with her. But she couldn't sit there all night.

His messy habits gave her an idea. Edging past the pile of clothing, she carefully crawled to the man's closet, groping around until she emerged triumphant with a handful of silk ties.

He was on his back, sprawled out beneath a thin sheet, giving Cassie easy access to his arms and legs. The patterned silk ties worked even better than rope. She slipped them deftly around his outstretched hands and both strong ankles, checking to make sure each tie was securely knotted to the bed frame. When he moved, each narrow band of silk would tighten firmly into place. She stood up and breathed a sigh of relief, glad he was in a deep, exhausted sleep.

"Wakey, wakey, Mr. Merlin," Cassie O'Connor said as she started to take a step back from the bed.

She didn't make it in time. A big hand shot out and very strong fingers wrapped around her wrist with bruising strength, preventing her escape.

"Let me go!" she ordered, trying not to let the panic he felt enter her voice.

He squeezed a little harder. "Why?" the man asked, his tone a bit puzzled and husky with sleep, but no less commanding.

A tiny derringer was suddenly pressed against the tip of his nose and a loud click sounded in the silence as she set the hammer back. "Does this answer your question?"

His grip didn't loosen as he studied her in the muted moonlight. Dressed all in black, her features weren't easily discernible. But in spite of her bravado, he could sense her nervousness and uncertainty, an unpredictable woman with a gun. She just might shoot him, and even a tiny bullet could do a lot of damage at this range.

"Take it easy, lady. I'm rather attached to my nose."

There was a loud knock on the bedroom door. "Jack," a masculine voice with a hint of a brogue announced, "we have an intruder in the house."

"No kidding."

The gun pressed more firmly against his nose as a reminder of who had the upper hand. "Tell him you know me."

"Do I have a choice?" The cold steel chilled his nose. "It's all right, Russ, I know her."

"Her?" The other man chuckled. "Well, now. If that's the way it is, I'll just give the alarms a once-over and go back to bed, shall I?"

"You do that, Russ." They heard his footsteps on the creaky stairs and then silence.

"Very nice, Mr. Merlin," Cassie said. "Now if you'll be so kind as to release my wrist."

Jack let go of her, slowly, watching as she stepped back and slipped the small gun into a pocket of her loose-fitting black pants. Then she stepped over to the window and opened the draperies, flooding the room with brilliant moonlight.

"What now?" Jack asked.

"We talk," Cassie informed him, dragging a leather-covered wingback chair closer to the side of the bed and taking a seat.

"Talk?" He sighed and looked on the silken bonds holding him captive on the bed. "How anticlimactic. I thought you might have something more interesting in mind."

She ignored his lascivious comment.

Her face was almost completely hidden in the shadows of the overstuffed chair, but he could still see her eyes. He'd lied to Russ. He didn't know this woman. A face he might forget, but not a smooth voice like hers, and he would never have forgotten those eyes, like cool, blue ice. They were gorgeous even in the dim light.

"The only thing I want from you right now is your undivided attention, Jack Merlin."

"How flattering."

"Do I have it?"

"You're not sure?"

Cassie was only sure of one thing: she had the right man. Flippant in the face of danger. No ranting, raving, or struggling against his bonds. A man with a far-from-sterling reputation, who didn't seem at all surprised to find himself tied up and held at gunpoint. From what she knew of him he was running true to form.

"Do I have your attention or not?" she asked.

"I'm all yours," he replied with an amiable grin. "So state your case."

Smug, egotistical bastard. According to her source she wouldn't have gotten away with this stunt if he hadn't been on the go for the past forty-eight hours.

"I want you to do something for me, and in return I'll do something for you."

He quirked one full, dark brow high, his gaze roving thoroughly over the length of her crossed legs. "Maybe."

"Shall I start with what you want, or with what I want?"

"I'm a selfish person. What do I want?"

"My silence."

"About what?"

For a moment she studied his relaxed pose, the burgundy-colored sheet covering most of his chest and body, his head resting comfortably against a pillow. He didn't realize it, but his carefree attitude was making this easier for her.

With a little luck and some time-consuming digging, she had finally managed to come up with enough on Jack Merlin to blackmail him into helping her. Then she'd had to come up with this plan of making him listen. Through it all, Cassie had wondered what she would feel when she actually confronted the man. Guilt? Maybe even a little pity?

Not a smidgen. Not now. A man as infuriating as this one deserved everything she could throw at him. "You have a very interesting past, riddled with inaccuracies and tall tales." She paused and tilted her head slightly. "Or are they actually shocking, accurate facts?"

"How can I answer that until you tell me what you think you know?"

He had the perfect poker face, devoid of emotion, giving nothing away at all. Though his voice was still roughened from sleep and his black hair tousled, his golden-brown eyes were sharp and alert.

"Eight years ago. Paris. Ring any bells?"

He shrugged. "I've been to France many times."

"You know what I mean. Or have you worked for so many governments you've lost track?"

"You're mistaken. I don't work for any government."

"No?"

"No."

Cassie wasn't perturbed by his denial. With Jack Merlin's background, she expected nothing less. It was going to be tricky, however, to convince him she had enough information to ensure his cooperation. After a moment of surveying each other in silence, she leaned forward in her chair.

"Allow me to refresh your memory. Eight years ago you were detained at Orly airport, trying to make a rather hasty departure. Are you with me so far?"

He shrugged again. "I was late for my plane. But the French don't like people running in their airports."

"Cut the humor, Mr. Merlin. We both knew why they prevented you from leaving the country."

"Do we?"

Cassie met his gaze, trying to stare him down. "The main thing is that you were detained, then suddenly decided to stay and enjoy a little of Paris in the springtime."

Jack yawned in her face. "I hope all this is leading somewhere. I'm sleepy."

Cassie jumped out of her chair and strode across the large room to the picture window, struggling to hold on to her temper, her hands clenching and unclenching inside her pants pockets. She'd worked too long and hard to blow it now.

Composing herself, she turned to face him once more. "Your French general let you off in return for a favor. And you're going to make the same deal with me."

"For the sake of argument, let's suppose I know what you're talking about. What do I get out of this so-called deal?"

"I told you. My silence."

Jack stifled the urge to laugh at her answer. Maybe she knew what she was talking about and maybe not, but he certainly wouldn't trust her to remain silent in any case. He could count the people he trusted on one hand, and she certainly wasn't one of them.

She intrigued him, though. It took a lot of work to come up with something on him, particularly that annoying incident in Paris.

"What do you want?" he asked.

All she'd managed to do was pique his interest and she knew it, but she would win in the end. "I want you to acquire something for me."

His eyes narrowed. "Go on."

"It might be rather difficult to get."

"How difficult?"

"It shouldn't be that tough for a man of your talents. It's in a bank vault, inside a lockbox."

Jack tried to sit up but couldn't. He'd momentarily forgotten about the position she had him in. "Valuable?"

"Valuable enough."

"Then go acquire it yourself."

"Why should I? It'll be so much easier to just use you. And if you don't agree to help me, I'll make your life as miserable as I can for as long as I can."

He settled back onto the bed with a disgusted sigh. "You keep threatening me with some kind of exposure. How do you hope to accomplish that? Who the hell are you?"

"Cassie O'Connor. I'm an investigative reporter, the eyes and ears of a curious public. And I've gathered enough bits and pieces on you to come up with a very shocking story, maybe even work it into a three-part piece. It makes utterly fascinating reading, be it fact or fiction."

"Makes?"

"I don't trust you, Jack Merlin. My article is written, and I've made arrangements to ensure that it will be printed if I don't make it out of here alive." Cassie pulled a piece of paper out of her pocket and held it up for him to see. "This is page one—it starts out with your name and address. You can't stop it from being printed if anything happens to me, now or later."

Another repeat of Paris, no solid evidence against him, but enough hearsay to make his now-quiet life unpleasantly public. Of course, the general had held a much better hand than Cassie O'Connor. However, romantic French soul or not, he didn't have a womanly body like Cassie's to persuade a man with.

"Why don't you untie me and we'll discuss this calmly, like adults?" Jack asked.

"We're doing fine my way. Are you going to cooperate?"

"Are you going to tell me what I'm supposed to be after?"

They stared at each other in silence, neither wanting to give way, the strength of their wills equally matched. Cassie finally returned to her seat in the comfortable leather chair and propped her black shoes on the edge of the bed, ankles crossed. She had the most to lose in this standoff.

"Documents," Cassie replied at last.

He didn't even blink. "Negotiable?"

"No!" She glared at him, her feet dropping to the floor with a thump. "Not everyone is as avaricious as you, Mr. Merlin. The kind of documents I'm talking about contain evidence to back up a story I'm working on."

A story... it was much more than that. But Cassie supposed it was as good a description as any for what she was doing. If she could prove her suspicions it would certainly be front-page news.

"Must be one hell of a story to make you break into my house," he said, his hard eyes boring into her. "You're not stupid enough to go after the Mob, are you?"

Cassie crossed her arms over her breasts and looked away. "If that's what it takes to see justice done."

"Great," he muttered, "I'm being blackmailed by someone with a Quixote complex. What windmill are you tilting at, Ms. Cassie O'Connor?"

"It doesn't concern you. All your job entails is retrieving those papers for me as soon as possible. I'll take it from there."

"How do I know you can be trusted to keep your silence?"

She turned to face him again and asked, "How do I know you won't betray me to the criminals named in those documents once you have possession of them?"

Jack nodded thoughtfully. "Now there's an interesting notion. What *would* stop me from doing that?"

Cassie was prepared for his question. It was time to divulge the one real hold she felt she had over Jack Merlin. When the going got tough, she wasn't sure if his obvious fear of publicity would be enough to keep him in line. But her research had turned up something—or rather someone—that would. Or at least she hoped it would.

"Your honor... and Patrick Rourke."

His eyes suddenly narrowed to slits, his muscles coiled taut like a tiger ready to spring. If she hadn't believed in the strength of the knots holding him down she'd have run for her life.

"Explain."

"At last, Mr. Merlin, I see I truly have your undivided attention." Cassie almost sighed with relief. Her gamble had paid off. "I have information that he's involved with the people I'm after. How and why I don't know—that's your problem."

Jack barely noticed her self-satisfied expression. She had him, she knew it, and he saw no reason to try to hide his concern from her. Rourke and he went way back, back to times he rarely thought about anymore. Could this story of hers get Rourke into trouble? Did he need help—again?

Putting a brake on that train of thought, Jack focused on the problem at hand. Cassie O'Connor. He had to admit he liked her style, but he still didn't trust her. She could be anybody, in league with any one of a number of his former enemies. Someone seeking revenge for wrongs he'd righted in Ireland. Maybe someone he'd stolen from to achieve those goals. Or it could be someone wanting to know the whereabouts of items he'd acquired more recently and sold for the right price.

He had enemies on both sides of the law. Maybe she was working for some government. This could all be part of an elaborate trap, set up to snare him.

Not that it made any difference. He had to find out what Rourke was involved in, which in turn meant going along with this woman—for the moment at least. But Jack had no intention of doing what she asked by himself. If he was going to get caught in some kind of cross fire, then Cassie O'Connor would be caught right along with him.

"I'll do it, on one condition."

"And that is?" She leaned back in the chair, her face completely hidden in the shadows again.

"You'll be with me, every step of the way."

This was not one of the problems Cassie had anticipated. After all, she was in his bedroom in the dead of night to get *him* to do the job for *her*.

After hitting one dead end after another, almost giving up because she lacked solid evidence, she'd finally managed to learn of the existence of the documents. She'd worked hard to find an expert to retrieve them for her, and now he was trying to put it all back in her lap.

She couldn't drop this project. But go with him? Actually break into a bank? Her mind felt numb. "I . . ."

"How far are you willing to go to get those documents?"

Cassie's resolve steadied. She glared at him. "As far as I have to, Mr. Merlin, and don't you forget it."

"Then it looks as if we'll be spending a lot of time together, Cassie. I won't do this job without you by my side."

It sounded to Cassie as if he was trying to take charge, and she didn't like it. "I hold the cards, remember?"

"And I hold the expertise, Miss O'Connor."

True. She wouldn't be here if he didn't. She knew that without his expertise she would never find out what had really happened to Brian Fenton.

Knowing that didn't make his ultimatum any easier to take, but it narrowed her options considerably. If she wanted the documents, she would have to follow his lead. And she wanted, needed, those documents, if she was going to find out who had murdered her best friend.

"All right, I agree to your condition, but only because I've decided it's not such a bad idea to keep a closer eye on you," Cassie said. "Remember who and what I am, Mr. Merlin. Don't try to cross me. I can have my eye-opening article on you printed so fast it'll make your head spin, and I will, at the slightest sign of deceit on your part."

"Take your own words to heart, dear, and don't cross me, either," Jack told her, his voice as cold and hard as a block of ice.

Cassie didn't want to find out what he did to people who crossed him. Having accomplished what she had set out to, she stood. She was more than ready to leave.

"Where do you think you're going? This discussion is far from over," Jack informed her. "Take a seat."

"You're not in a position to give orders."

"I am if you want my help." Cassie sat back down slowly. "Good. Now, how did you find out about me?" he asked.

Her chin tilted up. "I don't reveal my sources."

"Then I don't help you. It might be worth the publicity risk to eliminate you."

Cassie gulped quietly. What was she getting herself into this time? She decided to tell the story, but not name any names. "A fellow reporter heard the story at a party in France, about a man named Jack Merlin who was coerced into using his expertise to retrieve incriminating pictures for a certain general who was being blackmailed. It was a name I recognized in connection with the ownership of this estate. Since I was looking for someone with the sort of abilities you were said to possess, I put two and two together, did some more research and decided to come after you." She didn't add that she'd been absolutely desperate at the time, or that Patrick Rourke's name had also been mentioned, confirming the connection her informant had indicated later.

Jack nodded. "The reporter's name?" Cassie remained silent and he sighed loudly. "Do you want my help or not?"

Her voice was sharp. "I heard the initial story from a man named Brian Fenton."

"What else do you know about me and Patrick Rourke?"

Cassie hesitated, not wanting to reveal how weak her position really was. Publicity and his connection to Patrick Rourke were the only leverage she had.

"Spill it!" Jack demanded, straining forward. "And the truth this time, Cassie O'Connor."

"It is the truth!" Her hands clenched into tight fists as she tried to hold on to her temper. "I know you two have worked together before. I've been told you're like brothers. And I know his name came up in regard to the story I'm working on. That's all I needed to know to obtain your help."

"Good point." He leaned back, studying her. "I want to know why this is so important to you?"

Cassie sighed. "A few months ago that same reporter, Brian Fenton, committed suicide. At least that was the verdict of the coroner and police investigators," she began. "But I knew Brian. He wouldn't have taken his own life. He was working on something important at the time of his death and getting close to a breakthrough, judging by how excited he was."

"And you think he got too close? That someone murdered him to shut him up?" Jack asked.

"I do."

His eyes narrowed. "Your foolishness is beginning to make a little more sense. Was he your lover?"

"No! We were friends. Not that it's any of your business."

"Your motivation is definitely my business. Just what was your friend looking into that could've gotten him killed?" Jack wanted to know.

Again Cassie hesitated. "Oh, what's the use," she said at last. "He was very close-mouthed."

"You don't know." Jack stared at her for a moment, then asked, "How does his death tie in with these documents you want me to get for you?"

"I don't know...at least not exactly," Cassie replied. "After Brian died, an informant heard I was digging around, trying to find out what Brian had been working on. He contacted me, said he knew the truth about Brian's death, and that the proof was in a lockbox."

"And that's it?" Jack asked incredulously. "That's all you know? Your source tells you just the thing you want to hear and you fall for it?"

Cassie knew it was a shaky story, but she intended to stick with it. She did have more information than that, she just didn't think it was any of Jack Merlin's business. "Okay so it's odd," she admitted. "I guess I should also tell you he mentioned Patrick Rourke's name just when I was looking for some way to make sure you'd help me. I knew the two of you were connected, but that was the first I'd realized Rourke was involved in the story I was investigating. It gave me just the leverage I needed."

"This swamp is getting deeper by the moment," he muttered. "Don't all these coincidences bother you? Because they sure as hell bother me."

"Of course they bother me! But I know Brian didn't kill himself. And my informant is scared—you can hear it in his voice. Add to that the disappearance of Brian's notebooks and the cassette logs he kept of interviews, and my instincts tell me I'm on the right track." Cassie looked at him, suddenly feeling the need to make him understand her desperation. "Someone murdered my friend to shut him up, and I'll do whatever it takes to prove it. Wouldn't you do the same if the victim had been your friend Patrick Rourke?"

"I would," Jack replied. "I'll also do whatever it takes to protect him now. Remember that."

She wasn't fooled by his deceptively soft tone. She knew Jack Merlin was a dangerous man. Cassie stood up with studied nonchalance and walked to the bedroom door. "I think we understand each other. I'll be back tomorrow to discuss the plans."

"Hey." Jack lifted one leg off the bed as far as his bonds would allow. "Aren't you forgetting something?"

"I hear you're a very inventive man, I'm sure you'll manage to free yourself."

"Cassie, a word of caution." The insistence of his tone made her look back over her shoulder at him. Jack smiled at the way her fingers curled nervously around the doorknob. "Don't wear that perfume again. The dogs will attack if they catch your scent from now on."

"It's not my scent, Jack, it's the baby-sitter's. I'm pretty inventive myself. How else do you think I got past the beasts of Merlin manor?"

With that she disappeared into the darkness of the hallway, quietly closing the door behind her. Jack smiled in spite of his predicament. "This might be quite intriguing after all," he muttered under his breath.

He was still smiling a moment later when a panel in his bedroom wall opened on silent, hidden hinges, revealing one of the secret passageways which riddled the old house. A dark figure emerged.

"Do you want her?"

"No, let her go, Russ. She'll be back tomorrow."

"Of course she will. How could she resist such a charming lad as yourself?" A dim light came on in the room. "I heard most of what she said. You don't really know her, do you?"

"No. But I'm going to, as soon as you free me so I can get to my computer terminal to commission a report. And don't use your knife!" Jack ordered as a sudden flash of silver glistened in the light of the moon. "My wardrobe has suffered enough indignities for one evening. Have you checked on Bridget?"

"Sleeping like the little angel she is, with that guard dog close beside her," Russ replied, bending to look at the knotted ties around the other man's wrists. "That beastie doesn't like me, Jack. I thought he was going to make a midnight snack out of me just for entering her room."

Jack chuckled quietly. "I thought you liked dogs?"

"They have their place. Outside."

"It was your idea to give Bridget a living alarm of her own, if I remember correctly."

"And a good one it was, too. Until we get the rest of the electronics perfected, he stays, even if he does seem to find a resemblance between my rear end and rump roast." Russ muttered a Gaelic curse. "She ties knots like a sailor! That lass could give us lessons, I do believe."

"I wouldn't doubt it a bit, Russ," Jack said. She was one determined woman. What they could teach each other might turn out to be quite interesting. "Hurry up, will you? Or are you admitting to defeat by a woman, and an O'Connor in the bargain?"

"It wouldn't be the first time an Irishman was trounced good and proper by an Irishwoman. Speaking of which, these bits of silk look an awful lot like your good ties."

"They are," Jack answered, freeing his other hand.

"You're never going to get the wrinkles out."

"I don't want to get the wrinkles out. I'm going to save these ties as a reminder." Cassie had run up a debt this night, and Jack Merlin would eventually have his payment in full. "It remains to be seen whether they'll bring back pleasant or unpleasant memories."

Chapter Two

Cassie studied the man sitting behind the messy desk, trying to gauge his mood as he talked on the phone. He was only two inches taller than her own five foot six. His white hair was stylishly cut. At forty-six he was in excellent shape, and a local tanning salon gave him a golden tan year-round.

Stan Lockwood was a nice man most of the time, as long as you weren't asking him for anything and you did your job. Of course, to him that meant the twin impossibilities of no rewrites and never missing a deadline. But he didn't seem too vicious today. Yet.

"Stan, I'm going to need some time off," Cassie announced as he hung up the phone.

It was best to get right to the point with Stan, before he found a way to discourage you.

"Why?" her editor asked bluntly.

Stan liked Cassie. She did her work well, rarely asked for favors and gave him few headaches. And the combination of her black hair—today twisted into a simple knot at the nape of her graceful neck—a stunning pair of pale blue eyes and a creamy complexion made her quite pleasant to have around.

"I'm working on a story."

"So work on it here." Stan didn't like his reporters taking unexplained leaves of absence. And they never wanted to reveal what they were working on in the beginning, even to him. "Or have you developed an aversion to our happy little newsroom?"

Cassie shook her head in noncompliance. "This one's going to require all my concentration for the next week or two, maybe longer."

"How much longer?"

She had never noticed what beady little brown eyes Stan had when he was narrowing his gaze on someone. But she knew when to hold her tongue. With Stan, silence could be more than golden; on occasion it could be a diamond-encrusted weapon of the first order.

He picked up a sharp yellow pencil and began tapping it against his index finger. "I take it you don't know how long you'll really need. You people never do."

You people. That meant reporters. Though he'd been one himself once, and a good one, he now considered them the enemy. Cassie hid a smile and resisted the temptation to call him a turncoat.

"It's not the type of thing easily judged," she told him. No way would she beg for time off. She deserved it, and he was going to give in, not her. "Come on, Stan. This is me, remember? Have I ever let you down?"

"No, but there's always a first time. I don't suppose you would care to give me a hint of what's so important you want to leave us, your co-workers and loving boss, to fend for ourselves against a virtual flood of—"

"No," Cassie interrupted, ignoring his poor attempt to sound pitiful. "I wouldn't. I'm very protective of my leads and you know it, Stan." Brian had been like a brother to her, a soul mate. Someone she could talk to about anything, someone who had always been there for her. This time she was going to be there for him. She wouldn't let him down.

Stan was tapping the pencil annoyingly against the edge of the desk now as he considered her request. Part of what made Cassie such a good reporter was her unfailing tenacity in seeking out all the facts. Her equally stubborn nature and hot temper were well-known around the city. She was worse than a bulldog with a bone. Once her teeth were dug in, she just wouldn't let go, and those pearly white fangs were obviously into something juicy this time.

"Please don't tell me this so-called story is the same one you've been stewing over for months now?"

Her eyes flared open at his question. Stan hadn't become an editor by accident. He was well able to read his staff.

"All right. I won't tell you."

Stan groaned. "Cassie, we've been over this before. Brian Fenton committed suicide—there was a full police investigation." In a rare display of gentleness he added softly, "Let this one go."

"I can't." Cassie paced the room restlessly. "I knew him better than anyone." She stopped pacing, placed her hands flat on his desk and glared at him. "Brian didn't take his own life, Stan, any more than I ever would. Would you believe it if the police said I jumped off a thirty-story building?"

"No."

"Well, I can't accept that Brian did, either. I'll never accept it." Cassie resumed her pacing. "And don't give me that stuff about delayed-stress syndrome. I know Brian served as a reporter in Vietnam but he didn't have a problem with it."

"You don't know that."

She ignored him. "If anything, his time spent over there just made him stronger, more determined than ever to expose corrupt government employees." She turned and looked at him. "Do you know exactly what he was working on when he died?"

"We've been through this before." Stan sighed. "You know every story he was assigned, and the political arena is wide open. He could have been after almost anyone."

"What happened to his notebooks, his cassettes on those stories? Where is his laptop computer? The police didn't find anything in his apartment."

His voice was sharp. "I know they didn't. Brian could have left them anywhere."

"Fenton the fanatical? Don't kid yourself!" Stan looked surprised. "Oh, yes, Brian knew what you and others called him behind his back."

"He made few friends here," Stan reminded her. "As a matter of fact you were probably the only one."

Cassie felt compelled to defend him. "Brian was a loner, and a damned good reporter."

"He was also a constant pain," Stan replied. "It's not surprising someone wanted him dead."

"Are you admitting something?"

Stan glared at her. The muscle in his neck was twitching, a sure sign that she'd gone too far. "I'll forgive your outburst this time, Cassie. But remember, I had an easier way to get rid of him if I'd wanted to. All I had to do was fire him."

"It's no secret you wanted to, more than once, but his columns sold newspapers. That's always the bottom line."

Placing her hands on his desk, she leaned toward him and said, "The owners wouldn't let you get rid of him. But your fights were notorious around here, Stan."

Stan jumped up, gripping the sides of his desk as he leaned toward her. "You're pushing your luck, Cassie. Don't make accusations you can't back up. It's called slander, remember?"

"I'm not accusing you, Stan." Cassie stepped back, trying to calm her temper. After all, he could fire her. "Who was he gunning for in this town?"

"You just don't give up, do you?" Stan shook his head. "I don't know. Maybe no one. Maybe someone big. You were two of a kind in that department," Stan told her as he sat back down. "Brian didn't tell me a damn thing. But that doesn't—"

"Prove anything?" she interrupted. "No. But it does suggest a possible explanation, one I find far more acceptable than suicide. It suggests that Brian unearthed something really terrible, and that whoever he was investigating murdered him to keep it a secret." Cassie crossed her arms, her stance firm. "I intend to find out what those secrets are, Stan. With or without your cooperation."

Stan picked up the pencil and started tapping it again. Rhythm torture. "Cassie, Brian didn't pull any of his punches—he could analytically scalp someone without flinching and did so many times. He kept digging until he found proof of personal gain, sifted through every inequity in their voting stance and then gleefully exposed them to the public." He shrugged. "As you said, we sold a lot of newspapers that way. And he made a lot of enemies."

Stan's indifference infuriated her. "Dammit, Stan, he was murdered! And I'm going to prove it, somehow."

"Cassie, you know most of Brian's work centered on political heavy-hitters. If he did discover something—"

"Something worth murdering him over," she added.

Stan saw that it was pointless to argue with her. "I'd rather see you go on a nice vacation," he told her, "but since you won't listen to reason, go ahead. Take your time off and get it out of your system. But we're already short-staffed and I need you to finish those pieces on charity events before you go off on this wild-goose chase."

"But I—"

"Take it or leave it."

He gave her no choice. She needed her job. Besides, she wasn't about to let someone else finish what she had started. "I'll take it."

"I have other vacations starting in three weeks, you have until then. But I expect you back here even sooner if by some improbable chance you do come up with something." He jabbed the pencil at her to emphasize his next point. "And if you do find anything, remember which paper you work for."

Cassie was already heading for the door before he had time for second thoughts. She needed to get out of his office fast, before she broke down and cried. Talking about Brian this way had been hard, like ripping a bandage off a wound barely beginning to heal. Her feelings were still too raw.

"Thanks, Stan."

"Get the hell out of here." Though he hated to set a bad precedent by showing his concern twice in one day, he knew she had a tendency to leap into things and then look for the danger when it was too late to back out. So he said, "But do me a favor and be careful, will you?"

"I always am," she quipped, grinning at him to hide the tears welling in her eyes as she quickly backed out of his office and ran smack into the person trying to enter.

Cassie whirled around, catching the woman before she fell down. She also caught a whiff of the woman's unique, ultra-expensive perfume and groaned silently. Of all the people to run into.

"Oh! I'm so sorry, Mrs. Carlyle!"

The unexpected collision still had the older woman wobbling on her high heels. "I think you've broken my shoe," she said.

Cassie winced at the thought of what it would cost to have such pricey footwear repaired. "Let me help you to a chair."

"Mrs. Carlyle! What a pleasant surprise!" Stan strode forward with a big smile and took the woman's hand. He shot Cassie a withering glare and whispered, "Get lost. Fast."

Cassie beat a hasty retreat out of his office. Stepping on the toes of Mrs. Carlyle, executive editor, part owner of the paper and society matron, simply wasn't done. Pausing at the water cooler just down the hall from Stan's office door, she listened with her fingers crossed. Maybe Mrs. Carlyle hadn't had time to see who had committed the evil deed.

No such luck. "Wasn't that Cassie O'Connor?"

Stan, bless his parched little soul, murmured a vague but affirmative answer to her question and then tried to change the subject. "Now, what can—"

"I thought so. Who is she so fired up to investigate now?" Mrs. Carlyle inquired.

Cassie heard Brian's name mentioned and groaned, deciding to take Stan's advice and get lost in the hubbub of the newsroom. What she had just overheard was a perfect example of why she told Stan so little. In order to keep his job he had to answer to his superiors when they asked questions. If she kept him in the dark for the most part, then he couldn't very well pass on what he didn't know. Brian had been right. It was the only way to minimize leaks and keep a lid on exclusives.

"Cassie, dammit! Answer your own phone," George yelled across the sea of desks as she entered the newsroom. "The joker who keeps calling you hangs up whenever anyone else answers."

"Of course. Whoever it is obviously has good taste in reporters." Grinning, she plopped into the battered chair behind her desk and grabbed the black receiver. "Cassie O'Connor at your service."

"Cassandra?"

Her smile disappeared. "Elizabeth isn't here."

"Westheimer and Shepherd, five minutes."

Ignoring the curious eyes of her fellow reporters, Cassie left the newsroom immediately. She ran all the way to her car and broke every speed limit on the back streets trying to get to the designated corner in time. Why did he always do this to her?

Racing through the last intersection between her and the phone booth just as the traffic light turned from yellow to red, Cassie pulled to a screeching halt at the corner and jumped out of her car on the run.

She grabbed the ringing pay phone, breathless. "O'Connor."

"Are you making progress?"

"Some." She gulped in a deep breath of air. "Can't you move those documents? A bank vault isn't the easiest place to—"

"No!" the person on the other end of the line exclaimed. "It's too risky for me." His muffled voice grew more confident as he said, "I'm doing enough for you already. If you want the truth badly enough you'll find a way to get to the documents."

"I'm trying. But I still need the exact number of that lockbox," Cassie reminded him. "Please?"

If she had the number she might also be able to find out who owned the box before she broke into it, and in turn find out who and what Brian Fenton had been investigating. If. Maybe. Lord, what a mess Brian had left for her.

"You aren't ready for that information yet," the caller replied. "But time is running out. I can't control the movement of those ledgers. And you have no story without them. Mitch Johnson."

"Who?"

He hung up abruptly.

Cassie listened to the dial tone for a moment, then put the receiver back on its hook with a heavy sigh. "Great." Another name to track down. So far he had given her two others. One of those had been Patrick Rourke. The first name, Rusty Green, she'd thought was a joke, but research had shown that Russell Green, known as Rusty to his friends, was dead. He'd died in a construction accident two years ago.

How were these three men connected? *Were* they connected? What did Patrick Rourke have to do with them? Once she found out who the third man was she'd have more to work with.

She supposed she should count herself lucky. Cassie knew Brian had been working on something big when he'd died. He'd refused to talk about it, but he'd been very excited—yet another reason he didn't fit the profile of a suicide. The story had to be connected to his death, but she'd had nothing to go on except her gut feelings and a few of Brian's notes she couldn't decipher, until this anonymous tipster had somehow learned of her investigations and contacted her. She was onto something. Possibly something dangerous. But what?

Cassie returned to her car. Her thoughts were troubled as she drove toward Jack Merlin's home. Stan Lockwood's parting words were beginning to haunt her. Be careful? Of course she'd be careful. She always was. Or at least she always had been in the past. But Brian's death and her infuriatingly hesitant informant with his vague allusions to hidden evidence and smuggling had changed things.

And, as he had just reminded her, time was running out.

ON THE OTHER SIDE of Houston, a well-dressed man leaned back against the glass wall of an isolated pay phone. But he kept his back ramrod stiff, resisting the urge to slump. From a very early age it had been drilled into his mind that appearance was everything, second only to money.

Was he doing the right thing?

He pressed a monogrammed white handkerchief to his face as chills swept along his overheated body in the morning sun. Each time he talked to her it got worse. Even before he picked up the phone the heart palpitations began, the sweat of his brow and upper lip beading up to form tiny droplets across his face. Right thing or not, he didn't know how much longer he could keep this up. What if he got caught?

Stupid question. That's why he was taking every precaution he could think of. If he was found out he would be killed. Still, something had to be done. It had all gone too far.

Of course he could always back out, grab as much money as he could and take off for parts unknown. The O'Connor woman didn't know who he was, nor had anyone caught on to the double life he was leading. Some choice. He could betray his lover, his family or his country.

Which would it be?

JACK MERLIN LIVED on the outskirts of the city, and Cassie's research revealed he'd bought the run-down place he now called home five years ago. The old, two-story stone house was still undergoing periodic transformations. It was a venerable structure, with some history to it, and the *Houston Herald* had therefore tried to get the corporation that was listed as the owner to allow a write-up, but the answer had always been a very adamant, absolute no.

What had she gotten herself into? She knew Jack Merlin was going along for his own reasons, mainly to find out what his friend Patrick Rourke was up to. But whatever his other reasons, he was going to help her. That's all that mattered to Cassie at the moment.

She was, however, determined to find out everything she could about the man. If, as she suspected, this situation was dangerous enough to have gotten Brian killed, then it was very important to know Jack Merlin. Should he try to put his interests ahead of hers, she was determined to win.

Cassie slowed down as she approached one corner of the estate and watched the big dogs running freely across the grounds. The entire ten-acre property was surrounded by an eight-foot, black, wrought-iron fence, with sharp points on each vertical rod. There wasn't enough room for a dog to slip through, let alone a person. Cassie knew because she had tried once and almost gotten stuck.

She grinned, thinking of her nocturnal visit the previous evening. She now had a story she could tell her grandchildren—providing she made it through the rest of this scheme unscathed.

Sobered by the thought, she pulled around the corner and stopped at the massive black gates, pushing a discreet button built into the stone pillar.

A tinny voice issued from a hidden speaker. "Yes?"

"Cassie O'Connor."

"Park under the covered portico but do not get out of your car. The dogs are free. And I do believe they're a bit ticked off about last night."

The huge gates swung open, and she drove through. It didn't help her nerves any to observe how quickly they slammed shut behind her car. She was in now, with no way out; she'd tricked the dogs twice already and knew she didn't have a chance of doing it again.

The same could be said for Jack Merlin. She'd tricked him once, and Cassie had an uneasy feeling it could easily turn out to be once too often.

Chapter Three

Her nervousness increased as she drove up to the front of the old stone house and parked. But it didn't show. She'd had lots of practice at keeping her feelings hidden; a reporter who couldn't seldom lasted long.

Suddenly six snarling dogs surrounded her car, white teeth bared.

"Stay!" Jack commanded. Everyone of them sat. "Come inside," he invited in a deep masculine voice.

Cassie got out of her car and looked up the five semicircular steps to find Jack Merlin standing in an open doorway, his hands slipped casually into his pants pockets. Was this impeccably dressed man the same slob who left his clothing strewn everywhere?

He was wearing a navy-blue jacket, a cream dress shirt, a dark blue paisley tie and navy-blue trousers, his burgundy-colored belt a perfect match for his expensive shoes. And Cassie knew expensive when she saw it. She'd endured almost a year working for the fashion section of another newspaper at the start of her career.

"So we meet again, Miss Cassandra Elizabeth O'Connor."

The use of her full name immediately heightened her guard. No one used her full name, including her parents.

When Jack abruptly turned and walked into the house, she stepped carefully around the dogs and followed him into the large, empty foyer. She stopped to admire the grand curving staircase and the old marble floor. When she looked up she found a big man with short red hair and green eyes appraising her quite openly. Where had he come from?

Automatically she stuck out her hand and introduced herself. "Cassie O'Connor."

He nodded, but didn't shake her hand. "Russ Ian. You'll find him down that hallway."

It was his voice shc'd heard last night outside the bedroom. And, according to the story, Russ Ian and Patrick Rourke had been in Paris to help Jack Merlin eight years ago.

Walking down the hallway she passed a vacant room before entering a huge one with vaulted ceilings and a loft. It was decorated in a light, airy, modern Danish style with white walls, teak trim and few knickknacks. Against the far wall, arching windows placed high above eye level allowed natural light to pour in. Bookcases lined the opposite wall to an eight-foot level, then a short length of staircase led to the second-level loft, and the books started again, some leather-bound, some paperbacks, of all shapes and sizes. Did he buy them by the pound, she wondered?

"Have a seat," Jack said.

She sat down on a lemon-yellow love seat. Although she had dressed to look composed and secure, with her thick black hair in an elegant chignon, tailored black slacks, and a white blouse with a cinnamon print scarf draped over one shoulder, she felt her lack of trust and knew it probably showed in her eyes.

Cassie could feel the imprint of his gaze on her. He was sitting in a light gray leather chair and staring right at her. It made her nervous. She was usually the one pinning down the other person as she interviewed them; she didn't like being on this end of things.

"How long before we can acquire the documents?"

"That's up to you."

She pinned him with a sharp look. "What do you mean?"

"Before we go any further there are certain conditions you will agree to."

"Conditions? Last night there was only one."

He leaned back in his chair, rocking it gently. "That was last night. Today there are more."

"And if I don't agree?" She tilted her chin defiantly.

"You have no choice."

A discreet knock sounded on the open door, then a slender, dark-haired, young girl in jeans entered the room. She was carrying a tray, which held a plate of cookies and an elegant tea set. She put it down carefully on the teak-and-tile table in front of the love seat.

Turning toward Jack she curtsied deeply, holding out the skirts of an imaginary dress. "Tea is served, sir. Will there be anything else, sir?"

Cassie didn't believe it. His rough-hewn face could show emotion after all. Jack's golden eyes were sparkling in reaction to the girl's antics. She, meanwhile, struggled valiantly to keep the proper demure look of a servant on her small, gamine face.

At last the girl gave up and burst out laughing. "One of these days I'm going to beat you at this game, Jack."

He grinned at her. "At the rate you're progressing, I'll be safe for a very long time yet, Miss eleven-year-old Bridget. Probably until you're old and gray."

Some of the light went out of her green eyes and she tugged nervously on the hem of her shirt. "But you'll still be there, right?"

"I'll always be there for you." His voice was firm and positive, full of reassurance. "And so will Russ."

The name seemed to spark something positive inside Bridget and she smiled at him again. "I almost have him beat, too," she boasted loftily.

"What have we told you about stretching the truth?"

Bridget peeked at him, a sly urchin in a pink T-shirt and baggy jeans. "I didn't say what I'm almost beating him at."

Jack gave her a stern look. "You've been home too long, picking up bad habits. It's past time to ship you back to school, young lady."

Bridget wasn't fazed by his gruff manner. "I like it there, especially when you guys aren't home. But remember, I'm going to Kathleen's tomorrow. She has six baby kittens I can't wait to play with." His features were still unmoving. "You promised." Bridget pursed her lips into an amazing replica of a disapproving spinster's frown. "And one should never break a promise, once given. Right?"

"Right," he answered softly. "Never ever." He stared directly at Cassie.

"Or forget your manners, either," Bridget admonished. "Aren't you going to introduce us?" She took the opportunity to help herself to a cookie, shuffling from foot to foot and avoiding Jack's disapproving gaze.

"Cassie O'Connor, this little imp stealing our cookies is Bridget. You'll be seeing Ms. O'Connor here off and on until you leave for school. In the meantime, go help yourself to the cookies in the kitchen."

"Can't," Bridget said, grabbing another cookie on her way out. "I ate all the rest. Oh, it was nice to meet you, Ms. O'Connor, and I like your scarf. It's beautiful."

Bewildered, Cassie tried to make some sense of the sweet domestic scene she'd just witnessed. Bridget was obviously the child who made it necessary for Jack Merlin to have a registered babysitter on his payroll. Up until now, she had been too caught up in planning her raid on his house to think about his situation, and a virtual flood of questions came pouring into her mind.

Who was this young girl, and what relation was she to Jack Merlin? There was no family resemblance, but she could still be his daughter, though Cassie's research on him hadn't uncovered any family. Besides, Bridget hadn't called him Daddy. Was Bridget responsible for his penchant for complete privacy? She intended to find out.

"Would you pour, please, while it's still hot?"

She poured out two steaming cups of tea and handed him one. "Bridget's a very pretty little girl. Is she yours?"

Jack ignored the question. "To continue, the first thing you will promise is to never use my name in your work in any way, be it verbally or written. Not a word, ever, whether I get the documents or not. I'll do my best, but this isn't the kind of job that comes with an unconditional guarantee."

Cassie nodded. "As long as your efforts to obtain the documents are genuine, Mr. Merlin, you'll never see your past in print under my byline. Nor will I give the information to anyone else."

"The second and probably most difficult thing for you to agree to, is to obey all my orders. Without question." Jack could tell by the fire in her eyes that she didn't like that condition one bit, but he wasn't going to start planning anything with her unless he had her complete obedience. "I know what I'm doing," he told her, "and you don't, no matter how resourceful you think you are."

"For your information I do know how to take orders and follow them. As long as they make sense," she tacked on, her lips curling into a smile.

Her smile was really something, even the rather sarcastic one she was giving him now. His instincts hadn't been wrong last night; she was all woman. And probably all trouble.

Her defiance worried him, it could get them both killed. His voice turned cold, unemotional, cutting like a sharp knife. "If I give you an order, it's needed whether it makes sense to you at the time or not. You will do exactly as I say, when I say, without argument. Agreed?"

This man was arrogant—but Cassie needed him. "Agreed," she bit out through clenched teeth. "Anything else?"

"You will also promise to leave any other names I deem important out of this story of yours."

"No. Absolutely not!" Cassie put her cup on the table and stood up, her balled fists resting on her hips. "It's one thing to protect a source and quite another to hide fugitives from justice. Your request is totally out of line, Jack Merlin," she told him, her voice just as sharp. "You know it and I know it." He was trying to throw her off balance, but he wasn't going to succeed. "You are not going to harass me into agreeing to amnesty for any scum you happen to feel like saving. If you've got something on your mind, say it. Otherwise stop playing games."

Jack sat silently, contemplating her. At last he said, "Rourke walks."

"What if he's involved in something illegal?"

"Too bad. He walks, period, just like me. No names, no hints, not a peep."

"Who is he to you?"

"None of your business."

Without moving a muscle he managed to make her feel about an inch tall. He was asking her to let a man who might be a criminal go free, and he was well aware that if she needed him badly enough, she would do it. Jack Merlin knew his own worth very well.

"You leave me no choice," Cassie said.

"But you do have a choice, Cassie. Forget about this whole unsavory mess. Drop your story. Go find something or someone else to dig your sharp talons into."

Cassie glanced down at her clear, oval-shaped nails, then gave a bitter smile and shook her head. "Not a chance. Get used to the feeling of them digging into you, Mr. Merlin. Because they're in you to stay for a while."

He already knew that. Jack knew enough about human nature to recognize certain characteristics that he and Cassie had in common—stubbornness for one.

"No need to keep reminding me, Cassie, I get your message, loud and clear. I hope I've been just as clear?"

"You have my promise, if that's what you mean," she answered. "What's the big deal?"

"Do you remember what Bridget said about keeping promises?" Cassie nodded. "Good, because no one breaks a promise to me," he said, very softly. "Not without the most profound regrets."

She felt a chill slip down her spine and goose bumps covered her skin. Cassie was positive she didn't want to find out what he did to people who broke promises.

"Anything else?"

Jack leaned back in his chair, rocking it gently. "Who gave you Rourke's name?"

Truth or fiction? Which would help her more in this case? "I should give you a lecture on journalistic integrity for even asking that question." She smiled at him. "But, since it would be a waste of breath anyway, I guess I'll answer. I don't know."

"Are you telling me," Jack said, each word slow and distinct, "that you've gone to all this trouble, blackmailed me into helping you, and you don't even know the name of the person who's feeding you information?"

Cassie nodded. "You've summed it up very well."

"Of all the stupid, reckless . . ." He trailed off, muttering several choice expletives under his breath. "You are either a blathering idiot or you don't care about the value of your own life!"

"I beg your pardon!"

"And well you should. My life is involved here, too. This could easily be a trap set up by someone out to get you." Or me, he reminded himself silently. "I don't suppose you've thought of that?"

She struggled to remain calm. "Why do you think I decided I needed professional help?"

"You can say that again. It sounds to me as if you should have had your head examined."

She clasped her delicate teacup firmly. Her temper was close to boiling over. She'd about had enough of his condescending attitude.

Jack recognized the signs. He'd been married once to a woman with a wild temper. Cassie was obviously just itching to throw that cup at him. "Don't even consider it," he murmured. "Take a deep breath, get your temper under control, and put all your cards on the table. Now. Or you can take a hike, Cassandra O'Connor."

"Jack Merlin, I ought to—"

"Don't make threats you can't back up, lady," he said with deadly calm. "If anybody here has a right to be angry, it's me. You've invaded my home, blackmailed me, and now you're carelessly putting my life in danger." *And the lives of the people I love most in the world,* he thought to himself.

Cassie struggled to remain calm as she thought about what he'd said. Put like that, he did have reason to be angry. This time she would have to back down. She couldn't successfully pull this off without him. She was mature enough to handle her anger and him at the same time if she worked at it hard enough.

Taking a deep breath she said, "This hostility isn't getting us anywhere. I need your help. I didn't want to go to these lengths to get it, but I did. Now that I have I'll see it through, no matter what. Do you believe me?"

"I wasn't doubting your resolve, Cassie. Just your sanity." Jack glared at her for a moment, then leaned back in his chair. He sighed. "Okay. So let's have it."

"Have what?"

"The cooperation, dammit!" Jack exclaimed. "I need to know everything you know. And don't tell me you don't know what stories Brian Fenton was working on; you have your sources. What was your friend looking into that could've gotten him killed?"

Cassie hesitated. "Brian was a political writer, and he was working on several stories involving local politicians. He was checking the records of the new city council members, what they said they believed in while campaigning, compared to how they actually voted on issues. There was also a piece on illegal dog fights that he felt strongly about."

"Politics and dog fights? Good combination."

"We all work on pieces unrelated to our main departments," she explained patiently. "Brian wanted to expose the extent of the illegal dog fighting in the city. That piece ran in the Sunday paper two weeks after his death."

"So you think it wasn't related to his death?"

Cassie shook her head.

"What else was he working on?"

She thought for a moment. "He was delving into the backgrounds of candidates running for various statewide positions. Brian was always interested in exactly who benefited from how people voted and how much personal gain the candidate himself received."

"Any specifics?" Jack asked.

"Nothing solid." Cassie poured them each another cup of tea. "You can't incriminate someone because of who they socialize with at parties. I'm not convinced anyone would jeopardize his reelection campaign by killing a reporter to keep him quiet."

Jack picked up the cup of tea, weighing his words. "Not unless that reporter had uncovered something which would get him bounced out of office and into a jail cell."

"True. But what did he find?" Jack waited for her to answer her own question. "Oh, what's the use," she said at last. "I'm not sure what's going on."

"You're not sure." Jack stared at her for a moment, then asked, "You really don't know which story he was working on that got him killed?"

"No, I don't. My educated guess is the story was politically involved. Brian Fenton was respected in this town. He was always careful to have the proof to back up his accusations."

"That's probably what got him killed." Jack muttered, looking right at her. "How did Rourke's name come up in this mess?"

"My informant said a transaction involving Patrick Rourke would take place soon, one he felt should never be completed. He wanted to know if I knew who Patrick Rourke was. I told him I didn't, to see what he'd say, but I remembered the story Brian had told me and I went searching for more information after we talked." Cassie looked at him. "He told me the man was from Ireland."

Jack didn't like the implications. Her knowing about Ireland hit too close to the past he was trying to keep hidden. "What did you find out?"

"Nothing much about that. I checked every source. He isn't a known member of the war—excuse me, the so-called troubles—over there, on either side. Nor is he a politician. I even checked to see if he was an entertainment figure. He's not. But you know all this, don't you?"

Jack didn't reply. He just sat there staring at her, but now his forehead was creased in thought, not anger. So far, she knew nothing about Patrick Rourke, and he intended to keep it that way. "You said Brian Fenton's notes disappeared? Every trace of what it was he'd been doing?"

Cassie hesitated, then made her decision. He wasn't going to be able to help her if she gave him nothing to work with. "Not all of it."

He leaned forward in his chair. "What do you mean?"

"We used to joke around about where we'd hide really important evidence if we ever got our hands on any. Before the police got to his apartment, I slipped in with my key and looked around." Cassie glanced at him. "I found a plastic bag beneath the refrigerator with a spiral notebook inside. It wasn't much help, though."

He tilted his head to one side and asked, "How so?"

"The notes are in Brian's handwriting but they don't make any sense," Cassie told him. "They must be in some kind of code."

He frowned at her and muttered, "I want to see them."

"Excuse me?"

Jack waved her question aside. "Quiet, please. I'm thinking."

Cassie watched as he stood up and slowly paced around the room. She had no idea what he was thinking about, but it seemed a good sign. Apparently she had convinced him that her suspicions were well-founded.

But what did that matter? His part was to get the documents; as long as he helped her do that, she didn't much care whether he believed in her quest for the truth or not. Just as she was about to point that out to him, however, he stopped pacing and came to stand in front of her.

"All right," Jack said. "Before we go any further let me make one thing clear. Your threat of publicity bothers me, but Patrick Rourke's possible involvement is what got me involved. You may not like it, but you're not going to be able to get rid of me." He paused, then added, "And this is going to take time."

That was the one thing Cassie didn't have in abundance. "How much time? I got another call from my source just this morning and he told me the documents might be moved. He also sounded more nervous than ever. I'm afraid he's going to clam up on me before I can get the number of the lockbox out of him."

Jack arched his eyebrows. "You don't have it?"

"No. But I do have the location of the bank."

"Good. But you'll have to get that number out of him somehow, and if possible a key. In the meantime, however, I think we should do some more digging."

"What are you talking about?"

"Are you absolutely certain those documents will help you prove Brian Fenton was murdered?" he asked. "Or show what he was involved in?"

"I just told you I'm not certain," Cassie replied curtly. "But the documents are my only lead to answering either of those questions, so why don't we concentrate on getting them?"

"We will," he assured her. "I agree with you that the situation surrounding the death of your friend is odd. But we're going to have to proceed very carefully—it could be a trap. I have enemies and so does Rourke. And if Fenton *was* killed, your probing into his death isn't going to sit well with whoever murdered him, either."

He wasn't telling her anything she didn't already know. "If you're trying to scare me, Jack, you're doing a pretty good job. But I'm still not going to walk away from this."

"I didn't think you would. Neither will I. Rourke can take care of himself, but he sometimes jumps in before he checks the depth of the water. Just like you."

"Meaning?" she asked.

"I think we should keep looking for information that your informant isn't offering."

"So where do we start?"

Jack returned to his chair. "Three months," he said, thinking out loud. "I'm sure Fenton's apartment has been rented again. I don't suppose you know where his stuff is now, do you? Did his family take it?"

"Brian didn't have any living relatives, other than an ex-wife who remarried ages ago. It was a furnished apartment, so there wasn't much, but I took his things and put them in storage." Cassie closed her eyes, remembering. "I couldn't bear to sell it off or trash it, not yet. Maybe after I find out what happened."

"You still have his personal effects?" he asked. She nodded. Jack clapped his hands, startling her back to the present. "Now we're getting someplace!" With that he jumped up, grabbed her hand and pulled her to her feet. "Where?"

"In a miniwarehouse I convinced Stan Lockwood to rent for me near my apartment."

His eyes narrowed. "Who?"

"Stan's my editor at the *Herald*. He's a friend of the warehouse owner and got me a discount. But I told you I looked through everything," Cassie objected. "Twice. Once just after Brian died and again as I was packing it for storage."

"Maybe you missed something," he said, practically dragging her toward the front door.

"Are you saying I wouldn't know a clue if I saw it? I'm a reporter, Jack. I don't miss things like that."

Jack stopped and yelled up the stairs, "I'm going out for a while, Russ."

"Are you now," a disembodied voice asked. "Might I inquire as to where?"

"Fishing," Jack replied.

"Don't fall in."

Jack turned to Cassie. He was still holding her hand. "I'm not questioning your abilities, Cassie. But reporter or not, you were grieving for a friend at the time. It's not easy to take a hard, cold look at the remnants of a person's life. I know. I've done more of it than I care to think about." He opened the front door and ushered her out. "As long as you've gone to so much trouble to acquire my expertise, you may as well use it all. You drive."

She slipped behind the wheel of her car and unlocked the passenger side door for him. No doubt about it, she had hooked up with a very odd duck. Cold as stone one minute, warm as sunshine around the little girl, Bridget, and now tender in his response to her grief over Brian's death.

Again Cassie wondered what she'd gotten herself into. Once Jack had decided to help her, he had certainly jumped in with both feet. Then again, she *had* forced his hand. And he had made it clear he was going along for his own reasons, she reminded herself, mainly to find out what his friend Patrick Rourke was up to.

Whatever happened, she was now even more determined to find out everything she could about the man sitting in the car beside her.

"Take a right up here," Jack told her.

"I know how to get to my own neighborhood!" Cassie made the turn, then glanced at him suspiciously. "The question is, how do you know?"

He looked smug. "The same way I knew your full name, and that you are arguably one of the most tenacious reporters in Houston. Unlike mine, your life is an open book, Cassie," Jack informed her. "Or should I say an open newspaper?"

Cassie pondered this revelation and decided she didn't like the implications. Jack was silent, too, seemingly lost in thoughts of his own.

Chapter Four

Brian had been a man of simple tastes and few possessions, which made it possible for Cassie to lease the smallest and thereby least expensive storage compartment available at the miniwarehouse facility. She'd had to put it in Stan's name to get the discount, but she was paying for it, and as a reporter for the notoriously underpaid print media, price had been an important consideration for her.

On this hot Houston day, however, she'd wished she'd taken a space with a big garage-style door. This one had a regular door with hasp and padlock; it was secure enough but didn't allow much fresh air to circulate within the tiny enclosure.

It was easier for Cassie to let Jack be the one to go through the boxes. Sorting through Brian's things was just as tough on her this time. Each item she touched brought back so many memories for her. Some memories were happy, some sad, others touching, some downright annoying. It was a bittersweet experience and one she could have done without. She wiped a tear from the corner of one eye, irritated with herself for not having more control.

"This is crazy," Cassie said, sitting down on a cardboard box full of books. She leaned against one of the slightly cooler cinderblock walls and sighed. "It's too damn hot to be looking for a clue that probably doesn't even exist."

Jack wiped beads of perspiration from his forehead with the back of his hand. "I'm beginning to think you're right." He was crouched beside an open box, searching through the piles of old correspondence within. His suit jacket and tie were tossed to one side, shirtsleeves rolled up to his forearms in an effort to gain a little relief from the heat. "There's nothing in this one of any interest. How about the one you're sitting on?"

"Paperbacks. And I already looked through every single book, page by page," she told him. "Brian was a big mystery fan."

"Obviously," Jack muttered. He stood up and shifted a stack of boxes marked clothing out of his way to get to a much larger box in the corner. "And this one?"

She heaved herself to her feet and joined him. "Let me see. Oh. That's his beer can collection."

"His what?"

"Brian collected beer cans from all over the world. I thought it was a silly hobby until he told me it was worth about a thousand bucks. Some of them are quite rare."

"Did you look through it?"

She shrugged. "No. It was already boxed up. I didn't see much point. Shall we?"

"Might as well," Jack replied. He pawed through the collection of empty cans, chuckling. "Amazing. I didn't know there were this many beers in the world."

The single bulb overhead didn't provide much light. Cassie had to bend down to see inside the box, peering over Jack's shoulder. "That's a neat one. It's so big."

"Australians like their beer big and bold," he explained. Jack picked up the can and hefted it, his eyebrows arched in surprise. "Hey! It's full."

"It shouldn't be. Brian told me collectors punch a hole in the bottom and drain them. That way they can have a can that looks unopened without the risk of it exploding or something." Cassie took the oversized container from Jack, frowned, then handed it back to him. "I've heard of full-bodied beers, but isn't it awfully heavy?"

"You're right." He held the can up to his ear and shook it. Nothing sloshed. "Unless it's thick as molasses, this isn't beer."

"Then what?"

Jack studied the can for a moment, then twisted the top. It came off in his hand. "Well I'll be . . ."

"What's inside?" Cassie demanded.

Still frowning, he turned the beer can upside down and caught the cylindrical hunk of gray-white material that fell out, then examined it in the dim light.

"I've seen these before. It's a concrete core sample," Cassie told him. "The kind building inspectors take at construction sites to make sure the proper mixture and procedures are followed when a big foundation is poured." She grabbed his arm. "Like the foundation of a high rise!"

"Or a bridge or . . ." Jack trailed off, watching the color drain from Cassie's face. "What's wrong?"

"Brian died as a result of a fall from a thirty-story building, Jack. A building which had just recently been completed. What if he had been investigating construction fraud? What if someone—"

"Hold it," Jack interrupted. "Before you can jump to any more conclusions, let me point out that a newly built high rise is usually empty, especially here in Houston with its depressed market." He patted the hand holding his arm and added softly, "A man who really wanted to commit suicide would pick an empty building, Cassie. Less chance of someone spotting him and interfering."

Cassie jerked her hand back. "A killer would pick an empty building, too. For the same reasons," she returned, her anger bringing color back to her cheeks. "It fits, Jack. If Brian suspected fraud in the construction of that particular building, it would have been easy to lure him there. And why would he have gone to the trouble of hiding this sample if it wasn't important evidence?"

Jack nodded thoughtfully. "You have a point. But we don't even know yet if this concrete is substandard, and even if it is, would someone commit murder to cover up construction fraud?"

"People kill each other over a lot less, Jack."

"Yes," he admitted in a quiet voice, "they do."

Cassie saw the pain in his eyes, could practically feel the sadness that descended upon him. Perhaps he was only expressing sorrow about man's inhumanity to man, but somehow she thought his reaction was caused by something much more personal.

Just as she was about to ask him what was wrong, however, the door to the storage space slammed shut. Because the overhead light was wired to turn off automatically when the door closed, the small cubicle was plunged into total darkness.

"Was that the wind?" Cassie asked in a shaky voice.

"What wind?" Jack replied. "It's ninety degrees and dead calm out there." Grabbing Cassie's hand, he pulled her toward the door. It wouldn't open. "Where's the padlock?"

"In my purse."

"Well, something sure has this door wedged shut." He beat on it and bellowed, "Hey! There're people in here!"

No one answered. The warehouse cubicle had become a stifling, pitch-black prison. Fighting the urge to scream, Cassie said, "This is probably as good a time as any to tell you I suffer from claustrophobia. Can we break the door down?"

"Not unless you're also going to tell me you've spent some time playing tackle for the Houston Oilers," Jack replied. "You're paying for secure storage, remember? It's a very good door."

"Then what are we going to do?"

"Did Fenton have any tools?" he asked.

"Yes! I think there might even be a crowbar around here somewhere. Hold on." Cassie took two steps, tripped on a box and sat down with a thump atop a rolled-up rug.

"Be careful."

"Gee, thanks," she muttered.

Cassie blundered around in the darkness for a moment. Then Jack spoke again, his voice far from reassuring. "I think you'd better hurry, Cassie. There's gasoline coming under this door."

She could smell it now, a choking, blinding veil of fumes that got worse as she rejoined him at the entrance. Someone had pried up the rubber seal at the bottom of the metal door, a tiny sliver of sunlight spotlighting the gas as it flowed in like waves on a beach.

"Here," she said, handing him the crowbar. Grabbing clothing from one of the boxes she tried to stem the tide of gas flowing in while Jack worked on the door. He succeeded only in bending the side out far enough that they could see through the crack.

"It's no use," he informed her. "Somebody has parked a truck against the door. That's where all this gas is coming from." It had soaked through the clothes and was pooling around their feet now. Jack pushed Cassie toward the far corner of the narrow room. "Get on top of those boxes. Now!"

She jumped up. He dragged the rolled-up rug over and spread it atop her. "What are you doing?" Cassie asked.

"Protecting you from the flames. I've got to try to chop a hole in this cinder block wall."

"Flames? What flames?"

Her answer came an instant later as a roaring ball of fire crept under the door, following the trail of spilled gasoline. The room was suddenly ablaze.

Through the thick black smoke Cassie could see Jack hacking fiercely at the wall with his crowbar. He had managed to open a small hole through the hollow cinder block to the outside, but the fire used the increased oxygen to surge forward.

It was a race against time, Cassie realized. And Jack was losing. Cassie grabbed a wrench and began to chip away at the concrete wall next to him. Progress was slow and the fire kept creeping closer to them.

Suddenly Jack stopped beating on the wall, apparently seeing something through the hole they had made that scared the daylights out of him. Jack let out a yell, grabbed her around the waist and pushed her against the far wall, sheltering her body with his. "Look out!"

The entire wall crumpled inward in a spray of concrete dust and broken shards of cinder block as the nose of a blue car slammed through the wall. Jack didn't waste a moment. He grabbed Cassie and threw her and himself onto the hood of the sedan which immediately pulled back out the way it came. The furious blaze reached out in one last attempt to claim them, then settled for the puddle of gas beneath the truck blocking the storage room door.

A tremendous explosion split the quiet afternoon air. Twisted pieces of the abandoned truck rained down upon the totally ruined corner of the warehouse complex.

After the driver of the blue car had driven himself and the passengers on his car's hood a prudent distance from the inferno, he stopped. Slinging his brown leather jacket over his shoulder he got out and stood looking at the smudged, smoky pair. The knife in his pocket was close at hand, but he didn't think he'd have to use it. Whoever had started the fire was long gone by now.

"When you go fishing," the man said with a grin, "you certainly don't mess around."

Jack coughed and helped Cassie off the hood of the car. They were both unsteady on their feet. "You're a lifesaver, Russ. Literally. Did you see who did it?"

Russ shook his head. "No. I followed you here, then hung around outside the security fence, just to keep an eye on things," he replied. "But the driver of that truck made fast work of it. He was up against the door and gone in a flash, if you'll forgive the pun, with scarcely a pause to light a match." Russ turned to watch a fire truck roar through the miniwarehouse gate. Then he added, "If it's any consolation, I don't think he really had time to see who was inside when he torched the place."

"I don't think he cared," Jack said. "Otherwise he would have stuck around to make sure someone like you didn't ride to the rescue."

The day was hot even without the nearby fire, but Cassie still shivered. "You mean he wanted to destroy Brian's things?"

"Looks that way," Jack replied.

Cassie was hypnotized by the fire, watching as the flames licked out to thoroughly consume every remaining piece of Brian's life, reducing it to ashes, just as Brian had been. She felt a strong arm slip around her shoulder, offering her comfort as tears streamed down her sooty face. Spray from the fire truck hose sprinkled them in a fine wet mist.

"You'll always have your memories, lass," Russ told her.

Cassie nodded and took a deep breath. "I guess the arsonist got what he wanted."

Jack chuckled at her forlorn expression. "Is that a fact?" he asked, holding up the cylinder of concrete.

Russ smiled. "Let's get out of here while we still can."

SIGHING, the stylishly dressed woman eased her foot into a tub of hot water beneath her beautifully carved mahogany desk. Her big toe felt as if it was on fire.

"What was that?"

She placed the phone receiver back to her ear and said, "Nothing. It's just been a bad day. I'm soaking my foot."

"Somebody step on your toes?" the man on the other end of the line asked, laughing at his own joke.

"You're damn right," the woman snapped, knocking a red shoe off her desk. "And I'm counting on you to make sure it doesn't happen again. Did you destroy it?"

"Yes."

"All of it this time? You're sure?"

"I said yes, didn't I? There were some people in the way. I may have gotten rid of them, too."

"May have?"

"Hey! You didn't pay me to bump anybody off this time. When you called earlier today you just said destroy everything in the miniwarehouse, immediately."

The woman banged her desk with her hand. "Who were these people?"

"How should I know? My fee didn't include asking for names, either. You said make the stuff disappear and it's gone. While we're on the subject of fees—"

"You'll be paid," she interrupted curtly. "But don't take it and go off on a bender. I may need you again before this is all over. Do you understand?"

The man laughed. "Yes. I understand. And for an added price I'll tell you the license number of the car parked closest to the units I destroyed. Do you understand?"

The scum! She had no choice but to go along with him. "You've got a deal, give me the number." She repeated it back to him. "I'll be in touch," she said, then hung up.

The man was an ass. But he was good at his job, as men who enjoy their work so often are. And if the amount was right, he would do anything she wanted. Anything at all.

Right now, though, she needed a man of different talents. One who could find out what that nosy reporter, Cassie O'Connor, really knew. No one was going to be allowed to mess up her plans. She also needed to have this license number traced and she knew just the man for the job.

CASSIE SET THE PHONE receiver down and looked at Jack. Both of them reeked of gasoline and smoke. His cream dress shirt was streaked with sooty brown spots, ruined, his suit jacket and tie destroyed in the fire. She didn't look much better. Her once-white blouse was stained with dark splotches and varying shades of brown dust covered her black pants.

"The markings on that core sample are those used by AAA Labs here in town." She walked across the smooth slate floor and handed him a piece of paper. "That's their address and hours of operation."

Jack nodded. "Did the police find out anything from the ministorage manager?"

"Nothing useful. He claims the guy came barreling through without stopping."

Frowning, he asked, "How did he do that without destroying the gates?"

"They were already open, a vehicle had just entered and the gates hadn't swung shut. And no, he didn't call the police to report a trespasser. Said he wanted to check it out on his own first." Cassie sat back down at the opposite end of the large oval table and took a sip of iced tea. She'd already finished two others. Her throat was raw from smoke and gas fumes.

"And the vehicle?"

"A small, local gas delivery truck that was reported stolen just before the explosion took place. The driver had been knocked unconscious while taking his coffee break on the outskirts of town. Of course, I wouldn't have to be calling my own newspaper trying to piece this information together if you hadn't insisted on leaving the scene of the accident when no one was looking."

Jack leaned back in his padded chair. "We discussed this on the way back here. Do you really want us to spend our precious time—time you say we don't have—trying to explain to the fire department what you and I were doing?" He cocked an eyebrow high. "And also have to explain how Russ saved us."

He did have a point, but she didn't think it was his only reason. "Admit it, Jack Merlin. You don't want the police checking you out."

"They wouldn't find anything." Not in this country anyway, he thought. He held up the piece of paper, deliberately changing the subject. "We need to find out exactly what the letters and numbers on the core sample refer to. Any suggestions?"

Cassie smiled. "You break into the offices of AAA, and rifle their files."

"Try this—you break into their computer system and rifle their records." He almost returned her smile. "It'll be safer and easier."

She sat up straight. "What!"

"You heard me correctly."

His face was alive, his eyes twinkling. He was actually enjoying her dismay. "I don't like that look, Jack Merlin."

"What look?"

His face was void of expression now, but she still didn't trust him. "What evil plot are you hatching now?"

"You hatched this evil plot, not I." He ran his finger down the side of the frosty tea glass. "And you're sinking right up to your sweet neck into the mess. This is a job for a computer hacker and I don't think we have to go searching for one, do we?"

"What are you saying?"

"My report on you was detailed. You know your way around computer systems. Must come in handy in your profession."

"I don't like what you're implying."

"You don't have to like it. You just have to do it." He glared right back at her. "We'll use my system here."

She stood up. "For your information it's better to go into systems at night when they're not being fully used. Less chance of getting caught," Cassie explained curtly, though she had the feeling he already knew.

"Agreed." He sipped his tea, eyeing her. "I'm curious. Where did you pick up these particular skills?"

"From a person I interviewed for a series of articles. He was finally caught while deleting one of his credit-card bills from a system," she explained. "His ex-girlfriend set him up or they never would have caught on. He taught me a thing or two that never hit the papers.''

Jack understood; he'd learned most of his skills that way, too. "It's been a rough morning. Would you like to stay for lunch?" He didn't know who was more surprised by his invitation, Cassie or himself.

Eat? He had to be kidding! Her stomach was doing flip-flops. "Thank you, but not today, I have too much to do." She picked up her purse and scarf. "I'll be back here around eight tonight."

"They shut down at five," Jack reminded her.

"I know that, but first I want to take a shower and put on clean clothes. Then I need to find out if their system has the capability to trace the phone number of the person logging on to their system. If they do, then I don't want to use your computer system here."

"Thoughtful of you."

She shot him a withering look. "I'm protecting my own hide, Jack Merlin. I don't want this traced back to you or me."

"Of course, how foolish of me. You're only protecting me because I'm useful."

Cassie ignored his taunt. Someone had tried to kill them both today. The meaning of those words had finally sunk in and her nerves, usually strong as iron, were shaken. She desperately needed some time alone to gather her strength for whatever came next. And there was work to do. She still hadn't had time to check out the latest name her informant had supplied, Mitch Johnson. What was his connection? Was he dead or alive?

"I also have to finish the background work on my charity article later this afternoon." The lie rolled smoothly off her tongue.

"How much of the money from local fund-raising efforts actually makes it to the needy causes?" Jack murmured.

He'd managed to shock her. "How do you—"

"Money buys answers."

Few people knew the exact direction her series was taking and Cassie didn't like the implications of his knowledge. She glared at him. "Who?"

"What you're working on is common knowledge." Jack stood up. "Knowing your investigative background, the rest is my guess about what you're really after."

Cassie moved toward the door, annoyed with his smugness. "I'll see you tonight."

"I'll be here."

Jack watched her graceful exit. He'd shaken her up on purpose and he planned to keep doing it in order to keep her on her toes. They needed to be ready for anything. They'd almost died today and they still didn't know why.

Chapter Five

"I want that address."

"We're doing everything we can."

He felt the heat rising in his face, turning it to a mottled red. He ran a four-fingered hand through his short auburn hair. "You've had months to work on this!"

"We warned you from the beginning. Without some kind of starting point these things are quite difficult. People *can* remain successfully hidden in a city the size of Houston, especially if they don't wish to be found."

"Keep at it." He slammed the receiver down. No. There had to be another way. He'd spent months planning this, and even more time setting up the situation. All his work wasn't going to be wasted.

He waited impatiently for the operator to put his call through. "Has the general been contacted?" he asked.

"Not yet."

"I can't wait any longer. Pay a visit to him and use whatever is necessary to get him to comply with my wishes. Once he is contacted I want you with him when he makes the call, and I want it traced. I want that address."

He wasn't going to accept defeat the way he had once before. This time he wouldn't be the one to give in. Living in the shadows had grown distasteful and he had been on the run too long. He wanted his freedom.

"WHY ARE YOU looking at me like that?"

Russ wiped the speculative frown off his face and replaced it with an innocent smile. "Like what?"

"Forget it." Jack sighed and turned back to preparing dinner. "Did you take care of our leak?" he asked.

"It's in the works. The first revealing photo should arrive at the general's home tomorrow. His wife will have to personally sign for the envelope. At approximately the same time a copy will also arrive at his office, marked confidential and with your note enclosed. And, by tomorrow that same photo will be in the hands of the reporter we owe a favor to in Paris."

Russ's efficiency never ceased to amaze Jack. "Thanks, Russ."

"About time, if you ask me, which of course you didn't. But that's all right. You've had other things on your mind," Russ commented with a sly wink. He watched as Jack poured white wine into a bubbling sauce. "I really thought we'd have problems with the general much sooner."

"So did I. If the man can't keep his mouth shut, his career is over. I trust everything is arranged to send the next picture out tomorrow if we haven't heard from him?"

Russ nodded. "It is. Personally I think the one of the general with his wife's lifelong best friend should be sent out next. It's time that old goat had someone close to home threatening him on a daily basis."

"I agree," Jack said. "That particular photo won't hurt his career much, even if it's made public, but what his wife will put him through is even better." The two men grinned at each other.

"'Hell hath no fury like a woman scorned'—or betrayed," Russ said.

"True." Jack tested his sauce, nodded and changed the subject. "Did you have any problems with Nancy?"

Nancy was the registered baby-sitter they had hired to help out with Bridget when she was home from school. Russ grinned broadly. "Did you expect any? As we predicted, young Nancy was thrilled to throw away her present perfume in exchange for enough money to buy several more expensive brands."

Jack returned his easy smile.

Russ sat down in a chair at the kitchen table, fiddling with the silverware. He was about ten years older than Jack but as strong as a bull. An intense, rough-hewn Irishmen, with clear green eyes and red hair, who'd seen the inside of more than one mine in his youth and had the muscles to prove it.

But Russ had found a hidden talent for working with his hands in an entirely different manner. Eventually, though, his close friendship with Jack Merlin and Patrick Rourke had become instrumental in putting the zealotry of his younger days behind him.

But his talents were still honed, and now he was tempered by experience to use them more wisely.

"Speaking of women," Russ said, after a thoughtful silence, "Cassandra O'Connor doesn't really have enough on you to force your hand."

"She has the threat of publicity," Jack reminded him. "And I don't want publicity of any kind, you know that, Russ. The peaceful, quiet life I'm building here is what I want now, what I need. A place to return to and call home." He paused then went on. "I'm going along with her plans."

"And might I inquire as to the real reason why you need her? We're capable of protecting Bridget and helping Patrick on our own."

Jack was only sure about one of his reasons. He wanted peaceful anonymity above all else. The rest of his reasons were tangled up with Cassie and what she was. His report on her had been quite detailed and he actually saw aspects of his younger self in her. How she would laugh if he told her that!

He looked Russ straight in the eye, knowing he could lie to his friend, but also knowing he needed his counsel now as much as ever. "I really don't know why."

Thoughtfully Russ balanced a fork on the tip of his finger. "Could be a trap."

"With your help, my friend, there won't be anyone standing under the net." He paused, thinking of Cassie and her seemingly genuine idealism. "If there is one."

Russ flipped the fork through the air and caught it, perfectly balanced, on the back of his other hand. "I'm ready anytime. When do we start?"

"Tonight. We can—"

A small, delicate cough interrupted him. "Jack, Russ is playing with the cutlery again." Eyes shining with devilry, Bridget entered the kitchen and sniffed the air. "Are we having plain chicken without any mushy stuff on it, and plain potatoes?" she demanded.

Jack looked over at Russ. "Where did we ever find such a pristine young lady?"

"What's pristine mean?" Bridget asked, dragging a stool over to the stove and climbing up to look into the pan. She wrinkled her nose in dismay. "Gross!"

Jack reached out and gave one of her braids a gentle tug. "Go look it up in the dictionary."

"I don't know how to spell pristine," Bridget said, looking up at him with wide, innocent, green eyes, "so how can I look it up?"

"Work it out phonetically," Russ told her as he helped her down from her perch. "Go on now, lass, and no dessert unless you find the definition."

"What's for dessert?"

"There's only one way you're going to find out."

They both watched her scamper out of the room and heard her sliding across the wooden floor, her young voice high with glee. Russ shook his head and sighed.

"Are you driving her over to Kathleen's tomorrow?" Jack asked.

"Wouldn't miss the trip," Russ assured him.

Kathleen was Jack's housekeeper, and Russ was quite in love with her, but his convincing her of that had so far proven to be an insurmountable task. She'd been married and deserted very young and since had refused to love again. But Russ wasn't easily dissuaded. He'd declared his intent to win her heart with or without her cooperation.

Bridget returned, struggling with a book that seemed only slightly smaller than herself. She lugged the book over to the breakfast table and plopped it down, not seeing Jack wince as the spine hit the hard surface.

"That's a book, Bridget, not a battering ram."

"Excuse me."

"Are you sure you've got a big enough dictionary?" he inquired.

"It's a big word, so you need a big dictionary," she explained patiently. Her small hands began riffling through the pages as she looked for the correct spelling.

Jack watched as Bridget coaxed Russ into helping her find the word. Part of his need for privacy involved Bridget. He'd bought this place not just for himself but for her as well. She needed a great deal of reassurance and consistency in her life. And it was something Jack intended to provide for her for as long as she needed him. It was a wonderful feeling to be needed and loved unconditionally.

Ripples of girlish laughter filled the room as Russ began tickling her. She wiggled free and ran toward Jack. "Save me!" she squealed as Russ pounded the floor behind her.

Jack whipped the little girl up into his arms and hugged her close. "Found the word, did you?"

"Yes." She felt so safe and secure with him. No matter how busy he got, he always had time for her. Jack, Russ and Kathleen were her family now. And Patrick Rourke.

"Well, green eyes?" he teased.

"Yes, sir golden eyes," she returned impishly, bumping his nose with hers. "It means pure, things are in their natural state," she recited. "Adulterated."

Jack glanced over at Russ. His shoulders were heaving with suppressed laughter at her unknowing choice of words. "Unadulterated," he corrected softly.

"What's the difference?"

"Think about the prefix. The two are opposites. You like all of your food in an unadulterated, pristine state, no sauces added," Jack explained.

"I'm pristine, sauces are yucky," she sang. "If I eat all my vegetables I'll be as strong as Russy."

"Russy?" Russ demanded, trying to look fierce and failing miserably. "Russy?"

Bridget sniffed. "I had to make it rhyme," she informed him, doing a much better job of looking haughty than he was of looking mean. "Poets can do that 'cause they've got a license."

"They don't actually have a license, Bridget," Jack explained, laughing. "It just a term. Poetic license."

"That's what I said."

Jack took one look at her defiant expression and started laughing so hard he couldn't explain further.

Russ wasn't about to try. He was still wondering if he'd ever live down a nickname like Russy.

"Can we eat now?" Bridget asked impatiently.

Throughout the meal and until her bedtime, Bridget kept them fully entertained, falling asleep within minutes of crawling into her frilly canopy bed. The two men finished the joint effort of tucking her in and went to the study, taking full advantage of the peace and quiet.

"We need to track down Rourke," Jack said as he handed Russ a short crystal glass filled with a generous portion of Irish whiskey. "Cassie said he's unwittingly involved in whatever it is she's digging into."

"How do we know it's our own dear Patrick she's referring to? It's a common enough name."

"True, but Cassie's told me enough to make it seem likely. Do you know what he's up to right now?" Russ shook his head.

"Neither do I," Jack said, pouring a shot into his own glass. "But I'm inclined to believe Cassie."

"Put that much faith in the lass, do you?"

Jack laughed. "You know me better than that, Russ."

"Then what makes you so sure she's not leading you down the garden path?"

"Where she's leading me remains to be seen," Jack told him, giving him a sidelong glance. "But she's probably telling the truth about Rourke, especially considering his penchant for trouble. For one thing, she knew enough to balance her whole scheme on that one name, certain I'd cooperate with her for the chance to help him."

Russ almost spilled his liquor as he whipped his chair around to look at Jack, his eyes narrowing shrewdly. "What else does she know about? Does she know anything about who Bridget is or what happened in Ireland?" Russ asked.

"No. But her curiosity is aroused and she's persistent enough to be dangerous. With that mess in Paris as a starting point she's quite capable of digging up other facts as well. Working with her is the best way to control her."

"She could be holding information back," Russ warned.

Jack agreed. "I'm sure she is. But if Cassie knew anything more about our former occupation she'd have used it against me. Her position was far too weak."

"Are you sure you want to proceed with this?" his friend asked, looking as close to worried as he ever came. "Sounds like complete madness to me."

"Yes, I'm sure," Jack said, "I need to know exactly what she finds out and how she comes up with the information. If somebody other than the general is talking about me, I want to know who." Jack sipped his drink and shrugged his broad shoulders. "Bridget is always at risk, and since Cassie got Patrick's name from her anonymous informant, we have to proceed on the assumption he's somehow involved, too."

Russ nodded. "Then we're in this all the way."

"Agreed. Anyway, we'll plan this job like we would any other, camouflaging our backsides each and every step of the way. That's why I want Cassie involved up to her pretty neck."

Russ grinned. "As added insurance? Now that sounds more like the Jack Merlin I know and love," he said, laughing raucously. "Exactly what are these documents you're looking for?"

"She's not sure. But they're supposed to prove her friend Brian Fenton didn't commit suicide."

That news dispelled some of the good humor Russ had been feeling. There was no way Jack was going to let this problem drop, and that in turn meant Russ would have to look after him even more closely than usual. He swallowed the rest of his whiskey and stood up.

"That setup today at the miniwarehouse was done by a professional. He was in and out fast, used a stolen vehicle, burned all traces of his existence to the ground. I'd say these people don't want to be discovered."

"But were they actually after Cassie or was her being there a coincidence?" Jack asked.

"I don't know if they're on to her, lad, but the closer she gets the nastier they'll become. They may not miss next time," Russ warned.

Jack looked at him. "Then let's get started."

"I'll start tracking Rourke down tonight."

Barely aware of his friend's departure, Jack leaned back in his chair, his legs stretched out in front of him, the amber liquid in his glass swirling around the rim as he thought of Cassie. She was quite a woman, and he sincerely hoped she was going to start being more honest with him. He couldn't very well protect her if he didn't know all the facts. He tossed back the rest of his drink and got to his feet. There was work to be done.

He walked over to a pair of bookcases that had been swung away from the wall and through the white double doors that lay behind them. His hidden office was paneled in redwood. Plants were everywhere, the grow lights giving the room real warmth. His inner sanctum, Bridget called it.

Sitting down at his desk, he dialed a number from memory. It was a funny thing, he'd never met Harry face-to-face, but over the years he'd gotten to know her.

It was somehow comforting to know that Harry hadn't changed her phone number after all these years and the cackling laugh he knew so well was still vibrant.

"As I live and breathe—and let me tell you that's gettin' harder for me ever' day—I never thought I'd hear from you again, Jack."

He could hear the painful raspy wheezing as she took each breath. The sound seemed amplified over the phone lines. It had gotten much worse. "Didn't think I'd be calling you, either, Harry. Still in the same business?"

"Some things don't change. What ya need?"

"Complete plans of a branch bank in Houston."

"You, rob a bank? My, my! Fellow comes out of retirement and goes completely wild." Her wheezing chuckle turned to hearty laughter and then into a painful cough. "Give me the info on it," she ordered when she was able to talk.

Jack told her the name and location of the bank. "How fast can I get these plans?"

"Give me a day or two, Jack. I'll be in touch to set up the pickup."

"Okay. And, Harry, set the meet up for a woman." He heard a scratching on the line, followed by a banging noise.

"Sorry about that, there must be something wrong with my phone. Did you say a woman? You don't work with women."

"I do this time. You take care of that cough, Harry."

"Ain't nothin' they can do for me. But don't you worry, boy," she said, chuckling again, making Jack smile. "I got my successor all picked out and trained. I'm takin it easy in my old age."

"Good for you, Harry."

He leaned back in his chair contemplating who he should call next. The first two numbers he tried no longer belonged to people he had once known. It didn't surprise him. After five years what did he expect? He punched in another phone number, the unusual ringing tone was oddly familiar, as was the voice on the answering machine.

"State your name, phone number, method of payment and what you want."

Jack was brief. "You know who this is and how I pay. I want information on who might have been paid to kill one Brian Fenton. He was a reporter in Houston, Texas, died from a fall off a thirty-story building." He consulted his notes and gave the date. "And I need it yesterday." If Fenton had been murdered, then this contact—given enough time—would come up with an answer. But would it be soon enough?

He had started the ball rolling, but it wasn't moving fast enough for him. Banks were dangerous places to rob and the penalties high if one was caught. As far as he was concerned there were plenty of other places they could look for answers before he resorted to robbing lockboxes.

For starters they needed to find out exactly where that core sample had come from, but he needed Cassie to do that. He glanced at his watch, noting that she was already a half hour late. Still, he sipped his whiskey and waited. He'd spent most of his adult life waiting and he was good at it.

HER HAND WAS RESTING on the cradle of the phone. She had no choice. Someone had been going through private records that could be used against her. She had thought all the loose tongues stilled, but she'd obviously missed someone.

Through the years she had found it necessary to do a great many unusual things in order to keep the social status she valued so highly. It was the way she'd been brought up to do business. She dialed a familiar number.

"Do you know who this is?"

"Yes."

"I have a traitor within my organization, Mr. Knox. I need to know who it is. After you've given me his name I want to know who this person has talked to and what he has revealed about my family's business. Do you want the job?"

"That's all you want done?"

Her tone was sharp. "Do you want the job? A simple yes or no will suffice."

"I never accept a job without knowing exactly what is expected of me." He repeated his question. "Is that all you want done?"

"No. Once you've extracted the information from this person I want him killed." She didn't need to ask if he was capable of murder, she already knew he was. "Make it look like an accident," she added.

Anthony asked, "And the method I use for extracting the information you want?"

"I'll leave that to your discretion."

"What about the person he's talked to?"

"I want to know who it is first. The rest can be decided later."

"If it's anyone with a high profile the fee goes up accordingly," Knox reminded her.

"I am aware of your terms. Do you want the job?"

"I'll take it. Half up front."

"One third now, a third after the family informant is dead and a third when the whole job is completed. That's my only offer."

Knox expected this. They'd argued over his fees before and he'd never budged an inch. For her he charged top price. "Fine. Give me your list of suspects."

"There are only three who know enough to do any real damage." She gave him the names. "Be very sure of your findings, Mr. Knox." He could hear the smile in her voice. "Their continued good health depends on your accurate research."

"No need to worry. I'll get the right man."

Chapter Six

It was past eight-thirty. If Jack was like most men, the first thing he'd do was nag her about being late. Cassie didn't care. She drove slowly up the curving drive, still mulling over what she'd discovered that afternoon. Mitch Johnson was dead. Another construction accident and another victim. Where was all this leading? She hadn't been able to find any connection yet between the two buildings where the accidents had taken place. But then, she hadn't found out who actually owned those buildings yet, either.

Why had her informant given her this particular name? Was he trying to confuse her to hide his identity? If he was, then he was doing a magnificent job. Right now she felt as if she wasn't even close to finding out what Brian had discovered. Or who was responsible for his death.

The core sample might give her the answers she needed. If one of the men had died at the location the sample came from, then she might be on to something. What, she didn't know yet.

Russ was waiting for her on the front porch keeping the dogs at bay while she entered. "You're looking lovely this evening."

A blue and white crepe blouse was tucked inside navy blue slacks that hugged her hips. Her black hair was French braided. Cassie smiled. "Thank you." She glanced down at herself, then back at him. "Quite an improvement from earlier, wouldn't you say?"

"I would." Russ laughed. "He's waiting for you in the library."

Jack didn't even give her time to say hello before the questions began. "What did you find out?"

Cassie shot him a quick glance before remembering he knew nothing about the other names she possessed. "According to a friend of mine who is a computer salesman, AAA's system doesn't have the capability to backtrack who logs on."

"Good." He stood up and crossed to a computer sitting on a lovely rosewood desk. "Let's get started."

She was positive that the machine hadn't been there earlier today. She was fascinated by computers. "Nice machine!"

Jack pulled up another chair. "With the latest telecommunications software, too. I'll show you the quirks."

As he ran through the basic operating procedure the scent of whiskey was unmistakable to Cassie. Did he drink a lot? And why? Who was this man? His mysteriousness made him both intriguing and exciting, like forbidden fruit.

"Okay?" he asked, once he'd finished his explanation.

"Got it." He was also a good teacher. Cassie maneuvered her chair in front of the keyboard, then glanced at him. Their chairs were touching and when he leaned forward to point things out his shoulder brushed hers. "Don't you have something to do?"

He pushed up the sleeves of his white cotton crewneck sweater. "Yes. I'm learning how to break into other people's computer systems. And no, you can't get rid of me. I'm always open to new technology. Look at it as one of the prices you'll pay for using my expertise in other matters."

Cassie sighed. "All right, you can watch. Just don't ask questions." She elbowed him aside. "And give me space to work!"

For the next hour she worked in silence until she latched on to AAA's system. Then she probed deftly into its data base and brought up a menu of what it held. She continued working and eventually found what she wanted, but didn't like the results she finally came up with.

"It can't be," she muttered.

"What's wrong?"

"According to the file, all core samples from that lot number passed every test," Cassie informed him.

Jack frowned. "Strange. Why would Fenton have kept one of them, then? And taken such pains to hide it?" he wondered aloud. "What sort of project was the sample from?"

"A twenty-story office building," she said, standing up and stretching. "Gunther Construction Company was the builder. The name isn't familiar but I can find out more about them quite easily. I can also find out tomorrow if the inspector for that project is still working for the city."

"You think the test results may have been altered?"

She turned away for a moment and closed her eyes. The strain of working on the computer had dried them out. "Like you said, why would Brian have kept a sample otherwise?"

"Maybe he just suspected something, the lead didn't pan out and he never got rid of it."

"You didn't know Brian."

Jack couldn't help noticing the tightness of her back muscles, and the tension in her slender neck. He didn't think all of it came from pounding a keyboard for two hours, either.

"Why do I have the feeling you know something I don't?" Jack asked. "You have some other reason for suspecting fraud, don't you, Cassie?"

"Not fraud, necessarily, but something." She sighed. Decision time. Cassie wasn't entirely sure it was in her best interests, but at some point she was going to have to trust him. Jack's help was essential to her, and she couldn't expect him to work totally in the dark. "My informant has given me three names. Patrick Rourke, Rusty Green, and today, Mitch Johnson. Mitch Johnson died in a construction accident two years ago. Russell Green is also dead, from a similar accident. Satisfied?"

Three men, two of whom were now dead. Jack didn't like the odds. Suddenly, he was more worried about Patrick than ever. "Why didn't you tell me this to begin with?" Jack demanded, clearly angry.

"When I first contacted you I only had the first two names. I didn't think there was a connection to Brian's death until we found the core sample. And even now I'm not sure they're related. It's just a hunch."

Jack shook his head. "Give me a break, Cassie. Brian fell from a high rise. I'd say it's more than a hunch."

"All right! They could be related. *Could* be. But I don't have anything that puts all of the pieces together. Yet. I didn't tell you about it because there wasn't any reason to."

"From now on, could you let me be the judge of what is and isn't important to me, Cassie?" he asked her sternly. Secretly Jack was pleased. This was a sign she was finally starting to trust him, at least a little. But he wasn't going to let her off the hook. "Any little thing, no matter how insignificant it may seem to you, could jump up and bite us if we aren't careful. Is that clear?"

"Whatever you say...sir." The heavy sarcasm in her voice made him smile in spite of his anger. He pulled a map out of the desk drawer and set it on the table. "Where is this building?"

Cassie looked at the address she'd copied down from the computer screen, then located it on the map. She visualized the area. "I'm not positive, but I don't think this building was ever finished."

He nodded, and Cassie realized he was lost in thought. The more she was around Jack Merlin the more curious she became. Where did he come from? She'd thought he was from Ireland, too, but he didn't have an accent like Russ or Bridget. What nationality was he? And how was he related to Bridget?

Cassie intended to spend part of tomorrow afternoon trying to find out, after she made sure the interview with Mrs. Xavier was still on for that evening. Her duty to the newspaper had to come first if she expected to keep her job.

"Depending on what you find out tomorrow we might want to inspect the premises," Jack told her at last.

"Why?"

"If this is the same building we're both thinking of it's only half-built. Why wasn't it completed?"

She shrugged. "I don't know, but I can find out."

"Do that."

Cassie picked up her purse. "I won't be able to come over tomorrow evening. I have to interview one of the charity party givers at her gala event. But I'll call you if I find out anything."

"You're always ready to leave before you even get here." There was a gleam in his eyes. "Do I make you nervous?"

Yes he did, in more ways than one. But she wasn't going to bolster his ego. "You wish."

"Did you remember to bring those notes of Brian's you found?" he asked, letting the other subject drop.

From the intent look on his face, it was a good thing she had. "In my purse. Would you like to see them?"

"No, I just wanted to know where they were." His sarcasm wasn't lost on her. "Give them to me."

Cassie pulled the small notebook from her purse and tossed it at him, hitting him square in the chest. "Anything else?"

"Stick around while I look at these. Help yourself to a drink," he offered.

Jack was already studying the blue-lined pages when Cassie left the room, headed for the kitchen. She needed black coffee. Alcohol at this point would knock her out.

A single light over the kitchen sink illuminated only part of the room. The far end of the kitchen table was concealed by the shadows. Cassie opened cupboard after cupboard looking for coffee.

There had to be some, somewhere. What kind of household was this? She'd found the mugs and spoons and had nothing to go in her cup.

"Try the freezer."

She whirled around, her spoon and cup clattering to the counter. A familiar shape moved out of the shadows. "Dammit, Russ, you scared me!"

He chuckled. "A bit nervy are we, darlin'?"

Leaning back against the counter, she crossed her arms over her chest. "Now why would you think that?"

Russ crossed to the freezer and took out a jar of instant coffee. "Have a seat before you fall down. This'll be ready in a jiffy."

"Thank you." Cassie sat down and watched him mix the cup of coffee and put it in the microwave. When the bell tinged he pulled it out and opened another cupboard. "What's that you're adding?"

"A little something to quiet your nerves. Irish Creme. The best available in this country."

Cassie thought she detected a hint of wistfulness in his voice. "Do you miss Ireland?"

Russ set the cup down in front of her. "At times. Have you ever been there?" Cassie shook her head. "It's a truly beautiful country. Someday you'll have to visit."

"I'd like to." She sipped the hot coffee. "This is good." Holding the cup between both hands she continued, "I wanted to thank you for coming to our rescue today. And I'm sorry about the damage to your car."

"Don't give it a thought, the car's been through worse and it'll mend, a lot easier and quicker than people do."

He meant what he said. Looking Russ in the eye she asked, "You don't approve of what I'm doing?"

"I never said that, and I can understand your reasons. But you could have found someone else to do your dirty work."

Cassie gave him a tired smile. "People like you and Jack aren't that common or easy to find."

"Exactly how did you find us?"

"The reporters' grapevine. Brian Fenton heard it from a reporter friend of his who was living in Paris at the time. Apparently they both thought the story a great exaggeration on the general's part."

Russ looked at her quizzically. "Why?"

"Why wait eight years to tell the story? And why at a party with the media present?" She shook her head. "It didn't make any sense, especially considering what he was revealing wasn't exactly flattering. Why gloat about the incident?''

That very question bothered Russ, too, but he didn't let on. "Was my name mentioned?"

"As a matter of fact, it was. But what the general's story emphasized was the closeness between Patrick Rourke and Jack Merlin. And that Merlin now lived in Houston, Texas." She took a sip of coffee and continued. "The general did try to gloss over how he'd managed to persuade Jack into helping him out of his bind." Cassie grinned at him. "But reporters are like piranha, they can scent where the real meat is."

Russ chuckled. "That they can. Speaking of which, how did you find out Jack lived here?"

His voice was soothing, almost hypnotizing. For a moment Cassie gazed at him curiously, wondering where a big, brusque Irishman like him had learned such a subtle interrogation technique. Who were these men, and what had made them what they were?

"Diligent research." Cassie smiled, suddenly deciding to be honest. "Not really. I happened to come across it accidentally a few years ago and stored it away for future reference. It came in handy." His questioning look encouraged her to explain further. "There was a delivery being made here from a local department store, I recognized the name and noted the address. That simple."

Jack leaned against the doorjamb. They were talking quietly and he was hesitant to interrupt. For some uncanny reason, people—especially women—found it easy to confide in Russ. Rather than scaring them, his size seemed to reassure them.

"Another cup?" Russ asked.

"Straight coffee this time, I have to drive home tonight."

"Straight it is." Russ picked up her cup and glanced at Jack. "Quit hovering in the doorway. You want a cup, too?"

Jack held up his glass. "No thanks." He sat down opposite her, dropping the spiral notebook on the table. "Do any of these initials mean anything to you?"

"No, except under purely speculative circumstances." She took the cup of coffee from Russ. "Thank you. There," she said, pointing to one of the entries. "MJ. Mitch Johnson? Who knows? I could assign those initials to any number of people, but I have no basis to start with. They might not even be names for all I know."

He didn't like the way she wouldn't look at him. "You aren't lying to me, are you Cassie?"

"No." Both men were staring at her intently. "I'm not! Maybe if you spent your time deciphering it, and quit accusing me of wrongdoing, we'd get somewhere."

Jack chuckled. But he put his hand on the notebook. "I'm going to hang on to this for safekeeping."

"All right." She sipped the steaming brew, not at all worried. A copy of that notebook was in a very safe place. "I'll call you tomorrow when I find out more about that building."

"I'll be waiting."

Cassie gulped her coffee, more than ready to leave once again. Russ was comfortable to be around, but Jack tended to disturb her equilibrium. "Can I have your phone number?"

"What?" Jack looked at her, not comprehending her request at first. Then he chuckled softly. "You break into my home, blackmail me, and you don't have my phone number?"

She gave him a dirty look. "Just give me the number."

Jack took the notepad Russ handed him, both of them still chuckling. "Testy late at night, aren't we." He scrawled his number then handed it to her. "Do me a favor." He waited until Cassie met his look. "Memorize it before you leave."

"Okay. But I positively will not eat it when I'm done." She took the piece of paper and stared at it for a moment. "Got it," she murmured, then placed the sheet in Russ's outstretched hand.

"I'll see you out, Cassie," Russ announced. "We don't want the dogs nipping at your heels when you run to the car. You might trip over something in the dark."

Cassie followed him out of the room. "Why didn't you tell them to heel yesterday?"

"And deprive myself of such prime entertainment?"

"If you call that entertainment you're warped, Russ."

Jack sighed aloud as their voices faded into the background. As if Russ wasn't bad enough, now he had an accomplice in his pursuit of weird humor.

"Quite a lass," Russ announced, entering the kitchen.

"You like her?"

Russ straddled a chair, smiling at Jack's accusatory tone. "Yes I do. She's quite good at her job. Not afraid to go after what she wants or needs. But you already know that. She's also easy on the eye, charming, witty and intelligent." All his life Russ had made snap decisions about people. And he was rarely wrong. "What she said about the general's story rings true, and I don't like the implications. It makes absolutely no sense for him to speak up now.

He knows we have copies of those photos. Why risk our exposing him after all these years?''

"Maybe he was coerced.''

Russ nodded. "Probably was. But who?''

"Your guess is as good as mine. We have more enemies than friends.''

"Too true,'' Russ said. "If someone is after us we'll have to let them show themselves first.''

Jack stood up. "I agree. Anything on Rourke?''

"No. And with Bridget home from school it's not like him to not at least put in an appearance, for her sake. Besides,'' he added with a grin, "I put out the word that I'd kick his butt from here to Belfast if he didn't contact us.''

Jack looked at Russ. "Nice to see you still remember the old code.'' Jack smiled, but he was still worried. It was hard to believe that something could have happened to Patrick without him hearing about it. But it was possible. Where was Patrick Rourke?

The neon sign was flashing on and off to draw motorists' attention. It was also a constant irritation if one was sitting within the range of its obnoxious flashing light.

He eased his sore body into a more comfortable position. After the long, turbulent transatlantic flight, he needed a good bed, not the front seat of this compact car. But first he had to make sure that the kid he was trailing after wasn't going to be making any sudden moves.

Following him from the airport had been easy. They'd both gotten their rental cars at about the same time and the kid had made only two stops on the way here, one for fast food, the other for liquor.

Rourke glanced at his watch. Just past midnight. He'd been sitting here for three hours now and no one had paid the kid a visit. Rourke figured he was passed out cold by now. And there was an easy way to find out.

The phone number of the motel was plastered across the front of the red brick wall, another neon sign trying to lure people in. When the manager answered the phone, Rourke asked for the room number he'd seen on the white painted door. The phone rang again and again, but no one answered.

Walking into the office he booked a room for one night, right next to the kid's. Once inside his own room he crawled out the back window. The screen on the unit next to his had a hole in it already.

He eased the latch open, then quietly removed the screen. As he'd suspected, the kid had left the window cracked. Foolish mistake.

Inside the room he moved cautiously, the gentle snoring sounds leading him toward the bed. Rourke pulled a pencil thin flashlight from his pocket and turned it on. He flashed the beam of light across the kid's pimpled face. There wasn't even a flickering of the eyelids in response to the bright light. He was passed out cold, an empty pint of whiskey beside him.

Rourke hunched down, the light held between his teeth as he went through the flight bag on the floor. Inside a black velvet bag he found what he was looking for. But he didn't take anything; instead he left it right where he'd found it and went back to his room to get some sleep. The contents of that bag would eventually lead him to something worth even more.

Chapter Seven

"Making any headway?"

Cassie jumped. "Stan, don't sneak up on me that way." She had thought she was alone in the newspaper's basement, or *morgue* as many of them referred to it. She'd been there since early that morning and it was now late afternoon. Casually she covered up her notes, before swiveling her chair to face him. How long had he been there? He sat down on the edge of a nearby desk. "Any leads?"

"No, I'm not getting anywhere." With gentle fingers she massaged her tired, strained eyes. When she closed them she could still see the microfilm pages flipping past. "Why the interest?"

"I'm your editor."

She laughed out loud at that and even made him smile. Stan? Concerned? "Ha! Give me a break."

"I already have. One of our reporters spotted you and some guy in the area of that fire yesterday." Cassie didn't say anything. "You didn't arrange that fire to stir up interest in the story, did you?"

"What!" Shocked, Cassie jumped out of the chair. "You know me better than that, Stan. Or you should by now."

Their gazes locked and Stan couldn't miss the fury in hers. "Fortunately I do." He leaned back. "So, what were you doing there?"

"I live in that area, remember?" He was playing her along, Cassie realized, waiting to see how she'd react to his words. She sat back down. What was he up to?

"And you just happened to be there when the explosion took place?" he asked.

"What are you trying to say, Stan?" she asked suspiciously. His even voice was growing more irritating. "It's not like you to beat around the bush like this."

He folded his arms. "I talked to the police earlier today. Remember, that space for Brian's things was rented in my name. They asked me some unusual questions. Did I know who would want to destroy the last remnants of someone dead for three months? Or why? After all, he was working for me at the time he committed suicide."

Cassie winced. "What did you tell them?"

"Nothing, because I don't know anything, do I? I have a reporter who's investigating this, and the next thing I hear a storage unit is being blown up. What do you know?"

"Not a damn thing." Which was the truth. "Are the police sure the space you leased for Brian was the one targeted?"

Stan nodded. "Oh, yes. They also know a car smashed through parts of two other storage units to make a hole in the unit that Brian's things were in. Isn't that odd?"

Cassie struggled to remain calm. "It certainly is. Did they get the license number of the car?" An even better question was how had the person who'd tried to kill her and Jack yesterday found out the location of Brian's things? From Stan? Who else knew? And who else knew she was investigating Brian's death? The only other person she could think of offhand was Mrs. Carlyle. Stan had mentioned it to her. "Will you call me if you find out?"

Stan nodded and stood up to leave, then sat back down. "I'm worried about you, Cassie. You've always been tenacious, but this time it's like this story has possessed you. Why can't you let this go?"

"Because I'm the only one who cares."

He rubbed his hands over his face. He wasn't getting anywhere, but then he hadn't expected to. "Cassie, please be careful." He stood up again, slipping his hands into his pants pockets. "And if you need help, promise me you'll call."

She held up one hand. "Scouts honor, I promise."

"And keep me informed! That's an order."

Cassie saluted him, smartly. "Yes, sir. Will there be anything else, sir?" Why didn't he leave?

"Now that you mention it, you haven't forgotten about the Xavier thing tonight, have you? I don't have another reporter covering it," he added.

"Ah, so the true meaning of this visit finally floats to the surface." She smiled at him, unable to resist a little dig. "You're usually not so slow, Stan. Old age must be catching up with you." He frowned at her. "I haven't forgotten. I've even arranged to see her for a short time this evening."

Heading for the open doorway, Stan announced, "Good. Then I'll let you get back to work."

"Wait a second! Stop right there, Stan. What do you mean I'm the only reporter who'll be there? Why isn't the society columnist covering this?"

He turned around. "She has the flu."

"Stan, I don't have time to write some fussy piece on who wore what, by whom, with whom. I'm on leave, remember?"

"But still on the payroll," he informed her. "You have Mrs. Carlyle to thank for that, by the way."

Writing things like that were sheer torture for her, and Stan knew it. Cassie crossed her arms. "No! Absolutely not."

"You can at least give me a list of who's there, can't you?" Stan asked, then added, "in case the photographer misses anyone important?"

"I suppose I can do that," she conceded, "but nothing else. No dress descriptions, no—"

He held up his hands, interrupting her. "Okay, none of that, but I want a complete list," he ordered.

"Stan, why don't you just get a copy of the guest list?"

He smiled. "Good idea, you do that, but double-check it for accuracy before you turn it in."

Cassie watched him leave, feeling only slightly victorious. She'd learned the hard way with Stan. Get all the ground rules spelled out first. Getting a copy of the list would be easy, and then her job would be done. Later she would also have to thank Mrs. Carlyle.

Turning around, she resumed reading the material on the microfilm machine, the interruption already forgotten.

Stan walked silently back into the room. Cassie seemed completely unaware of his presence and he took advantage of her total absorption in the material to read over her shoulder. It took him a minute to figure out who she was studying.

"Hook family, huh?"

Cassie jumped out of the chair. "Stan, I'm going to clobber you! Didn't I just tell you not to sneak up on me?"

"Sorry." He didn't look the least bit sorry, but he did step back a few paces. "I just thought of something."

Her tone was terse. "What?"

"Brian's stuff. You had to tell the police where you were going to store it when you were waiting for his will to go through probate."

Cassie stood in front of the machine she was using, still trying to hide the screen. "Sure. That's right. Thanks. Now if you don't mind..."

"Do you think the Hooks have something to do with Brian's death?"

Cassie laughed. "What! Your mind is slipping, Stan." Still chuckling, she turned around and flipped the machine off, then put her notebooks inside her purse. "The Hooks are the last segment of the charity series that you demanded I finish."

He shrugged. "Just doing my job."

"Well, get out of here so I can do mine."

"I'm leaving," he announced, walking toward the doorway.

"And good riddance."

The rest would have to wait for another day. She needed to get over to the hall of records and do some checking before they closed today. Where was the time going?

Russ and Jack parked beside each other in the driveway. "Harry called earlier," Russ said as he climbed out of his car.

Jack closed the door of his Mercedes. "When's the meet?"

"You'll have to call her back." Russ grinned. "Bridget was with me."

Jack returned his smile, following him into the house. "And she does hear everything."

"Wants everything explained, too," Russ added. "It's best she's staying at Kathleen's for the next two days."

"I agree. How is Kathleen?"

Russ beamed. "Lovely as a morning rose ready to bloom. She'll be back here in a week or so. Her mother's leg is about mended."

"Good." Jack knew Russ had missed seeing her daily, and besides, the house needed cleaning. He relied completely on Kathleen to supervise that part of things for him. He headed straight for the phone in his office.

He sat down at his desk and punched in a phone number. "Harry, this is Jack Merlin. When and where?"

"Tomorrow at two." She gave him the address. "It'll be the usual routine. And I told 'em to expect a woman like you said."

He found the street address on the Houston map. Jack hadn't expected a good part of town, but you couldn't get much worse.

Cassie wasn't going to like this one bit. Hell, he didn't like it, either. But the meet was set and they'd stick to it. He wasn't breaking into anything without those plans.

Jack found Russ in the garage, trying to bang one of the new dents out the hood of his car.

Russ looked up, particles of blue paint clinging to his red hair. "What unsavory task needs doing now?"

"The meet is set for tomorrow at two. Will you check out the site for me? General layout, exits, that kind of thing." Jack told him the address.

Russ's shrill whistle made Jack jump. "Lovely part of town." Russ gave him a wicked grin. "Why don't you do it yourself?"

Jack grimaced. "Because I'm not big enough to walk into a place like that alone and back out again. In one piece that is."

"At least you know your limitations. Sometimes." Russ continued to bang on the car. "Cassie call?"

"Not yet."

Russ gave the car a good whack. "How's the bank?"

"It's an old bank building, but financially quite sound."

"Good." Jack made no move to leave and Russ sighed. "What else do you want me to do?"

"The usual stuff. Oh, I'll need a hat and oversized denim jacket for Cassie to wear, too. Sorry to lay all this on you, Russ, but I've got arrangements to make for our cover at the bank."

Russ glanced up from his banging. "Don't worry, I'll take care of everything. Just leave me a list."

The phone was ringing when Jack walked back into his office. He let the answering machine click on.

The voice he heard was female. "I . . . um . . . this is Ms. James. Uh . . . I don't want to alarm anyone but . . . I'm sorry, I'm the secretary at the school Bridget attends. We just—"

He grabbed the phone, shutting off the machine at the same time. "Jack Merlin. What's wrong?"

"I have instructions to call if there are any inquiries about Bridget Houlihan," she replied. "A woman called asking if we had a girl by the name of Bridget attending our school. She didn't know the last name but her description of Bridget was quite accurate. We, of course, said nothing."

The worry lines between his eyebrows deepened. "Did she identify herself?"

"No, but her phone manner was quite experienced."

"I appreciate your calling, Ms. James."

"Bridget *will* be with us at the start of next term?" Ms. James inquired.

"Of course. Thank you."

Jack strode out of his office, yelling at the top of his lungs. "Russ! Russ, we've got trouble!"

Russ came running asking "What's wrong?"

"Someone called Bridget's school asking about her."

"I'm going to Kathleen's. I'll get the car."

Jack ran to his office, grabbing a black sheath of narrow knives as a car horn began blaring nonstop. "Where's the damn gun," he muttered, tossing things aside in his haste to get to it. He ran out the front door to find Russ leaning on the horn. He handed the knives and gun through the open front window.

"Don't be so slow about it, lad," Russ shouted. "Go punch those gates open before I hit them. And call Kathleen. Warn her." The old blue car peeled out, dust and dirt flying everywhere.

Jack ran back into the house and punched in the code to open the gates. Then he called Kathleen, and talked to Bridget for a few minutes, assuring himself of her safety.

Once those tasks were completed he headed for his own car. He had his own ideas about who might have called the school, and he was going after her.

Chapter Eight

Juggling an overloaded sack of groceries, Cassie unlocked her front door, fumbled her way into the dimly lighted entry hall, then slammed the door shut with her foot. Silence greeted her.

Her roommate, Tracy, a roving supervisor for a major retail chain, was out of town opening another new store. Sharing the apartment worked well for both of them; neither spent much time at home, and the financial savings were important to Cassie.

Cassie was putting her groceries away when she heard a strange noise. Heart hammering in her ears, she listened for another sound. Complete silence. But she didn't move. Fear kept her immobile.

She had thought she was handling the stress of her present situation quite well until now. Had she made a slip somewhere and become the hunted instead of the hunter?

Her gun was in the bedroom, in the drawer beside her bed. It would be a long walk down that dim hallway.

If there was an intruder, she wasn't willing to take chances with her life. Her fingers curled around her purse and keys as she made the decision to run out the front door and call the police.

Cassie stopped as suddenly as she had started. There was a shadowed figure leaning against her front door. She turned, running for the only other exit, the patio doors.

"Going somewhere?"

The mocking voice stopped her cold. She turned to face the intruder.

He stared at her, unmoving. Cassie could practically feel his cold fury, even from across the room. "What—"

"Did you call Bridget's school this afternoon?"

"Well . . . I . . ." she sputtered.

"Yes or no? Her life could be in danger."

"Yes."

Jack crossed to the kitchen wall phone and punched in a number.

At last Russ answered the phone. Jack spoke quietly. "Russ, it was Cassie. I'll be in touch later."

Cassie could barely contain her curiosity. "Why is Bridget's life in danger?"

"You just can't leave well enough alone, can you?" He took two steps toward her and stopped. "Don't try it again. You have a question, ask. If you don't like the answer, tough. Is that clear?"

"No, it is not. I'm a reporter, it's my job to—"

"To get innocent children murdered?"

"What!" Cassie froze. "What are you talking about?"

"Bridget."

Cassie gave him a puzzled look. "But I don't know anything about Bridget."

"No, you don't, but that didn't stop you from trying to find out, did it? If you aren't damn careful Cassandra O'Connor, you are going to be the one responsible for Bridget's murder."

"Murder?" The meaning of his harsh words slowly sank in and her anger was replaced by concern. "Murder?" she repeated. "Why don't you calm down and tell me what's going on?"

"Calm down!" His fingers clenched and unclenched in frustration. "I've been cooling my heels in this apartment for over an hour waiting for you to get here. And you tell me to calm down!"

Cassie kept her distance. This was the most emotion she'd ever seen him show, and all of it was violent. "Why don't—"

"I've been sitting here, wondering if they had finally learned of Bridget's existence, found out where she was, what she saw. And you tell me to calm down. I'd like to wring your neck."

She gripped the back of the sofa, ignored his threat and kept her voice low. "Jack, you're yelling."

"You're damn right I'm yelling. At you and your stupidity. How did you find out about Bridget's school?"

Cassie sighed. Maybe answering his questions would help. "I followed Russ, Bridget and the baby-sitter into a department store and overheard the name of the school in the dressing rooms."

"Who else did you call or contact today? I want every single name," Jack ordered.

"Stan. He's my editor," she reminded him. "And a few other co-workers. I was also at the records department today, looking up births here in town. But it's hard to trace someone without the correct last name," she informed him.

The creases in his cheeks became more pronounced as a coldness settled over him. "But you tried, using all of our last names, didn't you?" Cassie nodded. "Who else?"

"Mrs. Xavier's office."

Jack looked up at the ceiling, then back at her. "Who the hell is Mrs. Xavier?"

"The woman I'm interviewing tonight for my charity article." Cassie paused before letting the next piece of information drop. "She runs a benefit for the Irish Orphan's fund each year."

Jack closed his eyes, trying to calm his temper. He had never hit a woman, and he didn't want to start now.

Cassie's interview for this evening just happened to be a woman who had ties to Ireland. Lately there were too many coincidences. What was going on? His voice softened and he spoke slowly. "What did you tell her about Bridget?"

"Nothing." His eyes popped open. "I only talked to her secretary," Cassie explained with a shrug. "At the time I hadn't thought about asking her for information."

"And you're not going to!"

Cassie dropped her shoulder bag and keys on the couch, but stayed safely behind it. She still wasn't getting within his reach. "Not if you tell me what I want to know."

"I can't believe you're this callous. We're talking about the life of an innocent child."

She sat down on the back of the sofa, one foot swinging back and forth, the other on the ground. "So you say. Why should I take your word for anything?"

"Because you need me if you're going to find out if Brian Fenton was murdered."

Cassie looked right at him and replied, "And you need me and my source to find out if Patrick Rourke is involved."

Jack stared at her, weighing his options. He didn't have many and she knew it, and he was positive she wouldn't let this drop without a damn good reason. "If Bridget were to die because of what I'm about to tell you, I'll come after you myself. Do you understand?"

"Yes. And I still want to know." Cassie had no intention of harming or bringing harm to the child.

"Bridget—" he paused, still hesitant "—Bridget's parents were gunned down in Northern Ireland. She saw it happen, and she can identify the men responsible." Jack held up his hand to stop her questions. "No one claimed credit for the execution, and her parents were involved in a great many things, most of them illegal."

"If Bridget can identify them why weren't they found?"

"Because no one knew who they were. Rourke came up with one name, but we couldn't find the man before we quit looking."

Cassie's mouth dropped open. "You quit?"

"We had to quit before we aroused anyone's curiosity," Jack said. "No one knew she was in the house that night except for the old couple who kept her when her parents went out of town. And no one came looking for her after the incident."

"Then why are you so overprotective? No one saw her."

Jack sighed. Would her questions never stop? "Sometimes, years later, unforeseen events cause people to check out previously overlooked details. Like what happened to the child of the couple you murdered?"

And if the rumors from Ireland were correct, that was exactly what was happening now. But Jack didn't intend to tell Cassie that. He still didn't completely trust her.

"How did you end up with her?"

"Rourke found her hiding in a closet. He got her out of the country that same night, brought her to Russ and me, then went back to find out what happened."

"How did Rourke get involved?"

"You just never stop, do you Cassie?"

"Come on, Jack, answer the question. I've already agreed to blanket amnesty for him, he's safe. And details like that drive me nuts."

"I think someone should drive you nuts for a change." His anger had started evaporating as soon as he'd known it was Cassie checking up on Bridget and not someone else.

"Okay," Jack answered at last, "Rourke was in a local pub and overheard something. By the time he found the house they were dead. Satisfied?"

"One more question. What did you have to do to get in here?"

"The lock on your patio can be opened with a credit card."

Cassie almost fell off the sofa as she whirled around to look at the doors. "Where's the doorjamb lock?"

"There wasn't one."

She could see that. Her eyes darted nervously around the room. "There should have been. I check it every night." Her eyes met Jack's. Panic and fear filled her face. "Someone else has been in here."

"Now, Cassie, you can't be sure." It was obvious that this had really shaken her up. "Is anything missing?"

She looked around the room. The television, stereo and VCR were all in place. "Not that I can see."

"Search the rest of the place," he ordered. Cassie didn't move. "Don't worry, no one else is here right now. I've been through the entire apartment."

Cassie returned moments later. "Everything seems okay, just like I left it."

"I found the lock under the curtains," Jack said, checking to make sure he'd installed the locking gadget correctly. "Are you sure it was locked and in place?"

"Positive. I've been paranoid about things like that since this mess started."

Some stranger going through her things bothered her more than she cared to admit. It left her feeling shaken and vulnerable, emotions she rarely had to deal with. Who had been inside her apartment? What were they looking for?

Jack saw her shiver again and crossed the room to stand close to her, instinctively encircling her in his arms. She leaned into him, letting his warmth and strength seep into her.

"It could have been your roommate."

Her voice was firm. "No. I talked to her last night. She won't be back for weeks."

"The apartment manager?"

Cassie glanced at Jack. "Possibly. It's easy enough to find out." She slipped away from him, found the number and dialed it. Tapping her foot, she waited impatiently while they checked maintenance records.

"No one from the complex was in here today," she told Jack, hanging up the phone. "So! What does that mean? Does someone think we're on to them?" she asked, rubbing her arms to stop the shivers. No wonder he was flippant in the face of danger, Cassie thought. It was easier to accept that way.

He squeezed her shoulders reassuringly. "I warned you this would be dangerous."

She leaned back against him, needing the comfort he offered. Things had been a mess for a long time now and without Brian to talk to she'd felt quite alone. Her best friend was dead. Was this how they had come after Brian? Or had Brian had no warning?

Was she going to be next?

"Jack, if the person who searched my apartment hadn't left that lock on the floor I'd never have known he'd been here. There's nothing out of place."

"It's the way professionals work."

"But why leave it on the floor?" She looked at him over her shoulder. "Would you leave the lock on the floor?"

"Not unless I wanted you to know I'd been in here. If he did that, I'd say he's hoping to shake you up enough to have you make a mistake and reveal what you're working on. Which is probably what whomever hired him wants to know." Strong fingers massaged her shoulders. "Another possibility does exist. Maybe he heard something and had to leave in a hurry."

"Jack, what—" The phone rang, cutting her off in midsentence. Cassie grabbed it, irritated by the interruption. "Hello."

"Cassandra?"

Her body sagged back against the kitchen wall. "Elizabeth isn't here."

"Same as last week. Five minutes."

"Damn, double damn!" Cassie muttered, looking around the room. Where had she left her keys? She ran across the room and frantically began searching for them among the sofa cushions.

"Your source?" Jack inquired.

"Yes. Where did I leave them?"

"Looking for these?" Her keys were dangling from his finger. "We'd better get going or you'll be late."

Cassie snatched the keys from him and ran out the front door, barely giving Jack time to exit before she slammed it shut and locked it. He steered her toward his car. "I'll drive. It doesn't bother me to break the law, remember?"

She didn't argue. There wasn't time and he did drive much faster than she; near misses with other cars didn't faze him.

Cassie barked directions like a drill sergeant, ordering him to take a left, then a right and another left. She led him through the back streets like a professional navigator, and he responded with consummate skill.

The phone was ringing when Jack pulled up. She was out of the car before he put it into Park. "O'Connor."

"Are you ready to get the documents? Time is running out." His voice was even more distorted than usual, making it hard to even to understand him.

"How can I be? I still don't even know their exact location! They haven't been moved, have they?"

"No, but until you're ready to—"

"No," Cassie interrupted. "This time, you listen to me. If you expect me to help you, you're going to have to cooperate. I'm the one doing your dirty work. Give me what I need to do it!"

Silence greeted her words. Had she gone too far? The events of the past few days had gotten to her, unnerved her usual calm approach to her work. She glared at Jack, who was practically standing on top of her, listening in on the conversation.

Finally her informant spoke. "How soon?" he asked curtly.

Jack held up four fingers. Cassie said, "Four days."

"All right." He gave her the box number, repeating it twice.

Jack was gesturing to her. She did her best to interpret. "When do I get the key?" she asked. Jack nodded his approval.

"I don't think that will be possible," her informant replied.

"I can't do this without the key. I'm taking chances, you have to take chances, too."

One minute stretched to two as Cassie waited for him to answer her. He suddenly spoke. "I don't know. There's more I haven't told you about." This was perhaps even worse than betraying family. In a way he was betraying his heart.

"What?" Cassie asked.

"They really are going too far this time, jeopardizing everyone's future in this country."

His voice was fading out. She pressed the receiver closer to her ear to hear him better. "What are you talking about?"

"Never mind. I'll try and get you the key. Lance Mizer."

"Wait!" The line went dead. "Dammit, I pushed too hard."

Jack held the car door open for her. "Maybe, maybe not. But we do have the box number and now we can find out who owns that box."

"You make it sound so easy," Cassie said, sliding into the front seat.

He closed her door and got behind the wheel of the car before he answered. "With enough money it can be. Who's Lance Mizer?"

"I don't know, the name doesn't ring any bells." Cassie looked at him. "That's how he did it before, just dropped the names on me like bombs. Except for Rourke. As you know, he was a little more specific on him. But this time I'll let you know right away when I find out who Lance Mizer is, okay?"

Jack started the car and put it in Reverse. "You do that. Where to now?"

Cassie glanced at her watch, groaning as she noticed the time. "It can't be seven! I should already be downtown keeping my appointment with Mrs. Xavier. Can you drive me?"

"The Irish Orphan fund-raiser?" Cassie nodded. "Is it legit?"

"Very. The accounting books are open. They're very proud of the way this thing is run and the money distributed. The bare minimum goes for administration cost. Mrs. Xavier's late husband began the whole thing."

Jack could almost hear the hesitation in her voice. "And?"

"He was an orphan himself, from Ireland. Like Bridget."

Jack didn't say anything, didn't look at her, just kept driving. Cassie chewed on her lower lip. An apology was due and he wasn't making it easy for her. And now that she knew the circumstances she didn't need anyone else adding to her mounting guilt.

"Look, Jack, I'm sorry if I've caused any trouble to come Bridget's way. But how was I supposed to know that her life might be in danger?" Cassie placed a hand on his leg. "Please believe me. I would never deliberately harm her."

Silence filled the car. "Jack, say something."

"I like the way your hand is caressing me, but unless you intend to let it lead to something more intimate I suggest you remove it."

Cassie jumped, pulling her hand back. It had seemed so natural touching him that way. For once she was at a loss for words. Her body was tingling with awareness, an awareness of him as a desirable man.

Jack accepted the ensuing silence, knowing his words had startled Cassie, just as her roving fingers had startled him. He'd known from the start that he was attracted to her, and the attraction was growing stronger. They both had a lot of thinking to do.

The lighted mirror on the back of the window visor projected a soft glow onto Cassie's face. Jack watched out of the corner of one eye as she transformed herself. First she touched up her makeup and applied more lipstick. Then, she added a broach at the throat and flipped up the collar of her gold silken blouse. It was amazing what those small changes could accomplish. She looked quite elegant.

Neither spoke until Jack pulled up in front of the lavish hotel she'd named. "Are you coming inside?" she asked. "This shouldn't take much time but there will be a ballroom-size crowd in there."

Jack thought about it for a moment. The chances of anyone inside knowing him were slim to none. Besides, he didn't want to leave Cassie alone to find a way home. Someone *had* searched her apartment this afternoon and they still had no idea who it was. If he stayed in the background it would be easy to slip out of the room unnoticed if he saw anyone he knew.

"I accept."

Chapter Nine

Cassie meandered through the guests, taking note of who was present this evening and at the same time looking for Mrs. Xavier. Jack had disappeared as soon as she'd gotten him through the door. She only hoped he wasn't lifting someone's jewelry.

"Come on, Cassie," she muttered to herself. "You're not being very fair. You don't even know if he's capable of doing that." Cassie smiled at a man who was looking at her strangely, then turned the other way. She had just been talking to herself out loud again. Jack was getting to her. Here she was, already making excuses for him, a man she barely knew. His revealing Bridget's past to her had touched her, and shown him in a different light. But she didn't have time to dwell on that, she needed to mingle and get her mind off him and back on the job.

The ballroom of the hotel was filled to capacity with people affluent enough to afford the high price tag required to touch elbows with the cast of a theatrical touring company and various soap opera stars. Every mode of dress was present, from formal, to avant-garde, to casual.

Cassie finally spotted Mrs. Xavier, but at the moment she was talking to the very person Cassie was trying to avoid. Mrs. Carlyle. Even though she knew she should take the time to thank her for keeping her on the payroll, she felt it was too soon after stepping on her toes to bring attention to herself. Besides, she wasn't ready to discuss her story with anyone. Cassie definitely wasn't going to interrupt that little gathering.

The third woman in their group was Mrs. Hook, Cassie's next charity article subject. All three had known each other for years and were quite close friends. Judging from the color and style of their hair they also all shared the same hairdresser.

The newspaper photographer winked at her as he passed, and Cassie grinned.

Cassie continued to mingle, making a complete circle of the room. It was impossible to see much through the dense crowd. Where was Mrs. Xavier now? All Cassie wanted was to do the interview and get out of there. There were more important things that needed her attention tonight.

A whiff of distinctive perfume suddenly caught and held Cassie's attention, teasing her senses. Who did that scent belong to? The information was on the tip of her tongue.

Someone squeezed her shoulder lightly, interrupting her train of thought. Cassie turned around. The woman behind her was slim and elegant in her black gown, the bodice encrusted with tiny seed pearls. Short silver hair glistened under the soft lights. Her face was almost unlined.

"Why, Mrs. Xavier, I've been looking for you."

"I know, dear. Please excuse my tardiness, but there are so many details to attend to at functions like these."

Cassie smiled at Mrs. Xavier, who was the epitome of Southern graciousness and charm. "I can only imagine. Could we find a quiet corner to discuss a few of those details?"

"Why of course. This way, dear." For the next fifteen minutes Cassie had Mrs. Xavier's undivided attention. The woman answered all of her questions with straightforward details and facts.

One of the most prominent—and good looking—members of Houston society, Allen Hook, finally interrupted them. "Pardon me," he said, smiling at Cassie before leaning over to whisper something in Mrs. Xavier's ear.

Cassie heard a name that made her eyes widen. She followed Mrs. Xavier's gaze as she sought out and found a cluster of well-dressed men.

"You'll have to excuse me now, Cassie, but I have other business to attend to. If you have any more questions just call my secretary for an appointment. She'll also be happy to get you a copy of our guest list for this evening."

Cassie thanked Mrs. Xavier for her time, waited a moment and then began discreetly following her across the room. Even though the other woman walked with a slight limp and was moving slowly, the crowd still prevented Cassie from staying with her for very long. Had she overheard Allen Hook right? Was that man really here?

Cassie looked around. Where was Jack? She needed to find him, and it wasn't going to be easy in this zoo. At last she spotted him and headed more or less in his direction.

He stayed off to one side, letting Cassie work her way around the room toward him. More than a few of the people there knew her, if the number of times she was stopped were any indication at all.

Finally she neared him and he slid his arm around her waist. "Looking for anyone special?"

"You!"

"How flattering."

She turned, placing both hands on his chest. "He's here!"

Cassie hadn't seemed the type to be stunned or excited by a movie or music personality. This side of her made Jack smile indulgently. "Who?"

"Patrick Rourke."

His fingers tightened around her waist, the open smile gone. "How do you know that? You don't even know what he looks like."

"True, but I overheard someone mention his name to Mrs. Xavier. Haven't you seen him?"

"No, but then he wouldn't expect me to be here." Nor would Jack expect Patrick Rourke to be in attendance, either. What was going on? "Let's mingle." They worked their way back and forth across the room but Jack didn't see him.

"Maybe he'll get in touch with you later tonight," Cassie said.

Jack didn't answer her. Patrick Rourke was a common name. It could be a coincidence. But Jack didn't believe it was. Why was Patrick here? And where had he disappeared to? Jack didn't like puzzles, especially ones involving Patrick Rourke.

"Let's get out of here. We still have work to do tonight."

AS THEY WALKED toward the exit, a hazel-eyed man watched them with great interest. Were his eyes deceiving him? Was it really Jack Merlin? What was he doing at a function like this?

Patiently the man waited until Jack turned his way once again. It was Merlin all right. One didn't forget a man who drove you to fake your own demise.

This was working out quite well. Serendipity. The woman would lead him right to Jack, saving him valuable time. This time he'd remove the threat forever.

He'd only had to ask three people who she was before someone had recognized her. Cassie O'Connor, reporter. Her address would be easy to come by.

Now he had to make some quick decisions and hope he made the right ones. He couldn't take any chances, not against Jack Merlin. He went to find a pay phone. But he had to wait a long time before anyone answered. He spoke softly.

"Be ready to roll within the hour."

"WHAT DID YOU FIND out today?" Jack was watching her carefully, gauging her response.

"We were both right—the high rise was never finished. And as far as I can tell Gunther Construction was an independent company."

"Was?"

"They no longer exist, due to bankruptcy," she explained.

"What about the inspector?"

"The inspector does still work for the city. I didn't have time to do any cross-referencing to find out if he served as an inspector on any of the projects where the fatal accidents occurred. But I intend to."

Jack nodded his approval. "Any other connecting links?"

"None that I've found."

"Okay," he said, turning to leave the room. "I want to check out the high rise tonight. Better under the cover of darkness than in broad daylight. Give me a few minutes to change clothes. Then we'll go by your place."

Speaking of which, something had been nagging her. "Wait a minute. At my apartment, earlier today," she reminded him, "you looked around a bit while I was gone, didn't you?"

"Yes." Jack turned and looked at her, his shirt hanging open. "What of it?"

Cassie's eyes widened a bit. Nice pectorals. But she quickly hid her interest behind another question. "You took the break-in so calmly. What did you find?"

"In your freezer you'll find two listening devices. One was in the living room under the coffee table, the other in your bedroom on the lamp. There's no way to tell how long they'd been in the apartment. Before you go to bed tonight put them back out," he advised. "If whoever put them in your apartment suspects we've found them, they might decide to come get their answers in person instead." He turned and walked out of the room.

Great! Her apartment was bugged. What had she revealed? And to whom? She needed more answers, not more questions.

WHEN THEY TURNED OFF the main highway onto a dark feeder road, a car followed them. The driver smiled. It looked as if they were going to make his job easy for him.

Rising high above them were the open square cubicles of an unfinished building, the steel beams rusting away. The ground was littered with construction debris left behind, booby-traps for anyone in a hurry.

Cassie slipped through the slit in the chain link fence right behind Jack, directing the beam of her flashlight on a faded sign. "Gunther Construction. They were one of the companies that lost everything when oil prices sank to nothing. Looks as if they abandoned this project completely, too. Not even a guard to watch over what's left of it."

"Lucky for us. Now we won't have to bribe anybody to let us take a look around."

"And just what are we supposed to look for?" she asked.

He shrugged. "I'm not sure."

"Great."

"Not much to see down here, though." The concrete floor beneath their feet was covered with dirt, old newspapers and other trash. Tumbleweeds littered the corners. Jack looked at her over his shoulder and smiled. "Did you get your exercise in today?" he asked, making his way to the west side of the building.

Cassie lagged behind. The stairway he was heading for was exposed, open to the air, and she didn't like the looks of it at all. She wasn't fond of heights.

"How high up are you going?"

"About midway." He looked down at her. "Coming?"

She put one foot on the first step and gripped the rusted railing firmly.

They started climbing up. Level after level, higher into the air, the ground a dark smudge below them. Cassie's knuckles were chalk white on the handrail now. A light breeze ruffled her hair. "This better be worth it, Jack. What do you hope to find up here, anyway?"

"I want to take a look around. Check out whatever's been done. Maybe I'll find some code violations."

He continually surprised her. "You know the correct sizes for this stuff?"

"I researched it." When they were about halfway up, Jack went through an open doorway back into the building. "There's a hole in the flooring to your left, there," he warned her as she joined him. "Unless you've got a strong nervous system, don't look down it."

Cassie took his advice, deciding to wait for him right where she was. Let him do the research for a change. She pressed her back against the concrete wall. It felt nice and solid, much better than wandering around on a floor with holes scattered hither and thither.

Everyone had their phobias, and height was one of hers.

Finally she worked up the courage to focus her attention someplace other than her own shoes. Other than the wall behind her, the building was open to the air, with only narrow columns of steel and a small raised ledge lining the perimeter to block her view.

The twinkling lights of the night city were all around them, stretching for miles in every direction. In the distance the sound of traffic hummed, an occasional honking horn disturbing the steady rhythm. After the hectic day she'd had, she welcomed the peace and quiet of this place. It was almost as if they were alone on a tiny island, and there was no way for anyone to disturb them.

A shadowed figure silently stepped off the stairs onto the level below her. He paused, listening, then moved to one of the steel girders. This job was more than worth the effort he was expending on hunting down his quarry.

Best of all, he'd soon be even with the man calling himself Patrick Rourke. Never again would he call expecting him to jump on the first plane to wherever he needed a job done. Or to sit in a strange city for two weeks, like he had here, waiting to find out who his target would be.

Cautiously, using the girder to steady himself, he stepped onto the perimeter ledge and grabbed hold of the one above his head, levering himself up to peer over it. He spotted his victims. They weren't together, which would make the disposal more difficult.

But not impossible. He'd get rid of the man first, then take his time with the woman. He lowered himself back down and started edging his way along the ledge toward Jack.

"CASSIE, COME HOLD this light for me."

Ready to fall asleep, Cassie blinked rapidly, trying to clear her tired, gritty eyes. She'd been up since six this morning and would probably get precious little sleep tomorrow.

She pushed herself away from the wall, but didn't move forward. He was all the way across that treacherous floor.

"Find anything?"

"Maybe." He flashed his pencil-slim flashlight at her.

Suddenly a dark figure loomed up beside him. "Jack!" Cassie screamed. "There's somebody—look out!"

Jack dropped flat to the floor as he felt someone try to shove him off the building. The man came down on top of him hard, knocking the wind out of him for a second. But when he felt himself being pushed toward the edge, Jack latched on to the other man's clothing and rolled back to the center of the high rise.

Both figures were dark-haired and dressed in black clothing. Cassie had her gun ready but couldn't tell one body from the other in the muted light. They were punching and pummeling each other as they rolled around on the floor. One of them managed to get on top, but the other hit him in the side with his knee and threw him off. Rolling apart, they jumped to their feet and started circling each other. Suddenly, one lowered his head and charged like a bull. The two men grappled, their battle taking them ever nearer the perimeter wall and the nothingness beyond.

Cassie couldn't just stand here, she had to do something. Jack could get hurt, even killed. Raising her gun in the air, she pulled the trigger.

The sound of a shot being fired startled both of them, and one man slipped, hit his knee on the ledge and tumbled over the edge of the building. Luckily the other caught hold of his hand, preventing him from falling into oblivion.

"Jack!" Cassie cried. Her fear of heights forgotten, she strode across the floor, gun at the ready.

"Yeah," he ground out through clenched teeth. His grip on the other man was weak. "I'm okay. But he's not."

And the man was well aware of that fact. "Help me up!"

Jack wrapped his arm around one of the steel beams to secure himself, but didn't pull the other man up. His voice was harsh as he gasped for air. "Answer some questions first." He took a deep breath. "Who do you work for?"

No answer. Jack shifted his grip on the hand that held the man suspended between life and death. "Answer me." Nothing. "This is your last chance," Jack yelled, threatening to loosen his grip. "Who do you work for?"

"All right!" He thought desperately, quickly, and chose the false name. "Patrick Rourke!"

"Try again and the truth this time. Or you're going to free-fall nine stories."

"Wait!" the man pleaded. Panicked, he spat out the name. "Flynn!"

Jack almost lost his grip on the man at the mention of that name from his past. "He's dead."

"No he's not, he's here in Houston." The guy sounded even more desperate. "Now pull me up!"

Jack didn't *want* to believe Flynn was alive. "What does he look like?"

"He's missing a finger, and he's about five eight, short auburn hair, hazel eyes!" the man replied quickly. "Now help me up! Please!"

Flynn couldn't be alive. He had died in a car bombing, killed by a mistake he himself had made. Or had he?

"Cassie, keep the gun on him," Jack told her. Then, he looked down at the man who had recently tried to kill him. "You're going to have to help—use your legs when you can."

Jack kept his arm securely wrapped around the steel beam as he struggled to pull the dangling man up over the side. But the leverage wasn't right. It wasn't working.

"Help me!" the guy cried out.

In an effort to gain more leverage, Jack positioned himself even more precariously. He pulled with all his might, and slowly the top of the man's head appeared. Too late, he realized that his attacker had gotten one arm over the perimeter ledge and no longer needed his help. Instead, his opponent suddenly yanked hard on his hand. Already off balance, Jack lost his footing and swung out over the abyss. Though he clung desperately to the beam, he couldn't prevent himself from slipping all the way down it until the ledge hit his armpit.

"No!" Cassie cried. She grabbed Jack's arm with one hand, pointing the gun with the other. "Stop right there!" she ordered the man.

He laughed and reached for Jack's dangling legs. Cassie fired, the bullet missing him by inches. Startled, the man stopped and looked her way. The gun was pointed right at him.

"I won't miss next time," she promised.

"Neither will I, lady," the man told her. With that, he grabbed the ledge with both hands and swung himself down to the level below. A moment later she heard him pounding down the metal stairs.

"He's getting away."

"Let him." Jack's voice was hoarse as it floated up over the edge. "I could use your help now. Quickly, please."

She set her gun down. "What do you want me to do?"

"Crawl over here, so I can see you," Jack replied.

The edges of the steel were gouging into the flesh of his arm, cutting off his circulation. When he tried to move his other arm up to grab the ledge, he felt his hold on the beam loosen. But he had to do something. Soon his arm would be numb.

She did as he asked, every possible inch of her body hugging the floor. With only her neck sticking out over the ledge she looked down at him. "Oh no." His feet were dangling in the wind and there was no way he could reach anything to secure his position. It was a long drop. She groaned, feeling dizzy.

"Don't look down, look at my eyes." He waited until she did as he'd asked. "Good girl," he praised softly. "Now, extend one hand out to me." She didn't comply. "Cassie, I'm not going to grab your hand, I'm going to throw you something. See this cord?"

Her voice was shaky. "Yes. What do you want me to do?"

"Grab the end of this, wrap it around the beam and secure it with the latch." He tossed the end at her.

She caught it. Wasting no time, Cassie secured the cord as he'd said. Then she tested the snugness before announcing, "Okay. What now?"

"Stay back, I'll do the rest."

The other end of the cord was attached to a strap around his waist. He'd used this lifeline enough in the past to trust it. So he slowly let his grip on the beam slip, until he hung suspended by the slender cord, and sighed with relief as he felt circulation return to his poor, abused arm. Once feeling returned, he grabbed the cord and started climbing, hand over hand, until he was sitting safely on the ledge again.

"Whew!"

Cassie sighed, too. "Pretty neat gadget, Jack."

"No well-dressed high-rise prowler should be without one."

Chapter Ten

Jack sat on the ledge and watched the dark figure run across the lot. "How nice. He waited to see if I was going to make it."

"Kind of him," Cassie agreed.

A few moments later they saw a car race away. They moved back from the ledge. Cassie breathed a deep sigh of relief and sat down on the floor, not caring about the dirt. Jack sat down beside her. It had been a close call.

She touched his cheek with her gloved hand. Sweat glistened on his face. His breathing was harsh and erratic.

"Are you hurt?"

"No." He lifted his hand to touch her; it was shaking and unsteady. "How about you?"

"Fine. Who was that guy?"

Jack shrugged. "If you can believe a near-death confession, he's one of Flynn's minions."

"Who's Flynn?"

Even in the darkness, she could see the glimmer of his smile, and heard his low chuckle. "Ah, Cassie, you don't ever change. Didn't you notice we were both almost killed a few minutes ago?"

"But we weren't killed. So, who's he after?"

Jack pulled his glove off, sliding his hand around her neck and guiding her mouth down to his. "Me," he whispered, before giving in to an urge he'd wanted to do something about for days.

Maybe it was the excitement of the evening or the realization that she'd almost lost him. But Cassie didn't protest, instead her lips parted and the kiss deepened. He tasted so good. As she leaned forward her cotton turtleneck pulled away from her slacks and she could feel his hand gliding across the smooth satiny skin of her back. His fingers were callused, the rough edges sending little impulses of shock deep inside her.

"I needed that," Jack murmured, his lips hovering over hers, skimming the tender skin with a feathery touch. "It's nice to be alive."

The touch of a cool breeze on her bare skin brought sanity back in a flash. "Jack, what are we doing? That man just tried to kill you."

"We were kissing. And that man intended to kill us both, or did you blank that minor detail from your mind?"

"No." Cassie closed her eyes, suddenly thinking more about the killer than the kiss. What was she doing? "This is crazy."

Jack sighed and let her move away. "You said it."

"Jack, who's Flynn?"

Nothing she said or did could have doused his desire any quicker. He fought the memories that tried to fill his mind. His voice was harsh, cold, reflecting the way he felt. "He's a cold-blooded killer who is supposed to be dead."

"But he's not?"

"I don't know." Jack sat up and pulled his gloves back on. "And Patrick Rourke's name is coming up more and more often, isn't it? First your informant. Then the fund-raiser. Now this guy, who supposedly has some connection to Flynn. I'm getting very confused, and I don't like it. Let's call it a night."

Who did Flynn murder? She wanted to ask, but it was obvious she wasn't going to get any answers out of Jack, at least not tonight. His face was grim, and a coldness had settled over him.

"What were you looking at when that guy interrupted you?" Cassie asked, changing the subject.

Jack rolled the flashlight toward him with his foot, then stood up. "Plumbing. If corners were cut, that's the first place it usually happens and the easiest for me to check. Come hold this for me," he ordered, extending the slim flashlight in her direction.

"Yes, sir," she muttered, taking it from him. Jack was back to normal, giving orders freely. She watched as he used a nifty little measuring gadget to gauge the diameter of the pipes. "Right size?" she asked.

"Yes." Jack was disgusted. "That pretty much leaves us where we started, doesn't it? Let's get out of here."

Cassie walked beside him to the stairs, her mind full of unanswered questions. But the long descent made her too jittery to concentrate. She felt much better when they were safe on the ground, picking their way around the debris.

As soon as they slipped back through the hole in the fence, Jack put his hand on her arm. "Stay here," he ordered.

Cassie watched while he walked all the way around the car, checking it over with his flashlight. Then he got down on all fours and poked his head underneath it in several spots. After that, he carefully inspected the hood, opened it and looked at the engine for a while, then closed it again.

"Let's go."

They were back on the highway before Jack spoke. "Would you consider staying at my place until this is all over? Your apartment leaves you too vulnerable."

She sidestepped his question. "You were looking for a bomb, weren't you?"

"Yes."

Cassie had known the answer before she'd posed the question. Hearing her suspicion confirmed out loud made it just seem more real. Who was this man? What was he involved in? Hell! Her problems were his now and vice versa, so whatever it was she was involved in it, too.

"Jack, tell me what's going on?"

"I don't know." He glanced at her. "I really don't. There are things I'll need to check out before I have any answers."

She had a lot to check out, too. Maybe all this wasn't even related to construction fraud. Perhaps the core sample was pointing in another direction. But where?

Only one thing was certain. It was now more imperative than ever for them to get the documents her informant said existed. Then she would have more pieces of the puzzle to work with.

"If there is fraud involved I wonder who's being bought off?" she mused aloud.

"I don't care who it is unless it has direct bearing on our problem."

"Aren't you even curious?"

"I don't have to be," Jack replied. "You have enough curiosity for ten people."

It was not meant as a compliment. He was worried. Their recent escapade was bringing back memories, both good and bad. What they were doing was dangerous, and he realized he was enjoying himself. He'd forgotten how much he'd liked living on the edge, taking physical chances, pushing his luck. This wasn't good. Bridget depended on him. He had too many responsibilities now to indulge in this sort of thing.

And Flynn brought added complications. As if Cassie's problems weren't proving difficult enough to deal with, now he had to find out if Flynn really was alive and why he'd chosen this particular time to come after him. And what of Rourke?

Cassie said, "There's nothing wrong with being curious."

His tone was purposely cutting. "It's what got your friend Brian Fenton killed, or have you forgotten?"

The words still hurt. No, she hadn't forgotten, but it didn't curb her curiosity, instead it fueled her desire to know more. It was part of what kept her searching for clues to Brian's death.

"I'm going to have that core sample tested at another company," Cassie told him. "It's the only way to find out if the concrete is substandard."

Jack changed lanes before answering her. He was weaving in and out of traffic, making sure this time they weren't being followed. "Good idea. Do you want me to take care of it for you?" he asked.

The offer was tempting. She didn't have the name or address of another company yet, and it would probably be expensive to have it done, too. But it was still hard for her to ask him to do something for her, even when she wanted to. "Okay," she finally said. "But I want to know the results as soon as you get them."

"Of course."

Jack glanced at her. He felt responsible for Cassie. Granted, she had brought a part of this mess onto herself, but if Flynn was after him he could be embroiling her in something she hadn't bargained on and certainly wouldn't be able to handle.

"Are you going to stay at my place?" he asked.

All she wanted right now was her own bed, some sleep, and a little time to think. "No, thank you."

"You'll be safer with me."

"Is that a fact. I was with you tonight and look what almost happened," Cassie said sarcastically.

"You know what I mean. My house is better protected."

She raised her eyebrows. "Oh, really? I got in, didn't I?"

"Dammit!" Jack blew out a deep breath. "All right. Do what you want. Just get a good night's rest. You're going to get the bank plans for us tomorrow, remember?"

"Thanks. That thought's just what I needed to help me sleep."

He dropped Cassie off at her place. She'd agreed to meet at his house tomorrow morning. Stubborn woman. Nothing short of brute force would have swayed her, and he didn't need to be beaten up anymore tonight.

Jack ached all over, but his mind was running at full speed as he slammed the kitchen door behind him and headed toward the library. "Russ, are you awake?"

"I would be now if I wasn't before." Russ came down the stairs, staring at the dusty, dirty figure before him. "From the looks of you, something must have gone wrong," he observed, following Jack into the library.

"A man tried to kill us on that high rise tonight." Jack told him about the near misses that night, saving the worst for the last. "The guy said he was sent by Flynn."

"Flynn's dead."

Jack was puzzled. "The physical description matches. And it's possible he's using Patrick Rourke's name."

"That sounds like Flynn." Russ frowned. "But how did he escape that bungled car bombing of his?"

"I don't know." He looked at Russ and bitterness filled his voice. "He probably set it up from the start. Knowing Flynn, he even went so far as to cut off his own little finger to leave amid the wreckage to give us irrefutable evidence of his demise. If it is Flynn he'll be out to settle old scores."

"That he will, only he'll become the hunted again."

Jack nodded his solemn agreement. Russ sipped at his whiskey, careful not to let his emotions show. They already had enough problems and he knew Jack would be emotional enough for the two of them.

"The general called."

"What did he have to say?" Jack asked.

"Cussed a lot, in French and English. It's all on the answering machine," Russ told him. "And if I understood him correctly he said he was forced to reveal the information."

That announcement got Jack's full attention. "By who?"

"He didn't say. And he didn't leave a number, either."

Jack drummed the metal arm of the chair with the tips of his fingers, thinking. "Send out the next photo. The one we discussed, and I'll add another note." He looked at Russ. "If he doesn't call us tomorrow with the name, send out two more."

"You think it's Flynn."

"It reeks of him," Jack said. "There have been too many coincidences lately for my liking."

"We don't even know if he's alive," Russ said sharply. "So right now concentrate on tomorrow." Jack didn't reply. "Did you hear what I said?"

Jack looked at him vaguely. "Yes."

"Well, snap out of it," Russ ordered. "The jacket and hat you wanted are upstairs. The walkie-talkies have new batteries and the rental car is reserved. Anything else?"

Russ was right. He needed to concentrate on tomorrow. "What about the layout of the bar?"

"Simple and straightforward." Russ showed him a diagram he'd drawn of the interior, explaining the setup carefully. "Are there any details for tomorrow's run that we left out?"

Jack thought about it. "No. I'll pick up the car first thing in the morning." Russ's continuing silence and glare spoke volumes. "You don't think I should let Cassie do this tomorrow?"

"You know me too well," Russ said. "I don't like using women for dangerous work—never have, never will. That's a rough part of town, even in daylight."

Jack agreed with him. He was beginning to care for Cassie, and he wished he hadn't set things up this way, but there was nothing he could do now. "It's too late to change the plans."

"I know that, lad, and I'll be nearby just in case anything goes wrong. And don't worry," Russ told him. "I left Sheba over at Kathleen's to protect Bridget. Now you're home, I think I'll go check on them."

Jack nodded. "Why don't you take the two Dobermans, as well. They can stay outside." He looked up at Russ. "If Flynn is alive he'll go for our weakest point, once he finds it." He stood up. "I'm going to send out coded messages over the ham radio for Rourke."

"See you in the morning."

Jack pressed the books on the top shelf, and the bookcases swung open revealing the double white doors to his office. The redwood walls and green plants brought him no peace of mind this evening. He sat down at the familiar console and flipped a switch.

Flynn. After all these years. Jack's determination now was no less intense than it had been then. If Flynn was alive he'd find him and destroy him.

"WHAT DO YOU MEAN, you failed?" Flynn asked. The call had awoken him from a sound sleep, but he was instantly alert.

"The woman had a gun. It was either pull back or get myself killed. I can try again."

"You're damned right you will. Merlin's address?"

"I didn't get it. He lost me on the freeway. You didn't tell me he was a professional."

"It shouldn't have mattered. You got careless. You'll be hearing from me again, so stay put. And don't leave town, or I'll hunt you down myself." Leaning back against the deep gold velvet headboard, he picked up a piece of paper with the reporter's address on it. He didn't necessarily want to use this woman. She had too high a profile, and he didn't want to bring any attention to himself.

He was still contemplating the possibilities when the phone rang again. "Yes," he answered brusquely.

"The general has been contacted, and the call made. He left a rather garbled message on Merlin's answering machine, in French."

There was a burst of static on the phone line. He waited for it to clear, smoothing his short auburn hair back with his free hand. "Don't worry about that, they understand the language. If you don't hear from them by tomorrow have the general call again."

"Consider it done. It's a shame you can't see this photo. Interesting. I didn't know the general liked boys."

He smiled. "No one did. He's managed to keep it secret until now." He was pleased. Soon he would have the information he needed. "Call me."

Rubbing his hands together, he grinned like a kid. "Yes! It's working out after all." He spoke to himself, there was no one else in the penthouse suite. Another few days and everything would be in place. "Soon, very soon."

And if this plan didn't work out, he still had another card up his sleeve. Would they be able to resist coming after the jewels?

Chapter Eleven

Morning sunlight streamed through the clerestory windows of Jack's airy library, but Cassie took little cheer from it as she paced restlessly around the spacious room. She'd been here for over an hour now. In that time she'd learned how to put in soft, brown contacts to change her eye color, used an instant tan lotion to give her skin a dark tint, and now she had lined crows feet around her eyes. The effect was quite startling. She looked like a young woman who'd lived a hard life, old long before her time.

All this to get a current blueprint of the bank building. She was on edge.

She'd been up early, researching Lance Mizer, only to find he was dead, too, another construction accident. Cassie didn't know who owned the building he'd fallen from but she intended to find out—along with which construction companies had been involved on each of the projects.

Cassie glanced at Jack, scowling. "There isn't an easier way to do this?"

"No." Jack was glaring right back at her, himself on edge after a restless night. "Our contact is expecting a woman this afternoon, and that's just what we're going to give him. It's too late to change plans now."

"Great," Cassie muttered, grabbing the directions to the meeting place from his cluttered desk. It was in a part of Houston that always gave her the creeps. "Are you sure there isn't a sleazier bar in town you'd like me to entertain this guy in?"

"You aren't going there to entertain him," Jack returned with equal sarcasm. "Besides, he chose the place, not me. Now listen carefully. After you enter the bar, turn left and walk straight to the rear. Sit down in the last booth."

She glanced up from the diagram on the desk. "What if there's already someone sitting there?"

"There will be. He'll be waiting for you," Jack replied impatiently. "Now shut up and listen. As soon as you sit down, place the brown envelope I gave you on the table. There'll be another envelope on the seat next to you. Pick it up without making a production of it, slip it into your jacket and leave. Got that?"

"Seems simple enough." As long as she didn't think about the area of town the bar was in or the sort of people who would be hanging around such a place. "What if something goes wrong?"

"There's a rear exit three steps from that booth. It will be unlocked. Get your tail out of there fast."

"Wonderful advice."

"And speaking of that pretty tail of yours," he added with a wry grin, "watch it. Men who hang out in bars like this one don't take no for an answer. As a matter of fact it excites them. So get in, get the envelope, and get out."

"Any other helpful hints?"

Jack stood up, his eyes narrowing as he contemplated her. She was dressed in dark, loose clothing, per his instructions. Her hair was pulled back tightly into a French braid. He had a bad feeling about sending her on this errand, but as he'd said, it was too late for him to go in her place.

"Here," Jack said, handing her a beat-up old cowboy hat and faded hip-length jean jacket. "Put those on. You want to look like you belong in that run-down bar."

The hat fit tightly, and the jacket loosely. Cassie sighed. "Gee, thanks." She bent to pick up her purse.

"Leave it."

"But—"

"This will fit in your pocket," Jack interrupted. He held his hand out. The gun he'd removed from her purse was in his palm. Cassie glared at him, furious.

"You went through my purse?"

"Of course. Who taught you to shoot?"

Cassie took the small automatic pistol from him and checked it with obvious familiarity. Then she engaged the safety and slipped the firearm carefully into her pocket before answering him.

"My ex-husband. And as you may have noticed, I'm a excellent shot. He wouldn't accept anything less."

There was a lot of animosity in her voice and Jack wondered about it, but there was no time to pursue the matter. He tossed her a set of keys. "Those belong to the brown rental sedan parked a few blocks from here. The license number is on the tag. Better get walking or you'll be late and blow the meeting."

Cassie turned on her heel and strode toward the front door. "Are the dogs free? Is the side gate open?"

"You worry too much!"

"I can't imagine why," she tossed back sarcastically, slamming the front door behind her.

Jack crossed the room and picked up a small but powerful walkie-talkie. "Russ, she's on her way down the drive."

"I've got her in sight."

"We'll meet back here."

He turned and ran up the stairs. Stripping off his clothes, he quickly changed into faded jeans, stained work shirt and tennis shoes. Then he used a heavy gel to slick back his thick black hair. He didn't like the effect, but it worked for his purposes.

Jack was halfway down the hall to check on Bridget before he remembered she was still at Kathleen's. And on Sunday they would take her back to school. Trying not to think about how much he would miss the little girl, he raced down the stairs.

THE LIGHT BROWN SEDAN had seen better days, with dents in all four fenders and a long scrape down one side. Cassie parallel parked it a few doors down from the bar. It fit right in with all the other hulks lining the old narrow street, likewise rusted by long exposure to Houston air.

She took a moment to accustom herself to her surroundings. They were far from pleasant. It was one of those blighted sections any large city contained, where everything was coated with the grime of neglect and even police cars traveled in pairs. Filth and debris littered the sidewalks and gutters.

Cassie studied the bar. If possible the place looked even sleazier than she'd imagined it would, its peeling, hot-pink paint garish in the bright sunlight. A broken sign dangled over the entrance as testimony to how little the owner cared about upkeep. There were two picture windows, almost black, patched with plenty of gray tape on each side of a dented, green metal door.

As much as she wished otherwise, Cassie knew it was time. She ran her fingers over the small gun in her jacket pocket for reassurance and stepped out of the car, leaving the door unlocked. Another car couldn't park in front of her because of the alley entrance. If she had to run out of there fast, she wanted all the help she could get.

Feeling conspicuous in spite of her disguise, Cassie walked to the front of the bar and pulled the heavy door open. The smell was fetid, indescribable, but at least the wave of air that hit her was cool. She stepped into the dimly lit interior, blinking her eyes rapidly to adjust to the change from full sun to darkened gloom. The place was surprisingly full for so early in the day—even for a Saturday. Stale smoke from cigarettes and cheap cigars hung in the hazy air, swirling amid the buzz of voices.

With her gaze carefully directed down at her shoes she made a sharp left beside the row of booths, walking quickly to the last one per her instructions. It was a long walk.

"Hey, cookie, where you going?"

"My, my, my."

A much younger Cassie had once dreamed of entering a roomful of people and leaving everyone stunned. This was not how she had imagined that dream. Apparently her loose clothing didn't succeed in hiding her feminine curves. Or had Jack been right about her walk?

She slid into the booth without looking back. Somebody started the jukebox and loud, blaring music filled the room. Sitting across from her was a heavyset man with a full beard, leaning against the dirty wall behind him. His dark hat was pulled down low over his face and he appeared to be asleep.

Scarcely breathing, her newly acquired brown eyes never leaving his face, she began sliding her right hand across the seat, searching for the package. It wasn't there. All she found were crumbs and ripped Naugahyde repaired with layers of sticky tape.

"The envelope," he muttered, not opening his eyes or moving a muscle.

Cassie placed the brown envelope on the table with her right hand. The man still didn't move. Something was wrong.

She looked up. A large young man was weaving from side to side nearby, bumping against their table. *"Señorita,"* he announced in a loud, slurred voice, "come dance with me?" There were more men behind him, encouraging him.

"Take her hand," one whispered, laughing, revealing stained and rotting teeth.

Cassie shrank back into the seat, carefully keeping her face shielded with the wide brim of her cowboy hat. She wanted out of there. Now. Where were the plans?

"Women!" another of the leering onlookers exclaimed. "They say no, they mean yes. Look at her. She wants it!"

The young man became more insistent. "Dance with me."

Fear clawed at her stomach. If she didn't do something fast, this could turn into a very ugly scene. She had no friends here. No one would help her. To top it off, her brown envelope was now missing from the table, and there was still no sign of the package she'd come for. She had to stall, she needed that package. Damn Jack for getting her into this situation. Next time she'd arrange her own meeting.

"All right," she agreed demurely.

"I told you so! Take her hand!"

Keeping her eyes down, Cassie slowly began to inch across the ripped booth, her mind reeling with a plan to get her out of there quickly. Her small gun wouldn't be of much use against this crowd. At the very least she had to reduce the odds. And she still didn't have the plans.

Just as she was about to lose control and make a run for it, her fingers came into contact with a thin package. All she had to do was get out of here with it and her mission would be a success. Victory was literally within her grasp.

Dipping into a reserve of courage she hadn't been aware of until now, Cassie clutched her prize and stood up. Without a second thought she leaned forward and shoved the swaying young man into his companions, charging forward with her arm straight out like a football player in sight of the goal line. Then she spun around and took the three quick steps to the back exit. It was there, just as Jack had promised.

It was also locked.

For a few precious seconds she fumbled with the latch before realizing the door was held shut with an iron bar. She swung it out of the way, pushed, and burst through into the daylight, followed by cries of angry outrage. Nothing had ever looked as good to Cassie as that sunny, garbage-strewn alley.

A foul stench engulfed her. But it was far better than the foul mood building behind her. She crashed through a pile of empty liquor boxes blocking her escape, kicking them out of the way and fighting to stay on her feet. It was like running a putrid obstacle course. Leaping over piles of trash and rotting garbage, dodging abandoned tires and machinery, she went flat out for the alley entrance and the safety of her car.

"There she goes! Get her!"

"Damnation!" she cried, her feet sliding precariously on slippery masses of goo. Her cowboy hat flipped off her head and into the mess but she didn't slow down.

Cassie ran straight into the narrow street and looked around in disbelief. Her car was gone. Someone had stolen her car! She whipped around as she heard the grumblings of angry men picking their way up the alley toward her. At least they hadn't been smart enough to come out the front door after her.

It was going to be a long run to the highway, Cassie thought, sprinting along the broken pavement and staying close to the parked cars lining the left side of the street. None of the sad, crumbling buildings along the way appeared to offer her sanctuary, either. Judging by the sort of people lounging in the doorways, she'd rather take her chances on the street.

A quick glance over her shoulder confirmed her worst nightmare. Some of those men were running after her. And a couple of them were quick. Real quick.

Fear and adrenaline kept her moving. She'd only run the equivalent of three long blocks and she was already tired, ready to drop. Jogging was not her favorite exercise.

Suddenly, the nightmare came into clear focus. One of her pursuers was much smarter than the others. A car roared past her and squealed to a stop, the driver's side door opening directly in front of her. Cassie was running too fast to dodge around the obstacle. She held her hands out to grab the top of the door and gritted her teeth against the impending impact.

She never touched the metal frame. A man's strong arms whipped tightly around her waist and hauled her into the car, bending her in two as he flung her over him and across the bench seat. Cassie bumped her head on the doorjamb and hit her hip on the window handle before landing in a crumpled heap on the floorboards.

"Stay down," a harsh voice commanded. Viselike fingers held her neck, pressing her face into the velour seat.

Great. Now she was being kidnapped!

Chapter Twelve

But what for? She heard the roar of the engine as the car burned rubber and took off like a rocket. Her abductor whipped the car around one sharp corner after another, throwing her around like a sack of potatoes. Still, she managed to tuck the envelope she'd held clutched in her hand up under her black turtleneck for safe keeping.

With a final bump and a powerful burst of acceleration, they were suddenly driving along smooth highway. The traffic sounded heavy, a possible distraction to the driver. Just as Cassie decided this might be a good time to pull her gun, the kidnapper's grip turned gentle, his fingers massaging the back of her neck, easing the constricted muscles with a magical touch. She couldn't help herself. A tiny moan escaped her parched lips.

What was wrong with her? His touch was doing strange things to her nervous system, her body responding in a very confusing way. Was she cracking up from the stress she had been under? Unsure of what to do next, Cassie held her breath, trying to force her beleaguered mind to function. How was she going to get away?

"May I get off the floor now?" she asked.

He withdrew his hand. Cautiously, staying as far away from him as possible, she got up and leaned her back against the door. Sitting out of his reach with her legs curled to one side, she studied him.

Both of his hands were on the steering wheel and he was looking straight ahead. He wasn't familiar, and yet he was. Those long fingers reminded her of someone also. But who? She didn't know any men who wore their hair slicked back in that particular style.

"Cat got your tongue, Cassie?" the man asked. "I never thought I'd see the day." He flashed her a wide grin. "What happened to your nice hat, sweetheart?"

Welcome relief washed over her. But her relief was short-lived, replaced by red-hot anger. How dare he scare her half to death?

"Jack Merlin," she seethed through clenched teeth. "You jerk! I could have shot you!"

"I see." He glanced at her and winked. "Then that pretty moan I heard must have been out of sympathy for my approaching doom, right?"

"Damn you!"

"Is that any way to treat your savior?"

Cassie crossed her arms over her chest and glared at him. "I was doing just fine on my own."

"Is that so? I'll remember that next time," Jack said.

She wanted to kick him. But he might just take her back to where he'd found her and she didn't want to prove her point that much. "What were you doing there?"

"Waiting for you to get into trouble. And by the smell of you I'd say you did."

Cassie stared down at her garbage-caked shoes. She'd probably end up having to throw them away and it was all his fault. Sarcasm flowed with her words. "What a vote of confidence."

He took the next exit ramp and began maneuvering into a light industrial district. "Actually you did pretty well, considering. But I got you into this, so it was my job to get you out."

Cassie was secretly pleased by his near-compliment, but tried not to show it. "Where did you find this car?" she asked, looking around with dismay. The interior was button-tufted crushed red velvet, with matching red fake fur on the dashboard and rear parcel shelf. Fuzzy black and white dice dangled from the rearview mirror. "It's really you. What do you do, cruise the streets each weekend looking for teenyboppers half your age?"

Jack sighed, holding back a smile. "If I was of a mind to cruise, dear, I'd do a lot better with my own car," he informed her.

She gave him a dirty look. "Oh, really?"

He drove behind a warehouse and parked beside a familiar Ming-green Mercedes sedan with dark-tinted windows, then tossed a set of keys into her lap.

"Just get in it and wait for me while I return this car."

Cassie uncurled her legs and got out, muttering under her breath as she went to the passenger side of his car and unlocked the door.

"Go here, wait there. It'd serve you right if I ran off and left you. Bossy jerk!"

"I heard that. Don't do anything you'll be sorry for, Cassie," he told her, holding the car door open for her.

"It might be worth it." She slammed the door in his knowing face, still fuming as she sank into the rich leather upholstery. Chuckling, Jack walked off in the direction of the warehouse.

Cassie ignored him and closed her eyes for a moment, savoring this hard-won moment of success. She patted the envelope beneath her shirt. This represented one more step along the twisted path toward her objective, brought her one step closer to nailing whoever had killed Brian. She was closing in on them; one hard, tiring step at a time. Soon Brian Fenton's reputation would be restored.

Stifling a yawn, Cassie tried to open her eyes but couldn't quite manage it. Jack had parked his car in the shade and it was cool, relaxing to her frayed nerves. Last night and this morning had left her completely wrung out, taking quite a toll on her both mentally and physically. In fact, she was exhausted. Her breathing deepened.

"Cassie, wake up."

Was that a male voice intruding upon her pleasant dreams? Were those masculine fingers pulling up the hem of her shirt, exposing her skin to cooler air? Her eyes popped open. It was a male, all right. A male with slick, greasy black hair.

She felt the envelope moving on her abdomen, leaving a tickling trail in its wake. Cassie clasped her arms over her stomach, trapping his hand along with the package.

"Back off."

"I can't. I seem to be stuck." The tips of his fingers caressed the smooth white skin beneath her breasts. "And for future reference," he added in a whisper, his warm breath tickling her ear, "this isn't a good hiding place when a man's involved. First place he'd want to look."

With a sigh she released his hand and practically fell out of the car. Unfortunately she couldn't get away from the memories of his touch as quickly.

Still a bit groggy from her unplanned nap, Cassie blinked and looked around, surprised to find herself back at Jack's house. It made her feel odd to think she had slept all the way there, with him right beside her, watching her. And the look on his face told her he knew exactly what she was thinking and was enjoying her discomfort.

"We should have used the servants' entrance," she said, politely removing her garbage-smeared shoes before entering the house ahead of him.

"Are you saying you're willing to be my servant?" Jack asked. He led the way to the kitchen, and so didn't see the obscene gesture she made in response to his question.

But Russ did. He grinned. "Ah! Ancient Celtic sign language!"

His friend looked at him as if he'd taken leave of his senses. "What?"

"Never mind. How did it go? I arranged to have the rental car taken back to the . . ." Russ trailed off when he noticed Jack's grimace of warning. Then he saw the fury in Cassie's eyes. "Oops. Put my foot in it, did I?"

"You stole my car?"

Russ shrugged his massive shoulders. "What did you expect, leaving it unlocked in that neighborhood? It was either me or the young hooligans Jack chased off. And he had enough to do already, keeping an eye on you."

"And you had it planned that way all along, too! I don't believe this." Cassie whirled around to confront Jack. "Was any of this necessary? Or was it all some kind of plan to scare me into total obedience?"

"If last night didn't scare you into that, nothing ever will." Jack looked at her for a moment, smiling, and then he asked, "Are you hungry?" He turned away, opening the refrigerator door and removing a large platter laden with meats and cheeses. "Help yourself. There's hot coffee and tea in the dual brewing machine on the counter, other things to drink in the fridge. Do you want mustard on your sandwich?"

"I want to know what's going on!" She sliced the envelope open and took a peek. "The bank plans aren't in here!"

"You're right. But I trust my informant. There'll be something in there to lead me to the plans. Meanwhile, we'll talk as we eat," Jack said. "Sit down and help yourself."

Cassie stared at the two men in growing disbelief as they took seats at the kitchen table and began assembling their meals. "I don't believe this!"

"Take it easy, Cassie. We know this afternoon was rough on you. You need to relax." Jack was layering cheddar cheese on top of crisp lettuce. "You may not be hungry, but Russ and I happen to be starving. Too much adrenaline always seems to affect us that way." He glanced at her briefly. "You ought to give it a try. It helps."

"Remember that time in Turkey?" Russ asked. "The three of us ate an entire leg of lamb and all the trimmings."

Jack grinned. "I remember. The owner of the place called us a trio of walking stomachs."

The three of them? Cassie was suddenly quite certain that the third person of that trio was Patrick Rourke. Her curiosity won out. She slipped off her jacket and sat down at the table. It just might be worth staying to listen to this conversation.

The food didn't look bad, either. She reached out and took a piece of cheese, nibbling it slowly. It tasted wonderful, as did the sliver of chicken breast she sampled next. Had she eaten yet today? When was the last time her stomach had been calm enough to handle much of anything?

And she was strangely calm, in spite of the suspicions whirling around in her mind. After all, Jack had been there for her, even if he had neglected to tell her about that part of his plan. There was something about Russ, too, a steady, rock-solid presence that was reassuring.

Was she safe in their hands? Probably, at least for now, and as far as bodily injury was concerned. The way she felt when Jack touched her, however, was another matter entirely, one she would rather not think about.

She made herself a sandwich and consumed it rapidly as Russ continued to talk about the different places and food they'd enjoyed, his soft brogue once again having an almost hypnotizing effect. Neither he nor Jack gave out any useful bits of information, other than revealing that they were well traveled, something she already knew. But Jack had been right. Eating helped.

"I thought you weren't hungry," Jack said, watching her finish her last bite of whole-wheat bread.

"I wasn't," Cassie replied, crossing the kitchen to pour fragrant black coffee into a large cobalt-blue mug. She sipped at the hot, flavorful brew. "This is very good."

"Thanks. What went wrong at the bar?" Jack asked, glancing at Russ.

Russ counted her transgressions off on his big fingers. "Her entrance was too slow, for one. And what a walk! Got the attention of every man in the place. Then she searched for the other envelope before revealing ours. No show of faith, delayed things a good two minutes." He paused, looking at Cassie with a smile.

"She did handle herself fine when it came time to run out of there, though."

"Gee, thanks," Cassie said. "But may I remind you we still don't have those blueprints? When will we go pick them up?"

"Lunch is over, so now's as good a time as any." Jack reached for the envelope and poured the contents on the table. A key pinged as it hit his empty plate. He examined it and said, "Bus station locker."

Russ took the key and stood up. "I haven't been inside a bus station in ages. Back in a few."

Cassie watched him leave, and then out of habit began loading the dishwasher, the messy kitchen a perfect excuse to keep busy.

Jack watched her, amused by her need for activity. "You could start a new trend," he murmured. "Two-tone skin."

Her hands and forearms were streaked with rivulets of white against the deep caramel of her artificial tan. It made her look sexy to him, quite erotic, like a pagan priestess of some forgotten tribe who painted herself to attract a mate. He sighed, knowing that wasn't her intention.

"Personally I think it makes me look like I've been playing in the dirt." Cassie picked up the soapy dishrag and rubbed it over her hands, restoring them to just one shade. "That's a little better."

"If you'd like to remove the rest, feel free to use the shower in my bedroom. Help yourself to whatever you need."

"Thanks."

After her shower Cassie explored the house. Jack seemed to have disappeared, and that was just fine with her. She had wanted to explore this house since first stepping inside it. There were six bedrooms upstairs and one down, the five full bathrooms all gleaming with shiny new fixtures. The kitchen and library were the only furnished rooms on the first floor, except for a large, white-painted room filled with modern exercise equipment.

Cassie returned to the library with a cup of coffee, ready to explore the bookshelves until Russ returned with the blueprints. She was on the second-level loft, perusing his books when the phone rang. Hesitant to answer it, she waited, but it didn't ring again. Jack must have picked up an extension somewhere in the house. She resumed her study of the books.

He walked quietly into the library and observed her for a moment. The sleeves of her black shirt were pushed up on her forearms, showing that the shower had removed all traces of brown makeup. Her black hair was neatly pulled back into a chignon. Slender fingers were busy skimming over titles and authors.

"You look much better."

Cassie turned around and gazed down at him. He'd taken a shower, too; his hair was back to normal, along with his clothes. "So do you."

He sat down in a chair, still looking up at her. "Russ has been unavoidably delayed." Seeing the stricken look in her eyes he hastened to reassure her. "Russ is fine, and he does have possession of the blueprints. We'll go over them later this evening."

Cassie walked down the steps toward him. "Did you find out who rents that lockbox?"

"Not yet. We should know by tomorrow. What did you find out about Lance Mizer?"

She picked up her purse. "He's dead, construction accident. It's a different building, though. And I still haven't come up with an ownership connection between them."

"Keep looking." Jack stood up and slipped his hands into his pants pockets. "Cassie, I still want you to consider staying here until this mess is straightened out. Any amateur could break into your place."

Cassie frowned. "I thought we'd gone over all that. Is there some new development you haven't told me about?"

"Let's just say some of your future problems could be my fault. You don't know what you're getting into."

"Then why don't you tell me what I'm getting into?"

He was tempted, but not until he knew more himself. "I will, once I know exactly what it is."

"Fine." She turned away, hurt by his unwillingness to confide in her. "Will you let me out? I have a newspaper story to finish."

Jack walked her out to her car. "If you change your mind, you're welcome here at any hour."

"I'll remember that. See you later this evening."

"ARE YOU SURE this time?" The man calling himself Patrick Rourke asked.

"Yes," she replied. "I should have possession within the next week, but knowing the delays we have already encountered, it could be the beginning of the week after."

He put his hand over the receiver for a moment, taking a deep breath and releasing it slowly. Patience, he reminded himself. The last thing he could afford to do was make this particular lady mad. At last he said, "It will have to do."

Her voice was cutting. "We will meet face-to-face before the charity party to discuss the new terms you've requested. And no more disappearing games like you played at the fund-raiser. This time we meet or both deals are off," she told him. "I want to see who I'm dealing with."

"As you wish."

"That's exactly right. It will be as I wish."

She hung up the phone, then sat quietly for a moment, gazing out her office window at the Houston skyline.

Chapter Thirteen

Russ returned home later that day and found Jack in his office, fiddling with some of his electronic gadgets. "Did the general leave a phone number this time?" Russ asked.

"Yes, and he's anxious to speak to us," Jack said. "Shall we see what he has to say?"

Russ sat down, watching as Jack dialed the long string of numbers. Then they waited patiently until they were put through to the general, who immediately began cursing.

"General, speak in English," Jack ordered. "You're on my speaker phone."

"Hi, Frenchie," Russ said, to let him know he was also present.

The voice coming over the speaker was coated with a heavy French accent, but his English was otherwise perfect. "Are you trying to ruin me! I did not do this on purpose. I was forced against my will."

"Keep talking, General. You haven't said one thing that would make me change my mind about circulating the rest of the photos," Jack told him. "Russ and I are having a very tough time deciding which ones to send—"

"No! No!" he yelled. "No more photos. Those already sent could ruin me."

"They were meant to," Jack informed him.

"I did not do this on—"

Russ interrupted him. "Cut the soap opera, General, or you'll have more photos tomorrow."

Russ looked at Jack and made a slicing motion across his throat. Jack shook his head no. He was well aware someone might be tracing this call. It didn't matter either way. They'd find out where

he lived sooner or later, and Jack wasn't going to sit around waiting for them to make their move in any case.

"No! I mean yes! I will tell you what you want to know. A man,
he held a knife to my throat, he threatened to torture and kill my
family one by one if I didn't cooperate."

"Who was he?" Jack asked.

"I do not know. He told me I'd chosen the wrong man to
blackmail. And he spoke like you, Russ. Your accent."

Russ closed his eyes. "What did he look like?"

"It was dark, I—"

"Frenchie," Russ warned, "you're about to earn yourself another photo."

"Please!" the general yelled. "Wait, I will tell you. He was
shorter than me, slender, but very strong, reddish hair. I think he
is a man who enjoys violence."

"You should know, General, seeing as you're a man just like
that," Russ pointed out.

"No, I am not like him. I do not receive pleasure from tortur-
ing others." The general suddenly began gasping for breath, then
coughed. "Excuse me. There will be no more photos?" he asked.

After a long silence Jack finally spoke. "You'll find out." Then
he abruptly broke off the connection.

After pouring a healthy shot of whiskey into each glass, he
handed Russ one. "Flynn?"

"Definitely. And I got the distinct impression the general wasn't
alone."

"Any word yet?" Cassie asked.

Jack swiveled his gray chair around to look at her. "Haven't you
ever heard of saying hello, how are you, before you begin the third
degree?"

"We've never been conventional before, why start now?" Cassie sat on the edge of the rosewood desk and took a sip of his coffee. "Who owns that lockbox?"

He leaned back in his chair. "I like your outfit, those jeans fit
you in all the right places."

"Quit stalling, Jack," she demanded, doing her best to ignore
the pleasure his compliment gave her. "You know who rents it. You
positively reek of smugness."

He took his time, placing one ankle on top of the opposite knee
before he answered. "Marilyn Hook and family." She looked
puzzled. "You recognize the name?"

Cassie nodded. "They're very prominent here in Houston. Political connections in Washington. They're one of the families I'm doing a story on concerning charity events and where the funds go," she explained, frowning. "This is weird! What would they have in their lockbox that could help me solve the mystery of Brian's death?"

"They're heavily involved in politics. You said Brian was mainly a political reporter. Maybe the documents your source has alluded to are proof of whatever wrong-doing he was investigating, proof they're keeping hidden to protect their own interests."

She arched her eyebrows. "That's entirely possible. Hiding things isn't new to the Hooks."

"How so?"

"Their fund-raisers aren't on the up and up. I'm not sure exactly how or how much, but I suspect they're skimming through administration cost. I'm also not that familiar with their various business interests, but I can find out a certain amount with one quick phone call."

He gestured toward his desk. "Go ahead." Her short-sleeved lilac cotton sweater followed the flow of her actions. A scarf in shades of purple encircled her throat, and beaten silver earrings completed her outfit. He liked what he saw.

"His wife says he'll be back soon, I'll call him later."

"Good. Russ is waiting for us in the kitchen." After they were seated, Jack asked, "Can you read blueprints?"

Cassie was sitting at the head of the kitchen table between the two men. The sheaves of paper with blue lines drawn in every direction were in front of her. "No, but it looks easy enough."

Russ laughed. "That's the spirit. We'll start with this section here." Cassie listened carefully as Jack and Russ explained the basic layout.

"Do you understand so far?" Russ asked her a short time later.

"Yes. What's next, alarms?"

Jack flipped another sheet of paper over. "No. Heating and air-conditioning ducts. We'll be using them as part of our entrance and exit."

Surprise showed on Cassie's face. "How wide are these things? Where do we gain access to them?"

Russ answered her, going into detail about the way they curved through the building and how narrow they could become on some of those curves.

They were both watching her like vultures when Russ finished his explanation, and she knew why. "Don't worry, I'm really not that claustrophobic. I promise not to panic and get anyone caught. Believe me, I can do this.''

"But you don't like heights," Jack said.

She leaned back. "True. What kind of heights are we discussing?''

"Three or four stories," Jack told her. "Russ and I usually just jump from from building to building, but I suppose we could tie a rope around your waist and toss you across." They watched as her face turned even whiter, and her lips pursed into a frown.

"Rest easy, lass!" Russ finally announced after a long silence. He was grinning like a mischievous kid.

Color returned to her face and she gave them both a condescending look. "Are you two *boys* through having fun? We do have work to do here.''

Jack was fighting back a smile as he turned another page over. "The basement.''

They went through papers one by one, answering all of Cassie's questions to her satisfaction. She learned something even more valuable as they continued to discuss what breaking into the bank would entail. Jack and Russ were professionals, and very thorough. They picked apart minute details, section by section and page by page, listing troublesome points on yellow legal pads.

Four hours later Cassie was more than ready to go home, her head so overloaded with facts and tiny details she felt like screaming. She was so tired she thought she could see lights flashing before her eyes.

No, lights really *were* flashing.

"Why did that tiny red light over the back door start blinking?" she asked.

Russ jumped up and hit the light switch, enveloping them in darkness. At the same time Jack grabbed her by the shoulders and pushed her down beside a row of cabinets.

"What's wrong?" Cassie asked.

"Stay here," Jack whispered. "Someone is breaking into the house.''

Cassie squeezed herself back into the corner. Where were the dogs? Not one had even barked. Had someone tranquilized all of them? That didn't seem possible.

She peeked around the corner, watching as Jack and Russ moved silently across the kitchen toward the interior of the house, talking to each other in sign language. Jack slipped through the doorway, followed by Russ. They paused, then proceeded in opposite directions.

Cassie couldn't stand not knowing what was going on. But as she stood up she heard a scraping noise at the back door. Immediately she sank back down into the corner. The doorknob was turning, she could hear it, and slowly the solid wood door slid open, revealing a stream of moonlight.

She held her breath and stayed in the shadows. A tall dark-clothed figure slipped inside, closing the door behind himself and moving stealthily into the kitchen. Cassie didn't see a weapon of any kind in his gloved hands.

What should she do? The intruder wasn't making any sounds. Where were Jack and Russ? She couldn't pinpoint their location in the house by sound, either. It was absolutely quiet. Her choices were limited. And sitting there idly until someone either rescued her or killed her wasn't one of them. She'd fight for her life.

Bending forward, Cassie peered around the cabinets. The intruder was in the middle of the kitchen now. What she needed to do was draw the attention of Jack and Russ, and at the same time get to the butcher knife in the wooden holder on the counter. The hard cold floor beneath her hands and knees gave her an idea.

Without a second thought, Cassie grabbed the back of a rolling chair and shoved it toward the intruder, following that one up with another and another. They rolled noisily across the floor as she leaped up. She reached the counter as the first chair almost hit home. The intruder jumped out of the way of the first one, but the second and third hit right on target. Unfortunately the impact wasn't enough to bowl him over.

Cassie grabbed the biggest knife, clutching it tightly in her fist as she raised it back over her shoulder. Two chairs now stood between her and the intruder.

Suddenly both chairs came rolling toward her and Cassie had to leap out of the way. It gave the intruder just enough time to aim a blow at her forearm. The knife went skittering across the slate floor. Cassie turned to run, but strong hands grabbed hold of her shoulders from behind. She slammed her heel into the arch of his foot but his grip didn't loosen any. Twisting sideways, she brought her knee up sharply. He managed to sidestep most of the blow, but it was enough of a diversion for her to escape his grasp.

She ran around the kitchen table, using it as a shield. They were an equal distance from the door. He was directly opposite her now. Could she make it?

Without warning he spoke, a trace of brogue coating his words. "I don't want to hurt you."

His voice was soft, reassuring. Cassie took a deep breath. She didn't believe him. And she was getting out of there while she still had a chance.

She ran for the door, pushing the chair at the end of the table in his direction to slow him down. The door flew backward and she was almost out when he grabbed hold of her by the sweater, pulling her back into the room. Cassie turned, landing blows wherever she could in her struggle to gain freedom.

Suddenly the room was filled with light and she was free. She turned around to find both Jack and Russ glaring at the intruder.

"And just what in blazes do you think you're doing?" Russ asked, his face a ruddy shade.

Cassie studied the man. His face was lean and hard. He had cold gray eyes and midnight-black hair swept back off his forehead. And there was absolutely no softness about him. She had thought Jack cold and hard in the beginning, but this man had him beat.

"Testing your alarm systems. They need work. And it was easy to override the circuit on the electric fence." He glanced at them, keeping one eye on the unknown woman. "Of course, I had an inside advantage. The dogs know me. Also your back door lock needs replacing; the front is good."

Jack looked at the man leaning against the doorjamb. "Where the hell have you been?"

"Around." Their accusatory looks almost made him smile. "Aren't you going to introduce me to the lady?"

"Cassie, this is—"

"Patrick Rourke?" she interrupted. The bleakness in his eyes disturbed her.

Rourke didn't bother to hide his surprise, his eyes opening wide. "Rourke, meet Cassie O'Connor," Jack told him. "She's a reporter by profession and a snoop by nature."

He looked at Jack, then at the woman who seemed so comfortable with him. "I see."

"It's a long story," Jack said with a loud sigh, easily reading his friend's questioning look. He glanced at Cassie. "I don't suppose you'd like to leave?" She was shaking her head. "I didn't think so."

"What happened in here?" Russ asked. Cassie's usually neat French-braided hair had strands sticking out all over, giving her a disheveled look. "Why are the kitchen chairs all over the place?"

Cassie and Patrick looked at each other, each waiting for the other one to speak and give their version.

Jack broke the stalemate. "Who won?"

"Neither of us," Patrick said, shrugging. "She did a good job of protecting your home."

"I was protecting myself," Cassie retorted. She bent down and picked up the knife from the floor, setting it on the table. "Are you all right?"

"I'll survive," Patrick said, then he looked at Jack. "I wasn't aware of any visitors."

Russ glared at him pointedly. "Well, if you'd taken the time to call us you just might have known about her." He looked at Cassie. "Why don't you go freshen up, lass."

His words were an order, not a hint. Though she was tempted to argue, she knew they wouldn't say anything with her present. "All right."

"I'm going to reset the alarms," Russ said, following her out of the room.

"A reporter?" Rourke asked after they'd left the room.

"Can I get us some tea before the inquisition begins?"

Rourke sat down at the kitchen table. "Lust?"

"You won't believe this one." Jack gave him a brief rundown.

"I like her style," Rourke told him, unable to contain his deep-throated laughter.

"Oh, you do, do you? Then you'll really love her job skills. Are you involved in a deal with the Hook family?"

The question stopped Rourke cold, his face suddenly blank, the crows feet around his eyes stretched taut. "What do you know?"

"Very little," Jack replied. He took a sip of his tea, gazing at Rourke speculatively over the rim of the cup. "Except that you're somehow involved, which is what got me involved with Cassie and her mess to begin with."

Rourke was worried. Had there been a leak? "Where did you get this information?"

"From Cassie. Her informant has chosen to remain quite anonymous but we've information which indicates he's probably somehow connected to the Hook family." Jack paused for a moment, then asked, "*Is* Flynn alive?"

Patrick didn't show any emotion. "Yes. He was spotted in Northern Ireland eight days ago, then London the day after. I've been trying to catch up with him since then."

"Then it really was Flynn who sent someone to try and kill Cassie and me the night we checked out that abandoned high-rise project."

"Lord," Rourke muttered hoarsely, "will it never stop! I think Flynn is—" He paused, then dropped the subject. "How did Cassie link us?"

Jack wasn't offended by Rourke's reticence. He knew many times the information Patrick had wasn't his to give. "Paris, the time you flew in to help me out. But don't worry. The general's loose tongue is no longer wagging. His wife found those photos we took as a precaution quite fascinating." Jack glanced over at the archway. "You don't have to listen at the door, Cassie."

"It's the only way to find out anything in this house," Cassie said, entering the room. She refilled her coffee cup, then leaned back against the counter. "So," she looked at Rourke, "are you and Marilyn Hook going through with some kind of deal, or not?"

Rourke choked on his drink, the hot tea scalding his throat all the way down. All he could do was stare at her, gasping for breath.

Jack smiled. "You get used to it," he told Rourke as a dull red flush climbed up his face. "It's an interviewing technique she uses a lot; shock them into answering before they have time to think. Her other one is just as deadly. For that she uses all her feminine charm to trick you into telling her what she wants to know."

"I'd prefer the second."

"Would you answer my questions?" Cassie asked.

"No."

"Are you involved?" Jack asked him.

Rourke hesitated, glancing at Cassie. "What is this? A tag team match?"

"Yes, if it will get me answers," Cassie replied. She sat down at the table. "If you are involved, try and find out who had a reporter, Brian Fenton, murdered."

Rourke didn't blink an eye. "Anything else, madame?"

"That will do for a start."

He chuckled and glanced at Jack. "Brassy, bold, a tough fighter. There's probably no stopping her."

Jack agreed. "My sentiments exactly."

Rourke stood up. "I have some business to take care of, I'll be back late this evening." He closed the back door behind him without making a sound.

Jack looked at Cassie. "I assume you called your friend again?" She nodded. "What did you find out?"

"The business interests of the Hook family are widespread, and all privately owned. Construction, real estate, oil and gas wells, electronics—they have fingers in many pies. And information on which companies they own is hard to come by."

"Construction? Have any of their projects gone bankrupt?"

Cassie put her feet up on the chair next to her and leaned back. "Not a one."

He gave her a puzzled look. "Isn't that unusual for the economy here?"

"According to Roger, very unusual. But they probably have the resources to bail themselves out if they choose to do so. Roger also said finding out their true financial position will be impossible. Sound familiar? It's not unlike your own situation."

He wanted to laugh. She never quit digging when she wanted to know something. "Can you think of any reason why they or anyone connected to them would have Brian Fenton killed?"

"No." Cassie shrugged. "I would think it'd have to be something more serious than construction fraud, though, and we don't even know if they're entangled in that, let alone murder. In short, we still haven't got a clue as to what's going on."

"True. I want you to find out more about the Hook family, try to narrow down who your source might be."

She laughed. "Wait a minute, Jack. Just what do you think you're going to do? Confront him and demand he give us the supposed ledgers?" He smiled. "It doesn't work that way. This guy is trying to protect his life. Even if we find out who he is, he's not just going to come out and hand over the information."

"Are you one hundred percent positive he won't?"

Cassie sighed. "No, but the odds are against it."

"It's still worth a try, and a lot easier than breaking into a bank, isn't it?"

This man had an annoying habit of being right too often. "I'll continue the research in the morning."

"Good. And don't forget, we do our first visual run-through of the bank tomorrow at noon."

She nodded, not letting him see the turmoil she felt inside. Tomorrow they would make a physical inspection of the bank and its premises. Cassie was on her way toward becoming a thief. "Anything else?"

"No. Be here by eleven. Dress expensively. Something that shows your legs would be nice."

Cassie saluted him, then made a rude gesture.

"Smart stuff. Get out of here. Unless you've changed your mind and decided to stay?"

"What? And disappoint whoever planted those listening devices? For shame. They've probably gotten very attached to hearing me brush my teeth."

THE WELL-DRESSED MAN leaned back against the plush living room couch and sighed. He was pretending to read a magazine, but was actually listening to a conversation taking place between two people in the nearby study. The woman, he was quite fond of. The man, he abhorred. That missing finger was . . . disturbing.

So was the anger in the man's voice. "Are you positive this guy didn't uncover our connection?"

"No, I'm not positive," the woman replied. "But Brian Fenton was a very tight-lipped reporter. If he did uncover anything, I seriously doubt he would have told anyone else."

"Then we'll go ahead as planned. Do you have a buyer for the jewelry lined up?"

"Yes."

"Good. I'll let you know when I'm ready. The timing on this will be critical," he told her. "Now, show me what you have on the other matter."

It grew quiet in the study. The man in the living room sighed again. Great. Now she was acting as a fence. Something would have to be done about that, and soon.

Chapter Fourteen

"This is Rourke, get Willie on the line." He was at a pay phone near the motel where he'd stayed last night. Before making this call he had checked on the kid. Sound asleep once more, passed out cold with his liquor bottle. Not that Rourke blamed him; the kid was in deep trouble.

"Willie here. Where the hell have you been?"

"We have a problem. His name is Flynn. He's using my name around town. And he's made contact with the seller."

A string of cuss words filled Rourke's ear. "First you disappear for a week," Willie exclaimed, "making my ulcer worse than ever, then you drop a bomb like that. You're not good for me, Rourke. We'll have him picked up," he ended on a sigh.

"It won't be that easy. You'll have to find him first. And he's good, Willie."

"Ain't you just bursting with good news. Okay," he announced with another loud sigh. "Where do we look?"

"If I knew that I'd serve him to you on a platter." Roasted, with an apple in his mouth, Rourke added silently.

The silence dragged on from one minute to two before Willie spoke. "There is no leak in my operation, Rourke.'

"Willie, knowing Flynn, he found out about this sale the same way you did. And your informant did turn up dead, by Flynn's hand no doubt. A bidding war might liven things up, help smoke Flynn out. And I want another favor."

"Naturally."

"Twenty-four-hour surveillance on an address here in Houston, until this mess is over with."

"I can't do that! We have no jurisdiction inside this country and you know it."

"Twenty-four-hour surveillance, Willie. Use your connections, or better yet tell your boss that's how I want to be paid this time."

"Damn free-lancers," Willie muttered.

"You've got that right, Willie. Free. I'll even give you a purpose for doing this to cover your hide. Flynn will probably show up at that address sooner or later."

"Well, why didn't you say so in the first place! I'll make arrangements with the local FBI field office. Who are we going to be protecting?"

"A child."

"Touchy. Is the child his?"

"No. I consider her mine, so protect her with your life, Willie. I'm a lot more dangerous than any of your bosses."

THEY WERE SITTING on the green grass under the large shade trees in the backyard, six kittens falling all over themselves as they explored the nearby area. Two large Dobermans were sprawled out a few feet away, their soulful brown eyes on the kittens. It was dark, but the area was illuminated by the yellow patio light.

"I missed you."

"I missed you, too, Bridget."

"When are you going to settle down, Patrick?" Bridget picked up one straying kitten and stroked it gently. "You could buy a place here in Houston? Or live with Jack?"

"Jack might not agree with you." Patrick smiled at her fondly.

"Yes, he would. He worries about you, I can tell." She picked up another kitten. "You could move all your horses here. Have them in one place."

"To Jack's place?"

Bridget giggled as he'd known she would. "No, silly, to a place of your own. Jack doesn't have any stables." She peeked over at him slyly. "Then I could stay with you sometimes." She looked at him, her green eyes begging for his understanding. "I couldn't stay there all the time because Russ and Jack need me, too."

So wise for one so young. And he knew how Bridget's mind worked. Let her get this out of her system. "Did you have a specific place in mind for me?"

Bridget grinned. "I'll be right back." She put the kittens on his lap and jumped up. The dogs followed her to the house, stopping at the back door.

Patrick absently stroked the tiger-striped kittens. Was she safe anywhere? They couldn't lock her away. What kind of life would she have then? They had to let her have enough freedom to grow up, could only protect her from so much.

Bridget returned. "Down guys." The Dobermans obeyed her command, resuming their previous position.

"See here," she thrust the want ads of the Sunday newspaper under his nose and knelt down beside him. There were several properties circled in red.

Patrick's eyes widened. "You have expensive tastes, Bridget Houlihan."

"But they'd be perfect for the horses," she explained.

"At these prices you'll have to sleep in the barn, too."

She pursed her lips. "I could help you out, I have plenty of money in my trust fund."

"Thank you for your kind offer but that money is for you and your education."

"But part of it's yours." She huffed her disapproval. "You put it there."

"For you and your future."

Bridget recognized that look. He wasn't going to listen to her, but there had to be a way. If he bought a place and settled down he wouldn't do dangerous things anymore. He wouldn't have time.

"I could loan you the money," Bridget bargained. "Your horses do win, sometimes. You could pay me back."

Patrick smiled. She wasn't going to give up and his humoring her was making the situation worse. "I have a better idea. You can look for a fix-er-upper like Jack bought, and in the same price range."

She frowned. "That's going to be much harder to find. With stables, too?" He nodded. "It won't have heating and air-conditioning like these," she warned, tapping his newspaper. "or a swimming pool. It probably won't even have electricity or plumbing."

He fought a grin. "That's all right. We'll tough it out at first."

Her sigh was long and loud. "All right." She rounded up the straying kittens before they climbed on top of the Dobermans. "Patrick, who's after you?"

"No one, yet." He tucked a stray hair behind her ear. She'd always seen through him. But all three of them had always tried to be honest with her. "We're just being cautious." His softened brogue was meant to reassure her and was only partly successful.

"This trouble isn't because of me, is it?" Patrick shook his head no. "But I'm your weak point, I'm what makes you vulnerable. Each semester at school they go over what we should and shouldn't do to help keep our families safe." She looked at him earnestly. "I know what to do, Patrick, I'll help you just like you've helped me."

He didn't smile or laugh. The situation now and in the near future was far too serious. Her safety might depend on her own actions. "Thank you, Bridget."

"Do you have time to play cards? I need to work on my poker game. The girls at school are getting better."

He watched her expertly shuffle the cards. "You aren't betting, are you?" She kept her eyes on the cards. "Bridget, remember the deal you made with Jack and me when we taught you these games?" The girl nodded, but didn't look at him. "We expect you to keep your word, always."

"Yes, sir."

"So how much did you win?"

A big grin filled her face and she looked up at last. "Six dollars and seventeen cents. We only play for pennies." Her smile faded at his stern look. "But I'm not going to do that anymore. I just won't play."

"Bridget." He waited, not fooled by her act for one moment. "This country is going to be taken by storm one day by quite an astonishing actress." He tapped her chin with his finger. "After you finish school."

"Not just the country. The world!" She grinned at him. "How 'bout if I promise not to get caught?" Patrick frowned and she frowned right back at him with a disgusted sigh. "I don't know why Russ thinks you and Jack are marshmallows. You two don't let me get away with anything, either."

"Then I guess we won't be going to the races next month."

"You promised! You—" Bridget closed her mouth. "Oh, you're teasing me. All right, let's play cards. Aces wild, jokers..."

Patrick shook his head in wonder. Actress, card shark, and yet still a sweet, sensitive child. What kind of monster had they created?

"Your report, Mr. Knox."

"I know who your traitor is," he replied, giving her the name. "What do you want done next?"

The announcement didn't surprise her. She'd suspected him all along, he was the weakest one.

"Find out who he talked to and what he revealed about the businesses. Then kill him. Immediately."

"I'll take care of it tonight. Anything else?"

"Not at this time." Marilyn Hook leaned back in her chair, rocking it gently. Blood ties should be unbreakable, but Lawrence had betrayed the whole family. He had to die to protect the rest.

IT WAS AFTER MIDNIGHT. The three men were sitting in the library. "Have either of you actually seen Flynn?" Russ asked.

"No," they answered in unison.

"Then it could all be hearsay." He thought for a moment. "Or someone could be trying to uncover Bridget's trail." Russ looked at Rourke. "Any more rumors?"

"None. Aside from Cassie, other than that one time in Ireland, no one has inquired into the whereabouts of Bridget Houlihan. The old couple told the man who called them what they were led to believe. Distant relatives picked up the girl the next day, promised to keep in touch, but never did."

"I have a bad feeling about this," Russ said. "Maybe we should take off with her again."

"She can't spend the rest of her life running away," Patrick returned harshly. "I should never have stopped searching for those killers all those years ago."

"The decision at the time was the best one for Bridget," Jack reminded him. "And it may still be the best choice. Especially if Flynn is still alive."

"He's alive. I can feel him. And the descriptions of him are too accurate." Rourke glanced at Jack, then Russ. "The man happens to be missing his little finger, too."

Russ jumped up, his ruddy face turning a deeper shade of red. "Dammit, Patrick Rourke, you try my patience!" he bellowed. "Why didn't you say so in the first place!"

Patrick wasn't fazed by his bluster. "The confirmation came in a short while ago. Don't worry. I'll find him."

"No, *we'll* find him," Russ corrected.

Patrick shook his head. "And what about Bridget? Who'll be protecting her? Her safety has to come first."

"We'll drop this mess with Cassie and—"

"No!" Patrick and Jack yelled at the same time but for different reasons.

Jack spoke first. "Patrick believes Flynn has some kind of transaction coming up with the Hook family."

"I see. And we know the lockbox belongs to the Hook family, too." Russ's mind shifted into high gear. "Who's to say Cassie's informant didn't give out the wrong lockbox number? Or it could be the right number and this is all a setup, orchestrated by Flynn."

"It is a possibility," Jack murmured. "And too much of a coincidence for my liking."

"Is Cassie to be trusted?" Patrick asked.

Russ looked at Jack before he spoke. "I say we can trust her." Jack nodded his agreement. "She really believes her friend Brian Fenton was murdered. And she's willing to break the law to prove it. A nice juicy story would also please her immensely." Russ sat down, his color returning to normal. "I've done some checking. No sizable deposits have been made into her savings or checking account and her balances are low." He chuckled. "They're always low. That lady likes clothes."

"Maybe we're giving Flynn too much credit," Jack said.

"Or not enough," Russ added harshly. He looked at Jack, then at Patrick. "We stalked him for three long years before we had proof of his death. Or so we thought."

Patrick didn't want to remember the past. And yet he could never forget it. It never left him alone. "So why is he surfacing now?"

"Revenge," Jack suggested. "We did kill his brother."

"No!" Russ yelled, pounding the nearby table with his fist. "We did not. Flynn sacrificed his own brother in the hopes of killing all three of us at the same time. He set that bomb himself, the timing on it was wrong and Flynn knows it. And he *chose* to use his only brother as the carrier. I hope it's eaten away at him all these years. I hope he's suffered as much as you two did when you lost your families in that bombing of his, and all the others who lost their loved ones because of him."

Jack didn't want to think about that time in his life. Recently he'd begun to believe he could successfully put all that behind him. It hurt to find out now that it wasn't going to leave him alone.

"But why come after us now?" Jack asked.

"It probably is revenge. He was forced to fake his own death to survive, leave his homeland, start somewhere else." Patrick shrugged. "It's eaten at him and after all these years he's found a way to get at us."

"Through Bridget?" Jack asked, his eyes narrowing.

Russ held his glass out to be filled. "Possibly. But that wouldn't completely satisfy him. What he wants is us."

"Do you think it's a coincidence that he's here in Houston right now?" Jack asked, looking at Patrick who shook his head no. "Who spotted him in Ireland?"

"Derry."

They stared at each other in morose silence. Derry was Patrick Rourke's childhood friend, and the man who had helped them get Bridget out of Ireland the night her parents were killed. They trusted him. Derry knew who Flynn was and what he looked like.

Russ sighed. "Not good."

"No, it isn't. And there's more," Patrick said, then waited until he had their full attention. "There have been two robberies in England in the past ten days. They were carried out by amateurs who couldn't possibly have planned them. Both times the target was a formal dinner party out in the country," Patrick explained. "Some of the pieces stolen are worth over a million each."

Russ whistled at that. "Pricey. But what's this got to do with Flynn or Bridget?"

"I think Flynn orchestrated the robberies," Patrick replied. "They were his style, from start to finish."

Jack interrupted him. "There hasn't been anything in the papers over there, or here. I wouldn't have missed something like that."

"You're right," Patrick said. "The victims and the authorities are afraid any publicity at all will spawn a rash of identical crimes. And the value of those pieces would become public knowledge, setting them up for additional robberies in the future."

Russ sat back down and looked at Patrick. "What is it you want to do? We haven't plied that particular trade in years," he reminded him. "And we don't need the money or have the time to mess with it right now. Even if Flynn is behind this."

"The jewelry is here in Houston." Patrick looked at the two men. "I want to steal it from Flynn."

There was a long silence. Finally Jack asked, "Where?"

Patrick pointed to the blueprints on the table. "Care to take a wild guess?"

That didn't please Russ at all. "It's a trap," he said. "This is too easy. I don't like it." He looked at Patrick. "How did you hear about the robberies anyway?"

"I was on Flynn's trail. Way behind on his trail," Patrick added wryly, "when I heard about the first robbery. The second one I found out about from an acquaintance. He was able to give me inside information on both robberies."

"Flynn may have paid him to leak the information to you. He could be trying to set me up. What else did he tell you?" Jack asked.

"They picked up two of the guys from the first incident for questioning, but they were killed by poison in their food before they revealed anything." Patrick moved restlessly in his seat. "Classic Flynn, all the way. Look, I followed a guy over here who tried to set bond for his friends. He's holed up in a cheap motel, probably waiting for someone to contact him. Today he took the jewelry to the bank. I followed him. The guy's not very smart, he's still a kid. All we have to do is get the key out of him. We've done this exact job before," Patrick reminded them.

Jack knew how Patrick's mind worked. "And I suppose you want Flynn to know we took his goodies?"

Patrick nodded. "Yes. And I want him to know that we know he's alive. If we're lucky, this will so enrage him he'll do something stupid. If this were meant to be a trap maybe we can see that he gets caught in it himself."

"It's a long shot," Russ warned.

"Do you have any better ideas? I don't intend to sit here and wait to see what he tries. You taught us to be the hunter, Russ, not the hunted."

After a thoughtful silence Jack asked, "Does he drink?"

"Like a fish," Patrick replied.

Jack gave him a grim smile. "Good, it'll make things easier. If we can find the right woman, we could have the key to his box by tomorrow night." Jack looked at Russ. "Do you agree?"

Russ sighed. "I still don't like it, but I agree. And I know just the person for the job. I'll take care of it."

His tone left no room for objections but that had never stopped Patrick or Jack before. "That won't be necessary," Patrick said. "I can handle this."

"Fine. Now let's get back to what's really important. Where will Bridget be safest?" Russ asked.

"Flynn knows where we are by now," Jack said. "But does he know where Bridget is?"

Patrick stood up and began pacing around the room. "Kathleen's home will be easier to guard, and the surveillance I have on it right now is—"

Jack interrupted him. "What surveillance?"

"I made a deal with the FBI," Patrick said.

Jack nodded and looked at Russ. "So, who is spending the night there, tonight?"

"I am," Russ said. "And no arguments, Paddy me lad. You look like hell. Try and get a good night's sleep for a change."

PLAY THE

LUCKY

CARNIVAL WHEEL

scratch-off game
and get as many as
SIX FREE GIFTS...

HOW TO PLAY:

1. With a coin, carefully scratch off the silver area at right. Then check your number against the chart below it to find out which gifts you're eligible to receive.

2. You'll receive brand-new Harlequin Intrigue® novels and possibly other gifts—ABSOLUTELY FREE! Send back this card and we'll promptly send you the free books and gifts you qualify for!

3. We're betting you'll want more of these heartwarming romances, so unless you tell us otherwise, every other month we'll send you 4 more wonderful novels to read and enjoy. Always delivered right to your home. And always at a discount off the cover price!

4. Your satisfaction is guaranteed! You may return any shipment of books and cancel at any time. The Free Books and Gifts remain yours to keep!

NO COST! NO RISK!
NO OBLIGATION TO BUY!

FREE! 20K GOLD ELECTROPLATED CHAIN!

You'll love this 20K gold electroplated chain! The necklace is finely crafted with 160 double-soldered links, and is electroplate finished in genuine 20K gold. It's nearly ⅛" wide, fully 20" long—and has the look and feel of the real thing. ''Glamorous'' is the perfect word for it, and it can be yours FREE when you play the ''LUCKY CARNIVAL WHEEL'' scratch-off game!

PLAY THE LUCKY
''CARNIVAL WHEEL''

Just scratch off the silver area above with a coin. Then look for your number on the chart below to see which gifts you're entitled to!

YES! Please send me all the free books and gifts I'm entitled to. I understand that I am under no obligation to purchase any more books. I may keep the free books and gifts and return my statement marked ''cancel.'' But if I choose to remain in the Harlequin Reader Service®, please send me 4 brand-new Harlequin Intrigue® novels every other month and bill me the members-only low price of $2.24* each—a savings of 26 cents per book. There is no extra charge for postage and handling! I can always return a shipment at your cost and cancel at any time.   180 CIH RDEZ
(U-H-I-01/90)

NAME_____
(Please Print)

ADDRESS_____APT. NO._____

CITY_____STATE_____ZIP CODE_____

39	WORTH FOUR FREE BOOKS, 20K GOLD ELECTROPLATED CHAIN AND FREE SURPRISE GIFT
15	WORTH FOUR FREE BOOKS, 20K GOLD ELECTROPLATED CHAIN
27	WORTH FOUR FREE BOOKS
6	WORTH TWO FREE BOOKS AND A FREE SURPRISE GIFT

Offer limited to one per household and not valid to current Harlequin Intrigue® subscribers.
*Terms and prices subject to change without notice.

More Good News For Members Only!

When you join the Harlequin Reader Service®, you'll receive 4 heartwarming romance novels every other month delivered to your home at the members-only low discount price. You'll also get additional free gifts from time to time as well as our newsletter. It's ''Heart to Heart''—our members' privileged look at upcoming books and profiles of our most popular authors!

If offer card is missing, write to: Harlequin Reader Service, 901 Fuhrmann Blvd., P.O. Box 1867, Buffalo, NY 14269-1867

Neither man spoke for a long time after Russ had left. Patrick finally broke the silence. "Do you think about her often?"

Jack glanced at him, then away. "Sometimes."

His voice was full of anguish. "The memories are fading," Patrick whispered. "No matter how hard I try to remember, they keep fading."

Jack heard and felt the agony his friend was experiencing. He'd felt this way himself. "Let them fade, Patrick, you have to let them go."

"I can't."

"Yes, you can," Jack told him. "You just don't want to. Nothing will ever bring your wife and child back. You have to make new memories, find new happiness."

"Like you have?" Patrick asked. "You set a great example."

Jack grimaced. "I'm trying."

"With Cassie O'Connor?"

Jack shrugged. "Maybe, maybe not. But I'm open to the possibility. You aren't."

"Cassie would be good for you. You need someone to keep your ordered life in constant turmoil, just like—" Patrick stopped himself, horrified by what he'd almost said. "God, Jack, I'm sorry."

"It's all right, Patrick. And you're right, Shannon did keep my life in a constant turmoil. I never knew what she was going to do next and I loved it, and her." Jack's smile was bittersweet. "She's dead, Patrick. And if I can capture only a glimpse of the happiness I had with her again I will accept that. I need someone in my life, a partner, someone to share things with, argue with, love."

Jack held a bottle and glass out to Patrick, but he shook his head. "No thanks, it's all too easy to slip back into past bad habits. My ears still hurt when I think of that first time we met Russ." They grinned at each other in shared remembrance.

Russ Ian had found them both in a local pub in Ireland, drunk, barely able to walk and getting beaten up. Russ had broken up the fight, pulled them up off the floor by their ears and dragged them to his room to let them sleep it off.

Over the next week he'd forced them to remain sober, gotten their story out of them and shown them that something could be done.

With Russ's help and guidance they began searching for the men responsible for setting the bomb that killed their families.

The bombing had been blamed on the strife in Northern Ireland, but they knew it had nothing to do with the unrest there.

Eight innocent people had died that day because of a personal vendetta. Flynn's vendetta.

Believing the end justified the means, Russ showed them how to steal from thieves. They'd made a good living returning stolen goods to owners for the reward.

It was a risky, quasi-legal but profitable business, and it gave them the money they needed to finance their search for the one man they couldn't catch. The elusive Flynn. He almost never carried out a job himself. He hired others to do most of the dangerous work. It had made him a hard man to catch.

They thought they'd succeeded once before, and they'd been wrong. But it wasn't going to happen again. Not this time.

Chapter Fifteen

"Remember what you're supposed to be looking for," Jack murmured in her ear, holding the door open so Cassie could precede him into the bank. It was twelve noon on the dot.

He was dressed impeccably, as always, the pale pink shirt looking crisp and stylish with his blue pinstripe suit, a subtle striped tie blending in perfectly. He looked rich, just like the bank.

It was an older building, with an ornate architectural style. Carved cornices flowed along the top of the high walls all around the ceiling junctures. Marble floors and counters gleamed, polished to a high sheen. They proceeded slowly across the lobby, past the tellers' cages, Cassie trying to spot any changes between the blueprints and the actual layout.

"Mr. Merlin, how pleasant to see you again." A thin, distinguished looking, gray-haired man in a three-piece suit stepped out of a glass enclosed office and shook hands with Jack. "Anything I can help you with today?"

"I require the use of a safety deposit box."

"Certainly, right this way."

He led them down a short flight of stairs to the basement, his pace brisk and businesslike. This area was just as ornate as the rest of the building, the marble tile floor gleaming. No one was behind the service counter, but a guard stood off to one side, watching the entrance to the safety deposit box vault.

"Have a seat, I'll get the manager of this section for you immediately."

"How does he know you?" Cassie asked quietly.

"I deposited quite a large sum of money here recently."

"Why?"

"You'll understand eventually." He stood up as the older man came back into the room, accompanied by a young woman.

His smile included Cassie. "Mrs. Harris will be assisting you, but if you require any further help, please don't hesitate to call on me."

They shook hands, then the older man left. Mrs. Harris turned to them. "If you'll come over to the counter I'll get your paperwork started."

Cassie was silent as they discussed the various box sizes and prices. When he had decided, Jack signed the identification card, scribbling his name across the form. It was illegible.

"Right this way," Mrs. Harris said, lifting a section of the counter up to allow them access to the boxes.

The heavy vault door was half-open, more than enough for them to enter. Fronts of gold-colored boxes lined the entire room. Indirect lighting fixtures ran along all four sides of the low ceiling, which was also colored gold and looked like solid metal. It was eerily quiet. Cassie imagined there was plenty of thick, utilitarian concrete behind the golden facade. Impenetrable.

Mrs. Harris found Jack's box, inserted her key, and watched as Jack did likewise. She pulled the long container out. "We have private rooms right this way, sir."

"How many rooms are there?"

"Three. But if things get busy we can make other arrangements to ensure your privacy," Mrs. Harris assured him with a congenial smile. She led them to a booth and put the empty box down on the waist-high table within. "Just let me know when you're finished." On her way out, the door closed behind her with a solid thump.

Jack opened his briefcase and swiftly transferred the contents to the lock box, then he looked around the room noting each detail. No cameras or microphones were visible. That didn't mean they weren't there, of course, though he doubted a privacy-conscious branch bank like this would have either the funds or the inclination to indulge in such a transgression.

His eyes swept over Cassie. She was dressed in an ivory-colored gabardine suit with an emerald-green blouse. A serpentine gold chain encircled her throat and small gold earrings adorned her lobes. Her hair was twisted into a sophisticated style. Cream high heels and a matching leather clutch completed her outfit. She looked elegant and sexy.

"I'm finished," he announced. "Would you carry this?" he asked Cassie, holding out his briefcase. She took the case and opened the door, allowing him to lead the way with the box.

"Right this way, sir," Mrs. Harris said, motioning to the open vault. They went through the procedure of locking his valuables up and wished each other a good day.

Cassie walked out the front door of the bank, breathing deeply of the fresh air. It was a beautiful day, full of sunshine and few clouds, the humidity not yet stifling, for a pleasant change. There must have been a high-pressure zone out on the Gulf of Mexico somewhere.

Jack opened the car door for her, then walked around the car and slid into the driver's seat, starting the Mercedes and easing his way into traffic. "Notice any changes inside the bank?"

"Structurally it appeared the same. You?"

"Small things, but nothing major. I'll dwell on it for a day or two and see what I come up with."

"We don't have forever!" Cassie reminded him sharply. "The documents could be moved at any time."

"It'll seem like forever if we screw up and get caught. Does the idea of ten to twenty in the state pen sound good to you, sweetheart?"

"No!"

"I didn't think so. We'll take every day and night we need to plan this thing properly."

His tone left little room for argument. And she knew he was right. Her nerves were on edge from visiting the bank. She had been waiting for someone to run up and arrest her prematurely, somehow reading her mind and deciphering her illegal intentions.

"What now?"

"We study the plans some more, look for potential problems, anything which might interfere with our mission."

So it was a mission now. Cassie wasn't sure she liked the nomenclature, but then again, she couldn't bring herself to think of it as a robbery, either. She glanced at her watch. "I need to check my answering machine."

"Expecting a call from your source?"

"Yes. And no, you can't speak to him!" Cassie was worried, she still didn't have the key to that lockbox.

Jack was still smiling at her clipped tone as he pulled up in front of a pay phone near a corner gas station. "Will this do?"

She threw him a withering look and got out of the car. What did he have to smile about? After dialing her number she tapped her foot restlessly, impatient with the slowness of her machine and the two eager-sounding men who had left messages for her roommate.

The next voice startled her. "Cassie, this is Stan. A member of the Hook family turned up dead this morning. Call me if you want the details."

Gripping the phone tightly, she forced herself to listen to the last message. It wasn't her source. And the tape was blank after that. There wasn't even the usual clicking sound present, signifying someone had called and then hung up without speaking. Ominous.

"Cassie, are you all right?" Jack was standing behind her, his fingers gently resting on her shoulder.

"Yes." Her voice was barely above a whisper, her lips dry. This felt bad, and her gut instincts were almost never wrong. "I need a quarter, please."

He handed her one, watching her as she dialed a number. There was a shocked, glassy look to her blue eyes, and her body was wound like a clock spring, the knuckles of her left hand white as she gripped the phone receiver.

"Stan, this is Cassie." She cocked her head to one side, closing her other ear with her index finger as a loud truck roared past. "Speak up, I'm at a pay phone."

Listening carefully, she didn't interrupt him once. She wasn't surprised that he'd remembered exactly who she'd been investigating that day in the newspaper's basement. Her eyes were opening wider by the moment while Jack watched, frowning.

"Thanks for calling, Stan. I'll be in touch." She dropped the receiver back on the hook and stared straight ahead, her already pale complexion now chalky white.

Unconsciously she swayed toward Jack, and he accepted the weight of her body leaning against him, wrapping his arms around her. He liked the feel of her in his arms, but her body was taut, brimming with tension, and she was barely breathing. It was as if she was afraid to take a breath lest she shatter into tiny pieces.

"What's wrong?" he murmured.

She took a deep breath and let it out slowly. "Lawrence Hook is dead. I think he was my inside source."

"You're positive?"

She nodded her head slowly. "Ninety-nine percent sure."

He led her back to the car and helped her inside. "How can you be that sure, if you've never met him?" Jack asked, his hands curving around the steering wheel as he waited patiently for her answer.

"I've been working on the charity stories awhile and I've done extensive research into the family from that angle." She leaned her head back against the car seat. "I spent my entire morning reviewing what I know and trying to put it together differently. The dead man was the only one high enough up in the family hierarchy to have access to the information I've been given who appeared to have any kind of conscience left." Glancing at him she asked, "And why else would he be dead?"

"An accident."

Cassie sighed. "Too much of a coincidence." She caught her lower lip between her teeth. "The police are still on the scene. I need to talk to them."

He started the car. "You could be wrong."

"Maybe." But she didn't think so.

"Give me directions."

Cassie glanced over at him. She was regaining her usual solid demeanor. "I can drive myself." Her fingers were smoothing over the rich brown leather of her seat restlessly. "He didn't die a pretty way."

"There is no pretty way to die. It can't be any worse than some of what I've seen." He pulled into traffic and headed for the freeway. "Besides which, there's no reason for either of us to view the body. Is there?"

"No." She relented and gave him the location, as well as instructions on the quickest way to get there.

They had to park a block from the canal. It seemed like everyone who drove by had to stop and see what all the commotion was about. It didn't help that the scene was close to a major shopping mall, and a half dozen police cars were a hard sight to miss.

Cassie started to get out of the car. "Coming with me?" she asked, looking at him over her shoulder.

"I'll sit this one out."

She flashed him a somber grin. "Don't fall asleep."

Jack watched her through an unusually crafted pair of minibinoculars as she carefully made her way across the brown grass in her high heels. This new development had him wary and on edge.

He scanned the area, but for what he wasn't sure. Most of the onlookers appeared to be just that, people looking for a little excitement in their otherwise dull lives.

Jack struggled with his own memories. A ghastly scene played over and over, mixing with the imagined stench of plastic explosive and the sound of screams. He closed his eyes, hard, willing the nightmare away. There seemed to be no chance of it leaving him alone forever, but if nothing else, he had gotten very good at making it go away.

His usual reaction to a scene like this was to run in the opposite direction. He was obviously in the minority in this crowd.

In his rearview mirror he spotted a tall man in jeans and knit shirt leaning against a tree, surveying the scene through binoculars not unlike his own. Jack fiddled with his, bringing the man into better focus.

"Well, now. What have we here?" he mumbled.

The guy was viewing the people in the crowd, not the police, occasionally putting down the binoculars to write in a small black leather notebook. Jack knew that if he waited long enough the guy would eventually lead him to his car and a possible means of identifying him.

"Nice legs!" a voice Cassie knew well called out. "You should come to work like that more often."

"Then what little work you do accomplish each day would become nonexistent," she retorted, accepting the teasing of her coworker with a knowing smile. He grinned back and they both settled down to work.

With the efficiency of an experienced reporter Cassie managed to elicit the vital facts she needed from various officials. They actually knew very little. No time of death had been established. No one questioned in the neighborhood so far had seen or heard much of anything. Since no motive had been established they were investigating it as a random act of violence. A mugging.

The one confirmed fact was the identity of the victim, Lawrence Hook. Cassie was almost positive he had been her source. And if she was wrong she still might never know the true identity of the informant because Lawrence Hook's death would most certainly scare him off.

One way or the other, she was in a fix. She still didn't have a key for that lockbox.

With difficulty Cassie moved through the swelling crowd in the direction of Jack's car. What was he doing? She couldn't see his face through the tinted windows, but his hand was outside the car, and he was motioning to her to keep walking. She was confused, but didn't break stride, going past the car and on down the street. Who knew what he was up to now?

Or what he might have spotted in the crowd. The thought made her shiver.

The mall was blocks away, long blocks, and walking them in her rarely worn high heels didn't improve her mood at all. To top it off, the day was heating up.

"Jack Merlin, you had better have a damned good excuse for doing this to me." She pulled open the outer glass door and stepped inside to cool air conditioning. Removing her shoes she massaged one aching foot, then the other, ignoring the few pointed stares she received from fussy patrons.

Let them look. Her eyes were on the accident scene, where the police now appeared to be sending the crowd on their way. Had Jack moved?

Jack stayed right where he was, watching the man study the dispersing crowd. As the last of the people cleared the area the guy flowed in with them, walking back toward the parking lot as part of the group. Very professional.

With unwavering patience, Jack waited for him to leave the parking lot in his late model sedan, then he eased the Mercedes into the flow of traffic, coming just close enough to read the license plate of the other car. He memorized the number and then drifted back among the slower moving cars behind him.

At the next intersection Jack executed a quick U-turn and went back to find Cassie.

"This had better be good, Jack," Cassie seethed, taking a special delight in slamming the car door. Her face was a becoming shade of pink.

"Write this down," he returned, rattling off the license plate number.

She read the numbers back to him, some of her anger dissipating as her professional curiosity took over. "What's up?"

"I wish I knew. While everyone else was watching the police and generally getting in the way, the man who left in the car with those plates was taking notes on the crowd." He shot her a quick glance. "You tell me."

Cassie shrugged, still hot and angry enough to want to goad him. "Could be a strange new reporting technique."

"You believe that?"

"No." She eased her high heels off and sighed softly, wiggling her toes freely in the plush carpet. The air conditioning was on full blast, the cool air relaxing.

"Sore feet?" She nodded. "I'll massage them for you when we get home," he offered.

Jack made the process of a foot massage sound very sensual and quite appealing.

"Why did you wave me on past the car?" she asked.

"He had his binoculars trained on you from the time you left the crowd."

"Maybe he liked my legs," she retorted.

Jack stopped at a red light and purposely stared at the length of leg made visible by the side slit of her skirt. "I can see why," he murmured, giving her an appreciative male grin as he slowly slid one finger up the nylon-encased thigh.

Cassie felt a need deep inside her come to the surface as his finger slipped to the inside of her thigh and down again to her knee. She tried to block out the pleasant sensations his touch evoked in her, but with little success. Business, Cassie reminded herself, they had a business relationship and that was all. Sure they did. Who was she trying to fool?

"What did he do after I walked past?"

Jack changed lanes before answering her. "He watched you cross the street, then he returned his attention to the crowd. Do you know someone who can trace the license number?"

"You mean you don't?"

"My connections are getting enough exercise as it is."

"I know what you mean." This story was costing her a lot of favors and at this rate she'd never be able to pay them back in one lifetime. But if she found out who killed Brian, it would be worth it. "I think I can manage to pull in another favor."

"Good. I want to know exactly who we'll be dealing with in the future."

Cassie looked at him. "What do you mean?"

"That man was a professional."

Curious she asked, "How do you know?"

They had arrived at Jack's house. Jack inserted a key into a small box, then punched in the code to open the iron gates. "Let's just say I've met his type before."

"Where?"

He parked the car under the portico and turned to look at Cassie. Her blue eyes never wavered from his piercing gaze. She was getting to him, managing to insinuate herself into his thoughts, bringing back memories of a feisty woman he'd buried long ago.

Involuntarily he reached out and slid one finger along the curve of her face. The same and yet so different. He wanted so much to have what she was so hesitant to give him. But the timing wasn't right. And over the years he'd found out the hard way that timing and patience were everything. If it was meant to be it would happen.

Cassie was studying him carefully. There was something in his eyes right now, a tenderness that surprised her. He seemed suspended in time, lost, revealing just a hint of vulnerability that she found immensely appealing.

His thumb caressed the delicate curve of her cheekbone, then glided down across the full curve of her lower lip. Cassie swayed forward and their lips met in a fleeting caress, like butterfly wings wisping across their skin. His hand curved around the nape of her neck, easing her closer, his mouth opening over hers.

They drank of each other with a greedy thirst that shocked and surprised them both, leaving them breathless.

"You . . ." She trailed off, her mind spinning with uncertainty. Why deny it? She wanted him. And yet there were still so many things she didn't know. "You never answered my question. That type of man. Where—"

"Ireland," he murmured, then suddenly he let go of her, his face hard. He got out of the car and walked around to open her door.

Cassie fumbled with her shoes, using the moment to pull herself together. Her breathing was uneven and her face flushed. What had come over her? What had come over him? In the flash of a second he'd changed from sensual softness to brittle, hard-edged steel. What had gone wrong?

She accepted his hand in getting out of the car and walked beside him into the library, both of them acting as if nothing had happened. A part of her wished that were true. But another part, a larger and steadily growing portion of her mind and body, wished the same thing could happen over and over again. And more.

"Use that phone to make your call about the license plate number," he said, his tone brusque. "I'll be back in a moment."

Jack was silently cursing himself. He hadn't allowed a woman so close in a long, long time and it had unnerved him. Right now he needed to concentrate. She was dangerous for him to be around.

"Russ, you home?" Jack called up the stairway, ignoring the elaborate intercom system he'd installed. He felt like yelling about something.

"You rang?" Russ asked, leaning over the balcony.

"Do you know where that new optical equipment catalog is?"

"I'll bring it to you," he said, and disappeared.

Jack entered the library to find Cassie talking quietly on the phone. She looked quite at home behind his desk, having removed her white jacket. Her silky, emerald-green shell top had minimal sleeves, revealing slender white arms, the rounded neckline hinting at the fullness of her breasts.

She looked up at him as she hung up the phone. "It's a rental car."

"Figures," Jack muttered.

"Here it is," Russ announced.

"What?" Cassie asked as Jack flipped through a catalog.

Jack showed a picture to Russ. "Found it."

Cassie joined them. She read the description of the item he pointed out. "The binoculars that guy had were also a camera?"

Jack answered her. "Yes. I knew they looked familiar."

"You did?" An interested gleam sparkled in her eyes. "Why? Do you own a pair?"

"No," Jack murmured, smiling. "His binoculars are a newer make than mine. Satisfied?"

"I'll just be on my way," Russ told them. "I have a few errands to run." Neither seemed aware of his departure.

"What happens next?" Cassie asked.

"Let's go over the bank plans again while our visit is still fresh in our minds. They're in the kitchen."

They spent the afternoon comparing notes, joined by Russ when he had completed his errand. Once again Cassie was impressed by the intensity of concentration the two men could bring to bear on a problem. She was exhausted by the time she left early that evening, more anxious than ever to get away from Jack and the subtle changes taking place in their relationship.

It was nothing obvious. After all, Russ had been sitting right beside her. But every now and then Jack had casually touched her, tucking a stray hair back into place, letting his fingers glide across her arm as he explained a point.

Cassie wasn't sure how to react. She liked his touch, but she didn't want any added complications right now. It was enough that they were going to visit the bank again tomorrow.

Please, she thought, *no more unpleasant surprises.*

"DID YOU TELL HER?" Russ asked later that same evening.

"No." Jack didn't look at him.

"Doing this my way, she won't have to worry so much. It'll all be over before she knows what's happened. Is everything arranged?" Jack asked him.

Russ was irritated and let him know it by his tone of voice. "Of course it is. Patrick has possession of the key to the other box and he'll be dropping it off sometime tonight. And I've already made you a copy of the bank's master key, from the impression you took earlier. That should save you some time, since you'll have to pick the lock on the Hooks' box. Are you positive you're up to it? It has been a while," Russ reminded him.

"I've been practising, but it looks as if I was wasting my time." Jack walked over to the answering machine and punched a button. "Listen."

The voice was Cassie's and she sounded excited. "Jack, Jack are you there?" There was a pause then she continued, "There was a package waiting for me when I got home! It's the key, Jack! Now, before you call me back screaming, the bugs are in the freezer at the moment. See? I'm learning. And don't worry, I'll be on time tomorrow. Good night."

"Looks like you're going to get your way," Russ muttered.

"Of course." Jack smiled. "Listen, there's more." He switched the machine on again.

The French accent was unmistakable. "Finally, I have found my courage. I want you to know that my last phone call to you was being monitored. They know your home address by now." The tape was blank after that.

"Interesting," Russ replied. "I'd say the general doesn't want any more photos released. And that he has found a way to bribe the reporter we sent copies to."

"I agree. He's earned a reprieve. That ties up one loose end," Jack said with a sigh. "Now all we have to do is tie up about a thousand others, starting with the bank."

Chapter Sixteen

To Anthony Knox the equation was quite simple. Power was pretty; wealth was wonderful; ergo Marilyn Hook was a good-looking woman. In a rich sort of way. Not gorgeous, mind you, but possessing all the beauty money could buy. He wasn't inclined to dwell on it much. She was paying him to do the work he loved and that was all that mattered.

"Why are there two pictures of this woman?" she asked.

Knox leaned over her desk to glance at the photograph in question. It was of a buxom blonde. "Binoculars with built-in cameras can be tricky to operate. My finger must have hit the button twice," he explained with a casual shrug.

It was a careless mistake to include two identical photos of the woman in the package he'd given her. She'd see it as a waste of her time. He didn't really care. Maybe she could make everyone else around her nervous, but not him. In fact, Knox couldn't remember ever having been nervous in his life. Marilyn Hook reprimanded him sharply. "I don't pay you to gawk at women, Knox." She flipped the photos over and pointed at the next picture just as she had with all the others. "Who is she?"

"An investigative reporter for the *Houston Herald*. Her name is Cassie O'Connor."

"I find it strange she would be working when she was all dressed up like this." Her voice gave nothing away. "Why was she at the scene?"

"That I don't know."

"Find out," she ordered. "As soon as you leave." She turned to the next picture.

Knox gave her the names and anything else he had on the rest of the people he had photographed. Luckily there were a few more duplicate shots and they weren't all women, thus saving him from the acid bite of her tongue. Marilyn Hook didn't make him nervous, but she could sure make him worry about a cut in pay, and he had expensive tastes to maintain.

There was nobody that odd or unusual in the photographs, just an everyday assortment of reporters and ghoulish thrill-seekers looking at his handiwork.

"Recognize anyone?" Knox asked when they had gone through the entire set.

"That's none of your business."

She looked at him through small black reading glasses perched on her narrow nose, not for a moment fooled by his youthful, boyish face. Behind those baby features lurked a very cruel man. A man whose greatest pleasure in life was seeing others suffer. His talents had been quite useful to her of late. But he had a smart mouth.

"If you didn't come so highly recommended, Knox, I wouldn't be using you," Marilyn continued, her words a clear insult. "Maybe your past employers have overlooked your crass behavior, but I will not. Is that clear?"

"Yes, ma'am," he answered, quite respectfully. He'd been plying his trade long enough to read people and figure out what they wanted to hear. And it didn't bother him to kowtow to someone, as long as he was paid.

She appeared almost appeased. "I expect the rest of that information today. We wouldn't even be having this conversation if you didn't get so carried away with your work. The next time I tell you to make it look like an accident, I expect an accident. You're dismissed."

Knox stood up and took his time leaving the room, hoping to irritate her a little. Sure, she was nice enough to look at, with her tall, slim build and carefully coiffed silvery blond hair. But her tongue wasn't the only sharp thing about her; she had the power and the mean spirit to sting like a wasp. This job couldn't end soon enough for him. Not, however, before she paid him the rest of his normal exorbitant fee. He had bills to pay.

Right now to earn that fee he had to find out why the O'Connor woman had been all dressed up, unlike any of the other print reporters. He'd also better check more carefully for any stories she was working on. Marilyn Hook hated surprises.

On his way out, he heard her terse summons to her male secretary. "Have Allen and Driscoll report to my office immediately."

"Two more lambs to the slaughter," Knox muttered to himself as he shut the office door behind him.

Alone, Marilyn Hook took a moment to reflect upon her present situation. There was too much riding on the outcome of this next deal for anything else to go wrong. And she really had thought Lawrence completely trustworthy, even more so than the others. Unfortunately, he had not revealed anything to Anthony Knox; instead he had proclaimed innocence till the end. Maybe she had miscalculated Lawrence's strength by a tiny bit, but he was no longer a problem; she'd had him taken care of, just as she'd been taught.

Marilyn looked fondly at the photos of her father and grandfather. They had both died over four years ago in the same crash, their small plane going down in an electrical storm. The loss had devastated her, for a short while, but she had a company to run. And she had a large, extended family who depended on her iron-fisted control of the income their various enterprises produced.

There had been no question as to who would take over as head. Her husband wasn't strong enough or ruthless enough to handle the job, and he had known in advance that eventually Marilyn would be the kingpin. She'd taken care of him, too.

Her ruthlessness surprised no one in the family. Marilyn, the oldest of four girls, had been groomed from an early age for this position, since her mother had never produced the coveted male heir. There had been sacrifices to make along the way, and Marilyn had taken each one of them in stride.

"I'm taking care of things, Poppa," she whispered, bright tears shimmering in her eyes as she stroked the photo. "Just like you and Grandpa taught me."

Marilyn was sitting at her desk, hands clasped together and looking almost serene when they entered her office. She immediately slipped into the well-polished role of a concerned family member.

"What have you found out about poor Lawrence?" she asked them, her voice wavering just the right amount.

"Nothing new," Allen replied. "The police are now calling it a random mugging. He was robbed."

"No clues at all?"

"Not a one," Driscoll told her sympathetically, reacting to the distressed grief he saw in her eyes. "They're doing all they can to find his murderer."

Marilyn nodded. "Look through these photos. Do you recognize anyone?"

Driscoll and his first cousin Allen were as different as night and day. Allen was tall, good-looking, muscular, and a very crafty accountant. And his ties to Leonore Xavier had often been useful to the family. Driscoll was short, balding, thin and a near genius with computers.

Marilyn Hook trusted these two men to a point. They had as much if not more to lose that she did if anything went wrong. Family ties bound them together even tighter. Lawrence had forgotten that his allegiance must always first belong to the family.

"I recognize a few of the television reporters but that's all," Allen replied.

"Same here," Driscoll murmured.

They looked at her, waiting for her opinion. "I didn't recognize anyone, either. After this next transaction we're going to stop any irregular activities for as long as it's necessary. Do you agree?"

"Maybe we should even hold off on this deal for a while," Driscoll suggested.

"We can't," Allen told him. "We won't be able to make all the payments without this sale and we can't afford to have rumors flying around that we're in a financial bind, like so many other prominent families in this town."

"He's right," Marilyn said. "We do have an important position to uphold. Once this sale goes through we'll have enough to tide us over for the next year. Don't worry. This is not a permanent way for us to do business. It has worked well in past years when money was scarce and it will serve us in the future, if need be."

"This Rourke guy is legitimate?" Driscoll asked.

"Very," Marilyn replied, smiling. Her teeth were as perfect as present technology allowed, like the rest of her.

"Are you going ahead with the charity event at the mansion next weekend?" Allen wanted to know.

"Why, of course! Poor Lawrence would want us to!" she exclaimed earnestly. "And after all, it does benefit those less fortunate than us."

"I don't know," Driscoll muttered, shaking his head. "The timing is rotten. How will it look to the rest of Houston society? I mean, a big funeral one week and then the very next week we have a party? It just isn't done!"

"It will be done by the Hooks. This is our yearly event and we must always maintain our position," she reminded him, her voice cutting. "Allen, make sure you get our usual cut."

"Consider it done."

"Good. Let me know if anything important turns up on Lawrence's, um, accident. I've assured the police that they'll have our full cooperation. I have another meeting in five minutes. I'll see both of you at the services tomorrow afternoon."

Allen stood up and picked up one of the photographs from her desk. "Nice legs. Who is she?"

"Cassie O'Connor, an investigative reporter."

He dropped it like a hot potato. "Never mind," he said, grinning. "What I don't need right now is another problem. See everyone later."

Driscoll followed him out, muttering under his breath.

"I don't like it. And I still think this party is a mistake."

THE KEY WAS BURNING a hole in her pocket of her teal dress as Cassie stepped out of the car and looked up at the imposing bank building, squinting slightly as the brilliant sun shone directly in her eyes. A light breeze ruffled the printed teal scarf draped around her neck. Tomorrow night or the next she was going to break into this place. She still couldn't believe she was actually going to go through with the plan.

"Ready?" Jack asked. He looked like a prosperous businessman in his navy-blue suit.

"Not really. It looks bigger today for some reason."

He chuckled and took her arm, guiding her into the bank. "Wait until you see it at night. Remember to look for the little details we discussed."

She nodded, unable to speak as she walked across the bank lobby with him at a very leisurely pace. They took the stairs to the basement the same way. To her, every casual glance in their direction became an accusing stare.

"Mr. Merlin, how nice to see you again," Mrs. Harris said. She seemed perturbed. "I'm afraid . . . um, could you have a seat for just a minute? I'll be right with you."

Cassie looked around the small space, the armed guard in his usual corner the only other person around. What was the delay? Her heart leaped erratically and her pulse began running full speed ahead. She felt as though the key was branding its shape into her thigh. They knew! Any moment the police would walk down those stairs and haul them off to jail.

"Jack!"

"Don't worry, dear," Jack said in a warm, soothing voice which was just loud enough to float easily across the service counter, "we won't be late for our appointment."

What was he talking about? Cassie looked over at Mrs. Harris, who was talking on the phone in quiet, urgent tones. What was going on? Time seemed to drag by, moving slower and slower until Cassie was sure she was going to scream. A door opened somewhere. Footsteps echoed in the quiet chamber. Cassie felt all the blood drain from her face.

Then Mr. Brown entered the room. "Mr. Merlin, I'm so sorry about this delay. It's rare that all our booths should be in use at the same time, I assure you, but it does happen. The lunch hour can be a busy time, you see."

Jack didn't say anything, his face void of expression as he waited for Mr. Brown to continue. Cassie was trying not to show how silly she felt. It was just a normal delay.

"I understand you're in a hurry and I hope my solution meets with your approval." He ushered them into the vault, where the guard was setting up a card table. "Would this be convenient?" he asked, quite obviously anxious to please this large depositor.

Jack looked pointedly at his watch. "It's fine."

Mrs. Harris brought in the card for him to countersign, and opened his box with her key. She smiled tentatively. Bewildered by all the personal attention, Cassie realized the old saying was true. Money really did talk.

"Now, we'll give you some privacy," Mr. Brown said. "Push hard on the vault door when you're ready to leave. The guard will assist you."

Cassie watched them walk out of the vault, feeling a momentary surge of panic as they closed the door almost completely shut.

She turned toward Jack who was visually inspecting the vault door. He nodded and walked over to the table. "I—"

Jack cut her off with a glare. "Ssh!" His briefcase was open and he was already inserting a key into the lock of a safety deposit box, his hands encased in light gray gloves.

Horrified, Cassie swallowed, the noise loud in her ears. "What are you doing?" she mumbled.

"Be quiet!"

"But that's not even the right one!"

He reached over and none too gently grabbed her arm, pulling her close. "Don't speak another word," he murmured in her ear, "the vault could be wired for sound."

Her eyes opened even wider when he deftly slipped out the long box and began pouring the contents into his briefcase. She peered around his shoulder. Sparkling gemstones of every color imaginable slithered past her eyes on their way into an opened purple velvet pouch.

The floor seemed to buckle beneath her. Jack was actually robbing the bank! She'd been set up, used, and there wasn't a damned thing she could do about it. He had covered his tracks so well, involving her every step of the way.

"Get a grip on yourself!" Jack ordered in a whisper. "Help me find the box you need." He consulted his gold Rolex watch. "We don't have much time."

What choice did she have? She was directly involved, just as he had planned all along. Waves of anger washed over her, but she did as she was told. If lady luck was with her she would get what she'd come for, the goal she had risked so much to achieve. There was too much at stake to fight the current now. And afterward? He had that planned as well. Keeping her credibility meant keeping him out of jail; everything would depend on her silence.

He pulled the box out and set it on the table, flipping the lid back. "What the . . ." Jack's mouth dropped open.

Cassie looked inside. The box was empty, except for a small, black computer disk. Cassie felt her body swaying as she looked at it. Where were the documents, the ledgers, the promised evidence that would prove Brian didn't kill himself? She'd risked her career and future for this?

Jack grabbed her arm and squeezed tightly. "Faint and we're done for, sweetheart. Pull yourself together. Do you want to take the disk?"

"Y-yes."

The disk was added to the growing contents of his briefcase. Moving efficiently, Jack returned the boxes to their proper slots, and then stripped off his gray gloves, throwing them inside the case as well before locking it up tight.

"Time to leave," he murmured.

Fury was at last winning out against the confusion and nausea she'd felt consuming her a short time ago. How dare he use her in this way?

Jack picked up the briefcase and moved toward her, grasping the back of her neck firmly with his free hand and pulling her up against him. His mouth covered hers in an arousing kiss, his tongue plunging deeply, drinking of her like a greedy, desert-parched traveler.

Cassie jerked back from his intimate touch, furious. "You're really getting off on this, aren't you?"

"Actually I'm getting you ready to walk out of this bank. A moment ago you looked ready to drop. I think you're sufficiently angry now to make it on your own."

"Don't worry about me!"

He walked to the door and surveyed the small room one last time before pushing hard on the heavy vault door. The guard was standing right outside, ready to offer assistance.

"All through, sir?"

Jack smiled and set the briefcase down. "Yes, thank you." He turned to Cassie. "Coming dear?"

In a way he was right. Cassie was too mad to be scared. She followed him out of the room and walked beside him as they left the bank, the briefcase in her hand.

He gestured gallantly with a wide sweep of his arm, holding her car door open. "Madam."

Cassie looked him right in the eye. "I'm going to wipe that smug, supercilious smile off your face when we get home, Jack Merlin."

"Are you indeed?" he asked, still smiling, his golden brown eyes sparkling with a wicked light. Adrenaline was singing through his veins, a positive charge from a job well done. "Is that a threat?"

"It's a promise," she said through clenched teeth.

Cassie wanted to wring his neck. He'd used her. And look what she'd ended up with: a computer disk. Her source had been quite specific about the evidence, and it was in paper form, thin old-fashioned ledgers. The disk wasn't what she'd expected but it might tell her something, if she could get it to read.

"No blows until we're inside the house," Jack ordered, parking beside the garage. "The dogs might misinterpret your actions and think I'm in danger."

"You are in danger," she assured him.

She marched toward the front entrance and had to wait impatiently while he unlocked the door. He simply smiled at her the whole time.

"After you."

Cassie was in the library before she realized he wasn't following her. She dropped her purse on a side table and went back to find him. He was at the top of the stairway.

"What do you think you're doing?"

Jack paused, one foot resting lightly on the top step. He turned to gaze down at her. "Going to my bedroom."

"We have things to discuss."

"Come on up," he invited, a pleased grin still plastered on his face. "I'm going to change clothes." His tie floated through the air toward her and landed on the marble floor at her feet.

When she looked up he was gone. Cassie climbed the stairs, reminding herself that murder was a serious crime. But was it any worse than the things she'd already done today?

Yes, it was. It would be much too kind of her to put him out of his impending misery. Some sort of slow, awful and continuous torture would be much better. She'd take her time and think of something appropriate.

His bedroom door was wide open but he wasn't in sight. Cassie walked across the room carefully, stepping over his discarded shoes. She picked up a solid pewter candlestick.

"Found your weapon?"

She whirled around, the heavy object held tightly in her hand. His suit jacket was gone and the crisp white dress shirt hung open to the waist, revealing glimpses of a smooth, well-muscled chest when he moved. With a valiant effort she managed to keep her eyes off his body.

"I'll use this," she warned.

"Really?"

"No." Cassie put the candlestick down, reminding herself once again that she didn't want to murder him. "But not for the reason you think. You're just not worth it."

"How do you know what I'm worth until you try me?"

She ignored him. "You used me."

"No more than you used me," he returned, leaning back against the door jamb. "You blackmailed me. Now I've got something on you, too. I'm a great believer in fighting fire with fire."

Though he appeared relaxed, Jack was ready to move fast. Her temper was unpredictable. He'd lured her up here on purpose. There were few things of value in his bedroom, at least of a size she could easily pick up and throw.

"And all the planning we did for the break-in tomorrow night?" Cassie asked, though she already knew the answer.

Jack confirmed it. "A ruse," he replied. "In case this whole mess was an elaborate trap." He had seen the disillusionment on her face when he'd opened the box to reveal nothing more than a floppy disk. She, at least, was who she appeared to be.

"What about the ordeal you put me through at that bar?" she asked, her temper simmering hotly as the implications of his words seeped into her brain. She moved toward him. "You told me it was for real!"

"It was real enough. We had to have the bank plans, not only as an important part of the cover-up operation, but as part of what happened today. And yes, we could have gotten into the bank the way we planned," he assured her, "but we'd never have been able to gain access to the inside of the vault. All that fancy talk about the safe and timing was mumbo jumbo."

Cassie couldn't believe she'd been so easily hoodwinked. "You put my life in danger for a cover-up? Damn you!"

Jack ducked an empty plastic water glass in the nick of time. "We had to mislead anybody who might have had us under surveillance."

For a moment he thought his logic had finally pierced her outrage. But she suddenly pulled off her shoes and took aim. A pair of high heels went flying. One missed. The other smacked him on the shoulder.

"Ouch!" Jack glared at her, but his eyes sparkled with grudging admiration. "Nice shot."

Cassie laughed grimly. "Stand still. I get better."

"Did it make you feel any better?" he asked.

"Not enough," she growled. He wasn't even upset! As a matter of fact he was laughing at her.

Cassie took two steps forward, the palm of her hand making contact with his face even before she'd realized her intentions. She'd never struck another person in her adult life. Not even her ex-husband. And it had been years since she'd been unable to control her tendency to throw things in a fit of pique.

He didn't move a muscle or step toward her.

Cassie felt uneasy, shaky from her bout of unrestrained rage. Much to her surprise, she was even starting to feel a little foolish.

"I . . ." Her hand had left a clear imprint on his tanned cheek.

"Feel better now?"

"N-no."

"Don't ever do that again, Cassandra." She was already shaking her head, needing no further warning than the look on his face.

Jack took a step closer, then another, backing her up against the bedroom wall. "Scared?"

"No." And she wasn't. Not in the way he meant.

He moved closer. "You should be."

She could feel the heat of his body, smell the masculine scent of his skin. There was no doubt in her mind. The escapade at the bank had excited him. He wanted her and he was trying to redirect her anger toward him in a sexual direction. The trouble was, he was succeeding.

His very presence was holding her captive. Her body hummed with a frightening need, a tension begging for release from its prison. But she was still furious with him and not about to give in, even though she wanted to.

Jack watched the conflicting expressions chasing across her face. He stared at her moist, barely parted lips, felt the unsteady rise and fall of her breasts against his chest with each short, gasping breath. With his tongue he teased her lips before slipping inside her warm moist mouth.

He jumped back fast. "Dammit!"

"Oh, you poor dear." She smiled at him innocently. "Did you bite your tongue?"

"Cassandra Elizabeth O'Connor! I ought to—"

"You've used me enough for one day, Jack Merlin. And you deserve a lot more than one little nip."

He smiled. "I agree. But I'd like it even more if you'd stick to nibbling my body, not biting. You have sharp teeth." Was his tongue going to swell up the way another part of his male anatomy was at this very moment?

Cassie didn't know whether to laugh or weep. There was no stopping him. Instead she turned and left the room.

Her derriere was swaying invitingly before him as he followed her downstairs. He almost reached out and touched her, but he stopped himself. She'd probably knock him down the stairs in her present mood.

She picked up her purse from the library table and held out an empty hand, palm up. "The disk please."

He didn't move. "Think about what you're doing, Cassie. Do you want to run all over town with this piece of evidence?"

Cassie did pause to mull it over. She sighed, disgusted, hating it when he was right. "I still want the disk."

"You can use my computer here."

She looked over at the rosewood desk, the surface was clean. "Where is it?" she asked, dropping her purse back on the table.

"You mean you don't know?"

"How could I?"

"You should patent that innocent look. I'm well aware you've searched most of this house."

Cassie crossed her arms and leaned one hip against the table, her head cocked slightly. "And found precious little. What kind of place is this, anyway? You and Russ seem able to come and go like wraiths."

Jack hesitated, and it troubled him. Flash decisions were an everyday part of his life. Why was he questioning letting her in on the secrets these walls contained? Was it because she was slowly slinking her way into his life, and he was uncomfortable with his feeling of responsibility for her? Or because another layer of his thick covering would be stripped away by what a certain room revealed to her? He wasn't really sure.

"Are you in there?" Cassie asked, stepping closer and peering into his eyes.

"Somewhere," he replied.

"Then come on," she demanded. "We don't have all day."

Jack had to smile. She was so sure of herself, and she had a right to be. He was going to reveal to her another part of himself, because he didn't want her seeking the advice of someone she couldn't rely on. Obviously he had come to value her safety more than his secrecy.

What did that mean? He had to admit it was more than lust he was feeling, more than the surface emotion of male protectiveness for a female. But he was not yet ready to confront what else it could be. Down that road lay pain.

"Over here." Jack walked across the room and touched a spot on the middle bookcase.

Cassie watched in fascination as the massive, book-filled shelves swung open on silent hinges, revealing white walls and a set of white double doors. He opened them and turned on a light. Beyond them was a room, the walls on each side covered in redwood.

The redwood paneling continued around the room, giving it a warm feeling. It looked like a large, modern office without windows, obviously the place from which he conducted his business—whatever that was. Large green plants under grow lights filled each corner. There were beige metal filing cabinets; an impressive looking computer; a telex and facsimile device; even a ticker-tape machine. He had everything he needed in this hideaway, including a communications center against the opposite wall complete with phone and a ham radio.

Cassie whistled. "This is quite a setup."

"It suits me. There are few distractions when I'm working and the doors are closed."

"I'll bet."

Cassie walked around the room, studying the equipment. Her fingers were just itching to get into those filing cabinets and find out what sort of work he did here, but the cabinets all came equipped with sturdy locks.

"These are the instruction books to the computer," he said, opening a hutch on the top part of the desk. "I'll go get the disk."

He left the doors open but that didn't stop Cassie. She was studying the computer printouts on his desk when he returned, silent as a big cat.

Jack would have been quite surprised not to find her snooping. "Interesting reading?"

"Do you play the stock market a lot?"

"Play is hardly the word," he returned dryly.

"You must make a good living at it."

He smiled. "Keep digging."

"I will," she assured him, moving back to the computer and sitting down. "When I have the time."

"That should be a while," he said, leaving the disk on a shelf within her reach. "Yell if you need help."

Cassie was disappointed. "You leaving me alone in here can only mean one thing."

"You've got it, sweetheart. Important documents that would reveal really pertinent or truly interesting information aren't kept in this room."

"You . . ."

But he was already gone. Cassie opened the first instruction manual and was soon immersed in the task of learning the interpretive program, losing all track of time. Then she started on a slow process of elimination, trying to get the disk to read. It was a difficult, engrossing problem; the program supported hundreds of formats.

"Any luck?"

Cassie jumped at the sound of his voice. "Not yet. Is that coffee I smell?" she asked, swiveling her chair around to face him. He handed her a big cobalt blue mug. She breathed deeply of the pleasing aroma before sipping the hot brew. "Thank you."

"You're welcome." He looked down at her notations. "I figured they wouldn't use anything common. Do you need help?"

"Only if the rest of these don't work out." She watched him sip his own coffee and had to grin. "How's your tongue?"

"Come a little closer and I'll show you."

"Thanks but no thanks."

Jack smiled, his eyes crinkling at the corners. "I thought you liked to play with fire?"

"I've been burned enough for one day, thank you very much," she replied with studied nonchalance.

He nodded and left. Cassie watched him walk away, confused by his erratic, on and off behavior. Of course, hers wasn't much better. And it wasn't just sexual confusion, either. She didn't like puzzles she couldn't put together and he was one of them. One minute nice and caring, the next sharp and cutting.

Where was it all leading to, anyway? She still didn't possess the necessary proof to print her story and her only lead, this little black disk, was being just as secretive about its contents as Jack Merlin was about his past. She was not, however, even close to giving up on either one.

Chapter Seventeen

"Where's Cassie?" Russ asked, taking a seat opposite at the kitchen table. Jack was studying a beautiful emerald necklace through a jeweler's loup. He appeared quite pleased with himself.

"In my office." He held up the necklace. "Take a look at this. You don't see stones of this quality very often."

Russ joined him. "Hmm. Nice." He looked up at Jack out of one eye, the other filled with the black jeweler's magnifying glass. "You showed her your inner sanctum?"

"Why not? There's nothing of value in there. Besides, she was bound to find it sooner or later."

"True. The lass has a bloodhound's nose for clues. But aren't you worried she'll get a vague idea of what you're worth?"

"Should I be?"

"You never know," Russ replied, grinning at him. "She just might decide you'd make great husband material and pursue you. You wouldn't stand a chance against her persistence."

"Fine with me if she throws herself at me," Jack muttered. "Speaking of persistence, did Kathleen turn you down again?"

"Of course." Russ shrugged nonchalantly. "She'll give in eventually, maybe very soon, now. I'm withholding myself."

"You're what?"

"Keeping my pants on, so to speak," he explained. "I'm at my wit's end, so it's worth a try."

Jack shook his head and laughed. "It might work, if you can hold out. She'll be back to tempt you soon."

"Not to worry. I'm strong." Russ held up the emerald necklace in his hand, studying it intently.

Jack spread the remaining contents of the purple pouch out on a large velvet cloth. Every piece was one of a kind, some very old, some new, but all quite distinctive.

Cassie was standing outside the door listening to their conversation. Which as usual revealed little.

"What are we going to do with them?" Russ asked.

Jack shrugged. "Let's throw them in the safe until we have more time to make a decision. Right now I'm too busy dealing with Cassie and her seemingly endless problems."

"I take it you didn't get the proof she needs?"

"No. All the box contained was a computer disk." Jack raised his voice. "Which she was busily trying to crack until a moment ago. Cassie, come in and have a seat, you'll be more comfortable."

It was uncanny, she thought, the way he could sense her presence. With a shrug she crossed the room, her gaze not wavering from his. After all, what did he expect of her?

Jack looked up at her and almost smiled. At least she was predictable in some ways. As usual she'd been snooping, listening at the door, and like any other person with an appreciation of the finer things in life, she couldn't keep her eyes away from the colorful sparkles sitting on the table.

Was he imagining it, or did he even see a hint of good old-fashioned greed? "See anything you like?" he asked.

Frozen, Cassie stood beside him, staring down at the loaded purple velvet cloth, her eyes opening ever wider as she took in each individual piece. Long ropes of pearls. Diamonds, emeralds, rubies, gold and silver, every stone imaginable, all in unique settings. She'd never seen a display like this, not even at the gala events she'd been required to cover for the newspaper.

"These must be worth millions of dollars," she whispered hoarsely, reaching out to touch an intricately formed peacock pin dotted with a multitude of different stones.

"Easily," Jack agreed.

"And they're all real?" she asked.

"Most of them."

Cassie picked up another piece. "How can you tell?"

She reminded him of a curious child, always wanting to know more. The trait served her well in her chosen profession. "We'll show you some other time," Jack said, feeling indulgent. "Did you have any luck with the disk?"

"What are you going to do with these?"

"Don't worry, Cassie," he chided, "you'll get your percentage of the gains."

She dropped the piece as if it suddenly burned her fingers and stepped back from the table. "No! I want nothing to do with your petty thievery."

"If she calls this petty," Russ murmured, "I wonder what she would consider a major haul?"

Cassie glared at him. "You know what I mean, Russ. I want nothing to do with any of that," she said, pointing to the jewelry. "You're both assured of my silence. But then you planned all along not to leave me a choice."

"I seem to recall you issuing me the same sort of ultimatum, Cassie," Jack reminded her.

She wanted to tell him it was different, that her slightly illegal actions were basically honorable and for a good cause. But she didn't open her mouth. When you compared the two, the bottom line was the same: blackmail was blackmail no matter the reason, and robbery was still robbery.

Or was it? In the world she had entered, Jack's world, the principle of right and wrong seemed to have taken on a new meaning to her. Right was still right, but sometimes you had to do something wrong to get there.

Confused by her own thoughts, she opted for a change of subject. "I got the computer disk to read," she announced.

"Is it any help?"

"I don't know yet. So far it doesn't make sense. I'm pretty sure it starts out with the cost analysis for different projects, but the names of those projects are in some kind of code. It looks like the same codes that are in Brian's notebook. It must be his disk. It's probably very basic, but I can't make heads or tails of it."

"Russ and I have some experience with codes. We'll take turns going through it, then compare notes."

"Do I get to eat first?" Cassie asked. "It's dinnertime and I haven't even had lunch yet."

Jack glanced at her. "What's more important, your story or your stomach?"

"At this moment, my stomach."

"Can you cook?" Jack asked.

"That depends," she replied, smiling sweetly at him, "on whether your stomachs are lined with cast iron."

Russ groaned audibly and Jack laughed. "You win. Show Russ what you've found so far and I'll cook us a decent meal, minus the indigestion."

"I thought you'd see it my way. Come along, Russ."

They worked through the late afternoon, eating while the entire disk was printed out with a laser printer. Then, taking turns, they studied the printed material.

"Dammit!" Cassie exclaimed, her temper short in spite of a full stomach. "This doesn't make any sense. I'm beginning to think the stupid thing was just left behind completely by accident. Or to throw me off course."

Russ nodded, rubbing his tired eyes. "I agree."

"Okay. Where does this leave you?" Jack asked her.

"Up the proverbial odious creek without a paddle."

He thought about the situation for a moment. "The paper could still print some of your story. The independent engineering check of the core sample isn't back yet. If it is below grade it'll be pretty obvious someone bought off the inspectors."

"Great story. I still don't know who killed Brian."

Jack tried to word his next statement carefully. "Cassie, have you seriously considered the possibility that Brian did commit suicide?"

"No, and I'm not going to!" Cassie grabbed her purse and keys. "I can see that I'm not going to get any more help here. Good night."

They watched her run out of the room and heard the front door slam. "Well, Russ. I handled that just dandy."

"Didn't you, though? You'll have to go after her." Russ looked at him. "Unless you think it's a wise idea to let her stay at home all alone?"

"You know it's not," Jack said with a disgusted sigh. "But she doesn't want to stay here. I already asked."

Russ sat down. "She's upset over the jewels."

"That's putting it mildly." Jack glanced up at him. "Try furious. The ledgers not being there sure didn't help anything, either."

"I bet not. Any messages from Patrick?" Russ asked.

"Not yet. Flynn should find out about the missing jewelry soon and that in turn should catapult him into some kind of action."

"I'm sure he knows who Cassie is and where she lives by now," Russ warned.

Jack stood up and walked out of his office into the library, pacing the large room restlessly. "I know that, and I'm heading over there soon." He thrust his hands into his pants pockets. "How much should I tell her?"

"Whatever you think she needs to know," Russ told him. "I'm not sure where Patrick is, so I'll be spending the night at Kathleen's."

Jack picked up his car keys. "I might as well get this over with."

He changed his mind repeatedly on the way over to her place. Just how much should he tell her?

Cassie peered through the peephole then opened the door and stood aside to let him enter.

Jack strode over to the coffee table, picked up one bug then he headed for her bedroom, returning a moment later with both of them in the palm of his hand. He placed them in the freezer before sitting down on the couch.

Cassie was still standing by the open door. "Did you bring the disk?" she asked.

"No."

"Then what are you doing here?"

"Close the door, I'm not going anywhere without you. Please," he tacked on belatedly when he saw the storm brewing in her eyes.

She closed and locked the door before sitting down in her favorite overstuffed chair. "Why are you here, Jack?"

"Because you're not safe here alone."

A mirthless laugh spewed forth. "Why should I believe you?" She curled her legs up beneath her. "Give me one good reason. You involved me in a robbery today. You stole someone else's property. And I refuse to believe you need the money."

"You're right, I don't need the money." Jack stretched his legs out in front of him. "And I don't intend to keep the jewelry, either. The owners will get it back."

Her disbelief was easy for him to interpret. "You're going to give it back?"

"Not exactly."

"Then what exactly are you going to do?"

He looked at her. "We'll turn it in, using a third party. For the finder's fee, of course."

"Why did you take it?"

Jack struggled with himself, still unsure of how much he wanted to tell her. "That jewelry we acquired today was stolen in the first place by accomplices of Flynn's. We took it in the hopes that it would force him into revealing himself."

"Then what will you do?" Cassie asked.

His face was cold, unmoving. "You don't want to know."

Cassie was momentarily stunned. "You—how can you? Why?"

"Because if we don't get him first, he'll kill us, one by one. And any others who get in his way. And he'll continue to ply his chosen trade, killing innocent people, for a price."

Cassie drew her knees up and wrapped her arms around them in a hug. "Why is he coming after you now?"

"I don't know."

With chin resting on her knees, she asked, "Are you telling the truth?"

"Why should I lie to you?" he countered.

"Because you have from the beginning," Cassie told him.

"No more so than you." Jack stretched his arm along the back of the sofa. "You haven't told me the whole truth, either. And you can cut the innocent act. From the very beginning you've known more than you ever told me. My report on you was quite detailed. You wouldn't have gone after this without some kind of solid evidence. Are you going to tell me what else you know?"

"If you'll tell me why you're so sure it's dangerous for me to stay here," she bargained.

He rubbed his fingers back and forth over the smooth velour couch cushion. How much did he want to tell her? "Flynn is alive. He undoubtedly knows where you live, who you are, and most importantly, that you know me. He'll see you as a weak point to get to me."

"Why does he want to get you?"

Jack tilted his head back and looked up at the white ceiling. "Because we tried to kill him, Russ, Patrick and I. And until recently we'd thought we'd been successful." He took a deep breath. "He was responsible for a bombing that took the lives of eight innocent people." Jack looked at her, his face grim. "He enjoys violence."

"Is Flynn his real name?" Cassie asked, curiously.

Jack rubbed his forehead, not believing what she'd just asked. At times he forgot that she was a reporter until she surprised him with some question. "No, it's not. It's a name he adopted. His real name is Liam Francis Dougell, but you won't find anything on him, under either name."

"Why is he coming after you now?" Cassie asked.

He sighed. "I don't know." Jack wanted her to understand more, but he couldn't bring himself to talk about that part of his past. Not yet. "We're trying to find out why he's resurfaced."

Cassie wanted to know more: who had been killed, how it had affected him, how he had coped. But she was sensitive to his pain and aware that he didn't want to discuss it. In time, if he grew to trust her, he'd confide in her. She could be quite patient, when she wanted to be.

Standing up, she walked into the kitchen and opened a bottom cupboard. Reaching inside, she pulled out a cookie sheet and placed it on the counter. Next, she pulled open a drawer and took out a butter knife.

Jack was leaning against the doorjamb watching her movements. "You're going to bake cookies?"

"No." She inserted the knife between the two metal sheets, running it around the edges to pry the pans apart. "Come pick this up, my hands are sticky from the corn syrup."

He gingerly picked up the flattened white paper sack, careful to not drag it through the syrup surrounding the rim of the pan. "Clever." Jack looked at the sack. There was a note written on it, and a signature. "Where did you get this?"

"From Brian's apartment, it was in the bag beneath the refrigerator also." She put the pans in the dishwasher and washed her hands. "The man who wrote that is dead."

"When?"

"The same date that's on the sack." Cassie leaned back against the sink, drying her hands with a towel. "He died in a construction accident. Supposedly his safety line broke loose."

"Who owns the building he was working on?" Jack asked.

Cassie set the towel on the counter before answering. "That's not the real key. Try who owned the construction firm—the Hook family."

"Then you've suspected them all along?"

She shook her head. "No, why would I? The letter states that there were codes being broken, but not what. There are plenty of employees who could authorize building code violations, pocketing the difference. What I'm interested in was what he implied he overheard that got him killed. And who he overheard talking. Just because the Hooks own the construction company, that doesn't mean they're involved."

Jack was puzzled. "Why would he send this to Brian? He was a political writer."

"I've though about that too. He may have known Brian, or read his work and liked it." Cassie paused. "Or maybe what he overheard was politically related."

"Are his initials in the notebook?" Jack asked.

Cassie glanced at him. "Yes."

"Along with the other men we know are dead." She nodded her agreement. "What does that tell us?"

Her tone was flippant. "That working in high-rise construction is dangerous."

"You're beginning to sound like me," Jack warned her.

"Heaven forbid." Cassie walked past him on her way back into the living room. "Have you received the results on the core sample?"

Jack shook his head. "Cassie, you can't stay here. It's not safe."

"Listen, Jack. I'm tired, it's been a very long day. All I want to do right now is go to bed. I have my gun for protection."

He took off a shoe, leaving it in the middle of the floor. "Fine. I'll sleep in your roommate's bedroom. And don't argue. You're not staying here alone."

"Suit yourself." She heard his other shoe drop as she walked down the hall toward her bedroom.

HE SIFTED THROUGH everything one more time in the hovel of a motel. Flynn wasn't going to like this. The kid he'd hired to bring the jewels over hadn't met him at the agreed time or place. Had he dared to fly the coop with the jewels? Obviously the kid didn't know Flynn, or he'd never have taken the chance.

Orange and blue flames shot from his lighter as the mattress stuffing began to burn. On his way out of the room he touched the flame to the drapes, too, the fire licking up them with alarming speed. He had to report, glad his only contact with Flynn was through the phone.

"Kid's gone, so is the key and the jewelry," he told Flynn a few minutes later, a safe distance from the burning motel.

"You found absolutely nothing in that room?" Flynn asked. The kid hadn't seemed that smart, none of them had, which was why he'd chosen that group to begin with.

"There was a piece of paper on top of the television with three stick figures on it."

Rourke. Flynn held his rage in check as he sat down on the edge of the plush coverlet. He'd underestimated them. The idea had been to use the jewelry to flush Rourke and Merlin out of hiding, not to let them steal it from right under his nose. This meant they knew he was alive and after them. They had his jewelry, worth millions even hot. Right now he needed that money bad. His lifestyle had taken its toll on his bank account. He had to get the jewelry back!

"The woman I told you about, Cassie O'Connor. Get her and call me immediately when you have her."

This time he would make them come to him.

Chapter Eighteen

The room smelled like the light misty scent she wore most of the time, subtly feminine and not overpowering. He was perfectly still as he listened to the night sounds of her town house. They were all strange to his ears, but one among them didn't fit. Silently he slipped into her room, closing the door behind himself. Gently but firmly he pressed his hand over Cassie's lips and gave her a little shake. With a soft sigh she curled toward his arm.

He shook her again, trying not to make any noise, his voice barely a whisper. "Cassie, wake up."

She woke in a daze from a deep sleep, to find a big hand covering her mouth. Instinctively she tried to break free, her teeth sinking sharply into the hand.

"Ssh! Damn!" He jerked his hand away. "It's Jack. Don't move. Someone's in your house."

"Jack? What?" Cassie froze in place, her pulse pounding erratically in her throat. "Are you sure?"

He placed his index finger on her lips and spoke directly into her ear. "Is your roommate due home?" Cassie shook her head. "You're absolutely positive?"

She nodded, her eyes opening wider as another muted sound was heard from the living room. "What was that?"

"Ssh! I want you to slide off the bed as quietly as you can. Stay on the floor until I call you." She could feel his strength, the readiness to fight emanating from him.

Cassie eased her way off the bed. She watched as Jack walked silently to the door and pressed his ear against it.

His body was wound tight, ready to spring. It could be a burglar, or a junkie on the prowl, but he doubted it. As a rule they were nonconfrontational criminals and seldom went farther than the first portable television or stereo they found. This one was looking for something else. He waited, listening as the first bedroom door was closed and the intruder made his way toward the next. Cassie's room.

Jack stood with his heels braced against the wall, his hand hovering above the doorknob, ready to jerk the door wide open. The average person tended to instinctively grab something when it was yanked away. With a little luck and a lot of help from him, the intruder would come falling into the room head first.

Heavy cloud cover diffused the moonlight, and there wasn't enough light for him to see the knob slowly twisting before the door began to open. Jack held his breath, not making a sound, waiting. Then he saw that the intruder was not the average person. The average person didn't carry a gun.

It came through the opening first, followed by the hand that grasped it and what looked to be a strong arm to back up the heavy recoil such an automatic weapon made. It was aimed toward the empty bed. Past experience gave Jack an edge in quickly changing plans. He slammed the door shut, wedging the forearm tightly between the two pieces of wood.

Whoever the intruder was, there was nothing average about him. He didn't yell, not a bit. What he did was struggle to break free, and his arm was every bit as strong as it looked. Jack held the door mercilessly against it with all his weight, then began bouncing against the door with his hip. It was a lot of punishment for a person to take, especially in stoic silence. As tough as he was, however, the mechanics of the situation were against the intruder; his fingers jerked involuntarily and started to go slack.

With his weight still against the door, Jack wrenched the gun loose from the other man's failing grip and tossed it onto the bed. He grabbed the arm with both hands, hard, letting his opponent know he wasn't the only strong person in the house. Then, in one fluid movement, Jack took his weight off the door and pulled ferociously, never letting up on his steel grip. The intruder came flying into the bedroom.

But he didn't fall. Jack kept pulling, using a Judo throw to flip him past and into the wall behind them. The man slammed against it head first, and yet still refused to go down, staying on his feet through some incredible instinct for survival. The blow had stunned him, though. Jack charged him before he could shake it off, hitting him square in the chest with one broad shoulder, knocking him to his knees. Having gained too much respect for his quarry to back off now, Jack stayed right on top of him and followed him down.

The guy was a fighter. They rolled across the floor, hitting each other, but the intruder was groggy and nursing his injured arm. His punches were thrown blind, while Jack took careful aim. He connected, a solid blow to the other man's jaw, and at long last got a startled grunt out of his opponent. Even then, all but unconscious, the intruder still managed to launch a fist at Jack's midsection.

It hit hard, but he'd made the mistake of using the wrong hand. He yelped in pain as the arm Jack had battered with the door seemed to crumple. Jack felt the man go limp beneath him.

"Damn!" Jack rubbed his bruised stomach muscles with a rueful expression. He got to his feet and found the gun on the bed where he'd tossed it. Aiming it at the intruder, he turned on the overhead light. The guy was out cold. "About time, too!" he exclaimed.

"Are you all right?" Cassie asked.

"Fine. Take this and keep an eye—"

She was already by his side, a handgun of her own trained on the man. "I've got him."

Jack grinned and cautiously approached the intruder. "Out like a light," he announced.

"You knocked him out?"

"Yes I did," Jack said with wry self-knowledge. "I let him punch me in the gut so the pain in his arm would knock him out. Great technique."

Cassie tried to soothe his wounded ego. "But you hurt his arm in the first place."

He nodded. "True. Still, I'd appreciate it if you didn't tell Russ the details." Jack quickly proceeded to bind the man's hands and feet.

Jack couldn't help but be aware of Cassie. She was sitting comfortably on the side of the bed in her yellow nightshirt, her legs crossed, the gun still pointed steadily at the prone form on the floor. She was quite a woman. The many facets of her nature never ceased to surprise him; he found himself equally surprised by his growing desire to learn every one of them, even if it took a lifetime.

"That's a nice bruise you're developing," Cassie told him, smiling.

"Witch." He smiled at her in spite of the little jabs of pain he felt here and there. "I'm going to drag this lump into the living room and make a quick phone call. Why don't you get dressed?"

Cassie hastily pulled on jeans and a red, short-sleeved cotton blouse. Her hands were shaking. Actually, her entire body was a quivering mass of jelly, her earlier bravado beginning to melt away.

This was not, she was sure, just a random burglary. But was the intruder's presence connected to her story on the Hooks, or Flynn? What other toes had she stepped on during her investigations? Someone was on to her, that was for sure, but why would the man come into her home to confront her about it?

There was only one way to find out. As soon as he woke up they would ask him, or the police would, whichever occurred first. At the moment it looked as if their uninvited guest would be out for some time.

Jack was talking on the phone when she walked into the living room. The intruder was on the floor behind the sofa, under his watchful gaze. All the drapes were closed. She looked around the room with dismay. This place would never feel the same.

Wide awake, Cassie started the coffee and stared at the clock on the kitchen wall. Five minutes after five in the morning. She looked out the window, seeing that it was still dark outside, dawn barely breaking across the horizon. If only daylight would come faster and lend a new look to the situation; in the predawn her thoughts were unsettling.

Had he come to kill her?

"Our friend is waking up," Jack announced.

Cassie poured out two cups of strong coffee and went to join him in the other room. "Did you call the police?"

"No." His voice was grave. "I'll deal with him myself."

"Jack!" A horrified look came his way. "You can't—"

He grinned at her, reading her mind. "Darling, I'm not going to kill him. Not unless he makes me, that is. I'm just going to have him kept out of the way for a while." His gaze grew even warmer. "Out of our way," he added.

"Who do you suppose he is?"

Jack shrugged. "Beats me. For a guy as tough as he is, though, he sure has a baby face, doesn't he?"

Awake now but dazed, Knox listened to their conversation with growing unease. He kept his eyes closed, ignoring the pain in his arm and trying to concentrate on what they were saying. The guy's name was Jack. If possible, Jack would pay for this.

From the way things sounded, though, it might not be possible. If nothing else, Knox was flexible, especially when it came to keeping his skin.

Where had he gone wrong? This was Cassie O'Connor's place. She had a female roommate who was out of town and no steady boyfriends. So where had this Jack guy come from and who was he? Whoever he was, he knew how to take care of himself, and that troubled Knox no end. What were they going to do with him?

"Jack, shouldn't we—"

He interrupted her. "Don't you think he looks like someone who could use a long rest? He's got a big bruise on his jaw and his arm is probably broken; hospitalization would be the best thing for him right now."

"Do you recognize him?"

"He's the one who was taking photos that day, the one who drove the rental car. According to his driver's license his name is Anthony Knox, but there are other identification cards in his possession as well." Jack grinned. "Since he likes aliases, we'll give him a new one and check him into a private psychiatric hospital."

"Wait a minute!" Knox cried out. He'd heard enough horror stories about those places. He might never see daylight again. "Let's make a deal."

It was odd talking to a disembodied voice coming from behind a couch, but Jack left him where he was. "What kind of deal?" he asked.

Knox didn't like the disadvantage of not being able to see who he was dealing with. It was much harder to tell how the negotiations were going by voice alone.

"I tell you anything you want to know, and you let me go free." There was a long, troubling silence. "Hey! You still there?"

"Who hired you?" Jack asked.

"Do we have a deal?"

"Anthony," he replied with a long-suffering sigh, "allow me to brief you on the realities of your situation. I could just kill you now and not worry about what you might know."

Cassie's eyes widened and she opened her mouth, but Jack cut her off by pressing his fingers firmly against her lips.

"What was that?" Knox demanded.

"A dissenting opinion," Jack said. "She doesn't like loud noises. It's all right, dear. I have my silencer, see?"

Knox squirmed uncomfortably. Nobody had ever been good enough to get him into this position before. For perhaps the first

time in his life, he was actually worried. Who was more dangerous? This guy or his present employer?

At the moment, Jack presented the most lethal threat. "All
right!" Knox said at last. "I work for Marilyn Hook."

"Surprise, surprise," Jack said sarcastically.

Cassie had managed to squash her own startled gasp this time.
"What are you doing in my home?"

"Looking for the story you're so secretly working on."

"Why at night? I'm almost never home during the day."

"I already tried that route, went through this place with a fine-
tooth comb twice and found nothing."

The thought made Cassie ill. She looked bleakly at Jack, who
gave her hand a reassuring pat.

"So you thought you'd try a little forced persuasion on a helpless female?" Jack asked him.

"No," he answered quickly. Too quickly. "All I wanted were her
notes on the story to see if there was any connection between her
work and my client."

"Why don't I believe you?" Jack asked.

"It's the truth!"

"And I'm an angel," Jack muttered. "Why did Marilyn Hook
hire you?"

This time the answer wasn't quite so quick in coming. "To find
out if anyone was investigating Lawrence Hook's death besides the
police."

"Why would she want to know that?"

"How should I know?" Knox shot back. "I just do the job, I
don't ask questions. Ask her yourself."

"What else?"

"She also wanted to know if anyone was investigating any of the
other family members."

"And what have you told her?" Cassie asked.

"Nothing, yet."

"Can we trust him?" Cassie asked Jack. The cynicism in her
voice was strong.

"No."

"I'm telling the truth!" he shouted desperately. "I haven't reported in to her since the photos were taken. Your name came up
as one of the reporters covering the story, and I've been busy trying
to figure out what else you were up to ever since. Really!"

"So you say," Cassie retorted.

"Just what are you up to?" Knox asked.

"Shut up, Anthony. This isn't a two-way street." Jack glanced at the clock, then at Cassie. "We're running out of time. Anything else you want to know?"

"A million things, but—" she raised her voice and asked the man behind the sofa "—have you ever been inside the Hook family mansion?"

Jack looked at her quizzically.

"No," Knox replied.

A soft knock sounded on her front door. Jack slipped into his shirt and went to answer it. Two big men dressed all in white filled the doorway. Behind them, a discreet looking van was parked at the curb, its motor still running.

"Good morning, sir. We're sorry to disturb you so early, but we were alerted you have one of our patients here?"

Jack pointed to the bound man behind the sofa. "We thought it best to tie him up, for our own safety."

"What about our deal?" Knox yelled.

"He's incoherent." Jack looked truly sorry for him.

"He usually is, according to his file," the second burly attendant said. "Tying him up was a sensible precaution."

Knox was having a fit, bouncing up and down on the floor like a beached fish. "Our deal!"

Jack shook his head sadly. "Be careful with him. I think he managed to break his arm somehow."

"His file says he is known to be violent."

"Hey, wait a minute! You've got the wrong—" A piece of white adhesive tape shut him up. He continued to make guttural noises while one of the men picked him up as easily as if he had been a child and carried him out to the waiting van. The other turned to Jack and Cassie.

"Sir. Ma'am. We're sorry for the inconvenience."

"That's quite all right," Jack assured him. "Thank you for your prompt attention on this matter."

"You're very understanding. Have a good day."

When they had gone, Cassie sat down on the sofa and stared at Jack, disbelief and puzzlement vying for top honors. "Where did you find them?"

He shrugged. "Ask Russ."

"Don't worry, I'm going to."

Jack walked into the kitchen and poured his coffee down the drain. "No offense, Cassie, but you make absolutely lousy coffee."

"It hadn't finished dripping," she told him absently. "And I'm out of milk."

"You're out of food period," Jack announced, entering the living room. "Frozen dinners aren't—" The deep furrows between her eyebrows stopped him in midsentence. "What's wrong?"

"Do you think he was sent here to kill me?"

Jack wasn't going to lie to her. "I don't know, but it's possible that was his intention."

He barely held back the next word on the tip of his tongue. *Eventually.* Why make it even worse for her than it already was?

"Do you think Marilyn Hook is wise to my investigation?"

"I don't know. It's conceivable she's just grown more cautious as time goes on, I suppose. Like hiring Knox to stake out the site of Lawrence Hook's murder." Jack frowned. There was more going on than met the eye. "Speaking of which, I think our friend Anthony wasn't quite candid with us on that point."

Cassie barely heard him. She was working on a puzzle of her own, and it didn't look good. "If she is on to me, then the evidence I need has probably already been destroyed or is now somewhere I can't ever get access to."

Her defeated tone made Jack smile. "Remember Cassie, never underestimate the overwhelming power and extent of someone's ego, whether in business or sex."

"Jack, I'm serious."

"And I think sex is a serious business. Especially if it involves you and me."

Cassie looked at him, surprised. "What! Quit trying to sidetrack me!"

"Is it working?" he asked, his golden eyes sparkling.

"No!" But she gave him a tiny smile, the furrows between her eyebrows easing. "Yes."

"Think about it, Cassie. Sometimes people grow so powerful they refuse to believe they can be caught. Or if they are caught they believe they're powerful enough to walk away without a scratch."

"Are you talking from experience?" she asked quietly.

He looked at her for a moment, his head tilted slightly to one side as he made a decision. "Yes."

"Someday," Cassie said, her voice soft, "I'd like you to tell me about it."

"Maybe."

Cassie changed the subject, not wanting to press her luck. At least it wasn't an outright no. And until she knew more about his past and what had shaped him, she'd never be able to figure out how he ticked.

"I have to admit that for once your messy habits came in handy," Cassie told him. He looked at her, puzzled. She pointed toward the floor. "Your shoes, that's what he tripped over, which in turn woke you up, isn't it?"

"You're lucky I'm so messy."

Cassie rolled her eyes, smiling, but something bothered her. "How did Knox get in here?"

Jack walked over to the low window; it was still partially opened. "He probably left this one open as a back-up entrance in case you discovered the patio lock was missing and put it back on. Which you did."

Cassie shivered as the implications of all this gradually began to sink in. The man had definitely meant to harm her in some way.

"I'm glad you were here," she told him simply.

Jack crossed the room and enveloped her in his arms, holding her snugly. The tremors running through her body were turning into quivering shakes. One tiny teardrop slid down his chest, only to be followed by another and another.

"It didn't happen," he whispered. "Dwell on the positive and not what might have been. Let it all out," he encouraged, gently stroking her back in a soothing gesture.

It wasn't fair for her to have to go through this. But at least she wasn't going through it alone. He'd seen so many sad tears in his lifetime already. They were a way of cleansing the soul and the mind, but they were always hard on him. He'd cried too many of his own.

Eventually Cassie lifted her head off his shoulder, her shakes subsiding. "You have nice broad shoulders, just made for crying on," she murmured, not looking at him.

He was still stroking her back, but his touch was changing, becoming more intimate. "I'm good for other things, too."

"I'm a mess, Jack." Her face was tearstained, her eyes pink and puffy. "You can't find me at all attractive at the moment." She paused, her voice hoarse as she asked him, "Can you?"

He slid his hand into her tousled black hair and turned her face toward him. "You're a beautiful woman, not afraid to show her emotion," he murmured against her lips, brushing his mouth across them. "I find you so attractive I can scarcely control myself."

A small laugh gurgled forth, and she smiled at him through residual tears.

He grinned and kissed the tip of her nose, before letting her go.

She looked at him, suddenly quite serious. ''Is your home still open to an invited guest?''

Chapter Nineteen

A major roadblock in the path of a desperately important story, life-threatening danger and a man who was driving her slowly to the brink of passionate insanity. Wasn't that enough to contend with? Did she have to put up with Stan's version of the Spanish Inquisition as well?

"You're absolutely positive you have the right person?"

Cassie groaned. "How many times are you going to ask me that question, Stan?"

He was striding nervously around his office. Cassie closed her eyes. The area between her ears was beating a drum cadence, which showed no signs of letting up, and the aspirin she'd taken earlier hadn't kicked in to ease the pain. She'd spent most of the day trying to figure out what information the disk they'd acquired from the bank held. It seemed like such a simple code. Why was it being so difficult?

"Just answer the question, dammit," Stan fumed.

"Yes, I'm sure," she replied, not opening her eyes.

"You do know exactly who she is, don't you?" Stan didn't wait for an answer. "Marilyn Hook has plenty of family money and more power than the electric company. For heaven's sake, Cassie, she's best known in this town for her charitable contributions! And her clout. She has two sisters, each married to a firmly ensconced Washington politician." His voice was growing louder with each word. "Connections? Thousands of them. She has unbelievable connections all over this country."

"I know, Stan," Cassie replied, massaging her temples with a circular motion. "Believe me, I know."

"We can't touch her without proof," he said. "I'll need rock-solid evidence showing Marilyn Hook is personally responsible."

"I know!"

"Without it, we can't print one word."

"Stop shouting!" Cassie's head throbbed. He was getting on her nerves and trying her limited patience. She did know how to do her job. "Don't you think I'm aware of that, Stan? I'm working on getting you the backup you'll need to go to print. What do you think I've been doing? Sitting around twiddling my thumbs and waiting for proof to fall in my lap?"

"Hell, I don't know," Stan grumbled, picking up his untouched cup of coffee and sipping it thoughtfully. "Do you have anything?"

She'd have to tell him something. "I found a piece of paper in Brian's things that indicates building code violations on a local high rise."

"What? Why didn't you tell me about it when you found it?" her editor demanded. He'd known of her research into the Hook family and their charity concerns, but hadn't realized she'd made any connections between that and Brian's death. "Why didn't—"

"I'm telling you now," she interrupted.

"Dammit!" Stan jumped up, growing even more irritated with her. "That still doesn't explain why you didn't come to me with the story!"

"Because I know my job, that's why. Proof, remember? I didn't have any. Besides the letter."

"You have a witness!"

Cassie shook her head, a knot of pain forming in the center of her chest. "He's dead."

"Dead?" Stan sat back down slowly, the wind knocked out of his sails. "How?"

"He fell from the high rise. It was ruled an accidental death. The police said his safety belt gave way. He died the day the letter was dated."

"Do you still have the letter?"

Cassie nodded. "Yes. It's written on the back of a white hamburger sack. He signed it, including his address and phone number." She closed her eyes for a moment, trying to dispel the memory. "I called right away. His wife knew nothing about what he might have discovered. He has two adorable children."

"Good Lord," Stan muttered. His expression became more gentle. "Why didn't you come to me, or go to the police?"

"Come on, Stan. You know me. I wanted to do a little more checking first, and the more I dug the more I found. But there's still not any solid evidence to actually implicate Marilyn Hook," she said, emphasizing the name, "in anything illegal. And she heads the family businesses now, has for four years."

"The police might have found something."

"Enough to get Marilyn Hook?" Cassie made a sour face. "With her connections she'd walk away totally free, with some minor employee taking the blame for her."

Stan sighed. "You're right. But if all this comes out you could be in serious trouble with the police."

"No, I don't think so." Cassie looked at Stan. "I did send copies of that sack to various policemen—anonymously. Then I called and made sure each of them had received their copy." Her grin was bitter, but smug. "I've got two out of the three men on tape, stating who they are and trying to find out my identity. They didn't reopen the investigation."

"Smart move." Stan thoroughly approved of her tactics. "You know, Cassie, it's always possible the police couldn't find any evidence to back up that information, either."

"Possible? I speak with the voice of experience when I say it's like pulling teeth to get something on the Hooks. Besides, even if they did find anything they'd most likely be stopped, taken off the case," she added bitterly. "You said it yourself, Stan. Political favors."

"Maybe. It's a very volatile issue, that's certain. You don't accuse rich, influential and politically powerful families of murder and corruption without being very sure of your facts." He paused for a moment, deep in thought, then asked, "How far does this go?"

"I don't know," Cassie admitted. "I haven't found all the pieces, Stan. The family company is private and partially buried in blind trusts. Records of their investments, earnings and losses aren't available to the public. And the pieces I do have don't add up."

"What do you mean?"

"The economy has hurt everyone, but the Hooks appear to be totally unscathed. Almost everyone else has cut back, but they're still spending money like they always have. And although their known sources of income have been practically wiped out, they're sitting on three completely empty high rises and paying the interest payments on time."

"Where," Stan asked, "is all that money coming from?"

She watched Stan's face very carefully as she told him, "Smuggling."

Stan's eyebrows went up. "What?"

"I can't prove it, but my inside source said the family was smuggling something to shore up their sagging income," Cassie said, exaggerating the truth a bit. What else could her source have been talking about?

"What are they smuggling?" her boss wanted to know.

"He wouldn't say." Nor would he. Ever. The Hooks had seen to that.

"I see." Stan's grin was sly as he asked, "You think that young kid who sent the letter overheard a lot more than just a scheme to violate the building code, don't you?"

"Yes." She shrugged. "In all honesty, though, it's just as possible he didn't. But I don't believe his death was an accident—it's too coincidental."

Stan shook his head and blew out a deep breath. "Unless someone in the know talks, you'll never get any proof that it was murder. You'll have to go after this from another angle."

"I am."

Stan looked at her curiously. She was wound up like a clock spring. What the hell was going on? "How are you going to get that proof?"

"Take it from me, Stan," Cassie replied, easing her clenched fists open. "You're better off not knowing. There is one little thing you can do for me," she told him as he stood up.

He eyed her warily. "What?"

"I want to do the advance publicity story for the Hook charity event," Cassie announced.

Stan sat down on the edge of his desk. "You're kidding me. You hate that kind of story."

"I'm serious. I want to do the interview at their home, with a photographer," she added.

His eyes narrowed. "What are you up to?"

"I just want up-close first-hand knowledge of the family." She shrugged. "What's wrong with that?"

He didn't know what she was up to, but he also knew he wouldn't be able to get it out of her, either. "You've got the assignment. On one condition. You keep me informed."

"Don't I always?" she quipped, standing up.

"Maybe you should think about a career in fiction," Stan returned dryly. "You're getting awfully good at telling lies."

Cassie grinned. "The interview is set up for ten tomorrow morning, right?" Stan nodded. "I'll be there," she told him, then turned and walked out the door.

She'd been furious when her answering machine had informed her that Stan wanted to see her today. Before five. If she still liked her job, that is. But, yes, this was going to work out just fine.

Stan watched her leave his office, her step as jaunty as ever. Not much slowed Cassie down. But this time she might be getting in over her head. And she'd be pulling the newspaper down with her. Stan picked up the phone, and dialed a number. One minute later he was on his way upstairs.

"Have a seat, Stan. What's the urgent problem that couldn't wait until tomorrow?"

Where did he start? Marilyn Hook and Mrs. Carlyle were old friends. "Cassie O'Connor is working on a story concerning the Hook family."

"I know that, Stan. Get to the point. My time is very limited today. Has she uncovered some impropriety with the charity function they give each year?"

"No, this concerns the Hook family businesses. Cassie is in the process of obtaining proof that they are involved in construction fraud, and possibly murder to cover up their activities."

Mrs. Carlyle sat back, stunned. "Murder! You are referring to the prominent Hook family here in Houston?"

"Yes."

She shook her head. "I can't believe Marilyn Hook would be involved in anything like this."

"She may not be involved," Stan replied. "It could be someone in her organization."

Mrs. Carlyle didn't believe that. She knew Marilyn Hook quite well, and if anything was going on Marilyn knew about it. Marilyn Hook kept a very tight rein of control over her domain.

She looked at Stan. "I'll need facts, solid proof before I'll allow one word to be printed. And even then we'll have to consult with the company lawyers before we make a move. The repercussions from lawsuits could ruin this paper. And worse, if we're not absolutely sure of the facts, our credibility could be sorely damaged."

"I'll be very sure of the facts before one word goes to print. When do we meet with the lawyers?"

Mrs. Carlyle ran a pale pink polished fingernail down her daily calendar. "Tomorrow, at ten, in my office."

Stan nodded and stood up.

"Thank you for bringing this to my attention, Stan. I appreciate the early warning."

He smiled. "Just doing my job." The phone on her desk rang and Mrs. Carlyle picked it up. "Yes? Oh. Tell her I'll be with her in just a moment." She looked at Stan. "I am still seriously considering the raise you asked for. Actions like this do make a good argument for giving it to you."

"Thank you."

"And, Stan, I want both you and Cassie in my office tomorrow at—" she looked at her calendar again "—two."

"We'll be here."

She watched him leave, then pressed the lighted button on line one. "Leonore Xavier! I was going to call you."

"PICK ANY BEDROOM you want, except Russ's," Kathleen told Cassie bluntly later that night. Her broad grin revealed perfect teeth. "Dinner will be ready soon."

Kathleen was a tall, big-boned woman somewhere in her late forties or early fifties. Her hair, still a brilliant orange-red color, was braided in a coronet around her head. The ruddiness of her smooth complexion went well with her friendly, sparkling hazel eyes. It was little wonder Russ was infatuated with her.

Climbing the stairway with a grin on her lips, Cassie decided she liked Kathleen quite a bit herself. The woman was as honest and blunt as Jack had said she would be. You didn't have to guess what was on her mind because she told you, just like Russ.

Cassie hesitated a moment at the top of the stairs, then turned toward the bedroom next to Jack's, the only other choice available unless she wanted to sleep in Bridget's frilly canopy bed. The other two bedrooms were completely empty, untouched by renovation.

After last night it had taken no persuasion on Jack's part to get her to move into his home for the next week or so. His security system was extensive; hers far too inadequate to protect her. Besides, as he'd pointed out, she was out of food.

Cassie took two steps into the bedroom and stopped. On the antique bedside table there was a single long-stemmed red rose in a slender crystal vase, a white card propped at its base. She read it.

"A good choice, although you're welcome in my bed anytime. Jack." An arrow urged her to turn to the other side. "Did you notice, it's thorn free?" The added note made her smile.

Was she that predictable? she wondered, opening the closet door to hang up her jacket. Her smile broadened. Evidently so. The clothes she'd brought over earlier today were hanging right before her eyes.

A booming voice from the intercom speaker on the wall brought Cassie out of her peaceful stupor. "Dinner's on the table," Kathleen announced.

Obviously Kathleen didn't believe the system worked unless you bellowed into it. Cassie entered the kitchen to find everyone seated and waiting for her. She smiled as her eyes met Jack's for a brief moment.

"I suppose this is a fine time to ask you if there's anything you don't eat," Kathleen said. "We're having red salmon tonight."

"I'll try almost anything once, and have found few things I can't gag down," Cassie returned just as bluntly.

Kathleen nodded and began passing the platters around the table. The meal flowed along with easy conversation. After a dessert of fresh fruit salad, Kathleen shooed everyone out of her kitchen.

Cassie followed Russ and Jack into the library. She wanted the answers to a few pertinent questions that had been plaguing her all day. "Russ," she asked, "how did you get those men to pick up our intruder this morning?"

He shrugged. "Tricks of the trade, lass."

She tried another tack. "Won't they know right away that he wasn't in that hospital before today? I mean, I'm sure you thought of that, tricks of the trade and all," she said with sarcasm disguised as innocence, "but somebody will surely figure it out eventually and let him go. And then he'll come after us."

Russ grinned. "Jack, this is one pushy woman you've found yourself."

"She found me," Jack returned with a matching grin.

Cassie ignored the exchange. "Answer me."

"A person could get lost for a long time in that place," Russ assured her. "Don't worry about it."

"What place?"

"That's not something you need to know," Russ told her.

"Is it really a hospital, or just somewhere you two send people who get in your way?"

Russ glared at her. "Keep asking and you may find out."

"In other words, you aren't going to tell me anything?"

"Right you are," Russ answered, and promptly changed the subject. "Any luck with the disk?"

Cassie sighed loudly. It would take a bulldozer to get anything out of Russ once he'd changed the subject. "No," she said, standing up. As she moved toward Jack's office, she told them, "I'm going to spend a few more hours with it."

"She's getting awful antsy," Russ murmured as Cassie left the room. "She needs all her wits about her right now."

"The incident this morning really shook her up. And she's worried her entire story won't ever be printed because she lacks solid proof." He shook his head, feeling a disturbing mix of apprehension and admiration. "Nor will she settle for just getting them on building code violations."

"It's obvious she's becoming obsessed with nailing Marilyn Hook," Russ agreed. "It's more than just the story to her now."

"She was obsessed with it before we met her, and it's taking a stronger hold on her each day." He paused and looked at his friend curiously. "And I thought you were withholding yourself from Kathleen. She's back today."

"Changed my mind," Russ mumbled gruffly, burying his red face in a magazine.

Jack schooled his features, trying not to laugh out loud. Evidently withholding himself had turned out to be more difficult than Russ had thought. Jack hoped he found something that worked soon. No two people seemed more suited for each other, and he couldn't imagine anyone else who could stand up to Russ the way Kathleen did.

But in a way he would regret the union. It meant he'd be living here alone, except during Bridget's visits from boarding school. It would be wonderful if she could be around all the time, but the child psychologists over the years had thought it best she stay in the school. Everyday routine was of vital importance at this stage; they'd been told that over and over again. There were times when Jack wondered if they knew what the hell they were talking about.

Bridget loved the school, the companionship of friends her own age, the constant activities that were planned for them. There were all kinds of lessons, too, including music, art and dance, almost anything they wanted or needed was made available to them.

Except love, parental love, *his* love.

But he wasn't so selfish he'd put her life in danger. The most important thing now was her safety, just as it had been five years ago when they had brought her into this country. Bridget was safe there; the school was small and specialized in taking care of and educating children whose parents were considered targets, politically or for some other reason. Her needs still had to come first, even at the expense of his own.

"I think I've got it!" Cassie crowed, coming out of his office. She was rubbing her hands together in glee. Jack and Russ looked up at her expectantly. "If you reverse the numbers at the top of each file they represent addresses for various projects the Hooks have been involved in," she explained. "I've matched up almost half the files with addresses I know about."

"Is this a private party, or can anyone join in?" Patrick Rourke stood in the open doorway, his hands buried in his pants pockets.

Russ groaned. "How'd you get past the alarms this time?"

"Kathleen let us in," he said, walking into the room. "Fed me, too."

"Bridget all right?" Jack asked.

Patrick sat down in the vacant chair opposite the love seat. "Fine, she's in the kitchen with Kathleen." He looked directly at her. "You mentioned the Hook name. What did you find?"

"Probably not anything as interesting as you found." Cassie sat down on the lemon-yellow love seat. "Interested in a trade?"

They stared at each other as worthy opponents, looking for weaknesses. Finally Cassie draped her legs over the end of the sofa and arranged the pillows behind her head to a more comfortable position, ready to wait him out. After a restless night and such an early wake-up call a nap would be wonderful.

Patrick continued to stare at her. She seemed quite comfortable in Jack's home. In the past five years, he'd never once seen a woman in this house. That meant she was important to Jack, especially if he allowed her access to his inner sanctum. He was going to have to tell her enough to keep her safe from harm.

"All right. The FBI and the CIA have a file on Marilyn Hook."

Cassie almost fell off the couch. "What's in it?" she asked, sitting up straight.

"Your turn."

So that was his game. "We retrieved a disk yesterday." All three men smiled at her word choice but she ignored them. "It holds the cost run-down on some of their projects. I'm not far enough into it to tell if it will reveal bribes or kickbacks. Your turn." Her eagerness for information was evident.

"How many people do you suppose have died accidentally on their construction sites in the last three years?" Patrick asked her.

Her mouth dropped open. "More than four?" she asked.

"Try six or more." He'd managed to stun her into total silence. "You knew about some of them?"

Cassie nodded. "Four of them. Three of the names came from my informant, who I have reason to believe is dead, also." She looked at Patrick expectantly. The man was as tight as a clam. "What else does her file contain?"

"An informant says she killed her husband."

Cassie looked puzzled. "But he died of a heart attack."

"Supposedly. According to their tipster, she gave him a drug, which worked against his heart medicine and stopped his ticker cold. Sweet lady."

"Sure, that fits. They didn't perform an autopsy," Cassie informed him, "and they'll never find out one way or the other now, because his body was cremated."

"Clever."

She cocked her head sideways, oblivious to everyone in the room except Patrick. "Do you know when the file on her was opened?" Cassie asked, speculating on how he'd come up with this information. Most likely quite illegally.

"How old is she?" Patrick returned, only half in jest. "The anonymous tips in the active file are recent, within the last three years. What else do you know?"

Cassie brushed a stray hair back before answering. "I couldn't find any evidence, and my source said it would be impossible to trace, but he implied there was some sort of smuggling going on. In his last call he seemed to be worried about something that would be jeopardizing this country. I just put the two together myself, but I have a hunch the Hooks may be involved in smuggling information."

Jack let his surprise show. She had been holding out on him. One of the five richest, most politically active families in Texas selling secrets? It was hard to believe they'd go that far. Arms he could understand; some of the biggest names in the country had gotten wealthy dealing in weapons.

"Wait a minute. Are you talking about government secrets?" Jack asked, entering the conversation.

"I don't know. But they have the connections and the means. According to my source, somewhere hidden in the myriad of companies they control is a small import-export business."

Rourke looked grim. "Did you get the name?"

"He said he didn't have that information." Her sour expression conveyed her disbelief. "But he did say the company wasn't registered as being owned by anyone in the family. They're up to their rear ends in dummy corporations."

"Smart move," Jack murmured. "Tracing it will be next to impossible without a name or some kind of clue giving us a place to start."

"Oh, I think we have a place to start," Russ chipped in. "Flynn. He's the one buying. Isn't that right, Patrick?"

Patrick looked at him. He should have known Russ would figure it out. He could see it in his eyes. "Maybe."

"What's he buying?" Cassie asked.

"I can't answer that."

"Can't or won't?"

"Won't," Patrick told her.

"Have you come up with anything on Flynn's location?" Jack asked.

Patrick shook his head. "Nothing. I'm still hoping the loss of the jewelry will make him do something rash."

"What about the kid we got the key from?" Russ asked.

"He's in a safe place." Patrick stood up. "I'm going to get some sleep."

"You can use my room," Russ announced, standing up, too. "Bridget and I will be at Kathleen's. And not one word out of you, laddie," he told Jack, shaking a finger at him.

Rourke followed him out of the room, leaving Cassie and Jack alone. Silence filled the space between them, and Cassie grew more uncomfortable. What was he thinking about?

He was making it harder for her to ignore her own desires. Each time she saw him, he would casually touch her in passing, let his fingers trail down her arms, across the back of her neck—but that was it, nothing more. She didn't like the way he upset her equilibrium; the way his slightest touch sent her nerve endings soaring out of control. It wasn't easy to ignore those signals when your entire body was practically beating you over the head with them, forcing you to take notice.

"What are you doing tomorrow?" Jack finally asked.

"I have a newspaper assignment at ten. I'm doing the publicity story on the Hook family for their charity event."

She'd managed to shock him. "Is that wise?"

"It's an assignment, Jack." Cassie shrugged. "Something I have to do in order to keep my job."

He studied her facial expressions. "You asked for it, didn't you?"

Jack was getting to know her too well. "So?"

He'd had a chance to think since early this morning, and had come to a few conclusions. "Don't let your animosity show," Jack warned. "I think Marilyn Hook sent Knox to check up on you because you were snooping around."

Cassie had come to the same conclusion. "What if she knows I'm out to get her?"

"I think if she was wise to what you're really up to, she would have blown up your place with you in it instead of messing around with Knox. Easy enough to fake a gas explosion."

Cassie closed her eyes and moaned.

"But if you irritate her," Jack continued, "or ask any questions that don't seem pertinent to the charity ball and auction . . ." He let his voice trail off to indicate the seriousness of his warning.

It wasn't necessary. "I know. She could change her mind and take me out just for fun. Don't worry. I'll be completely professional, a bipartisan member of the press, showing no emotion or feeling at all."

"Don't take it too far. You've been looking around and she knows it. She'll expect you to be interested. Just—"

"I know!" Cassie exclaimed irritably.

The dryness of his tone irritated her. She didn't need to be told to look before she leaped, or watch what she said.

She tilted her chin in defiance and told him, "I'll be in my room. I brought some work home that I need to get through tonight."

Jack walked into his office and sat down at his desk. The scent of her perfume still hung in the air. It was a struggle for him to concentrate on the work before him.

Three hours later he stood up and headed for the stairs.

There was no answer to his knock on her closed bedroom door. Entering the room quietly, he found Cassie in bed, sound asleep amid a sprawl of papers and notes. Her pale violet nightgown was more revealing than the one she'd worn last night.

Jack gently removed the pen from her hand and gathered up the loose papers, putting them on a nearby chair. He took the two extra pillows from behind her head and watched as she settled herself more comfortably, curling on her side, her loose hair caressing her pale cheek.

He trailed the back of his hand down across the smooth curve of her face. She didn't move when he slid the narrow string strap of her gown back up on her shoulder. What she needed right now was some sleep. They hadn't gotten much last night and she had a big day tomorrow. He had to get out of there now if he was going to stop himself.

What he really wanted to do was crawl into bed with her and sensuously awaken the fires he knew burned inside of her, but he didn't. Instead he pulled the covers up over her bare shoulders. With a resigned sigh he turned out the light and left the room.

Tomorrow was going to be a rough day and she couldn't afford to make any accidental slips of the tongue. He planned on having her around for a long while. How long he didn't know. Cassie was the first woman he'd met since his wife who made him even want to contemplate marriage, maybe children. He'd forgotten how nice it was to have a woman to talk to, someone to argue with, someone to come home to. Someone who simply made you want to come home.

Could he take that chance again? Love someone without reservation, share their aches and pains, the ups and downs of everyday life? He didn't know. He wanted to, but wasn't at all sure he was strong enough to take the chance.

"THE WOMAN DIDN'T return home. She's at Merlin's place."

Flynn brushed his auburn hair back, an evil grin spreading across his face. "That's all right. I have another even better plan." His sources had come through for him. "This will take a day or two to set up. Be there when I call."

He set the phone down, trying to contain his jubilation. Bridget, his passkey to the three men. He'd found their weakness. He didn't know or need her last name. All he needed was her location, and he now knew that, too. The housekeeper's address had been difficult to come by but a little careful surveillance always worked wonders.

However, this was going to take careful planning or the trap he wanted to spring on them might turn around and ensnare him. He could afford a few more days. His prize was worth that and more.

Chapter Twenty

Cassie made it through the interview on Wednesday morning without a single slipup. The two sisters who showed her around the Hook mansion were charming, beautiful and gracious hostesses. The family was willing to have any and all parts of their stunning home photographed if it would help raise money for their favorite charity, the children's hospital.

As it turned out, Cassie needn't have worried about meeting Marilyn Hook. She stopped in briefly as Cassie was concluding the interview, but was on her way to a business appointment and didn't have time to chat. That was fine with Cassie. The less they saw of each other the better.

She was a pretty woman and quite charming herself, though she perhaps worked at both attributes a bit too hard. For all her apparent sincerity, she still made Cassie nervous, wondering what was going on behind her carefully made-up eyes.

Appearances could be so deceiving. People in the know were agreed on one thing: her biggest fault was her inability to ever admit she'd made a wrong decision, a fault she had in common with her deceased father and grandfather. She was always undaunted when it came time to place the blame on someone and equally merciless when she fired them.

Reason enough to steer well clear of her until all the facts were in hand. Cassie felt a great sense of relief when the tour of her home was over.

The next few hours she spent searching for further Hook subsidiaries but had little luck. Though she had plenty of sources to contact for information, she'd grown more wary of whom she could and couldn't trust. Did everyone owe the Hooks favors?

As she made her way toward her editor's office, Cassie continued to mull over the gossip and facts about Marilyn Hook. Was she really the mastermind behind all this? Could she have killed her husband? And if so, why?

Cassie closed the door behind herself and sat down in a chair facing Stan, who was on the phone as usual. He talked a moment longer then hung up.

"What do you have?" he asked.

"Nothing new. It's two o'clock and here I am. The message you left on my machine said something about a meeting?"

Stan leaned back in his chair, twirling a pencil. The paper needed a big story at present; newspaper publishing was always a race, and the competition was gaining on them. He stood up and announced, "Mrs. Carlyle wants to see us both in her office, right now."

His news surprised Cassie. Frowning, she followed him out of his office. He opened Mrs. Carlyle's door for her and waved her in ahead of him. She entered the plush, airy room, then stopped in her tracks.

Jack Merlin was sitting in one of the three armchairs arranged in a a semicircle in front of Mrs. Carlyle's desk. What was he doing here?

If her eyes could throw daggers, Jack had the feeling he'd be dead right now, or at least seriously wounded. There would be a backlash from Cassie because of his presence here, but he'd decided it would be worth any price as long as she was safe. Cassie sat down in the chair next to him, refusing to even look his way.

"Let's get started," Mrs. Carlyle said, after everyone was seated. "Stan has kept me updated on your work, Cassie, and we met with the company lawyers this morning. I need to know exactly what your story will be about."

Cassie struggled not to squirm in her chair. It was a toss-up as to who she wanted to strangle first, Jack or Stan. "I can't be that specific at this time. Additional information may be forthcoming."

"Then let's run a photo of the hamburger sack letter on the front page along with what we do know," Stan suggested. "And print the new information as it comes up."

She turned in her chair toward Stan. "What about the proof you demanded I get? All I have right now is one young man's version, and he's dead." She leaned forward, glaring at him as his words sank in. "Wait a minute! What's this *we* stuff?"

"The paper will pay to have a sample test run on the concrete from that building when you bring it in," Stan replied. "And we can hire experts—"

Cassie shook her head. "That won't be necessary, I've already arranged for a test. And I have confirmation that the plumbing is below grade in that particular building." She paused. "Although all the results aren't back yet, it appears that some of the Hooks' more recent projects are also involved."

"You're sure about this?" Stan asked skeptically.

Her tone was indignant. "Of course I am. They've managed to use the same city inspectors for each and every one of their projects. Which isn't easy in a city the size of Houston."

"Were they paid off?"

"They had to have been," Cassie replied. "How could they move on to the next phase of construction, let alone the next building without code approval?"

"Can you substantiate that claim?" Stan asked.

Cassie sighed. "No. I don't have any actual proof the inspectors were paid money by the Hook family itself. They wouldn't make payoffs by check."

"And it's hard to trace cash," Stan said sarcastically before she could utter those exact words. "Right?"

Cassie ignored him. "They did have to sign and certify the work was satisfactory and met code. I've got copies of those records. And we all know," she said, suddenly remembering that others were present, "they weren't doing their jobs properly in the first place if they gave their okay. So we do have proof to back up that accusation," Cassie finished triumphantly.

"Then we're going to print," Stan informed her.

"No!" Cassie cried, glaring at Stan. What was going on? Why was Stan in such a hurry to get this printed?

Her editor looked at her intently for a moment, then leaned forward and tapped the placard on Mrs. Carlyle's desk with the pencil he always seemed to have in his hand. "See that? Unless someone changed it while we weren't looking, it says you take orders, not give them."

She needed more time. And she knew just how to get it. "Should we print the big story before or after we run the photographs and article about the upcoming charity event the family sponsors?" Cassie asked dryly.

"The assignment was one you asked for," he informed her, albeit with a wary look in his eyes. "And you've had work shelved before. This is one of those times."

"Stan, this is a charity event, held to raise money for the children's hospital. Little babies! If we print this now there won't be any money raised this year." She sat back, a concerned look on her face and turned her appeal to Mrs. Carlyle. "And how—"

Stan was furious. "Cassie . . ." he warned.

"And how will our loyal subscribers interpret our actions when the rival papers rake us over the coals for poor timing and bad judgment?" Cassie asked Mrs. Carlyle.

Mrs. Carlyle didn't say anything. She simply arched her eyebrows and looked at Stan. He broke his pencil. "Cassie, cut the crap! I know when somebody's trying to manipulate me. State what you want."

"I want to hold off on this story until after the charity event on Friday night." She looked at him. He wasn't wavering. "You can even announce that we sat on the story until after the benefit. That'll puff up our image. It's only a few more days, Stan!"

His beady brown eyes zeroed in on her. He never liked it when someone pointed out the obvious to him, especially when it was something he should have seen himself. And in front of the executive editor, at that. He pulled another pencil out of his pocket and started tapping it irritably on the arm of his chair.

"I'm inclined to agree with Cassie," Mrs. Carlyle suddenly announced. "We have to think of our public image."

Stan was still glaring at Cassie. He knew Mrs. Carlyle would make the final decision. "Tell me why you want to wait that long?"

"By then I'll either have the proof I'm after, or I won't ever be able to get it. Did you know there are some people who believe Marilyn Hook killed her husband?" Cassie asked, adding a bit of bait to her lure.

There was a shocked gasp from Mrs. Carlyle, but Stan was clearly not impressed. "So what?" he snapped. "The man was cremated, Cassie. There isn't a body to check for evidence. Anything else?"

She'd forgotten about Stan's memory for facts. "There is a chance," Cassie said, leaning forward in her chair to make her point, "a very good chance, that the family has dealt and is still dealing in the selling of classified information."

It was a quantum leap from hunch to very good chance. Jack cleared his throat, indicating his disapproval. Cassie ignored him. She knew what she was doing.

"What!" Stan was shocked. "Government secrets?"

Cassie hid a smile as another pencil bit the dust. Got him! Now to set the hook. "I might be able to back up that part of the story by this Saturday. But if we print what I know now, the evidence on the other will be buried forever.''

Stan was practically beside himself with excitement. She could tell because he looked ready to strangle somebody. "If another paper gets wind of this story in the meantime you can kiss your job goodbye,'' Stan threatened.

"I've kept my research quiet so far. If it gets out it won't be because of me or anything I do,'' she returned swiftly.

"Keep it that way,'' he ordered.

Jack had been listening intently to the newspeople, drawing his own conclusions from their heated conversation. It was all very enlightening. Calling Stan Lockwood had been a good idea. But he didn't like what he was hearing. He knew exactly what Cassie intended to do in order to get that proof she so desperately wanted. And it was not only dangerous, it was extremely foolish.

"Are you behind her one hundred percent?'' Jack asked, his voice soft. "If she gets the proof you need, will you print the story in its entirety, no matter who is involved?''

"Of course,'' Stan assured him, eyeing him with intense curiosity behind Cassie's back. Exactly who was this guy?

Obviously, this was the type of man who interested Cassie. He looked capable of handling her wrath, and that was good, because Stan knew Cassie had always made a point of keeping her work and her private life separate. She was going to be very angry her lover had called him.

"And why not? If she's right we'll have an exclusive no one can touch,'' Stan continued. "The public always has a right to know what's going on. Especially if it involves their tax dollars.''

"What do you mean?'' Cassie asked, sitting up straight.

"It's nice to know I can still get the jump on you every now and then. A Hook family subsidiary was awarded the construction contract for the new elementary school in Austin last night. They break ground in two weeks.''

Some of the color drained from Cassie's face. "Oh, no.'' Would they dare go so far as to use shoddy building practices on an elementary school?

"Cassie, these are very serious accusations,'' Mrs. Carlyle told her. "Unless we can acquire documented proof, I don't believe the paper can ever print the entire story.''

"I still think it might be better to go ahead and run with what we have,'' Stan said, contemplating the facts they already had. "Chances of us ending up with actual proof that they've sold government secrets is nil. And there's always the chance of a leak.''

"The leak won't come from me, or Jack. So who does that leave?" Cassie asked, glaring at Stan.

Stan's face turned red, the blue veins standing out prominently against his white hair. Mrs. Carlyle resisted the temptation to smile. Cassie was a go-getter, and her work was good, but sometimes she went too far.

"I agree," Jack said with authority. "The chances of her actually getting hold of any documented proof is nil."

Cassie turned and looked at Jack. So much for him being in her corner. She hadn't expected Jack to be behind her one hundred percent on this, but his attitude surprised her.

Turning back to face Mrs. Carlyle, Cassie announced quietly, "I think I can come up with what we need. All I'm asking for is a few more days. It will give me time to further document what we know so far, and to verify what Stan has found out."

Mrs. Carlyle leaned back in her chair, her fingers forming a steeple as she looked at the three people staring at her so intently. This was a difficult decision to make. Marilyn Hook and she had been close friends for years. But that wouldn't sway her final decision, at least not much.

She looked at Stan. "At this time I believe it's in the best interest of this newspaper to sit on the story."

Stan leaned forward, opening his mouth to protest. Then suddenly he changed his mind and sat back in his chair.

Mrs. Carlyle continued, "I want to consult with the company lawyers again. Repercussions for this could be devastating if we're not careful." She smiled. "Besides, if there is an even bigger story out there, then this newspaper wants it, exclusively."

No one protested her decision. Everyone present knew Mrs. Carlyle had the final say. Stan nodded then stood up and left the room. Jack followed him.

Cassie breathed a sigh of relief. "Thank you."

"Just get me that proof," Mrs. Carlyle told her, smiling. She liked Cassie, she'd been a go-getter herself once. "By the way, have you come up with anything on Brian Fenton?"

Cassie let her disappointment show. "Not yet." But with this added time there was still hope. "I am still working on it, but this came up along the way," Cassie explained, trying to cover up the real purpose behind her needed delay.

"Keep at it," Mrs. Carlyle said. "He was a good journalist."

"Yes, he was, and thank you," Cassie told her once again before getting to her feet and heading for the door.

Mrs. Carlyle watched Cassie leave the office, already contemplating her next move. The phone rang. "I asked you to hold my calls. Oh! Put her right through, and cancel my four-o'clock appointment. Leonore, what perfect timing!"

Stan was talking to Jack when Cassie caught up with them in the hall. "Maybe you can talk some sense into her. I've never been successful," Stan said.

"I don't take on impossible tasks," Jack returned, shaking hands with him. "Thank you for allowing me to be here. Ready, Cassie?"

He was going to pay for doing this to her. And for the odd way her boss was looking at her. She wanted some answers and Jack was going to deliver them. After reassuring Stan again that she would keep him informed, she walked out of the building with Jack. No one interfered with her job!

"I'll meet you back at the house," Cassie told him. "We have to talk." She slammed her car door in his face. Was her past coming back to haunt her?

Her ex-husband had caused enough problems at her first job to last an entire lifetime. Handsome, dynamic, sixteen years her senior, Marcus had easily swept her off her feet. Cassie had been completely infatuated, a very young, naive twenty and fresh out of a small-town college when she married him. How idealistic she had been!

Sharing the same journalistic fervor, everything was rosy for them until her job began taking up more and more of her time. As her reputation grew, his initial encouragement and pride in her work turned to scorn and dismay. He was a possessive man, and in time he'd become even more dominating, wanted to control every detail in her life.

It had taken Cassie a long time to accept that her marriage wasn't going to work out. Once her decision was made, though, she'd found another job, in another city far away from his influence. Immersed in her new surroundings, driven by pride and stubborn self-confidence, she'd built a strong career bit by bit.

It would take a very special man to accept her dedication to her work. So special she doubted he even existed. And no man was ever going to interfere in her work again. Not even Jack Merlin.

By the time she reached his home, she was calm. At least the dogs were getting used to her. They'd come running up the drive, but once they'd seen it was her they'd turned and run away again.

"Jack," she called out, entering through the front door. "Where are you?"

"Need something?" he inquired, coming out of the kitchen.

His recklessly fast driving had given him time to change clothes. He was dressed casually in gray slacks and a cotton shirt. "We're going to talk," she said. "Right now!"

He shrugged, then turned and walked away. "Come into the kitchen, I'm fixing dinner. What's up?"

Cassie followed close on his heels. "How did you know about the meeting today?"

"I accessed your answering machine with a gadget of mine. It goes through tones until it finds the code for remote playback of messages," Jack explained. "It sounded like a good opportunity to meet your boss, so I called him up and convinced him to let me sit in on the meeting."

"How?"

Jack shrugged. "I told him we were lovers and I was worried about the story you were working on."

"You what! How dare you!"

"Did you expect me to tell him the truth? Hi! My name is Jack Merlin and I'm being blackmailed by one of your reporters. She's in way over her head. Would you please try to talk some sense into her?"

Her temper flared at that statement. "Listen very carefully. Only I decide what is and isn't good for me," she informed him coldly. "Remember that in the future."

He picked up a carrot and efficiently sliced it into thin slivers. "You're not the only one involved this time, Cassie."

He had a valid point, but she didn't let it sway her from her goal. "What else did you tell him?" she demanded.

"You don't trust Stan completely, do you?" he asked.

"I don't trust anyone completely. He has been trustworthy so far, but that doesn't mean a thing. As you well know, everyone has a price, you just have to find it," she added cynically.

"That's exactly why I wanted to meet him. You work for him. He was bound to enter the equation sooner or later, and I wanted to get a look at him," Jack explained. "Marilyn Hook and her family own a good cross section of people in this town. I want to be sure that this story gets out, that it doesn't fall apart like those buildings of hers will someday."

Cassie was touched by his concern, but it couldn't excuse the way he'd gone about showing it. "Then why did you side with him?"

"I didn't side with him. I simply agreed with him that your chances of getting the information you need to bring down Marilyn Hook aren't good. Besides," he added, "it's very dangerous."

Jack was slicing up celery. He added it to a full bowl of various sliced veggies. She watched him dump the vegetables into the hot wok and stir-fry the colorful mass, returning some already-cooked chicken to the pan.

"I know it's dangerous," Cassie said, when he finished the noisy task. "But that's not your problem."

"*You're* my problem," he told her. He divided the contents of the wok onto two plates and sprinkled toasted sesame seeds over each one. Then he set the plates on the table and pulled out a chair. "Have a seat."

Cassie cautiously tasted the concoction, unable to identify most of the vegetable slivers. "This is good."

"Thank you."

She gave up questioning him for the moment, content to enjoy the meal in silence. Cassie was still angry with him for what he had done today, but there wasn't any reason to fight about it on an empty stomach.

When they were through, they went to the library, where she proceeded to take up where she'd left off. "Stan seems to want to stop me from further investigation into this. That's not like him and it worries me."

Jack leaned back in his chair, rocking it gently as he said, "I had Stan checked out."

Her eyebrows arched. "And?"

"He's as clean as a man can get and still be human. He has a strong sense of conviction and has never backed down on a story, even if it meant losing his job, which he did once."

That was one story she'd never heard about her boss. "Do tell."

"It was at a smaller paper, years ago. He printed a story, over the objection of his superiors, about an affluent politician buying his son's way out of numerous tickets and a drug bust. The man was influential enough to have him fired."

Cassie sipped her coffee. "What else?"

"He's divorced, likes lots of women and doesn't live beyond the means of his salary."

"And is a horrible gossip," she added. "He'd never let loose with anything that might give a story away, but he loves office dirt."

"I see."

Jack waited silently while she drained her coffee cup and then trained her brilliant blue eyes on him. Now they were getting to the true root of her anger. She was mad because Stan had seen them together, and because Jack had given him the impression they were lovers.

"Is that the problem?" Jack asked. "Cassie, with all the other things you have to be concerned about, how can you worry over a little gossip?"

"I'm not," she objected coolly. "It just makes trouble for me at work, that's all. Trouble I don't need. The problem is you." Cassie glared at him, her jaw set. "You're interfering with the way I choose to do my job. Just like my ex-husband did."

"Point made," Jack said, very softly. What she had just told him about her ex-husband was a revelation. Now he understood her reactions to his presence earlier today. "You're right, I am interfering. But you're taking too many chances in tracking down this story."

She scowled at him. "It's my job. The one I chose and the one I intend to continue doing."

Jack picked his words carefully. "Cassie, you need to realize you may not find out who murdered Brian Fenton. If that is the case, then you need to accept the story you already have. Construction illegalities."

"No! That's not enough to get Marilyn Hook!" Cassie exclaimed, using her hands to emphasize the point. "All that would do is incriminate some poor slobs who were following orders to keep their jobs. The real dirt won't touch her, because everyone around her knows what would happen to them if it did."

"Cassie, you're becoming obsessed," Jack warned.

Her eyes flared with anger. "She's guilty."

"You don't know that for a fact!" he told her, his own anger rising to the surface. "And going after those ledgers is a fool's stunt. Turn your information over to the FBI or the police and let them deal with this. Accept the story you already have."

"No! I still don't know who killed Brian Fenton!"

"Dammit, Cassie! Can't you get it through your thick skull? You could get killed!" Jack bellowed.

Russ had been listening to them unobserved and decided he had better enter the fray before they resorted to physical violence. "Are we having a mild disagreement?" he asked, entering the room. Neither answered him as they continued to glare at each other. "Lovely evening." He poured himself a shot of whiskey. "And what might you be up to now, Cassie?"

"She wants to keep searching for the ledgers."

"I can answer for myself," Cassie snapped.

Russ held up a hand in a placating gesture. "Where might these documents be kept, Cassie?"

"I plan to start with the mansion."

"Now isn't that the stupidest idea you've ever heard, Russ?" Jack asked sarcastically.

Cassie jumped up. "I've had enough of this. I'm going home. Don't get up, I can see myself out." She turned and walked out of the room, brushing past Russ.

"I'll handle this," Russ said as Jack stood up to go after her. "You've already put your foot in your mouth enough for one day."

Russ found her upstairs, throwing things into a suitcase. "Sure you want to do this?"

Cassie looked up from packing. Russ was leaning against the white doorjamb, his arms crossed. "Yes."

"Think about the last time you were home and what happened. There are other men like Knox out there, just waiting to be hired." He gave her a moment to remember then asked, "Are you safe at home?"

She knew she wasn't. "Do you know where Flynn is?"

His face tightened. "No, but he'll show up sooner or later. That's one of the reasons Jack is so worried about you." He hesitated, then spoke. "Cassie, if Jack didn't have feelings for you, then he wouldn't care about what happened to you. But he does care."

She sat down on the bed, an unfolded blouse in her lap. "Jack doesn't understand. Yes, I've come up with a great story. But I still don't know who killed Brian."

"He understands more than you realize. But he's worried about you, he knows what Flynn is capable of, and others like him. And he likes you, even though he doesn't want to admit it." Russ moved slowly into the room.

She was twisting the blouse in her hands, restlessly. "What did Flynn do?"

Russ stood in front of her, running one hand through his short red hair. "That's not my story to tell, Cassie. There's too much I don't know about how Jack felt, how he still feels inside. He has to be the one to tell you about his past, not me." Gently he pried her fingers off the blouse she was twisting and took it from her. "I like this blouse on you," Russ told her, setting it on a chair. "So I'd rather you didn't destroy it."

Cassie smiled. "You're a strange man, Russ Ian."

"I'll take that as a compliment." He held out his hand to her and she took it, her hand small in his large one.

"You do that," she told him, standing up. "We have work to do."

He grinned. "Lead the way."

"Oh, I intend to."

"You're determined to do this, right?" Jack asked, when they walked back into the room.

"Was there ever any doubt?" Cassie asked. "I've narrowed down where the ledgers could be to the Hook mansion. I don't think they'd keep them in an office safe."

Jack's eyes had taken on a certain sparkle. If she was determined to do this, she wasn't doing it without him. "I wonder how well it's guarded?"

"We'll find a way in," Russ assured them.

Cassie was getting the same sort of queasy feeling in her stomach she'd had when she saw him pilfering the lockbox earlier. It was a helpless feeling, and she didn't like it one little bit. "Wait a minute, you two!" Cassie looked from one to the other. "There's an easy way in," she told them. "They'll be holding their annual charity ball at the mansion this Friday night."

"She's already got this figured out," Russ told Jack.

Cassie refused to look guilty. "Yes." A shiver of excitement mingled with her uneasiness. "Their ranch is another possibility. They hold an auction and buffet there the next day. People fly in from all over the country. If I don't find what I need at the mansion, then checking out the ranch will be easy. It's a very splashy affair."

Jack found himself murmuring, "Do we need invitations for this charity ball?"

Cassie shook her head. "No. The entrance fee is two hundred dollars a person, and it must be paid in advance. But I can get you in on my press pass."

"That won't be necessary," Jack told her, "the money goes to a good cause."

Cassie nodded and added, "You can even specify which wing of the hospital you wish it to go to."

"How democratic," Jack said, making a face.

He had the funny feeling that if the Hooks were involved, not all of the money collected would go to where it was supposed to. Why was it that Cassie kept getting him into situations where he was practically forced to commit a crime in order to do a good turn? As lovely as she was, her unrelenting pursuit of the truth could be hazardous to his health. Nevertheless, his mind was already hard at work on the problem. "We're going to need the layout of the house."

Cassie crossed the room and picked up the sheaf of papers under her purse, then returned to the love seat, spreading them out on the coffee table. "I've sketched some diagrams already."

Russ and Jack sat down on either side of her and studied the drawings. "Not bad," Russ murmured.

"Not bad at all," Jack concurred. "Let's see. The way I figure it, once inside we can—"

"Wait a minute!" Cassie exclaimed. "Whose plan is this!"

"Do you want the evidence you need to print your story or not?"

"Of course I do, but—"

"Then you'll need help. And we're saving you the trouble of blackmailing us again," Jack told her. "Or finding someone new to pick on."

For the next hour they concentrated on entrances, exits and possible escape routes, Russ coaxing her into remembering forgotten details before they decided to give it a rest until the next day.

Cassie went up to bed early, to get some much-needed sleep. Jack lingered in the library, continuing to look over her diagrams. Russ came back into the room.

"What's wrong?" he asked, sitting down.

"She's getting too wrapped up in this, and damned if she isn't dragging me along for the ride. I wish she was a little more aware of the possible pitfalls."

Russ shrugged. "It happens. When you get too close to an issue or a person, you lose your sense of perspective."

"Tell me about it," Jack muttered. He was no longer seeing Cassie or the problem she presented quite so clearly himself. "Are you spending the night at Kathleen's?"

"Yes, and I won't be back tomorrow, either." Russ grinned at him, his eyes sparkling. "Are you sure you're going to be safe here all alone with her?"

Alone with Cassie. Now there was an intriguing thought. "We'll be fine," he replied with a smile of his own. "Just fine."

Chapter Twenty-one

Traffic was still heavy when Cassie finally left the office late the next evening. It had taken her a lot more time than it should have to write the article on the Hook family mansion and the upcoming charity event. She'd had to weed out her personal opinion and ever-growing animosity toward Marilyn Hook. The children's hospital could use every dime it could get. In the end the piece had come out clean and well-written.

She also felt a twinge of conscience about leading Stan on with the government secrets deal. Getting anything on that transaction was wishful dreaming, even providing there had been any truth to the accusation in the first place.

What she needed right now was a hot bubble bath to soak away the tension.

Cassie parked her car beside the garage, then made her way upstairs swiftly, not wanting to face Jack. Thoughts of him had drifted in and out of her mind as she'd tried to concentrate on her work today. She'd given some serious consideration to the undeniable attraction between them and had come to a decision.

It wasn't going to go away. It was not just pure carnal need. Other emotions had begun to enter into the equation. There was only one way to find out if Jack felt the same way: give in to the desires she could feel churning within her even now. That was a dangerous thing to do, but so was this entire situation. The fact of the matter was, with all the threat around her, considering all the other things she was fighting for and against, battling her own sensuality seemed pointless.

She wanted to give in. *Needed* to give in. For once in her life, she had decided to do something without questioning it to death. The next time Jack looked at her in that sly, inviting way he had, he was in for a big surprise.

But all she wanted to do at the moment was soak away her worries. She pulled on a short terry robe and went into his room, relieved to find it empty. The deep bubbling water felt delicious. Cassie closed her eyes and relaxed.

Jack climbed the stairs slowly. Cassie was swiftly becoming a very important part of his life. He'd felt a renewed burst of energy late this afternoon upon realizing that she would be returning to his home tonight. He knocked softly on his bathroom door.

"Come in."

Jack arched his eyebrows at her tone of voice. Of all the possible responses he had anticipated when planning to interrupt her bath, a sultry invitation wasn't one of them.

"Are you hungry?" he asked softly, setting the tray down on the broad side of the tub. "You've been up here for almost an hour."

Her eyes opened sensuously, then reached over and picked up one of the wineglasses on the tray, sipping the golden liquid carefully as she peeked up at him. His white shirt was unbuttoned to the waist, the cuffs turned back, his hair pleasingly tousled. He sat down on a wicker stool close to the tray and plucked a red grape from the stem. With a touch as light as a summer breeze he brushed the cool ruby grape across her lips.

"Grapes?" Her blue eyes were twinkling, full of desire and mischief.

"I couldn't resist," he murmured, popping the orb into her open mouth. "But I draw the line at peeling them for you."

She chewed and swallowed the tasty fruit. He fed her grapes and cheese and bits of crackers, teasing and cajoling her until he was satisfied she was full. No one had ever pampered her this way in her life. And it was a side of him she'd never seen before.

All her senses were tingling and aware of him. Deep in her loins her body ached for him, for the sensual pleasure and relief from frustration he could provide.

"Join me?" she invited, her hand rippling across the cooling water. Jack's eyes went wide. "Or would you rather I join you?"

She chuckled throatily when he stood up and grabbed a towel, holding it out for her. Cassie rose from the bath, stepping gracefully out of the sunken tub and into the waiting towel. He wrapped her tightly in his arms for a moment, inhaling her feminine scent, enjoying the sensations aroused in him by her soft curves pressing against his hard body.

She sighed. It felt good to be held, touched all over. Jack meticulously dried every inch of her, starting with her feet and working his way up. Cassie was a quivering mass of sensual emotions by the time he was done, barely able to stand up without holding on to him.

"Take your hair down for me," he murmured, stepping back away from her tantalizing form.

Jack watched as she raised her arms, her firm breasts rising with the motion. One pin and then another hit the floor with a pinging sound as she began unbraiding her hair. Slender fingers combed through the loosened mass, brushing the silken tresses up and out across her bare shoulders, her gaze never leaving his.

"Gorgeous," he breathed. The dim, glowing lights illuminated her in a pool of rosy light. Reaching out, he stroked a sleek black strand across her cheek, his golden gaze taking her in. Her skin was damp, soft.

He seemed mesmerized by the sight of her, almost unaware that Cassie was undoing his pants. She pulled his shirt off his shoulders. It dropped to the floor, along with the rest of his clothes.

"Impatient?" he asked as she tugged on his hand, leading him into the bedroom and the cool, waiting sheets.

"Past ready," she moaned as his hand slid across her most sensitive parts.

His tongue dipped inside her ear, his warm breath a caress all its own. "I want to be sure this isn't against your will," he crooned, continuing to caress her.

Cassie rolled on top of him, taking complete control, burying him deep inside of her with a smooth, erotic motion of her hips. "Are you satisfied now?"

"Not even close."

Fingers dug into her buttocks as she moved atop him. He moaned softly as she teased him, again and again until she brought them both to satiation. Then they fell together into a deep, dreamless sleep. Danger seemed a million miles away.

THE HIDDEN DOOR opened silently, its hinges well oiled. Like the professional he was, the man entered the room the same way, without a sound. Then he paused. He was good, but there was no way he could make it across the old wooden floor without it creaking loudly in the quiet of the night. The deep, even breathing of his quarry didn't put him at ease; he was well aware of Jack

Merlin's skills. And right now he didn't want to end up on the floor finding out who was the better fighter.

Listening, he realized that Jack had company. What was going on? Then he grinned wickedly and threw caution to the wind as his mind filled with evil intentions. He took a single, soundless step toward the bed.

Then he whistled, a low-keyed tone floating around the room, followed by the sound of a bird chirping away quite happily. He only hoped Jack remembered the code.

With a groan Jack eased his body away from Cassie's warmth. "Cut it out, Patrick," Jack groused softly. "You'll wake her up. I'll meet you in the library."

But Cassie wasn't quite as far gone as he'd thought. "What's up, Rourke?" she asked, her voice sleepy but firm. After pulling the sheet up to her shoulders, she turned on the bedside lamp.

"Damn," Jack grumbled as he pulled on a black and gray velour floor-length robe. He glanced at Cassie and found her eyes riveted on Rourke and the hidden passageway in which he stood. He was dressed in dark clothing, his face lean and hard.

"Did you locate Flynn?" she asked.

Rourke didn't bother to hide his surprise. He looked at Jack, then at the woman so comfortably ensconced in his bed.

Jack sighed loudly. "We'll talk downstairs."

"I could use a drink," Rourke said, then left the room.

Jack glanced at her. "I don't suppose...." She was shaking her head. "I didn't think so." With a shrug he walked toward the no-longer-hidden door and disappeared into the passageway. He could hear her scrambling out of bed as soon as he turned his back.

"What does she know about Flynn?" Rourke questioned as Jack walked through the open double doors behind the bookcase.

"Mind if I get a drink first?"

Rourke gave him the one he had ready, a dark eyebrow arched high. "Well?"

"She doesn't know everything, but I had to tell her a certain amount in order to protect her." He brought Patrick up to date. The other man shook his head in amazement.

Jack took a sip of his drink, gazing at Rourke speculatively. "What's wrong?"

"I've seen him."

"Where?"

Rourke finished his own whiskey in one gulp. "You know I've had people looking for him." Jack nodded. "They located him at a local hotel. He had the penthouse suite. When I arrived they had his room staked out, but he must have known something was up. I caught a good look at him as he drove away,'' Rourke spoke hoarsely. "There was no way I could catch him. His left hand was on the outside of the car. He didn't have his little finger.''

Jack closed his eyes for a moment as unpleasant memories washed over him. "Did he see you?''

"I don't know.''

"Did they find anything useful in Flynn's room?''

Rourke stared into his empty glass. "Nothing he'd come back for.''

"Dammit,'' Jack murmured. "What now?''

Rourke grimaced and leaned back against the liquor cabinet. "I don't know. Getting a lead on Flynn is going to be even harder now.''

"He knows we have the jewelry,'' Jack mused. "So he's going to have to make his move soon or risk more exposure.''

Rourke nodded. "I hope it's soon.''

Jack glanced toward the bookcases. "Still listening in doorways, Cassie?''

"It's more interesting that way,'' Cassie said, entering the room with graceful aplomb. She'd brushed her hair and slipped on black slacks and a silky black and white geometric-patterned blouse.

"So,'' Cassie said, casually taking a seat and swirling her chair around to face Rourke, "are you and Marilyn Hook going to go through with the deal, or not?''

All he could do was stare at her.

Jack smiled. "Honest, you get used it,'' he told Rourke.

"Did you find out anything about Brian Fenton?'' she asked, brushing a strand of hair back out of her eyes.

Rourke hesitated. "Nothing yet, but I have been checking it out.''

"Thank you,'' Cassie said, her voice soft with gratitude.

Jack sat down in the chair next to Cassie's, but his eyes were on Rourke. "Are you attending the party at the Hook family mansion on Friday?''

"I might be.'' Rourke's face gave nothing away.

Jack smiled. "I figured you'd say that. Just so you know, we'll be there. We're going to try to get the evidence Cassie needs to nail Marilyn Hook. Either way, all or part of her story is going to be on the front page of the Sunday paper.''

"Thanks for the warning. I'll wrap things up before then if I can,'' Rourke replied. Setting down his glass, he turned to leave. "Russ wants to talk to you. He and Bridget are at Kathleen's.''

Rourke made a face. "I'll pass. He's ticked off because Bridget let slip that I took her to Disneyland last month, and the horse races," he added with a tight smile.

"No wonder he's mad," Jack returned dryly.

The three of them often clashed on Bridget's upbringing. Russ had definite ideas about what was good for a child and what wasn't. Horses were fine, and Bridget loved to see them run, but betting was not on his list of good influences for an impressionable young girl.

"She's doing quite well," Rourke said, his facial muscles relaxing slightly, softening as he thought of the little girl. "Quite a young lady."

"Heard any more rumors?"

"No, but that doesn't mean she's safe."

"I know."

"I'll be in touch," Rourke promised, then he left the room.

Jack swiveled his chair to look at her. "Hold the questions, Cassie."

"Can I at least ask about the secret passageways?"

A small smile appeared, crinkling the corners of his eyes. "The former owner had those built in when the house was originally constructed."

"Haven't you ever wanted to know the true background of the former owner and builder? What did he have to hide?"

"No. Some mysteries are better left unsolved. It's more fun that way. But I'm sure you don't agree."

She was shaking her head in disgust. "You have no curiosity, Jack Merlin."

"Yes, I do," he said, standing up when she did. "I'm very curious as to what you have on underneath that blouse."

She gazed at him, her stance and tone challenging yet provocative. "Why don't you come closer and find out?"

"I'm going to," he assured her, taking a step forward for each step she took back. "Have you ever made love in a secret passageway?"

"No, I haven't."

Jack pushed a button and the bookcase swung shut behind him, leaving them in total darkness. "Then this will be a first for you."

"Everything I've done with you is a first, Jack Merlin."

"I'm glad to hear that," he murmured, before his mouth covered hers. "Mmm. Curiosity does have its good points."

Chapter Twenty-two

The next night Cassie rolled over in Jack's king-size bed, waiting impatiently for him to come back. Russ had said the phone call was urgent.

What could be wrong? She sighed and looked at the clock on his bedside table. It was two in the morning, and at the moment she was too comfortable to go eavesdrop. Jack would either tell her what the call was about or he wouldn't.

Her fellow reporters would probably say she was slipping, losing her nose for news. Cassie knew better. Something had happened to her all right, but it had nothing to do with her instincts. If there was one thing she had learned over the years, it was that you couldn't argue with the facts.

She knew she might never find out as much as she'd like about Jack Merlin's murky past, but it was beginning not to bother her so much. Somewhere along the way, she'd realized that she could trust Jack; and she'd accepted that she loved him. What would happen next remained to be seen.

Cassie was lost in her pleasant thoughts when Jack stalked into the room, dropping his robe on the floor as he headed for the walk-in closet. "I've got to leave."

"What?" She sat straight up in bed, frowning at his brusque tone of voice. "What's wrong?"

"You'll be here all alone. Five of the dogs are still here, but they know you so that won't be a problem."

"You can't leave! The charity ball is tonight!"

He came out of the closet buttoning a shirt. "I know, and I'm sorry. I'll try to make it back in time if I can. If you have any questions, pull up the file on my computer marked Manor."

"Where are you going that's so—" But before she could finish her question he was gone.

JACK BARELY MADE IT into the car before Russ took off like a rocket down the driveway toward the open gates. Neither spoke the entire way to Kathleen's house. Patrick was there, they had surveillance on the place, what else could they have done? Sent Bridget back to school? Was she any safer there? Was she safe anywhere? Jack tightened his seat belt as the speedometer hit one hundred and ten miles an hour. Would they make it in time?

"Get down," Russ ordered as he took the next corner into the residential area. They were all ranch-style homes, one level with attached one-car garages. Russ pressed a button on the dashboard and the garage door swung upward, closing after he was inside. It was pitch black. Both of them crawled out the passenger side of the car, waiting.

A small chirping sound filled the air, followed by a whistle and then more chirping. Jack chirped back, then waited for the reply, which came immediately.

"It's all right. The dogs are sleeping it off in the back yard." Both of them moved cautiously to follow Patrick into the house to find Bridget and Kathleen waiting for them at the dining room table. Russ had persuaded Kathleen's mother to go on a trip to Florida with friends at his expense. It was one less person to keep track of.

Patrick was worried, and it showed as he spoke softly. "I've arranged for someone to follow you out of here, Russ. They'll deal with anyone who gets in your way or tries to follow you. Jack and I will stay here."

Bridget sat quietly in her chair close beside Patrick. "Are the dogs all right?" she asked, fear making her sound far younger than her years.

"Yes," Jack murmured soothingly, crossing the room to hug her. He pointed to the piece of electronic equipment on the buffet against the wall. "See that thin red stick wiggling up and down across the half circular white background?" Bridget nodded. "What that means is someone has tranquilized them so their breathing is very slow right now. They'll probably sleep until morning, but they'll be fine tomorrow."

Bridget wrapped her arms around his neck and hugged him. "I love you," she whispered in his ear.

"I love you, too," he whispered back. "But it's time to go," Jack said.

Patrick had already put their suitcases in the car and had Kathleen hidden in the back seat. "Remember what I told you," he said to Bridget as she scrambled onto the floorboard in the front seat.

For a fleeting moment her small hand rested on his rough cheek, then she curled into a ball on the floorboards, as he'd directed.

Jack turned out the lights while Patrick made sure nothing entered the garage while the car left. "Are the dogs really going to be all right?" Patrick asked in a hushed voice after he'd locked the door leading into the house.

"You know I don't lie to Bridget. As far as I can tell they're just drugged. If the readings don't get worse, they'll be fine by morning. We can wait for Russ to call in before we take them to the vet to be checked over."

Silence filled the room until Patrick uttered an oath. "All right, for once your blasted love of gadgets has paid off, Jack. There. Are you happy?"

Jack chuckled in spite of the dangerous situation. "Yes. Considering how much I know you hate my 'toys,' as you call them, I am. Admit it, those collars that measure pulse and respiration on the dogs are absolute genius."

"I wouldn't go that far," Patrick returned dryly. "But I will admit that they worked this time."

Jack was happy with that concession. The collars were actually to be used for dogs with health problems. They were not unlike what could be used on humans. Both a loud beeping noise and flashing red lights alerted the owners if their pet was having respiratory or heart problems.

Which was how Patrick had known that someone had tranquilized the Dobermans. And how they could be sure that someone would be making their play tonight.

"How long before they come?" Jack asked.

"Give them another hour, maybe two," Patrick replied. "Most people would be in a deep sleep by then."

Time ticked by slowly. Neither man spoke. As they'd suspected, the enemy came in through the sliding glass doors. There were two of them, and they never saw Jack and Patrick. But they did feel the blows to the backs of their heads that rendered them unconscious. Patrick and Jack eased them to the floor, staying down themselves, waiting to see if more were coming. None did.

The phone rang, and Patrick answered while Jack finished tying up the two men. "Yes."

"Your friends are safe," Willie told him. "And you were right, Flynn was watching the action from a safe distance. Unfortunately he got away. But not without having to shoot two of my men. They were lucky he didn't kill them."

"Thanks, Willie. You can come get these two. I want everyone cleared out of here by daylight if possible."

Rourke set the receiver down, then looked at Jack. "He got away, but at least Bridget is safe."

Jack wasn't surprised. "Then let's get the drugged dogs to their veterinarian," he said, scratching Sheba.

"Go ahead. But after that we're going to have to answer Willie's questions, and it may take all day," Rourke warned. "I'll help you get the dogs out to the car, then find out where you can meet us."

THERE WERE PEOPLE everywhere, and they were enjoying every ounce of Hook hospitality their two-hundred-dollar entrance fee could buy. Not that it was a swinging bash by any stretch of the imagination, but there was a lot of reserved dancing, hors d'oeuvre nibbling and not-so-reserved drinking going on. This was a high-fashion, high-budget crowd, there to see and be seen. When the light was right, Cassie almost had to squint so she wouldn't be blinded by the sparkle of all the opulent jewelry.

Mingling wasn't hard for Cassie; she had attended enough of these occasions to be an old hand at small talk. Being a fairly well-known member of the press didn't hurt, either. It was a far cry from a television spot, of course, but most of those present were not averse to seeing a kind word about themselves in the *Houston Herald*.

In fact Cassie found the publicity seekers gave her more trouble when she tried to slip away unnoticed than any of the security staff. It was a relief when the society columnists arrived with their photographer and took the pressure off her.

Dressed to the nines herself, she also had a problem with one or two gentlemen who had more on their minds than getting their pictures in the paper, but she finally got rid of them, as well. Excusing herself to visit the powder room, Cassie drifted down a back hallway, glad to leave the party behind.

A few moments later she was standing in Marilyn Hook's quiet study, having achieved her objective so easily it frighten her.

No guards, and no locks on the oak file cabinets, either. It took Cassie what seemed to her a long, nervous time to discover why.

The woman had a big ego, but she wasn't a fool. There were records in abundance, even some on the construction companies under her control, but nothing even the slightest bit incriminating. And no sign of what her informant had promised: ledgers containing the day-to-day bribes, payoffs and substandard materials orders.

"Damnation," Cassie muttered.

She found the wall safe, even made a halfhearted stab at opening it like some television sneak thief, but it kept whatever secrets it contained tightly locked up. Though she knew it was insane, that she should rejoin the party and be happy she hadn't gotten caught, Cassie couldn't shake her obsession. To her, half a story wouldn't do.

It was Marilyn Hook who was responsible, and it was she who would pay, personally, without the slightest chance of starting up again when the heat died down.

Another thought caught hold of Cassie's imagination. What if Marilyn wanted the evidence near her, where she could take it out and gloat over it before she went to sleep at night. Maybe it would be locked up, but maybe it wouldn't. Either way, Cassie had to go see.

She left the study and went boldly toward the staircase leading to the upstairs bedrooms. As she had thought, the upper levels were off-limits to guests; a burly security man stood on the second-floor landing, looking alert and calm.

What now? Unlike some of the other guards, he didn't appear at all intimidated by the well-heeled gathering, so she doubted she could bluster her way past him. Force was out as well. The guard was so big he'd probably just laugh at the tiny little derringer she had in her clutch purse.

Maybe she could charm him. Cassie decided it was worth a try, and better than standing in the hallway where someone was bound to come along and ask her what she was doing. She stepped out of the shadows and walked across the marble floor heading for the foot of the stairs and trying to look as if she owned the place.

"Going somewhere?"

Cassie whirled around, her heart in her throat. "I—"

"I like your hair that way."

Jack was gorgeous in a black tux, and it fit him to perfection. His white shirt was pleated and starched, tiny black onyx buttons forming a neat row down the front. His hair was like ebony, sleek and swept back along the sides.

Heedless of the people milling around the massive foyer, he reached out and rested his hands lightly on her waist, taking in the view. She was the most beautiful woman he'd ever seen.

She had French-braided her hair into an elaborate style, with a long string of pale-pink pearls woven in and out of the dark halo crowning her head. Her arms and throat were bare. The beaded black bodice of her gown draped across her breasts, the beads forming a small vee at her waist. Black cashmere flowed from the tightly beaded bodice right down to the tips of her delicate black high-heeled sandals.

"Good plan," he said.

Cassie felt light-headed, relieved, excited and furious at the same time. "Excuse me?"

"Charming your way past the guard," Jack explained, leaning close to whisper in her ear.

"You think so?" she murmured, sliding her arms around his neck, unable to stop herself.

"I know I'd let you go anywhere you wanted to go." If he stayed this close to her for a moment longer he'd cause a scene for sure. He kissed her lightly then stepped back. "But you can never tell about guards. Let's get a drink and talk this over."

"All right."

They moved away from the staircase arm in arm, mixing in with the crowd and accepting two glasses of champagne from a passing waiter. As she sipped at hers, Cassie tried to regain her emotional footing. Granted, he was there now, but that didn't excuse all the worry he'd put her through. For a short time she'd actually felt guilty because of her anger. But she was justified and she knew it.

Jack started to put his arm around her waist and she pulled away. "It's about time you showed up," Cassie said, glaring at him. "I was sick with worry."

"About me?"

She looked away. "Why should I worry about you? You obviously weren't worried about me or my story."

"What I had to do was much more important than a story, Cassie," Jack told her, his eyes flaring with anger now, too. "But this isn't the time or place to discuss it. Besides, you appear to have made up your mind already, so why bother?"

"I'm amazed you came at all."

Jack stiffened. "I thought you might need help. I guess I was wrong." He started to turn away.

"Don't you dare leave, Jack Merlin!" Cassie exclaimed quietly. She grabbed his arm. "I—"

"Need me?"

"Yes!"

Though their heated conversation was quiet, they were still on the receiving end of some curious looks. Jack took her arm again and moved to a less-crowded corner of the ornate room.

"The study didn't yield anything I can use," Cassie informed him. "So I was on my way up to her room."

His expression spoke volumes. "Right up the main staircase in front of everybody?"

"You said it was a good plan," she replied defensively.

Jack sighed. "I was momentarily deranged," he muttered. What an understatement. This woman was driving him stark raving mad. He couldn't believe how close he'd come to ignoring his duty to Bridget and staying with Cassie. But now he knew Bridget was safe and he was free to return. "All right. We know her bedroom is the next place to look. I don't suppose you thought of using the servant's staircase at the back of the house, though, did you?"

"Damn!" Cassie closed her eyes for a moment. She'd forgotten the back staircase was even there. It didn't help her mood to have it pointed out to her so smugly, however. "It's probably guarded."

"We won't know until we try." He handed her his drink. "Stay here. I won't be long."

"But—"

"Don't worry," he said.

He wound his way into the crowd, leaving Cassie to fume alone. She finished her glass of champagne and had started on his by the time he returned.

"Well?"

Jack nodded. "Guarded. But I've arranged a diversion," he told her, glancing at his watch. "Come on. Let's work our way back toward the kitchen."

Just as they reached the broad hall leading to the larger of the mansion's two kitchens, a man dressed in white with a chef's hat perched jauntily on his head came toward them, wheeling a cart bearing a beautiful chocolate bombe. An assistant followed with a similar cart, which held crystal serving plates and gleaming silverware.

"Any trouble, Vincent?" Jack asked.

"Not a bit, sir. Madam Hook's caterers think it's a wonderful gesture," the chef replied as he went past. "Besides, they were running out of hors d'oeuvres."

Jack and Cassie lingered near the entrance to the kitchen long enough to hear the appreciative remarks of the guests behind them, then made their way to the back stairs. The guard there looked much less enthusiastic than the others Cassie had seen. He was also quite rotund, as if kitchen duty was his favorite security post.

"Did you ask?" the guard queried as they approached.

Jack nodded. "The guy on the front stairs said it would be okay, as long as you bring it back here to eat it. He'll cover for you a few minutes while you get some."

"Thanks a million! Chocolate's my favorite!"

He waddled away. Jack and Cassie wasted no time in climbing the narrow stairs to the upper levels. "That was pretty smart, Jack," she said with grudging admiration.

"I arranged it before I left. I mentioned it in the computer files, but I guess it would have been wasted if I hadn't made it back."

So he hadn't forgotten her completely. He had made plans for this night in spite of his emergency. It made her feel better, though she still wanted to know what had been so important that he'd left her.

"No, it wouldn't," she told him. "Chocolate's my favorite, too."

Chuckling quietly, Jack led the way to Marilyn Hook's bedroom. Cassie could be a royal pain sometimes, but he liked her sense of humor under pressure.

"Hold it," he said as she reached for the doorknob.

"Why?"

"It might be rigged into the alarm system." He checked the door thoroughly, ignoring the way Cassie was fidgeting nervously beside him. "Okay. Let's get this over with."

They went inside. Cassie had seen the room on the tour she'd taken, but it still took her breath away. It was more of a presidential suite than a bedroom, with thick carpeting, antique furnishings and more richly woven silk than she'd ever seen in one place.

"Is—"

"Ssh!"

Jack pointed to the walls, then his ear. Cassie nodded. The walls might have ears. Together they began to search the room. Jack's expertise in such matters became quickly apparent when he found the wall safe in scarcely over a minute.

Cassie crossed the room to where he stood looking at the safe with deeply furrowed brows. "What?" she whispered.

"I can't open it," Jack whispered back.

"Why not?"

He shrugged his broad shoulders. "I'm not really much of a safe cracker, Cassie. I have a little gadget for listening to the tumblers," he said quietly, patting his jacket pocket, "but this model has silenced ones. We need an expert. I'm sorry."

"Damnation!" Cassie's face was growing redder by the moment. "I haven't come this far to give up!"

Jack put his hand over her mouth. "Calm down! Maybe she keeps the combination around here somewhere. A lot of people do, you know. Shall we look?"

Cassie nodded and he released her. She went over to search the magnificently carved bedside tables, while he set about checking the drawers of an equally ornate dresser. A heavy scent hung in the air, teasing her senses. There was a cut crystal perfume bottle on the dresser. She removed the stopper and sniffed it. Why was it so familiar?

No time for that now. Long seconds ticked by. Jack was just about to force Cassie to admit defeat when he heard her smother a squeal of joy.

"Jack!"

"Ssh!" He turned to see her standing by the bed, a dark red leather-bound ledger in her hands. "Well I'll be—"

There was a sound in the hallway outside the bedroom door. Then the doorknob rattled. Paralyzed with fear, Cassie watched in horror as the door slowly opened.

That was when Jack jumped on her, knocking her flat on her back as they sprawled across the bed. "Oh, baby," he groaned, his hand rubbing the length of her nylon-clad thigh. "You're the greatest!"

Chapter Twenty-three

"Animals!" Marilyn Hook cried. "Stop that disgusting behavior and get off my bed this instant!"

Jack looked over his shoulder at her, doing his best to ignore the way Cassie was struggling beneath him. Even in this predicament her movements were exciting him and he didn't think Marilyn Hook would be one bit sympathetic to his aroused condition.

In fact, her eyes were twin pools of gleaming rage. "Stop it I said! Two-hundred-dollar riffraff! I'm going to have you locked up and the key destroyed!"

Jack waved at her. "Hi! Why don't you stop yelling and join the party, gorgeous?"

For a brief instant Jack thought he saw her look at him with a degree of interest. Then she took a deep breath and yelled for help. "Knox! Get in here!"

Cassie finally succeeded in pushing Jack off her. He rolled to one side and sat up. She did the same, her panic clearly displayed in her wide blue eyes. "Knox?" she asked weakly, looking at Jack. "Did she say Knox?"

"Couldn't be," Jack muttered in reply. "He's—"

"My heavens!" Anthony Knox exclaimed as he stepped into the room in formal dress. "What do we have here? Cassie O'Connor and her pet arm-breaker caught in the act."

Marilyn Hook peered at Cassie. "Why, it's that snoopy reporter! Do you know the man with her, Knox?" she demanded, regaining her composure and aura of command.

"We weren't formally introduced," Knox replied, "but I know him well enough." He had his gun out now, and looked perfectly capable of using it left-handed. "Hello, Jack. Nice place you sent me to. Very restful. I'll be returning the favor very soon, though I have a much more permanent resting place in mind.''

Suddenly Marilyn howled like a wounded she-wolf. "My ledgers! Put that down, you trollop!" she cried, advancing on Cassie and pointing a bejeweled finger at her. "Knox!"

"Yes, ma'am," he said, crossing the room close beside her. He put the gun to Jack's temple. "Stay nice and still, pal."

"Give me my ledger!"

Cassie hugged it against her breasts. "Never! You're going to pay for all the horrible things you've done, you harridan. I'll see to it! The whole world—"

Marilyn slapped her, leaving a bright red welt on her pale cheek. Jack started to stand up and Knox jabbed him viciously with the barrel of the gun.

"Go ahead, Jack. Give me an excuse."

The older woman was surprisingly strong. Tears of pain stung Cassie's eyes, but she held them back, glaring at her adversary with open hatred. "You murderous old hag!"

Marilyn slapped her again and yanked the ledger from her grasp. "You're not going to tell anyone anything. You're dirt. Nothing more than media scum! What do you know about the way the world works? I've only done what I had to do, the way I was taught—"

"You're crazy!" Cassie shot back. "Building death traps, killing anyone who gets in your way. And now you're going to build a school and murder innocent children, all for the sake of money! If your father and grandfather taught you that, then they were psychopaths just like you!"

Marilyn Hook's raspy breathing caught in her throat with a gurgling sound. "Kill her," she said in a quiet, strangled voice that made even Anthony Knox shudder. "Blow her brains out. Right now."

Jack tensed, ready to snap Knox's other arm like a twig if he so much as moved in Cassie's direction. But Knox just stood there, his gun never moving from Jack's head, gazing at his boss with a smile of perverse fascination.

"I can't do that," he said.

"I gave you an order! Kill her! Kill them both!"

Enjoying Marilyn Hook's red-faced hysteria, Knox grinned and spoke to her calmly. "Come on, Marilyn," he said, using her first name with obvious relish. "The who's who of Houston is downstairs, remember? I can't just blow them away here in your bedroom. We'll do things my way this time."

"I warned you about your insolence!" Her lips were drawn back over her white teeth in a horrible snarl. "Either kill them or give me your gun and I'll do it myself!"

Knox laughed. "As interesting as that would be to watch, I wouldn't hand you a loaded gun on a bet, Marilyn."

"She insulted my Poppa! She has to die!"

Cassie grabbed Jack's hand and squeezed it, terrified by the insane gleam in Marilyn Hook's eyes. The woman was completely unbalanced—a cunning, highly intelligent woman with an ego a mile wide, who felt the world revolved around her, and who would destroy anyone who dared oppose her without a trace of guilt or remorse.

"Don't worry," Knox said, his tone soothing. The old bat was nutty as a fruitcake. If he wanted to get paid and stay out of jail, he had to convince her to see things his way. He turned his gaze to the pair on the bed. "They'll both die. But not here, and not with a gun. We need an accident, don't we Marilyn? Something clean and untraceable, like the others?"

The change in her was immediate, as if some switch had been thrown in the pressure cooker of her brain. Right before their eyes Marilyn Hook became another person, calm and collected, right down to her ingratiating smile. Cassie shivered as she watched and held Jack's hand tighter still.

"Yes," she replied. "Of course. An accident."

"We could take them out to one of the construction sites and—"

"No!" Her voice cracked like a whip. "Stupid! She's obviously been snooping into that part of our operation. Even as dim-witted as they are, the police couldn't fail to make a connection this time. We were lucky enough to get away with faking Lawrence's mugging."

"You're right," Knox admitted. She might be crazy, but she wasn't dumb. "I'm all ears. Boss."

"That's better," Marilyn Hook said, lifting her chin in a haughty gesture of reproach. "We're having a party here. The who's who, as you called them, are nothing but a bunch of liquor-gulping sots."

Knox nodded, his eyes taking on a feral gleam. "I've got you. We pour some booze down their throats, stick them in their car and fake a drunk driving accident. Perfect!"

"Naturally." She glared at Knox, shaking a warning finger at him. "But not too drunk. I want them cognizant. I want them to know exactly what's happening to them as they die, Knox. Do you understand?''

''I wouldn't have it any other way,'' he assured her, laughing as he looked at Jack. ''On your feet, lover boy. You and your snoopy girlfriend are going for a ride.''

''You'll never get away with it,'' Jack told him. He stood up and helped Cassie do likewise, watching for any opportunity to get the gun away from the other man. The time would come, and he would be ready.

''Cassie's boss knows we're here.''

''That's right!'' Cassie said. ''He knows all about you and the story I've been working on.''

In a quick movement that made her gasp, Marilyn Hook grabbed Cassie's face. ''What does he know! Tell me or I'll claw your eyes out, you meddling tramp!''

Cassie shook her head, wrenching free of the older woman's grasp. ''Everything! They've tested the steel and concrete of your latest projects. They know what you're up to and they'll stop you. Killing us won't do any good.''

Marilyn Hook tilted her head back and laughed. ''Is that all? Who did you think you were dealing with? They can't link me to any of that personally. Not without this,'' she added, putting the ledger back in its hiding spot. ''Oh, I'll be inconvenienced, but a person with my connections will ride out the storm virtually unscathed. Why, now that you've warned me, I can probably even stop your paper from printing one word about me.'' She reached out and patted Cassie on the cheek. ''You poor dear. How you've wasted your time! But you were wrong, you know. Killing you will do a great deal of good. It will make me ever so happy!''

With that she waved a hand of dismissal at Knox and left the room to rejoin her guests, an expression of calm, dignified assurance on her carefully made-up face.

''She's mad, Anthony,'' Jack said. ''You know that, don't you? She'll be caught all right, and she'll drag you down with her.''

Knox jabbed the gun into his ribs. ''Of course she'll get caught. Eventually. But not until I've been paid, pal, I'll see to that. And if you think I'm going to hang around afterward you're as crazy as she is. Now move. Down the back stairs.''

They started toward the door, Cassie beside Jack and Knox right behind them, his gun digging into Jack's lower vertebrae. The need for silence was on their side, but Jack didn't fool himself; if push came to shove, Knox would kill them right then and there.

Cassie said, "Don't do this, Knox. Turn yourself in. Marilyn Hook is finished and you know it."

"Do I? All I see are two snoops who made a pretty desperate attempt to get some evidence on her and failed. I think she's right. I think she can get away with it." He chuckled, but kept a close eye on them as he followed them downstairs. "Either way it doesn't matter. I'm doing you two because I'm going to enjoy it. I'd kill you no matter what she said."

"But, Knox—"

"Shut up! One more word before we get outside and it'll be your last, both of you."

They had little choice but to do as they were told. Knox marched them out into the darkness, taking them to the makeshift parking lot, which had been set up for the guests who had driven themselves. The limousines and drivers were out in front of the mansion; this area was quiet and deserted. Jack made one attempt to get a step ahead of him, and got a painful jab in the spine for his trouble.

"Try that again and I'll put a bullet in you. Just one, so you can watch your dear Cassie die first. That's your green Mercedes there, isn't it?"

Jack thought about denying it, then thought of the pistol he had in his glove compartment and said, "Yes, that's it. Look, Knox, if it's money you want . . ."

"Nice try, Jack, but I'm faithful to one employer. And like the lady said, killing you is going to make me ever so happy!" Though the cast on his right arm made him clumsy, he managed to reach into Jack's pocket and get his car keys while still holding the gun on Cassie. "Get in. Oops! Wait a minute." He opened the door and fished around in the glove compartment, coming up with a stainless steel pistol. "Naughty, naughty! Now you can get in. And take this with you."

Jack looked at the bottle of bourbon the other man produced from his jacket pocket. Knox would try to make him drink most of it, then spill the rest on his clothes. Then he would probably knock them both out and drive them to some convenient drop-off or bayou to finish the job. The police might even buy it, for a while at least, until they linked the accident with Cassie's story on Marilyn Hook.

It wouldn't work. But that didn't bother Knox. He wanted them dead and didn't care what happened to his insane boss, as long as he got his money out of her before she went down. That would take a while even if she didn't find some way of keeping Stan Lockwood from going to print with what little he had. And worst of all, she would still probably walk away clear. He'd seen powerful, wealthy people do it before. The waste of it all suddenly got to him.

"I should have killed you," Jack said, his eyes glinting in the thin light of the moon.

Knox shrugged. "We all make mistakes, pal. Now get in the car and start drinking before I put a hole between your eyes. You, too, lady. It's a shame I don't have the time to have a little fun with you first. You've got a nice pair of legs on you."

Something snapped in Jack's mind. He wasn't going to let Knox's job be this easy. He lunged at the other man, grabbing his left hand and forcing the gun into the air. Startled, Cassie ducked down behind the car. She heard the odd, coughing spit of the silencer as Knox squeezed the trigger.

Then she heard another noise. It was a heavy thud, like a sack of garbage hitting the ground. She peered over the fender and saw she hadn't been far wrong; Knox was lying face down on the pavement. Two men stood over him.

"Thanks, Patrick," Jack said.

"Anytime. Just glad I happened to see you two mingling earlier. When you disappeared I thought you might have gone to get the goods on Marilyn and decided I'd better keep an eye peeled in case you ran into trouble."

Cassie joined them. "What are you doing here, Rourke?"

"Is she like this all the time?" he asked Jack.

Jack nodded and put his arm around her waist. "I'm afraid so. Thank the man for saving our lives, Cassie."

"Thank you. Now answer the question."

Rourke chuckled. "I'm supposed to be moving in their circles so I won't attract suspicion," he said, then shook his head and sighed. "It's a good thing, too, but I'll have to find somewhere to stash this guy until my deal goes through. I think he got a look at me."

"The deal? Is it taking place soon?" Cassie demanded, her hands on her hips. She was still shaking, but desperate to salvage something from this horrible evening.

"None of your business," he replied with an amiable grin.

"Look," she returned sharply, "I'm glad you came along when you did, even though Jack seemed to be doing pretty well by himself—"

"Gee, thanks," Jack interjected.

"But I came here to get evidence to back up a story and I'm not going away empty-handed," Cassie continued. "She's a murderer! We can't go back in there, but we found out where she keeps her secret ledgers. Can you get them for us?"

"No."

"Cassie," Jack told her before she could object, "you can't ask him to do that! He's got his own troubles. I'm sorry, but you're just going to have to take the story you already have on her and run that. Maybe it'll rattle her so badly she'll tumble all the way."

"And maybe she won't!" Cassie exclaimed.

"Keep your voice down!" He looked around to make sure no one was coming to investigate. "We've got to get out of here. Either you come willingly or I'll carry you!"

"Dammit, Jack! I—"

He cut her off with a ferocious look.

With a final glare at both men, she turned on her heel and did as she was told. She knew Jack well enough now to know he meant what he said.

"What are you going to do with him?" Jack asked Rourke.

"Stuff him in my van, I guess. He'll hold there well enough until I can figure something else out. Things are going to start jumping around here pretty quickly now."

Jack nodded. "Okay. I'll help you get him there."

"Thanks." They lifted the unconscious henchman between them and started off toward the back of the estate. "Jack? I hate to ask you this, but..."

"Just name it, Patrick. We owe each other so many favors I've lost count. What do you need?"

"You mentioned a story Cassie's going to run?"

"It's not much, but it's all she has now."

Sitting in the car, Cassie heard Jack's remark before the two men carried Knox off into the darkness. "You can say that again," she muttered to herself. "It's all I have."

But would it be enough? It would have to be. And perhaps Jack was right. Maybe the few things they could prove would lead to more, until Marilyn Hook's empire fell like the deranged house of cards it was.

This failure left a bitter taste in her mouth. It had been her last hope. Those ledgers were supposed to reveal who had killed Brian Fenton. And now they were gone. Or were they? Why couldn't she go back in there and try again?

Cassie was out of the car before she realized what she was doing. With Knox taken care of, all that stood between her and those ledgers were a few guards and Marilyn Hook. She could handle both. Taking a deep breath, Cassie walked in the back door.

When Jack came back from helping Rourke, he found the car empty.

Turning, he ran straight into the house, just in time to see Cassie bending down to whisper something into the rotund guard's ear. The guy's stomach jiggled with laughter as he stood aside to let her up the back stairs.

Jack couldn't think of a single way to charm his way past the guard as Cassie had. He lacked the necessary cleavage. Slipping out the back door, he paced around the wooden patio, glancing at his watch nervously. She had two more minutes, then he was going in after her. And if she came out sooner, he was going to strangle her for causing him so much worry.

Cassie swiftly made her way up the narrow back stairs. She paused on the upstairs landing but no one was in sight. Inching forward, she peered around the corner and studied the crowd below her. Finally she spotted Marilyn Hook talking to a group of people on the far side of the room by the piano.

The ledgers were almost hers. Moving quickly she made her way down the hallway to the bedroom. Once inside, she scooped the ledgers up and went back the same way she had come, meeting no one as she hastily made her way down the servant's staircase.

The little guard smiled at her as she walked past. Chocolate glistened on his teeth as he ate another piece of chocolate bombe. "Good night and thanks," she told him.

Cassie slipped out the back door, euphoric, the ledgers held tightly in her arms. She never saw the arm that reached out and curled around her waist, jerking her off balance. As she opened her mouth to scream a hand clamped down tightly over it, pulling her backward.

"Don't you ever pull such a foolish stunt again," a raspy voice whispered in her ear. "Now let's get the hell out of here."

Cassie was shaking, furious with him, but she couldn't protest because Jack was dragging her across the back lawn toward his running car. Once inside, however, the drawn, worried expression on his haggard face made her realize he had more on his mind than her disobedience. She started to ask, then decided her questions could wait until they got home.

It was a very quiet, tension-filled ride. Jack barely glanced at her the whole time, as if he knew what she was thinking and was trying to make a big decision.

As he ushered her through the front door and into the library, Cassie could see the struggle taking place within him. She sat down, watching as he poured them both drinks. What was wrong?

"Here." Jack handed her a short-stemmed crystal glass filled with an amber liquid. "Drink some of this."

Cassie sipped at the strong whiskey, letting the fire of its potency sing through her veins. Finally, when she couldn't stand the silence any longer, she asked, "Are you going to tell me why you had to leave so suddenly last night?"

"Someone tried to kidnap Bridget."

His news shocked Cassie. "Is she all right?" Jack nodded. "Was it Flynn?"

"Men hired by Flynn. And they got away. She's with Russ and Kathleen and they'll do whatever it takes to keep her alive and unharmed. We've learned not to take unnecessary chances."

Cassie could imagine the hell he was going through. Bridget meant so much to him. "What are you going to do?"

Jack shrugged. "Wait. That's all I can do right now. By tomorrow night Rourke may have Flynn."

"Jack, that doesn't explain why you didn't just tell me about it when you left."

He wouldn't look at her. "Cassie, I haven't had to explain myself or my actions to anyone in a very long time. And I knew you'd ask questions."

Cassie was hurt by his words. "And I didn't deserve an explanation?"

"I didn't say that!" Jack jerked off his tie, and unbuttoned the top button of his tux shirt. "Explanations aren't easy for me."

She already knew that, she'd had too few of them from him. But there was more of her involved now. Her heart. It was time to press for some answers. "What was the event you spoke of that destroyed your trust in the world?"

The bomb went off in Jack's memory. Sounds assaulted him, filling his brain with screams, shattering glass and the lethal whir of flying splinters of broken wood. Jack turned away from her, pressing his hands to his eyes until the horrible images faded. Almost losing Bridget brought it back with a vividness he hadn't felt in years.

His face had gone deathly pale. Cassie started to get up to go to him. "Jack—"

"No."

He waved her back to her seat, feeling vulnerable and exposed, unsure of how to relate to her the most difficult pieces of his past. There was no way to candy-coat what had happened, not if he expected to give her the real answer to her question: what had made him the man he was.

Jack's voice was shaky and he didn't look at her as he said, "My wife and five-month-old daughter were blown to bits in an explosion when terrorists bombed a local grocery store in Ireland. The eight people inside the store never knew what hit them, thank God. The dead also included Rourke's wife—pregnant at the time—and his two-year-old son."

Cassie recoiled as if slapped, afraid she might be physically ill. She covered the news everyday, had seen enough destruction to last her a lifetime. But she had never lost someone close to her. Her parents, brother and sister were all alive and well in Kansas.

No wonder, she thought. He was protective, reclusive and intense, afraid to talk about his past or commit himself to a woman. No wonder. "How did you ever cope?"

"I didn't. Not at first. Rourke and I didn't know each other until then.... We met at the hospital. Neither of us had any family left. Together we went on a drunken odyssey. I don't remember most of it, and what I do I wish I could forget. I refused to face or accept what had happened."

Cassie waited quietly, patiently, hoping he trusted her enough now to continue. And he did, seemingly taking some comfort from the telling. His voice grew stronger as he spoke. "I had been living the perfect life, I just didn't know it. I had a wife I adored, a beautiful daughter, a job that paid well. Good friends. It took a tragedy like that to make me see what I had. And to appreciate the value of a good friend."

Cassie nodded. "Russ?"

"None other."

He paused again for a long time and she finally prompted him gently. "Go on."

"Russ gave us something to live for, put a sense of purpose into our lives." Patiently Jack explained how Russ had found them and some of what occurred later.

"That's where you learned your, um, skills?" she asked.

"Some there, some later," he replied. "We made enemies. Eventually we found it wise to leave the country. Men with little to lose do some pretty unusual things to survive, Cassie. We all got very good at finding things and people, and at balancing on the legal line." Jack looked at her intently. "Some things I can't talk about. Do you understand?"

"Yes, I understand."

Cassie was well acquainted with legal balancing acts now. He had done what he had to do in order to save more innocent people, as she hoped to do with Marilyn Hook, who was a sort of terrorist in her own way. As for how he had dealt with them and the things he had done later, she didn't want or need to know. Like her own transgressions, they were better off left in the past.

Jack was looking at her. "I suppose you do at that."

She was beginning to know Jack Merlin quite well, and she knew something else was troubling him. She had the uneasy feeling it didn't have anything to do with his past or Bridget. Cassie realized that left her. "I know it was a crazy thing to do, Jack. But I had to have those ledgers."

"I know." He sighed. "You weren't hurt. That's all that matters."

"Then what's wrong?"

It was not an idle question. He had been in some tight spots before, had been forced to do some terrible things, but what Rourke had asked him to do tonight could be the worst.

What he had to tell Cassie could easily put an end to their tentative relationship. The temptation to put it off was great. What he really wanted to do was take her in his arms and make love to her until they were both exhausted.

But to do so would not only be deceitful, it would be using her in the worst way possible, delaying the inevitable just to have her in his bed tonight. And it was inevitable. He could lose Cassie for taking charge like this, but she and Rourke could both lose their lives if he didn't.

His troubled expression disturbed her. "After this you may not want to know me at all." He ran a hand over his face with a tired sigh. "Cassie, you're not leaving here. You have to keep a lid on this story about the Hook family businesses until Rourke gives the okay."

For a moment Cassie just sat and stared at him, not at all sure she had really heard him correctly. Perhaps the whiskey had affected her more than she'd thought.

"What did you say?" she asked quietly.

"You can't let the story out yet. You can't even let Stan know you've got the proof until—"

"You've got to be kidding!" Cassie interrupted. "I'm not going to back off now."

He understood her anger. "I'm talking about delaying the story, not killing it."

"No! No one interferes with my work, Jack. Not you, not Rourke, nobody!"

She jumped up from the love seat and started to leave the library. Jack caught her by the arms and spun her around, holding her in place. Her gaze seemed to spit blue flame all over him, burning his heart.

"You're not going anywhere. Rourke can't have any kind of leaks at this point. It could cost him his life. Hell," he added desperately, "it could cost you your life! The deal is set for Saturday at midnight. You'll keep quiet and out of sight here until it's all over."

Cassie jerked away from him. "Stop telling me what to do!" she exclaimed loudly. "You know my story won't even appear until after the deal goes through, so what's the problem?"

"What if someone working at the newspaper owes the Hook family a favor and tips them off in advance?"

She stepped back, folding her arms. "That won't happen."

"You can't be sure of that and you know it." He tried to reason with her. "Look, if anything blows this deal, Marilyn Hook is in real financial trouble."

She stared at him mutinously. "So?"

Jack wanted to shake her. "Think, Cassie! She's unpredictable and explosive at best, and is liable to lash out viciously at Rourke or anyone else within range if that deal goes sour."

"I have her ledgers, Jack! She'll find that out soon enough and start cutting her losses anyway, probably before Rourke's deal even takes place!"

"She may find out, but she won't know it's you who took them, because Knox won't be around to tell her we escaped. If anything, she'll probably think Knox took the ledgers to blackmail her and will focus her attentions on finding him," Jack told her. "She'll dig in, not run. Unless you or Stan tip her off as to what really happened by moving on the story too soon. The thought of the public probing into her affairs at such a crucial moment will spook her for sure."

Cassie wasn't buying his logic. "Ordering people's deaths is hardly the act of someone easily spooked, Jack."

"It's the act of a volatile woman with a screw loose somewhere. You insulted her poppa. And you were meddling. She wanted you out of the way for a lot of reasons, and I think this deal is one of them. At the moment her world is in a delicate balance, Cassie, and I can't let you do anything that might upset that balance."

Cassie's mind whirled. This couldn't be happening. "How can you do this to me, Jack?" she asked in a whisper, tears of rage forming in the corners of her eyes.

He didn't answer her. The words seemed stuck in his throat. He'd never liked sacrifices, especially when he was the one on the losing end. And he was losing her; he could tell by the way she was looking at him. Every bit of her hard-won trust in him was floating away.

"You didn't even consider the option of telling me the facts and letting me make my own decision, did you?"

"I thought about it," Jack replied. "But you're obsessed with this thing. Your life is more important than any stupid job, Cassie!" Jack exclaimed.

"Dammit, Jack!" She pulled free of his grasp and backed away from him. "It wasn't your decision to make!"

Jack closed his eyes for a moment, so angry at her he wanted to bellow like a crazed bull, so much in love it scared him. He couldn't let her put her life and Rourke's in danger for a story. Any story. And even if she never forgave him she'd still be alive and he could always hope that one day she would come to understand his actions.

When he opened his eyes again she had turned her back on him. His voice was soft but firm as he told her, "It's out of your hands now, Cassie. I gave Rourke my word. If all goes well Rourke should contact us by midnight tomorrow. You can leave here soon after and still get your story in the paper."

"I see." Her voice was lifeless, flat.

He reached out to touch her, thought better of it, then added, "It'll be over soon, Cassie. Please try to understand."

"It's already over, Jack." Bitterness coated her words. "Don't kid yourself. I understand why you're doing this. I even agree to your terms. But don't you see? It's not what you're doing, it's the way you're doing it that counts. I really thought you were different, that you could handle my doing my job without interfering. I see I was wrong. Again."

With that she walked out of the library and up the stairs to her room, the ledgers in her arms. Jack Merlin was just another mistake, a man she wished she'd never met and wanted to forget she'd ever known.

Chapter Twenty-four

Cassie went to bed, taking the ledgers with her. She studied them page by page, and disappointment over what they held slowly engulfed her in despair. The books did contain names, dates, payoffs, kickbacks paid in order to get jobs. But there was no mention of any smuggling operation.

And nothing on Brian Fenton.

She had failed.

Late the next morning Cassie got dressed. After gathering up her notes and the ledger she went downstairs, intending to work on the word processor in Jack's office.

She arrived just in time to hear Jack lying blithely to Stan Lockwood over the phone. No, he certainly had no idea where Cassie was or what she knew. But she had mentioned another possible source and had probably decided to give it one last shot.

He lied so well. Why had she believed him? Because she wanted to, that's why.

Jack noticed her standing there as he hung up the phone. "Good morning. Afternoon, actually." Rather than answer, she just glared at him. "I see you have all your notes there."

"Brian Fenton wasn't mentioned in the ledgers."

"I'm sorry, Cassie." Her disappointment was an almost tangible thing, and there was nothing Jack could do to help her. "This news isn't going to make you feel any better then." He turned on the answering machine.

A high-pitched male voice blared forth. "To date I have been unable to obtain any information on who had Brian Fenton killed, or who did the actual killing. As usual, if I don't hear from you the search will continue."

Cassie refused to look at Jack. Maybe she had been wrong, maybe Brian *had* committed suicide. But she didn't want to accept that, couldn't believe it.

Her anger and despair made her lash out at Jack. "Some help you've turned out to be."

"You're welcome to work on your story here, if you'd like," he told her, ignoring the acid bite of her tongue. "Are you hungry at all?"

"No. Since you're being so kind as to let me work, dare I ask you to leave me alone so I can do it in peace?"

He stood there for a moment, then turned and left the library without another word. Cassie sat down in the seat he'd just vacated. It was still warm from the heat of his body. She felt like crying.

No, she wasn't going to think about him right now. There was work to be done. Even the bits and pieces she had were quite a coup. She had a story to write. With all the energy she could summon up she began working fiercely. At last the story swallowed her, and Cassie was able to forget everything for a while.

"Feeling better?" Jack asked an hour later. He was leaning against a bookcase, gazing at her uneasily.

Cassie shrugged. "I'll survive."

Jack knew she would, she was a survivor. He set a cup of steaming coffee on the desk and left quietly, heading for the kitchen. At least cooking gave him something to do.

It was a long evening for Jack. Cassie scarcely noticed the hours slipping by. She was so absorbed in her work that when the phone on the office desk rang, all she could do was stare at it owlishly. Jack came in and answered it, listened for a moment, then frowned and handed the receiver to Cassie.

She glanced at her watch. It was twelve-forty in the morning. Judging by his voice, Rourke was every bit as drained and tired as she suddenly felt.

"Is Jack listening in?" he asked.

Cassie glanced at Jack, then quickly away. "No."

"Good. I have the feeling he's not going to like this. I've got an exclusive for you, Cassie, but there's a string attached," Rourke told her.

She sighed and rubbed her eyes. "I don't make deals, Rourke."

"It's good. Better than anything you planned on. But you'll owe me a favor and I'll make damned sure you live up to it. Now, do we have a deal, or do I call one of the other papers?" he asked brusquely. "Hurry. I can't sit on this for long."

A favor? Great! With all she owed what was one more. And a little tickle of instinct told her she would rue the day if she didn't take him up on this.

"Okay. I accept."

As Jack watched, wondering what his good buddy Patrick was up to now, Cassie started furiously scribbling down notes, her eyes getting wider by the moment. Jack tried to see what she was writing, but she turned her back to him. Finally, just as he was about to yank the phone away from her, she passed him the receiver and got to her feet, gathering her notes as she went. Rourke spoke briefly with Jack and then hung up.

"May I leave now?" she asked.

Jack nodded as he placed the receiver back on the cradle. "Yes, but—" She cut him off by leaving the room.

He walked with her out to the car. "Cassie—"

"No, Jack, not now."

He watched her leave, feeling confused but somewhat encouraged. She hadn't said never.

"Please don't take too long," he whispered to the darkness.

FOR THE FIRST TIME in her career, Cassie stopped the presses. The Sunday paper was delivered late and had a few typos, but the bold headlines made up for the inconvenience. Marilyn Hook and some members of her family had been arrested by the FBI for attempting to sell a famous piece of art stolen by her father during World War II. Over the years the Hook family had sold various other pieces to private collectors as the need for money arose. The intended buyer of the piece had expertly eluded the FBI trap. Hook family members couldn't be reached for comment.

On Monday the front page featured a picture of a hamburger sack bearing a letter from a young construction worker who had allegedly witnessed the Hooks' involvement in construction fraud. An investigation into his death was pending.

Because Cassie had already done extensive research, her paper had an astounding lead over the other media. Day after day under her byline Cassie reported another piece of the story she'd worked on for the last few months. She was on all the national news stations, an instant celebrity herself.

As the story unfolded, Jack watched and worried from afar. He was happy for her success. She'd worked hard and she deserved all the rewards coming her way. But he wanted her for himself. How long would the media make a circus out of her? How long could she stay mad at him?

Lately, to keep his mind off his troubles, he had taken to stripping the ancient wallpaper off the walls of the spare bedrooms. It was a filthy, grubby job he detested but he found it preferable to lying in bed unable to sleep. In the wee hours of the morning, a man in the throes of unrequited love would do some weird things to exhaust himself so he wouldn't have to think.

CASSIE STARED at the latest information she'd managed to glean out of her contacts. The puzzle pieces weren't fitting together as they should.

Anthony Knox had made a deal with the authorities and was talking freely about his murderous pacts with Marilyn Hook. But he had steadfastly refused to admit to killing Brian Fenton or blowing up the miniwarehouse.

Marilyn wasn't doing much talking, but she could hardly deny her involvement in construction fraud. There was damning evidence aplenty. After making copies of the ledgers, Cassie had gladly turned the originals over to the proper authorities.

Yet there was still no hint of the smuggling her source had alluded to. And the most troublesome point of all, Marilyn Hook had obviously not known it was Cassie and Jack who were on to her until the very end. Evidently Knox hadn't been lying; for Marilyn also denied having known anything about Brian's death.

That meant they must have gotten too close to something—or someone—else. It didn't make sense, but her informant had made it clear that someone among the Hook connections knew Brian had been investigating them—and had him killed. And Cassie wasn't giving up until she found out who and why.

Her informant had seen to it that Brian's trail had led her to the Hooks and construction fraud, but she was getting the distinct impression he had stumbled onto something much worse. But what? Did it involve Flynn? Smuggling? And if Marilyn Hook knew anything about it, what had her too scared to talk about it even when she needed to plea bargain?

Unable to answer those questions, Cassie asked herself some even tougher ones. Other than the police, who knew the miniwarehouse was full of Brian's possessions? Stan Lockwood.

Who had known enough about what she and Jack were doing to feel threatened? Stan Lockwood. Who had been aware of Cassie's decision to investigate Brian's death? Stan Lockwood.

Had he betrayed her? Cassie couldn't believe it. Despite her protests, Stan had told Mrs. Carlyle everything from the very beginning. And Mrs. Carlyle was a good friend of Marilyn Hook's.

The idea was crazy! But Cassie had to check it out anyway. She looked around the empty newsroom. Everyone had gone home for the day. Including upper management. Her office would be empty. The temptation was too great for her to pass by.

Cassie stood up and, with her doubts in tow, headed for Mrs. Carlyle's office. Knocking loudly on the door, she waited for someone to answer, but no one did. The lock wasn't that easy for someone of her meager talents to open, but she managed it.

Closing the door silently behind her she proceeded into the office. The first thing she saw was a broken red shoe, the same shoe Mrs. Carlyle had been wearing the day Cassie had stepped on her toes. At least she hadn't asked her to replace or repair it.

Cassie sat down at the desk, turned on the green-shaded lamp, and pulled the first file drawer open. Methodically, she went through each file, each drawer. Nothing. Disgusted, Cassie bent two hair pins and unlocked the long narrow drawer above her legs. It contained all the usual office paraphernalia, a few personal items and slender vial of perfume.

She picked it up and sniffed the bottle. The scent was familiar. Where had she smelled this recently? Suddenly a light turned on inside her muddled brain. Marilyn Hook's bedroom. Mrs. Carlyle and Marilyn Hook wore the same perfume. Why hadn't she noticed this earlier? It was a connection, but it didn't tell her a damn thing. The women were friends. And had been for years. So they liked the same perfume. So what?

Still, as she took another sniff, some other memory tickled her senses. Cassie couldn't put her finger on it but she also couldn't get it out of her mind.

She looked at the vial. It was an exclusive scent, not a brand name. Perhaps if she knew who had it formulated in the first place, the other pieces would fall into place. The address on the bottle identified a location in a small but expensive mall. Cassie glanced at the large round clock on the far wall of Mrs. Carlyle's office. If she hurried, she could make it there before they closed for the evening.

She walked into the perfumery's door at two minutes before closing time. The clerk gave her a congenial smile, but Cassie knew the young woman was ready to leave. This could work in her favor.

"Hi, I won't keep you long." Cassie handed her a piece of paper with the information from the label written on it. "I'd like some of this perfume."

The woman took the piece of paper and went into the back room. Cassie looked around the exclusive shop. It was tiny, the stained-glass windows surrounded by intricate bevels making it appear larger. An antique side table served as a counter between the clerk and the customer. Off to one side elegant chairs were set around a small table, giving the impression of coziness. Other than the sign on the door nothing revealed what this shop actually was. There were no soaps or scents one could pick up and sniff.

"Excuse me." The clerk waited until Cassie turned to face her. "This perfume is on our restricted list. No one but the originator of the scent may buy it without authorization."

Cassie kept an innocent expression as she walked toward the other woman. "You couldn't sell me just a tiny bit? My lover is absolutely captivated by it."

"I'm sorry, that's just not possible."

Cassie pretended to think about that for a moment, then asked, "Could you possibly make me a perfume quite similar, tonight?" For a fleeting second the woman allowed her dismay to show and Cassie felt she could read her mind. It was quitting time.

"I can't give you the exact same scent and you have to understand that even one tiny difference in the formula could result in a completely different reaction to the senses. It would be better for you to let us take a few days, and formulate a scent exclusively for you, for your skin and your man."

The woman was good. She had Cassie almost convinced she needed a scent formulated just for herself. Unfortunately it wouldn't solve her problem. She needed a name, not a perfume. "I don't know, he's so attracted to this particular scent I'm not sure anything else would do." Cassie hesitated a moment, then asked very softly. "Can you tell me who owns the rights to this perfume? Perhaps I can persuade the person to allow you to sell me some of it."

"It's worth a try," the clerk said, smiling. "Let me get you the information." The woman was back in less than a minute with a business card. "I can tell you right now, your chances of getting him to agree aren't good," she said, handing Cassie the card.

Cassie looked at the name, then glanced up at the clerk, her surprise showing. This was a connection she hadn't anticipated. "I've heard of him and his family."

''Lately there isn't a person in Houston who hasn't.'' The woman walked toward the door, gently but firmly ushering Cassie out. ''If you don't have any luck, come back. I'm sure we can develop something that would be perfect for you.''

Cassie smiled. ''Thank you. I will.''

Why hadn't she seen this sooner? Cassie resisted the urge to jump up and down for joy. Instead she walked sedately back to her car. Allen Hook. She repeated his name again and again. If he was the one, then some of the odd pieces were beginning to fit into the right niches.

The temptation to pick up the phone and call him almost overwhelmed her, but common sense prevailed. She had to think this through. This wasn't the time to make reckless moves.

Chapter Twenty-five

Cassie was sitting in Stan's office the next morning when he arrived. She'd had plenty of time to think things over and make plans.

"Good morning, Stan."

Stan set his cup of coffee down, then sat behind his desk before asking rudely, "What do you want?"

Cassie smiled at him. "You're such a lovely person first thing in the morning, Stan. Get up on the wrong side of the bed? Or was it the wrong one?" He frowned at her and Cassie's smile widened. "Have some coffee, Stan. You're going to need it."

"Cut the chitchat," he ordered. "State your case, then get out of here. And wipe that smile of your face."

Unable to stop herself from smiling, she leaned back in the chair, waiting for the right moment. "Did you betray me, Stan?" He choked on the swallow of coffee he'd just taken, his face turning red.

"What!" Grabbing a tissue he wiped his mouth and chin. "What are you talking about?"

Her smile was gone. "Everything I told you from the very beginning concerning Brian, you told to Mrs. Carlyle. Didn't you? Not just what she needed to know. *Everything*."

He looked at her quizzically, not understanding her accusing tone of voice. "Of course. She's my superior."

"I put my trust in you, Stan. And you betrayed me."

"Betrayed you?" Stan shook his head. "Cassie, what in the hell are you talking about?"

"Mrs. Carlyle is a close friend of Marilyn Hook's. I told you, you told her, and she in turn told Marilyn."

Stan was shocked. "That's a load of garbage, Cassie."

"Oh, is it? Who else knew I was specifically investigating the circumstances surrounding Brian's death? Who else knew where Brian's things were stored? Where I lived? What I was trying to find out? Only two people—you and Mrs. Carlyle."

"That's preposterous, Cassie."

"Is it? Then help me prove it." She leaned forward in her chair. "I was in that miniwarehouse when someone set it afire, Stan."

His eyes opened wide. "You're serious!"

"I've had my home broken into, searched, and bugs planted there. Anthony Knox paid me a midnight call and wanted to kill me. He worked for Marilyn Hook. All the pieces fit, Stan."

He sat there, stunned by her announcement. "Cassie, I don't know what to say."

"You owe me, Stan, and I've come to collect."

Stan didn't answer her right away.

He was eyeing her warily now. "What do you want from me?"

"A favor. I want you to come with me to meet someone. Going alone would not only be foolish, it would be dangerous. And I want a witness."

"When?"

She stood and pulled his phone toward her. "Right now. But first I have to make a call."

Cassie dialed the number she'd memorized last night. After having her call switched from one office to another in the process of tracking him down, her quarry finally came on the line.

"Hello, how may I help you?"

"Cassandra?" Cassie asked.

His stunned silence told her exactly what she wanted to know. "You're supposed to say Elizabeth isn't here," Cassie reminded him. He didn't answer her. "We'll meet by the merry-go-round in the park in ten minutes. If you're not there I'll tell the police you're involved in the mess up to your ears."

Cassie set the phone down. "We'll have to run."

Stan sprinted out of his office behind her and through the newsroom, ignoring the startled looks the rest of the staff gave them on their way out.

"I'll drive, I've done this before." Cassie was backing out of the parking space before Stan had both feet in the car. "Put your seat belt on," she ordered, stepping on the gas. Her little car flew forward into an opening in the heavy traffic. The breeze coming through the open windows cooled them some in the morning heat and high humidity.

They sped through the industrial area and into a housing district, Stan holding on for dear life.

"Who are we meeting?"

Cassie took a corner too fast, her car skidding into the other lane on the loose gravel. She maneuvered it back before answering. "Allen Hook."

"Why?"

She stomped on the gas, racing through a yellow traffic light. "If I'm right he's my original source, and someone else's source as well." Cassie pulled to a screeching halt under a shade tree beside the park. Opening her purse, she took out her gun.

"What are you going to do with that?" Stan asked, staring at the shiny blue-black steel.

Cassie smiled. He was almost squealing with nervousness. She checked the gun, then put it back into her purse. "I don't know how Allen's going to react. It's wise to be prepared." Jack Merlin had taught her that. "Come on, let's walk over to the merry-go-round. And don't speak unless I ask you to."

They were almost at their destination when a man stepped from behind a tree, startling her. "I chose well," he said. "You stopped the witch cold." He smiled. "You never suspected it was me, until now, did you?" She shook her head slowly. "No one would ever suspect Allen Hook of betraying his family or jeopardizing his income. Lawrence, yes. Poor Lawrence. But not me."

Cassie shook her head again, stunned but relieved. It really had been Allen Hook all along. Until this moment she hadn't been absolutely sure. He was good-looking, flamboyant and had a reputation for being out for a good time and living life in the fast lane. Right now, however, he looked much older than forty-one years.

"How did you discover it was me?" he asked, leaning against the huge tree, his fingers laced behind his back.

"I was looking for a connection between your family and my newspaper. I found one. You have exclusive rights to a perfume worn by both Marilyn Hook and Mrs. Carlyle."

He congratulated her quietly. "Good work. What do you want now?"

"I want to know what else is going on."

A stunning smile was flashed at her, a smile that had broken many a heart. "You expect me to give you a reward for a job well done?" he asked.

"No, I want the rest of the story you promised me," she told him. "The whole truth."

"What else could I possibly give you? You have the disk from the safety deposit box and the ledgers," he added. Her eyes jerked open wide. "Yes, I put Brian's disk there on purpose, to see how far you'd go to get a murderer. You didn't disappoint me."

She was nervous. Perspiration stained her printed silk blouse. He seemed too complacent to her. "You chose me for my tenacity. I'll focus it on you if I have to. What else do you know?"

He didn't answer her, wouldn't look at her.

"Look, Allen. I intend to expose you to the public in full. I have a witness," she reminded him, indicating Stan who was standing quietly off to one side. "You knew what was happening all along, but didn't try to stop it. You're as guilty as Marilyn is."

"No, I'm not!" he protested vehemently, gesturing with his hands as he explained. "Yes, I knew about the inferior construction materials, but I didn't know about her murdering construction employees who threatened to talk, until the last one." He rubbed his eyes, remembering. "I overheard Marilyn ordering his death." Shaking his head, he sat down on the grass, his hands clasped loosely between drawn-up legs. He looked up at Cassie, squinting from the bright sun. "I was too late. He was dead when I got to the site."

Cassie sat down beside him, her purse in her lap. "Why won't Marilyn talk, plea bargain?"

"She doesn't dare. There's someone else involved she's more afraid of than the police...."

"Who?" Cassie asked.

Allen considered the question. "All right, Cassandra, I'll make a deal with you. One last tip, but to get it you have to agree to keep me out of your story. There are three women I gave that scent to. Think fund-raiser."

"Fund-raiser?" Marilyn Hook. Mrs. Carlyle. Both were fund-raisers in their own right. Her eyes went wide as she made the connection. "Leonore Xavier!"

"Bingo," Allen agreed soberly. "Lenny's been pulling Marilyn's strings for a few years now. First she helped her with some shady loans when the oil glut hit, then she showed her a few unethical business practices to help things along. Finally she used Marilyn's complicity in the illicit schemes to slowly take hold of the Hook empire."

"Why didn't you try to stop them?" Cassie asked.

Allen gave her a sad smile. "You don't understand. Lenny Xavier and I have been lovers off and on for years. I was in this with Lenny from the beginning. I was bargaining for complete control of the Hook empire."

"Then why feed me the information to put them away?" Cassie asked, puzzled.

"I draw the line at murder."

Cassie knew there had to be more to it than that. "What else?"

"I knew you were good." Allen plucked a blade of grass and chewed on it thoughtfully. "Lenny was getting carried away. At the rate she was going, there weren't going to be any businesses left for me to take over. So I decided both women would have to go."

She drew back from him. "What do you mean?"

"Oh, I never intended to kill them, just expose their business practices." He paused for a moment. "But Marilyn was still family. All I intended to do was have her take a fall for the construction mess, not the murder. They were all ruled suicides or accidental deaths anyway," he explained.

Cassie couldn't keep the sharp sting out of her voice. "They were still murders."

"I know, but Marilyn was family," Allen replied. "Anyway, I knew Lenny would back off when she saw the ax was ready to fall on Marilyn. She wouldn't want to be implicated with her. Then I planned to step in and take over the family businesses—clean them up and run them right."

"What went wrong?"

"Between them they didn't let me know enough of what was going on." He sucked in a deep breath, then slowly let it out. "I didn't know, or figure it out, until Brian Fenton turned up dead."

Cassie blanched at the mention of Brian's name. "You were feeding Brian information?"

"Yes." Allen plucked another blade of grass. "I had always admired his work. He was a good reporter and he discovered a lot based on the tidbits I was feeding him."

"Who had him killed?" Cassie asked.

Allen shook his head. "I don't know, it might have been a joint effort. Lenny was keeping things from me, helping Marilyn to cover things up, introducing her to the sort of people who would comply with her wishes." He looked at Cassie, needing her to understand his position. "They didn't give me a chance to stop them."

"What's Lenny going to do now?"

Allen dropped the blade of grass and leaned back on his hands. "She's going to give an electronic schematic she purloined from a Hook defense contractor to a man named Patrick Rourke. They used the Irish fund-raiser as a cover for their meetings. Lenny had to be sure this guy was legitimate.''

"Did you say *give*?"

Allen nodded. "Yes. Her dear departed husband supported the cause in Ireland for many years. Though Lenny loved her husband in her own way she couldn't see parting with cash, her cash. So she came up with another plan to deliver what her husband had promised.''

"Which explains why Mrs. Xavier wouldn't let go of the Hook empire," Cassie said. But Patrick Rourke? She didn't think so. "Can you describe the man you know as Patrick Rourke?"

He did so. Cassie felt a chill run up her spine in spite of the heat. It wasn't Rourke. But she thought she knew who it was. Flynn. Explaining the situation to Allen Hook might spook him, though, so she kept quiet.

Allen moved restlessly. "I think Brian discovered this, too."

"Do you know for a fact that they had him killed?" Cassie asked, desperately.

"No, but I know Lenny knew about him. She and Patrick Rourke were discussing business once and his name came up."

"When did you decide to let me help you out of this mess you'd created?''

He smiled grimly. "Aptly put. Once I knew Lenny knew about Brian, my suspicions were aroused. I began keeping much closer tabs on her. We became lovers again. Lenny ordered the mini-warehouse destroyed." Allen paused and for the first time he acknowledged Stan's presence. "She was acting on information provided by Mrs. Carlyle."

Stan glanced at Cassie. Had she been right all along? Was Mrs. Carlyle involved, too?

"Lenny knew I was investigating Brian's death?" Cassie asked "Through Mrs. Carlyle?"

Allen crossed his ankles. "Indirectly. The two of them have confided in each other for years. And Lenny never gave Mrs. Carlyle any reason to doubt her trustworthiness." Stan breathed an audible sigh of relief. "Still, all Lenny knew was that the paper was looking into Brian's death, not who. It wasn't until Lenny and Patrick Rourke compared notes one evening that she knew it was you. Rourke had tried to have your friend Jack Merlin killed, and you were with him."

"I can't believe you didn't speak out. Try and stop them."

"I considered doing so, and I'd about decided I would have to come forward and tell you everything." He paused. "Then Lawrence ended up dead."

Cassie brushed a trickle of sweat from the side of her face. "I thought he was my source."

"I knew you would. And I didn't want to end up just like him. At the time I didn't know if it was Marilyn or Lenny behind his death. I only knew it wasn't the random mugging the police thought it was."

Cassie's voice grew loud with censure. "So you were just going to let them get away with all they had done, and were planning to do?"

"I didn't know what to do and I didn't have to decide. You were on my side, you weren't going to give up. Because of your continuing investigations you showed Lenny how much of a dead weight Marilyn was turning out to be, along with her hired gun, Anthony Knox. And because of her own failures to stop you she was more than ready to throw Marilyn Hook to the wolves. She anonymously tipped off the FBI about the art deal, so that Marilyn would get caught."

He was partly right, but the FBI had already known about the deal from Patrick Rourke—the real Patrick Rourke. "Wasn't Lenny worried that Marilyn would tell all?"

Allen chuckled. "And dig an even deeper grave for herself? Not likely. Lenny can be quite a charitable soul when she wants to be. But she's ruthless to her enemies, especially right now. The gout in her big toe has been acting up and she's hell to be around."

"If she should learn of this meeting, she'll consider you an enemy, too." Cassie was already formulating a plan.

He was suddenly more cautious. "And?"

"I want to set Lenny up."

Allen sat up straight. "You're crazy!"

"And I need your help," Cassie told him.

He was shaking his head. "No way, that's suicide. My own life is more important than seeing justice done."

"Oh, is being killed by Lenny better than suicide?" Cassie asked. "If she finds out you've talked to me the results will be the same."

Allen knew what she said was true. And nothing prevented Cassie from exposing him. She hadn't accepted his terms yet. "All right. I'll do it, on one condition. You guarantee me my freedom. I'll do whatever I have to do, but no charges will ever be brought against me."

"I'm sure that can be arranged."

LEONORE XAVIER was so naive, Flynn thought. He wasn't even involved in the situation in Ireland any longer. But she didn't know it. She'd found his name amongst her dead husband's papers and had proceeded to contact him through the method described.

At first he'd been hesitant to respond. But greed and revenge had won out. Using Patrick Rourke's name was a twist he'd particularly enjoyed, and the woman had accepted his change of name easily, completely understanding his need for anonymity considering his supposed activities. She was going to give it to him, believing him a courier for the causes her husband believed in. But he didn't intend to turn it over to anyone. He would sell it, and keep the proceeds all to himself.

Too bad he couldn't get the jewelry back, too. That was completely on his shoulders. It had been a foolish mistake on his part to use the bank recommended by Leonore Xavier. But he would have to salvage what he could.

Chapter Twenty-six

Just how far did Mrs. Xavier's reach extend? Cassie couldn't be sure, but felt there was one person she probably could trust. Patrick Rourke. He wanted Flynn, he had the FBI connections she needed, and besides, this was her chance to return the favor she owed him.

Unfortunately, now that Russ, Kathleen and Bridget were in hiding, the only way Cassie could think of to contact the elusive Patrick was through Jack Merlin. As personally distasteful as that would be for her, she had no choice.

After numerous phone calls and repeatedly getting the answering machine, Cassie finally got through to him. She gritted her teeth and said, "Jack, this is Cassie."

"At last! I was beginning to think you'd never talk to me again. Cassie, I'm sorry, I—"

"Save it," she interrupted. "I'm only calling because I have to. Can you contact Patrick for me?"

There was a long silence. When Jack did speak, his tone was defiant and much cooler than it had been only a moment before. "I can. But not unless you tell me why."

"I need his help."

"Why?"

Though tempted to yell, Cassie just sighed and began to explain patiently. "Because I need contacts that only he has." There was another lengthy silence. He was waiting for more. "It concerns Flynn."

"Flynn! Cassie, I forbid—"

"Dammit!" she exploded. "You can't forbid me to do anything! I need to talk to Patrick. Soon. If you really are sorry for what happened before, prove it by having him get in touch with me.''

Again it took a while for Jack to answer. "All right," he agreed reluctantly. "But—"

"No. This time, you have to promise to keep out of my way. I mean it, Jack. Don't interfere with my work or it'll be a cold day in hell before you hear from me again!''

Cassie slammed down the phone, angry but triumphant. After the way he used her, it felt good to give him a dose of his own medicine. Though it was a gamble, she felt certain her threat would force Jack to do just as she asked.

She was right. At six that same day Patrick Rourke was pounding on her apartment door. She opened it and stood back to let him enter. He didn't look happy.

"What do you need?''

Cassie came right to the point. "I need your FBI contacts. Do you want another chance to get Flynn?''

"Explain," Patrick said, sitting down on the sofa.

Quickly and concisely Cassie told him everything Allen Hook had told her about Flynn and Mrs. Xavier. "Are you interested?''

"You know I am.'' His haunted gaze sought hers. "What do you get out of this?''

Cassie didn't waver. "I'll find out who killed Brian Fenton. And I'll gain immense satisfaction from seeing the people responsible arrested and tried for murder." Patrick seemed to understand her feelings.

"How soon will the exchange take place?''

"Tomorrow night. They finished work on the schematic today. She should have one in her possession by then. Allen Hook will keep me informed.''

Patrick leaned back into the cushion. "You want to be there when they're caught, don't you?''

"Yes. I'll promise to stay out of the way, but I won't tell you the place unless I go along.''

He stood up. "I'll see what I can do, but I'm making no promises.''

"I guess that'll have to do." Cassie walked him to the door. "But, Patrick, please don't tell Jack about this.''

Patrick looked at her in silence, then pulled the door shut behind himself. He wouldn't promise not to tell. He was already late for dinner at Jack's and it might well be impossible to keep this from him.

As he'd expected, Jack didn't give him much choice. The moment he stepped into the living room, Jack glared at him and demanded, "What's going on?"

"Cassie asked me not to tell you about it." Jack's expression indicated that he wasn't taking that news well. Patrick continued. "But, I didn't promise I wouldn't. Sit down, Jack. You're not going to like this one bit." Patrick explained the situation.

Jack's face was grim. "You're right, I don't like it. It's too dangerous. Flynn is too unpredictable."

"I agree, but it's not your decision or mine to make." Patrick looked at his friend compassionately. "You can't rule her life."

Jack knew Patrick was right. He'd already made one gigantic error in that direction. "I'm going to be there, too." He stopped Patrick before he could protest. "In case either of you need me."

"You can't interfere," Patrick told him, waiting until he had Jack's assurance that he wouldn't before continuing. "I need to use the phone to set this up."

Jack nodded. "Patrick, how does she look?"

"Determined."

Patrick walked into the inner sanctum and sat down to make a call. The phone rang several times before someone finally answered. "Willie, I've got some wonderful news for you. You're not getting any sleep tonight."

The next morning Cassie met with the FBI for five hours of intense questions. Once Allen had been assured of his own freedom he'd told Cassie everything he knew. And now Cassie became a willing fountain of information.

She told the FBI that according to her informant, Lenny Xavier had possession of the schematic, and the exchange was to take place tonight, at the airport. With some checking they verified that one Lian Francis Dougell, alias Flynn, was booked on four different flights out of Houston, all eventually culminating in London.

Cassie had clearly stated her intention to be at the airport, and short of detaining her, they couldn't stop her from appearing in a public place. Reluctantly they agreed to leave her alone, as long as she followed their directives.

The airport was crowded with people coming home, others leaving, still others waiting to greet or saying goodbye to loved ones. Allen Hook kept his word to Cassie, informing the agents anonymously when Lenny Xavier left her home.

Cassie stood by one of the agents, listening in on his earphone. "She's been spotted coming in through the luggage area and is now on the escalator going up to level one. Khaki-green jumpsuit, wide gold belt, matching necklace. Red high heels. She's carrying a thin red clutch bag. No disguise. She matches her photographs.''

The agent looked at Cassie. "Stay out of the way, and don't mix with the crowd. If she recognizes you, she'll panic. And if that happens, her contact will get away."

Cassie nodded. "I'll stay back."

Jack Merlin and Patrick Rourke were monitoring everything from a security center, along with a few of the FBI men and some people from airport security. There was a whole wall of view screens revealing scenes from around the airport.

"Any sign of her contact?" Patrick asked.

"No. With the information you supplied I think we can all agree he'll be disguised in some way," a burly agent replied. "What we've got to do is see through it."

Jack had located Cassie on one of the security cameras, and his eyes were taking in her every movement. "What about the women's rest rooms?" Jack asked. With his size Flynn could get away with looking like a woman.

"They're all covered by female agents."

The waiting was almost intolerable. They were so close. Cassie was determined not to fail. She would get the answers she wanted, Flynn would be stopped, and Brian would be avenged.

"She's off the escalator and heading left. She appears completely at ease."

The agent beside Cassie began walking in that direction and she stayed discreetly in his shadow.

Cassie suddenly grabbed the coattail of the agent in front of her and moved up beside him. "The stocky woman in the cream seersucker pants outfit. She's missing the little finger on her left hand. And she's carrying a red clutch bag."

"Got her. Now stay back," he ordered, then relayed the exact description and position to the others. "Watch for an exchange of purses, I repeat, watch for the exchange of red purses."

Cassie slowed down. She didn't want to interfere or bungle things for the agents but her eyes were glued to the woman in cream.

The sound of Jamaican music was becoming louder as they moved in the direction of its source, a big chrome boom box. Four tall black men dressed in tropical printed shirts and shorts were standing around it, dancing and putting on an impressive show.

Cassie was so distracted by them that she almost missed the exchange of purses. Running forward she grabbed the agent's arm and cried, "The exchange has taken place!"

He nodded and waved her out of harm's way. "Move in!"

As agreed, Cassie stayed back, watching as a swell of agents, dressed in every conceivable style, moved in on Lenny Xavier. At that very moment Flynn realized he'd been set up. He pulled a gun from the pocket of his pantsuit and began firing wildly. The agents shifted their entire attention to him.

"Hold your fire! I repeat, no shooting. There are too many bystanders!" one agent yelled.

Flynn ran down the corridor, still firing blindly. People were screaming, crying hysterically and diving for cover as the shots went on and on. Mrs. Xavier, meanwhile, took off in the opposite direction.

Cassie was more frightened than she had ever been in her life. She knew this woman was almost as dangerous as Flynn. But after all Cassie had been through to arrange things, nothing on earth was going to be allowed to prevent the capture of Lenny Xavier. She ran down the corridor, pushing her way through the chaos.

Did Lenny have a gun? Probably. Cassie had hers, too, but decided not to produce it unless absolutely necessary. Instead she grabbed Mrs. Xavier from behind, pinning her arms to her sides and wrestling her to the ground.

"You're not going anywhere," Cassie spit out through clenched teeth. "Except to jail."

"Let me go!"

Lenny struggled like a wildcat, but Cassie held on for dear life. At last the other woman ceased her thrashing and started to cry. Someone touched Cassie's shoulder.

"Are you okay?"

Jack was kneeling beside her, and his hand cupped the side of her face gently. Her eyes went wide with total surprise. "I'm fine. But Flynn—"

"I know. I'll be back."

Cassie watched him jump up, his running form not far behind Patrick's. They leaped over dropped luggage and crawling people in their pursuit of Flynn. There were agents in front of and behind them, all after the same person. At last, the agent Cassie had been following came over to join her. He slipped handcuffs onto Lenny Xavier. One down, one to go. How could he possibly get away?

Jack and Patrick were running side by side. "He's going to take a hostage," Patrick warned.

"I know. He'll get boxed in and use whoever he can to stay alive." Jack gasped for breath. "Should we back off? Some of these people are going to get hurt."

"Even if we back off, the agents won't." As they approached the end of the terminal they slowed to a walk.

Flynn was standing a few yards away, in front of a door marked exit, and he had an arm wrapped around a terrified young woman's throat. His gun was pressed into her temple. "Stay back, or I'll kill her," he threatened, his brogue thick. "Move back!"

The agents were doing as he requested.

"Keep moving." Suddenly he shoved the girl forward, and she floundered wildly, knocking the red purse out of his hand.

He slipped into the stairwell, abandoning the red clutch in his haste to get away. Jack and Patrick pushed their way through the throng to get to the stairwell.

On the stairs they found his cream top, and a few steps later a brown wig. At the next exit the seersucker slacks lay crumpled on the ground. The exit led to the baggage pickup area and from there to an underground parking garage.

They looked at each other. "We'll never find him here."

Jack agreed with him. "No, we won't. They can check every car and plane leaving here and they won't catch him." Together they climbed back up the stairs and into the crowd of people, neither expressing their feelings.

Flynn had gotten away. They didn't have to tell her, she knew it from the expressions on their faces. She walked up to the two men, slipping between them, one arm around each of them. "Come on. Let's get out of here. If they have questions, the agents know how to contact us."

Together they left the terminal, walking out into the daunting heat and high humidity of the summer evening. The air conditioning in Jack's car was a welcome relief.

Patrick slouched in the back seat, his eyes closed.

Jack could feel the intensity of Cassie's gaze focused on him. When he glanced over he found her blue eyes filled with compassion. But he didn't speak. He couldn't right now. Jack was ready for Flynn's segment of his life to be over. It was time to begin anew. But he couldn't, not with Flynn out there, still a threat to all of them.

Cassie's hand squeezed Jack's thigh, then she left it resting there, its warmth bringing some comfort to him on the ride back to his place.

Cassie walked into the house behind the two men and headed straight for the phone. She called Rourke's FBI contact and spoke with him briefly. When she hung up the phone, she saw that Jack was leaning against the doorjamb and he looked tired, as if he hadn't been sleeping well.

"Hello, Cassie." He spoke her name ever so softly.

She had on an outfit he hadn't seen before. A deep rose blouse and charcoal-gray slacks; her customary scarf, this one a rose and light gray print, was hung bandit style around her neck. The marauding reporter. Her hair was neatly French braided, but he could see faint lines of exhaustion around her pale blue eyes.

Jack tried to smile. He couldn't believe how incredibly nervous he was. "You look hungry."

"What an opening line," Cassie said, looking up at the ceiling and doing her best not to laugh. "As a matter of fact I am. I've missed your cooking."

"Is that all you've missed?"

"No." She met his intent gaze. "We need to talk."

He hesitated, then plunged ahead. "Cassie, I'm trying not to be so overprotective, but it isn't easy for me. You've come to be a very important part of my life. And I don't want to lose you."

"Do you understand my position?" Cassie asked. "I can't live with someone who wants to run my life."

He nodded. "I didn't interfere with your operation today, even though I wanted to. Your being there was dangerous, but I didn't interfere."

Cassie felt like smiling. It was time. Jack hadn't tried to stop her today, even though he'd obviously known Flynn would be present. He really was trying. She did smile, and her words carried no sting. "I knew Patrick would tell you."

"He was my friend first," Jack said, moving toward her. "It was his duty." He stopped in front of her and pulled her into his arms, holding her close. "I've missed you."

Cassie wound her arms around him. "I've missed you, too," she murmured, her mouth finding his. They drank of each other greedily again and again.

"Jack?" Cassie whispered in his ear. "I have a story to write."

He stopped unbuttoning her blouse. "Now?"

She nodded and stepped back. "I need to go back out to the airport while the FBI men are still there, to gather the information I need to finish the piece."

Jack watched as she buttoned her blouse. "I don't think I like your job."

"Jack," she warned, her blue eyes flashing.

He smiled. "Just kidding. Come on, let's get this over with." He grabbed her hand, intertwining her fingers in his as they headed for the car. Suddenly he stopped and pulled her toward him. "Later?"

"That's a promise," she whispered before kissing him again. "Right now, I need to get out of here while I still can," she said.

"Wait just a minute! Where do you think you're going?"

"You left your car at the airport when you came back here with me. Were you planning on taking a taxi out there?" he asked innocently as he walked out of the house.

"Okay, I'll let you come along this time," Cassie said, as he opened the car door for her. "But just this once."

He bit back his next words and walked around to the driver's side of his Mercedes. He knew Flynn might still be at the airport. And Flynn knew who Cassie was. A link to them, a vulnerable point. Knowing Flynn, he was long gone, but Jack wasn't going to take any chances with Cassie.

"I forgot to ask," he said, changing the subject as he approached the highway entrance ramp. "Did Leonore Xavier admit to having Brian killed?"

"Not yet," Cassie told him. "But she will. Either she'll take the fall for it, or she'll admit it was Flynn."

"Flynn!"

Cassie nodded. "Allen Hook said they both knew about Brian. And one of them stopped him." She paused, then added, "By the way, Leonore said the red purse she gave Flynn was empty. At the last moment she'd actually had a touch of conscience and found she couldn't betray her country."

Her hand was gently kneading the muscles of his thigh. Whatever else happened, she had achieved what she set out to do—to find Brian's killer.

And along the way she had found something else. Love.

"I just realized something," Jack said, changing lanes on the highway. "You left your story behind to come with me earlier."

"Just then, you needed me. So I came."

Her words went straight to his heart. At times he'd doubted whether he could ever be more important to her than her career. Now he knew he was. It made him feel better, as did her teasing fingers.

"If you don't stop doing that," Jack warned as her fingers grew more daring. "I'm going to pull this car to the side of the road."

Mischief filled her eyes. "Is that a promise?"

Epilogue

"So, are we in agreement?" Patrick asked, looking at the two men for confirmation.

Russ spoke. "There's really very little choice."

"None," Jack confirmed. "We can't let Flynn run free."

Cassie sat on the love seat, listening as they discussed their plans. She hadn't spoken since they'd begun. She wanted Flynn stopped as much as they did.

According to Leonore Xavier, Flynn had personally taken care of Brian. Was she lying? They didn't have Flynn yet, but Brian's murder had been fully acknowledged. She'd seen to that; no one believed he'd committed suicide now.

"We'll use your home as our base," Patrick said, looking at Jack. "You're going to have to stay here, and be our link to each other."

Jack nodded. There was no other choice. Not if he wanted to be here if Cassie needed him, too.

"Russ and Kathleen will take Bridget. I think we're all in agreement that she's too vulnerable, too much a sitting duck at this estate."

Russ spoke. "We'll take her on a tour of the United States, via car, boat and airplane. It will be a good education for her, and also keep her out of harm's way."

"And I," Patrick Rourke said, standing up, "am going hunting. Flynn isn't getting away this time."

Harlequin Intrigue®

COMING NEXT MONTH

#131 BLACK MESA by Aimée Thurlo
To the Tewa tribe, Black Mesa was sacred land. Navajo FBI Agent Justin Nakai had traveled a long way to reach it—to see his old friend John Romero—only to find the man missing and John's beautiful friend Kelly Ferguson under attack and suspicion. Neither Justin nor Kelly was willing to abandon John without a fight. They could only hope their separate talents and their newfound love would be enough to protect them on the dangerous path they followed together.

#132 PAST TENSE by Tina Vasilos
For months, Samantha Smith had successfully eluded two men who knew she'd witnessed a murder. Now, the murder victim had turned up safe and sound in Tony Theopoulos's hotel—and Samantha faced a dilemma. Could she trust Tony? Could their sharp minds and keen instincts unite to piece together what really happened that fateful night in Montreal? Or would her gamble on the perceptive hotelier lose Samantha the deadly game of cat and mouse, and spell checkmate?

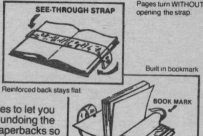

HARLEQUIN Temptation.

The Pirate
JAYNE ANN KRENTZ

At the heart of every powerful romance story lies a legend. There are many romantic legends and countless modern variations on them, but they all have one thing in common: They are tales of brave, resourceful women who must gentle and tame the powerful, passionate men who are their true mates.

The enormous appeal of Jayne Ann Krentz lies in her ability to create modern-day versions of these classic romantic myths, and her LADIES AND LEGENDS trilogy showcases this talent. Believing that a storyteller who can bring legends to life deserves special attention, Harlequin has chosen the first book of the trilogy—THE PIRATE—to receive our Award of Excellence. Look for it in February.

AE-PIR-1

A compelling novel of deadly revenge and passion from Harlequin's bestselling international romance author Penny Jordan

POWER PLAY

Eleven years had passed but the terror of that night was something Pepper Minesse would never forget. Fueled by revenge against the four men who had brutally shattered her past, she set in motion a deadly plan to destroy their futures.

Available in February!

Penny Jordan